THE FOOTSTEPS CAME CLOSER

A man in his early fifties appeared, brutal looking with a high forehead and piercing blue-gray eyes. He wore a gray suit and stared at the prisoners. Then he turned to two guards and spoke with them in Russian.

"See?" Carter said to Sinden. "We're going to get out of here." Even Sinden looked hopeful for a moment.

But the Russian instead unfolded a strip of plastic beneath his arm. Then he started to pull it across his chest. It was a butcher's apron.

Carter's eyes went wild with terror when he saw the Russian draw a pistol from within his coat. Then the sound in his ears was the same as in his throat: a scream. A scream straight up from Hell itself.

THE FINEST IN SUSPENSE!

THE URSA ULTIMATUM (2130, $3.95)
by Terry Baxter

In the dead of night, twelve nuclear warheads are smuggled north across the Mexican border to be detonated simultaneously in major cities throughout the U.S. And only a small-town desert lawman stands between a face-less Russian superspy and World War Three!

THE LAST ASSASSIN (1989, $3.95)
by Daniel Easterman

From New York City to the Middle East, the devastating flames of revolution and terrorism sweep across a world gone mad . . . as the most terrifying conspiracy in the history of mankind is born!

FLOWERS FROM BERLIN (2060, $4.50)
by Noel Hynd

With the Earth on the brink of World War Two, the Third Reich's deadliest professional killer is dispatched on the most heinous assignment of his murderous career: the assassination of Franklin Delano Roosevelt!

THE BIG NEEDLE (1921, $2.95)
by Ken Follett

All across Europe, innocent people are being terrorized, homes are destroyed, and dead bodies have become an unnervingly common sight. And the horrors will continue until the most powerful organization on Earth finds Chadwell Carstairs — and kills him!

DOMINATOR (2118, $3.95)
by James Follett

Two extraordinary men, each driven by dangerously ambiguous loyalties, play out the ultimate nuclear endgame miles above the helpless planet — aboard a hijacked space shuttle called DOMINATOR!

Available wherever paperbacks are sold, or order direct from the Publisher. Send cover price plus 50¢ per copy for mailing and handling to Zebra Books, Dept. 2297, 475 Park Avenue South, New York, N.Y. 10016. Residents of New York, New Jersey and Pennsylvania must include sales tax. DO NOT SEND CASH.

THE KHRUSHCHEV OBJECTIVE

CHRISTOPHER CREIGHTON and NOEL HYND

ZEBRA BOOKS
KENSINGTON PUBLISHING CORP.

ZEBRA BOOKS

are published by

Kensington Publishing Corp.
475 Park Avenue South
New York, NY 10016

First Zebra Books printing: May, 1988

Printed in the United States of America

*This book is dedicated to the men and women
of the "M" Section and their Chief, "Charlemagne,"
sometimes known as Admiral of the Fleet,
the Earl Mountbatten of Burma;*

*Also to his cousin, Marie Nikolayevna,
and her grandson, Alexis,
now the Guardian of the Imperial Throne
of All the Russias;*

*To Major Sir Desmond Morton,
the first director of "M" Section;*

*And to "Crabbie,"
Commander Lionel Crabb, OBE, GM, RNVR,
Order of the Soviet Red Star,
upon whom, when the chips were down,
most everything depended.*

"I've got a little job tomorrow.
I'm going to get my feet wet."

> Commander Lionel Crabb, RNVR,
> to drinking companions
> Portsmouth, April 17, 1956

". . . [It] would not be in the public
interest to disclose the manner
in which Commander Crabb is presumed
to have met his death . . ."

> Retired Prime Minister
> Anthony Eden, 1960

". . . It is worth noting that the
English weren't above trying to
spy on their guests."

> Nikita Khrushchev, 1970,
> in reference to what became
> known as the Crabb Affair

FOREWORD

The broad base of this story is true. Christopher Creighton is a real person, as real as Winston Churchill, Louis Mountbatten, Lionel Crabb and Nikita Khrushchev. But the story is here told as a novel. There are reasons.

On the occasion of a state visit to the United Kingdom by Soviet leaders Nikolai Bulganin and Nikita Khrushchev, and during the attendant stay of three Soviet warships at Portsmouth harbor, an incident occurred that has never been truthfully explained. Shortly after dawn on April 19, 1956, Soviet sailors observed a frogman floating between the battle cruiser *Ordzhonikidze* and the destroyer *Smotryashchi*. A vehement Soviet protest followed, protesting "spy activities" so close to naval vessels on a "friendly visit." The British Admiralty issued a statement that the frogman was its own retired Commander Lionel Crabb — never again to be seen alive — who apparently had been examining the hull of the *Ordzhonikidze* with neither the knowledge nor the authority of the Admiralty. This slender truth covered a multitude of larger ones.

Fourteen months later the badly decomposed body of a man in a black diving suit — identified as that of Crabb — washed ashore at Chichester harbor. The incident at Portsmouth was recalled, and the entire episode became known as the Crabb Affair.

For many years attempts have been made to learn the whole truth of what occurred. Questions were frequently posed to Prime Minister Anthony Eden and his successors. On each occasion, those who have served as Prime Minister have declined to answer on the grounds of national interest.

In 1970, Admiral of the Fleet, the Earl Mountbatten of Burma, consented to Christopher Creighton writing a book telling exactly what transpired. Both men were intimately involved in the incident. Creighton suggested that the story might be best told as a novel, which would allow him flexibility with certain details that could never be revealed. Second — and more significantly — some names, places, sequences and identities had to be disguised. Certain participants from several nations preferred, all else being equal, to live safely and quietly into the next century.

Mountbatten accepted these conditions but added two of his own. He directed the story not be told until a quarter century had elapsed from the operational date. And it most emphatically was not to be told while he was alive.

Twenty-five years elapsed by 1981. Tragically, Lord Mountbatten's second condition was fulfilled before the first. He was, as the world knows, murdered in

1979 by assassins claiming allegiance to the Irish Republican Army. But the slaying has never been placed in its proper historical perspective.

The motive behind it had been revenge. Revenge for Lord Mountbatten's involvement in the Crabb Affair, and his success in foiling the attempt to assassinate Bulganin and Khrushchev and destroy the Russian warships.

N.H.

ONE

France, 1955.

The tiny village of Mégve lay thirty miles southeast of Geneva, nestled cozily into a quiet, remote corner of the Haute de Savoie. It was perched almost at the peak of an unnamed mountain, ten miles west of Mont Blanc, the grand old *dame* of the French Alps. From Mégve, the imposing white face of Mont Blanc was visible on any clear day. From Mont Blanc, Mégve was a dot visible only to the initiated.

Yet among those with the financial resources to muster a skiing holiday among Europe's smarter set, as well as the athletic prowess to challenge one of the region's more demanding slopes, Mégve was one of the most popular and least publicized resorts of its day. Some things were better off as secrets.

The trails of Mégve snaked unpredictably down the south face of the mountain. Three miles below the gondola station that marked the height of the trails, the main *pistes de ski* diverged. There they met a rocky plateau that formed a small unexpected peninsula of land which was quite apart from the ski terrain. Signs discreetly marked it PRIVÉ, and as a private domain it was an almost whimsical one. Most skiers stopped to remark upon it at first encounter, then continued on, ignoring it thereafter. For beyond the signs insisting upon privacy and past the rough road which led to Albertville farther down the mountain, and surrounded by the heavy boulders and trees, was an exquisite villa. It was splendid, elaborate and turreted, dark wood and white brick. It was in fine repair, and its glass windows winked and sparkled in the winter sunlight. Here, it proclaimed, lived some wealthy hermit who had withdrawn from — or at least wished to be ignored by — civilization. The villa existed in an isolation that was more Himalayan than alpine: the retreat of a moneyed recluse, most observers concluded, if it were the home of anyone at all.

At four-thirty P.M. on Thursday afternoon, December 12, a sunset the color of fire embraced Mégve and stretched across the entire valley of the d'arbois. Outside the villa, as was always the custom, two guards stood by the main entrance. Their existence was as improbable as the villa itself as they, too, would have been more appropriate to another time, another place. They were Cossacks. Tall, ferocious, strapping bearded men, laden with muscles beneath their heavy parkas. At their sides, they carried Walther automatics in black leather holsters.

At this hour, darkness would quickly follow the sunset. Only the swiftest skiers could complete their final runs before actual nightfall. This simple fact left the slopes to only the best Europe could offer. So as was their custom, the guards watched the skiers in-

14

tently at this hour. It was one of the best free shows of athletic ability on earth.

On this afternoon, two skiers in particular caught the notice of the guards. They were a woman and a man, she in a light blue suit, he in a red: almost as if they were dressed to draw everyone's attention. They had already passed several times this afternoon. But they were again spectacular as they descended the main trail. In unison, they completed a series of traverses and evolutions upon the most relentless moguls of the mountain's face. Then they turned directly upon a path which led toward a rocky wall at the villa's perimeter. They skied straight on and sped toward a modest cliff which skiers of near-Olympic caliber used as a jump. Here they executed a back turn, came out of it, joined hands and hit the jump at full speed. They flew over the northeast extremity of the villa's low wall, and landed gracefully back upon the slope, their hands still joined. Next they separated and raced each other down the eastern trail.

The two Cossacks, who had seen much in their time, had rarely seen anything quite like this. They craned their necks to follow the striking red and light blue figures as they grew smaller against the white downhill *piste*. In doing so, the guards relaxed their attention upon the western side of the trail.

With unerring precision, four more skiers appeared from out of the blinding sunlight. They leaped over the wall at the other edge of the property and landed with a crunch at the forecourt of the villa.

The Cossacks whirled immediately, drawing their weapons. But the first two intruders were already upon the bearded giants, their ski sticks raised like lances. Yet these weren't ski poles at all. Rather they were elaborate spears, each equipped at the base with a sharpened foot-long steel shaft.

A lunge by the first assailant caught the nearest Cossack in the chest. The blade slashed upward toward the neck, ripping through goose down and releasing a torrent of blood. Almost simultaneously, the next attacker caught the second Cossack flush in the throat — then through the heart — with another spear. The two assassins twisted their weapons sideways as the Cossacks crumpled in agony. Seconds later, other spear thrusts completed the murders with merciful suddenness.

. Now the four intruders kicked off their skis. They pulled light Sten guns from their shoulder haversacks. One man remained in the forecourt. The other three walked slowly to the villa, their faces hidden by ski masks.

The apparent leader reached to a large brass knocker on the main door. He rapped firmly three times.

After a moment the door opened. There stood a startled male servant and two more Cossacks. For a moment those in the household stared at their visitors in disbelief. Then the intruders opened fire, driving their victims back against a finely papered wall and killing them instantly.

The gunmen crossed a hallway and opened a door. They entered slowly, their guns leveled, but expecting little more opposition. They stood in a large open area which comprised a living room, a bar, a library and a dining area. Candles illuminated the room — again suggesting another century — and by a far wall

16

was a hearth blazing with an enormous wood fire.

Within the room, turning in shock toward the intruders, were an elderly man and woman dressed formally for dinner. They stared. They were considerably frightened but at the same time appeared resigned to the situation. There was also one more person: a woman, slightly younger. She faced the fire, her back to the visitors.

The leader of the assassins moved toward her. When the elderly man moved out to obstruct his path, the woman turned and raised her hand.

"It is all right, Mikhail Petrovich," she said boldly. *I* will deal with this."

The leader stopped. The woman stared at him. She was very handsome, short, graying and in her fifties. Her eyes were large and blue. She wore a dark navy blue silk gown, a string of pearls and matching earrings. Upon the third finger of her left hand was an antique gold ring bedecked with both diamonds and rubies. In its center, as the leader looked to see, was a gold cross surmounting an Imperial crown. The woman held her head high and was quite unafraid.

The leader spoke with a Prussian accent. "Marie Mikolayevna?" he asked.

"That is my name," she answered in lightly accented English.

The intruder clicked his heels. He nodded his head a single time from the neck, the Coburg bow. "Madam," he said with deference.

"What do you want with me?" she asked. Her eyes sparkled with contempt.

"Madam," he said. "Your cause and the cause of my commander have now become the same."

17

She looked him up and down. "I cannot conceive of any cause that could be shared by us."

"I am sorry I am not permitted to present you with the details at this moment, Madam," he answered, "but my master wishes to tell you himself."

"And who is *he?*" she snapped.

The man was silent.

"*Where* is he?" she demanded. "Have you the courage to tell me?"

"He orders me to escort you to him at once," the man said.

Nikolayevna turned back to the fire. "You will have to kill me. I will not allow you to escort me anywhere."

"Madam," the intruder countered, "I am ordered to further inform you that we keep constant surveillance on an apartment house in Cannes. It's called the Palais des Dunes."

"Alexis?" she whispered, looking back. For the first time she betrayed concern.

"Yes, madam. Your grandson. The Prince Alexis. If you do not come freely with us, he will be seized and killed."

Slowly, Nikolayevna walked away from the gunman. She approached a small table. On it was a large antique crystal decanter. She filled three matching brandy glasses, handed one each to the old man and old woman, and kept one for herself. She raised hers. "Good health, my dear friends," she said to them in Russian. The three of them drank their brandy in one gulp. Then, following her lead, they flung their crystal snifters into the fire. The glass shattered and the surplus alcohol whooshed in the flame.

18

Marie again faced the man who had come for her. "That is the eternal flame of Russia," she said gently. "Someday it will come and devour you."

The man was unmoved. He waited.

"If you wish me to accompany you," she continued, "you will agree unconditionally to the safekeeping of my friends. Count Nesterov. And his sister, the Countess Irena."

"My commander would easily agree," said the intruder. "My men will pack your things. Your journey will not be long. Nor will it be difficult."

"Will we be returning here?"

"No. Never."

Marie sighed and nodded sadly.

Countess Irena brought Marie a long, cowled fur coat and placed it across her shoulders. Then Marie led toward the door, her elderly friends behind her. In the hallway she stopped by the bodies of the two Cossacks and the slain servant.

Gently and in turn she knelt by each. She made the Orthodox sign of the Cross and said a prayer in Russian. No one hurried her. Then she kissed each of the slain men on the mouth. Outside, in the forecourt, she repeated the gesture. It was almost dark. She was unaffected by the condition of the bodies.

In the driveway it was almost dark. But from the lights from the villa, she could see two trucks and three cars that she had never seen before. Ten additional men had arrived with them. She ignored them. Silently she slid into the back seat of a waiting black Mercedes-Benz. Nesterov and the Countess Irena got in with her. A driver started the car and moments later the vehicle began to move. Four men followed in the second car, a dark green Rover with French license plates. The leader of the gunmen was one of the four.

The man who remained spent the next several hours loading the contents of the villa into the two trucks. It was midnight when the task was complete. A steady snow was falling. Then they closed the rear doors of the trucks and the two vehicles started downward on the road toward Albertville. Only two men were left behind.

These two dragged the bodies of the Cossack guards into the villa. They poured gasoline throughout the building. They stepped back, closed the doors and threw a pair of ignition grenades through a downstairs window.

The ground floor of the whimsical old villa erupted in flame. The windows blew out. Within seconds a ferocious blaze engulfed the entire structure.

The two men ran to the edge of the domain where a two-year-old Porsche waited. Its engine leaped to life and as the flames spread, the sports car began a swift, nimble descent of the mountain. The snow intensified. But far from impeding the conflagration, the storm shrouded it. The isolation which had protected the fanciful villa for so long now ensured its destruction.

The early ski patrol the next morning found only a pile of simmering bricks and rubble where the exquisite residence had once stood. The discovery was stunning. It was as if the villa had had magical qualities all along, an alpine Brigadoon or Camelot which had no disappeared as unpredictably as it had existed.

Upon close examination, however, the charred rubble suggested otherwise. French police unearthed five corpses, figments of no one's imagination. But no identification was forthcoming, nor was any explanation. The property itself was registered to a bank account in Switzerland. It was as if those who died—much like those who had lived there and those who had come there to commit such atrocities—had risen from a shadowy underside of the real world, one of invisible identies and unwritten codes and laws, a demimonde populated by men and women who roam the earth like so many breezes, leaving little behind them as evidence of their existence.

Yet in the waning days of 1955, these people were very real, indeed. The events of the following year, 1956, would clearly attest to that forever.

TWO

December 1955, New York.

Among the three other musicians in the quartet, the opinion on Christopher Creighton was less than unanimous. Greene, the drummer, saw Creigton as a fraud who, despite the conspicuous British accent, had probably never been to London in his life. Billy Mills, the saxophonist, concurred and viewed the quartet's leader as a slightly more than ordinary pianist. Mills made it clear that his own membership in the group was only temporary. "Gonna get me something better real soon," he announced each week, and he even had a theory about the sketchiness of Creighton's past gigs. "Probably been in jail, man," he'd say to anyone who'd listen.

Maurice Cairnes, the bass player, was a more cultivated fellow by anyone's standards, having served six months in the U.S. Navy Reserve after the peace in

1945. Cairnes saw a subtle genius in the way Creighton toyed with the keys of a piano. He saw the group's founder as an accomplished jazzman but had a further observation. Creighton, Cairnes said, had the bearing of a sailor. Once he mentioned it to Creighton himself.

Christopher only laughed. "All Brits are sailors," he answered.

"But were you Navy? That's what I'm asking," Cairnes pressed.

"What you've go to remember, Maurice," Christopher hastened to point out, "in England, almost everyone is in the Navy. There's no point of land that's more than sixty-five miles from the sea."

Cairnes raised his eyebrows. "Funny kind of place that's completely surrounded by water," said Cairnes, gently teasing. "Hard to feel real safe."

"Makes me nervous right now," Creighton said, going along with it.

"Now?"

"Surrounded by water. Manhattan Island. Could get flooded out any minute."

Cairnes began to laugh, a deep resonant rumble.

"Wouldn't be telling you if it weren't so," Christopher concluded. It was a strange comment. Telling things that weren't so, living deceptions and false identities, were things that he'd been at home with for many years. It had begun back during the war. The *big* war, the one that had been over for more than a decade.

At thirty-one, Christopher Creighton was a slim

24

figure of a man. He was tall with long legs and an agile gait. He had a high forehead, dark blue eyes and a square jaw. In his usual gray slacks and a crewneck sweater, he was visibly strong around the neck and shoulders. Hardly a typical pianist.

"I think he's a cop," said Billy Mills, the saxophonist. They were playing a gig at a sleepy joint on New York's West Eighth Street. Creighton, who'd assembled the group in March of 1955, had not yet arrived that evening.

"Cops don't talk like that," Cairnes reminded him. "He's English."

Greene, the drummer, glanced up. *"Something's* funny," he said.

When Christopher entered, he was unduly quiet and clearly preoccupied. Over in England, it seemed, the government had changed. On the fifth of April, 1955, Churchill resigned. Anthony Eden succeeded him. Creighton appeared to take it personally.

"A great man forced into retirement solely by the weight of his years," Christopher pronounced sadly, dropping a New York *Herald-Tribune* into a wastebasket.

"Why's this Winston Whatshisname so important to you?" Bill Mills asked. "What's it mean day to day for a piano man in New York?"

Christopher simmered and opened his mouth to speak, but two conflicting images silenced him.

Churchill: In his bunker beneath London during the war, like being below decks in a battleship, protected by a five-foot ceiling of concrete and steel, shoulders hunched, stocky legged, arms akimbo as he stood in his solicitor's black-and-stripes—a short black jacket and pinstriped gray trousers; he wore a dreadful scowl, a spotted blue bow tie and, once or twice, a Colt revolver.

And, *Churchill:* years earlier, 1935 it was, Christopher's mother's landlord in Kent. He was nothing more than an aging, retired parliamentarian even then, a bulky fat man who more often than not sat on a terrace bundled in a heavy coat dabbling with oil paints on a canvas, all the time carping about Herr Schicklgruber. He was still an M.P., but no longer a minister with any effective power. Five years later, when Christopher was sixteen, Churchill—returned to office as First Lord of the Admiralty—would send Christopher into Belgium as a spy.

For a moment, Christopher entertained the fantasy of explaining this all to his newly found cohorts. There was this interlude around 1939 to 1945, he fancied saying to them. But then he supposed they were too young to remember. And anyway, they were American. Hitler had never been on their doorstep. Luftwaffe bombers had never rained fire and death on their cities. Why, they'd never . . .

He dismissed the impulse. "I've got the urge to take this group to England sometime," he said instead. "Play some small jazz clubs there, right?"

"London?" Cairnes asked.

"London for sure. Maybe Brighton in the summer. Southsea. I know where the right clubs are."

But no one went anywhere that summer. In July

they played a successful two-weer stand at Father John Bartholomew's on Bleecker Street. Father John himself, all six-foot-three, three hundred pounds of him, owned the place, tended the bar and claimed to be a defrocked Presbyterian minister. He also claimed to be tickled to death over the cash register receipts during the two-week visit. Accordingly, he offered the band a forty-week contract. They accepted. Father John's became a home away from home in September.

It was a cozy, small crowded place, one flight down from the sidewalk, with a caricature of a hulking Father John painted by a neighborhood artist above the doorway. A neon Knickerbocker beer sign flashed in each of the two windows and faced upward toward the street. The musicians played on a wooden stand behind the bottles of the bar—there was just enough space for three and a half of them — and Father John roamed the private side of the bar like a caged bear. He was a big, pleasantly profane, dark-haired mustachioed megalith of a man with tremendous forearms and fists. Simultaneously, he was the kindest soul in the West Village as well as the most adept owner-bouncer south of Fourteenth Street. He was a man's man, with six children, and Creighton loved him. He also ran one of the best establishments of its sort, ranking just half a rung below Eddie Condon's, Marie's Crisis Café, Juluis' and the Cafe Wha? Creighton's quartet played New Orleans jazz with a pinch of Chicago sprinkled in—this through the grace of Billy Mills, who'd once done eight months in Cook County Jail—and the sound was electrifying. The

27

cover charge was two dollars, and the beer (Knickerbocker, Rheingold or Krueger) was both cold and reasonable: six bits at a table, four bits at the bar. For
Christopher, there was only one odd association: with
its cramped quarters and its inevitable blended odors
of sweat, beer and cigarette smoke, Father John's reminded him of the atmosphere on a submarine that
had been forced to remain below the surface past her
normal limit. But then again, submarines rarely provided live jazz of Basin Street caliber. Submarines,
Christopher recalled, rarely provided good music at
all.

In October the weather turned colder and so did
Christopher's blood. When little whirlpools of dead
leaves coiled and hissed at him on quiet Greenwich
Village sidewalks, he thought back to the war. He
relived incidents in which he had nearly died, and he
saw the faces of men he himself had killed. Ghosts
pursued him, as they did every year at this time. He
found himself talking Father John into pouring him
an extra scotch much earlier in each evening at the
piano. It occurred to Christopher that he should have
been at his happiest playing the music he loved, far
from the mayhem and intrigue that had already
scarred his youth. He was finished with all that, he
kept telling himself. He had retired from the active list
of the Royal Navy in 1952, although he still remained
on the Reserve list and subject to immediate recall.
He'd do best to find himself a pretty, sympathetic

woman and maybe have a family.

Then he laughed ruefully at the very idea.

Love. He wasn't sure he knew what it was all about. The Royal Navy had been his entire adult life, and he supposed he loved the service. But as far as women were concerned, he had never found the right one. *I love you* were words he hadn't spoken since he was a teenager. He wondered if he'd ever say them again. He wondered if he'd ever want to.

Too much time to think, he told himself. And he had too much time to worry, also. That's what was wrong right now. That, and the fact that New York was too quiet. His life was proceeding *too* smoothly. Out of somewhere in the past, he began to believe, would soon step an enemy who'd demand a day of reckoning—or a friend who'd demand a day of action.

He was certain of it. So he began to take the old precautions: the extra chain lock on the windows of his Bank Street apartment, the hair left each day one foot from the floor, pressed against the doorway and the doorframe, the shirts in his dresser left in a precise order than an intruder wouldn't remember and the scissors and letter opener left in his desk drawer in a geometric pattern that a prowler there could never re-create. On Bank Street he memorized the license plates of cars that were familiar and belonged there, and took an extra-hard look whenever he saw a closed van with a trifle too much aerial.

Weeks passed. Nothing. At Father John's, his anxiety persisted. The feeling was unbanishable now, this sense of urgency, this burning all over his skin which seemed to radiate upon him from a shadow that he never saw. Something was imminent. What?

Then, one night a week before Christmas, he confirmed the fact that he had imagined nothing. Christopher was playing at Father John's — the quartet was now further crowded out by a small Christmas tree, Father John's one remaining homage to his alleged Presbyterianism — when the band brought a smooth ribbon of music to a perfectly disciplined stop. An eccentric two-bar drumbeat from Greene punctuated it in high style. There followed a smattering of applause.

Christopher's gaze wandered around the room and an icy draft hit him. Someone had opened a front window to disperse the smoke. Through it, his gaze settled upon a single woman who was seated at the end of the bar and to the side of him. She was very pretty, with short, light brown hair. More important, she was holding in her hand — Christopher had caught a perfect glimpse of it — a small photograph. He saw her looking directly up from it to him.

At their eyes met, her hand discreetly covered the photograph and she returned it to her purse. She looked to one side, away from Christopher, and initiated a conversation with a pair of men in business suits who seemed more interested in talking to each other. Then she gathered her coat and purse. A minute later she was out the door. She had never looked back to the stage after the moment he caught her watching him.

Christmas came and went. Then New Year's was over. Nineteen fifty-five had become fifty-six. Christopher waited. Nothing happened, except Father John asked if he could extend the quartet into July. Christopher hedged.

On the sixth day of January, Christopher crossed a cold deserted Abingdon Square at a few minutes past three in the morning. He wore an old navy duffelcoat and pulled it close to him. The wind was sweeping fiercely in from the Hudson River. The sidewalks were icy. But strangely enough, Christopher was on a high. The band had played superbly since mid-December. Even the personal antagonisms had drifted aside. Christopher mused upon it as he turned onto his block. Then he saw the car.

The first thing he noticed was that the auto was parked directly in front of his building, its motor running. He knew he'd never seen it before—a blue Oldsmobile with the garish high fins that were currently in style—and even the license plate jogged nothing in his memory. Then as he walked closer he saw that there was a single occupant seated on the passenger side. Seconds later, as he continued to approach, he saw that the occupant was female.

A young woman, he sensed, at that.

Creighton watched the car. No need to cover his back; he'd been guarding it for several days. There was no one behind him. He knew.

The car window rolled down and the woman looked his way. He recognized her—as he half-expected to—from Father John's. Their eyes met and she considered him with mild disapproval for several seconds.

"I thought you were going to keep me waiting all night," she said. Christopher's defenses were up. It took him not a moment to decipher her accent.

"You're English," he said.

"Scottish, actually, sir."

Christopher noted the purposely appended "sir." "I don't suppose you'd like to tell me your name," he said.

"James, sir."

He moved between two cars parked on the curb. He could see her hands, which were empty, and he could see that there was no one else in the car.

"Why are you calling me 'sir,' Miss James? Or is it Mrs.?"

"Neither, sir. It's Second Officer Jemima James, Women's Royal Naval Service. I'm attached to Room 39."

She produced an ID and handed it to him. He glanced at it without reaction. Room 39 was Royal Naval Intelligence in Whitehall. But hundreds of people knew that, not all of them trustworthy.

"So?" he asked. The card appeared to be authentic. He handed it back to her.

"So I'm here to apprise you of your travel arrangements," she said. "*Peter* Hamilton, I believe, sir?"

The name froze him. No more than a dozen individuals knew his cover name from the war. And those who knew were highly placed indeed.

She handed him another ID. "This one's your own,

sir. Quite up to date."

He stared at it. Royal Naval Intelligence, and their attention to the most minute detail, never ceased to astonish him. *Peter Hamilton:* Although it hadn't become his cover identity until September 1940, the name had first appeared on the Navy List of 1935. From then on it had been judiciously weeded and planted. Fellow officers, who were forever scrutinizing the List and appointments, would have no cause to remember one their own appointments and wonder why they couldn't recall a Peter Hamilton having been there.

So much came back. Under this cover, Christopher had assassinated a Vichy admiral in Algiers, Christmas Eve 1942. In another December in another part of the world, Christopher had planted a bomb that had destroyed an entire submarine and annihilated its crew; and in Berlin, four years after the end of the war, Christopher had escaped death only by being able to prove that he was Lieutenant Commander Peter Hamilton and not Christopher Creighton.

And now here it was again, complete with a current photograph. How they'd managed that, he'd never know. Then he saw the entry against rank. "I've been promoted?" he asked.

"You have, sir. Lieutenant commander to commander, with effect from January first of this year."

He held her in a gaze as cold as the wind off the river. "Why?"

"Maybe it's because you're good at your job, sir."

For a moment Christopher was spellbound. The

most attractive woman he'd seen in months was spinning an unfathomable story to him. Meanwhile, it was past three in the morning and he was slowly freezing. If she was to be believed, he'd been recalled to the Active List. But why? And by whom?

She leaned slightly toward him and lowered her voice. "If you're questioning your orders, sir, I'm instructed to say that Christopher Robin is to report to Charlemagne. And that I'm attached to M Section."

And then he knew. Christopher Robin had been his own operational code name with Churchill's own select intelligence unit—M Section—that had operated since the mid-1930's. But "Charlemagne"?

The Holy Roman Emperor had had twelve knight errants under Count Paladin. The senior naval officer now code-named "Charlemagne" had named some of his own officers after the count—Christopher had been one. But he'd kept the regal code name for himself. First, "Charlemagne" had never been a member of M Section, whose members took their own code names from the A.A. Milne characters. And second, the man himself was a direct descendant of the Holy Roman Emperor.

"Of course," Christopher said at length. "I should have known at once. Lord Louis. Admiral Mountbatten."

His eyes left her for a moment and settled on a pair of duffel bags on the back seat of the car. Then it dawned on him: the bags were Royal Navy standard issue. His. She saw him looking at them.

"An aircraft is waiting at Idlewild, sir," said Second

34

Officer James. "So I took a small liberty. I packed your things."

THREE

There was a stopover in Bermuda.

It was balmy at the landing field when they stepped off the airplane, a relief from frigid New York. A British naval attaché took an exhausted Christopher and Jemima to a special house just outside St. George. From a discreet distance four Royal Marines in civilian clothing covered the iron gate that was the only official access to the grounds. Four more staked out the perimeter.

Christopher changed into lighter clothing, cotton slacks and a sweater. He took a chair on the veranda at the back of the house, which had a view of the ocean.

He was not hungry for lunch. It was early on a Sunday afternoon and the parish was quiet. He read a local newspaper and day-old *Telegraph*. He spent much time staring at the water. He accepted tea when a waiter brought it at four o'clock. But there was still too much time to think.

The clouds covered the sun. He shivered. The waves before him blurred and time spiraled.

1942. By the summer of that year, Christopher was well known behind German lines. Working under Churchill's orders and posing as a young English traitor, Christopher sold to the Abwehr a report that laid out in detail the impending raid on Dieppe. Admiral Wilhelm Canaris, head of the Abwehr, had been skeptical about Christopher's information, but defending Wehrmacht divisions were put on alert anyway.

At the hour and date foretold by Christopher, the British invaded. The Wehrmacht responded, heaving everything in their arsenal at their attackers. The Commonwealth soldiers, mostly Canadians, who weren't driven back to their landing craft died or were wounded on the beach. Four thousand of them, due to the information that Christopher had passed.

The raid had confirmed Creighton as the Abwehr's top spy. And Churchill wrote off the casualties to a much higher purpose. The teenage spy would later pass erroneous information through the same Abwehr channels, and tens of thousands of Allied soldiers would survive D Day thanks to the sacrifice of four thousand in 1942. That was the type of numbers game Old Winston was playing.

Dieppe. Christopher sipped his cup of cooling tea and stared at the other side of the same Atlantic Ocean.

The Combined Operations force, the soldiers who waded into the sights of the waiting German guns, had Mountbatten as their commander in chief. Creighton had last seen Charlemagne in 1951. It promised to be some sort of reunion.

Creighton could hear the guns again, very clearly at first, then very faintly. Damn this fatigue that was overcoming him. On the veranda in Bermuda, Christopher closed his eyes, nodded, and . . .

A hand on his shoulder gently shook him. "Sir?" A woman's voice spoke softly. "Wake up, sir."

Christopher's eyes flickered, then blinked open. It was evening. He had been dozing for at least two hours.

"I gave orders that no one was to wake you," Jemima James said. "You'll need to be rested on arrival."

"Yes. Of course." He gathered his senses. Jemima now wore a tailored two-piece suit of dark blue wool, a light green blouse and a pink scarf. The look was practical, though not severe.

"It's seven o'clock, sir," she said without glancing at her watch. "There's a splendid place in Hamilton called Fisherman's Cove. Their specialties are rockfish, lobsters and savories. I'd love some company for dinner."

The restaurant was plushly appointed, one flight up, with picture windows overlooking Hamilton harbor. The tablecloths were white and the tableware silver. The staff was formally attired.

"We may be working together when we return to England," she said. "Or maybe not. It's subject to my senior officer's approval. That's you, sir."

"Which puts me squarely on the spot, doesn't it, Miss James?"

"Perhaps." She smiled and looked more attractive than he'd yet seen her. She sipped her rum punch, smothered in Angostura bitters, then looked up. "You'll see my service records," she continued. "But should I tell you a few of the basics now?"

"Why not?"

Her eyes glowed. Deep aquamarine emeralds. The soft pink light of the restaurant only enhanced her.

"I come from a military family," she began. "My father was a colonel in the Free Polish Air Force. During the Battle of Britain, he flew with the RAF, commanding one of the Polish squadrons. He won a D.S.O. and D.F.C."

Christopher nodded. He'd known the groups of heroic Poles who'd fled Hitler and flown for England. "Then you're Polish," he said with some surprise.

"Half. My mother's Scottish. Her name is James. My father's name was Jablonski. Once we came to England, we changed it to James. It pleased my mother no end." She paused momentarily and something in her eyes changed. "Papa died in 1948," she concluded. "Bitter and disappointed."

"Over the fate of Poland?"

"That," she allowed, "as well as the treatment of Free Poles in England. All the Free Polish forces were prevented from taking part in the Victory Parade, you'll recall. No one wanted to offend the Russians."

"I remember," Christopher said. "It was disgraceful. Bloody politics."

"Well," she continued, "when I was old enough to get my higher certificate, I was accepted for Girton College, Cambridge. I read European languages. Russian. German. French. Granted, my background gave me a head start."

"Indeed it must have."

"In my last year, I became interested in foreign affairs. My supervisor suggested that I join the Royal Navy."

Christopher smiled. He'd never met two people in his life who'd shared the same progression into the Senior Service. "Extraordinary," he said, knowing what was coming next. Language specialists with Cambridge degrees didn't float around on scows for their entire hitches.

"At my first Admiralty selection board interview," she said, "a senior officer said they were earmarking me for Room 39. I didn't even know what it was at the time. But luckily the director of Naval Intelligence agreed with him. So here I am." She opened her hands an acquiescent gesture. "It's not a dull life, certainly."

He had to agree and would have liked to have told her how well her suit flattered her. But this wasn't the moment.

"Here I am listening to your CV, and I don't even know what the job is. Do you?"

"Russians," she said after a pause. "These days that's the only kind of job I get."

The waiter appeared with the starters.

It was early morning, January 25, 1956, when the

41

royal Navy aircraft touched down at HMS Daedalus, the Royal Naval Air Station at Lee-on-Solent. It lay between Southampton and Portsmouth in the south of England. And the base, like every Royal Navy establishment, took the HMS in its official title, much as a ship would.

The runway had just been cleared of snow when Christopher and Jemima emerged into a cold, English dawn. There was a uniformed Wren (Women's Royal Naval Service) driver waiting for them. She saluted and opened the door of the transport. They climbed into a black Rover.

"Now where?" he asked.

"Portsmouth, sir," the Wren answered. "The fastest and most direct route. Up to Alverstoke, then toward the south of Gosport and into HMS Dolphin at Fort Blockhouse. From there you take the captain's barge across King's Stairs at *Victory.*"

Gosport, and the road that led to it, was gray on this winter morning, setting the mood perfectly. First there was Haslar Royal Naval Hospital, where Christopher had once left his appendix. Then, just on the hospital's periphery, there was a Victorian mansion. Monckton House, he recalled with a grin. The Wrennery during the war. Great parties, he might have told Jemima, mostly during the fighting. He pondered those memories as the car covered the last quarter mile to the Fifth Submarine Flotilla at HMS Dolphin.

At the main gates, a petty officer came forward. He took IDs and scrutinized them carefully. As their car drove through, he gave a crisp salute.

In another five minutes, after a brief call on the officer of the day, Christopher and Jemima were aboard the captain's barge. Everywhere, as they crossed the harbor, the waters summoned up ghosts of men Christopher had known in the forties. He lifted his gaze to the low, gray cloud cover and Jemima stood a few yards away, trying to read his mind. He forced a smile. Then there was the vibration of the barge coming alongside.

Christopher turned and his heart jumped. There, suddenly visible through the mist, was HMS *Victory*. He'd almost forgotten. *Victory,* commissioned in 1778 and still commissioned now, was the crown jewel of the British Navy. She had been Nelson's flagship in 1805, the vessel from which he commanded his fleet as he simultaneously vanquished the combined fleets of France and Spain at Trafalgar. The sight of the majestic old ship and its one hundred four guns always inflamed Creighton's imagination. Nelson had perished from a sniper's bullet on the quarterdeck before the battle had ended: one more ghost that haunted Portsmouth. The huge white ensign flying at her stern, sent a thrill through him. He felt he was home. Protected.

"We're due in Nelson's cabin at 0900," Jemima told Christopher. He nodded. The barge completed securing alongside. They had one hour to be ready.

Creighton ate breakfast, showered and changed into uniform, one which bore the three gold lace stripes of a Commander. He allowed himself a long, critical look in the mirror. *Commander, RN*. He shook his head and grinned. This would take some getting used to.

It was 0847 when he arrived in the quarters once used by Admiral Nelson. He stood there alone and in awe. The great cabin of *Victory* was gigantic, occupying the entire aft section on the centre level of the ship, stretching from beam to beam. The afterpart contained a large panoramic series of framed windows. Christopher wondered how the glass had been replaced after battle. A large oak table with matching chairs stood amidships, ornate late-Georgian candelabra upon it. To starboard hung an oil portrait of Emma Hamilton.

It was half history, half shrine. Christopher glanced to the port side and saw Nelson's brass-fitted writing desk and, above it on the bulkhead, a pair of early eighteenth century double-barrelled and rifled pistols. He was just about to be swept away again by the majesty and authenticity of the ship, when Jemima came in and turned on an electric light.

Creighton frowned. Then his gaze fell upon her. Gone was her civilian clothing and in its place were an impeccably tailored dark blue jacket and skirt, a crisp white shirt and black tie, black nylons and shoes. Eight burnished buttons marched smartly down to a trim waist. On her cuffs were the two distinctive blue braid stripes of a Wren second officer. Her hair was worn neatly close to her head, standing off from her collar.

But what his eyes settled upon was something else altogether. Above her left breast she wore the red and blue stripes of the George Medal. It was an award for acts of uncommon valor. His eyes moved quickly away, but she caught him observing it. She hadn't picked it up, he knew, by playing marbles. It was 0859.

"Quite a place, isn't this?" he asked, breaking an awkward silence.

"Ever been here before?" she asked.

He nodded. "A few times during the war."

"This is my first time."

"But probably not the last," he was about to say. But the words never came out, because he heard the ship's bells strike 0900 to the accompaniment of the bosun's pipes on the gangway outside. The gunner and petty officers gave the traditional compliments for an officer of flag rank: an admiral. These were followed by brisk footsteps on the deck outside.

Noisily, the door burst wide open. Mountbatten swept in. Christopher and Jemima came smartly to attention.

For a moment, Mountbatten and Creighton simply looked at each other. The First Sea Lord was in his fifties now, much grayer than when Christopher had last seen him. But he was sharply featured and handsome as ever. He was like a great actor making his entrance, charging the stage — in this case Nelson's great cabin — with his vitality, his determination, and the sheer force of his presence. He was immaculately turned out, and his admiral's blue uniform had a

45

holiness to it, nine rows of ribbons on his left breast and six full inches of an admiral's gold braid on each cuff. His face was keen and eager—fashioned, it seemed, by the outlandish places where he'd served his country. His eyes were slow-burning and censurious, sharp as thorns as they drew a slow bead and settled upon his male visitor. His grin was positively wolfish.

"Hello, Creighton," he said.

"Good morning, sir."

"Good of you to come." His voice was resonant with the timbre of the upper classes, his speech quick. Framed by the eighteenth-century door, Mountbatten seemed strangely tall. A thousand images formed before Creighton as he watched Lord Louis. Mountbatten and Creighton's father had been together briefly at Christ's College, Cambridge, where they became fast friends. That was how the relationship between Christopher and Mountbatten had begun. From age twelve to sixteen the younger man had grown up in Hampshire, just fifteen miles north of Broadlands, the Mountbatten estate. Christopher had always been like a nephew.

"Did you have any bother getting here, Christopher?"

"None, sir."

"I should bloody well hope not." His blue eyes were set and intense now, quiet and focused like a pointer's. "I don't send Wren second officers off to North America just for fun, thought I can't imagine that they don't have some along the way."

46

Jemima's expression was unwavering. Mountbatten winked in her direction.

"How are you this morning, Miss James?" he asked.

"Very good, sir."

"Yes. So I see. Now get outside the cabin. Stand by and wait till I call for you."

She turned abruptly and stalked to the door. She closed it noisily while shooting the Sea Lord a withering glare. Creighton suppressed a schoolboy smile.

"Right, then," Mountbatten continued, ignoring her. "Let's have a seat."

By a seat, he meant they were to occupy Nelson's table, with him at the head. Mountbatten removed his cap and flung it onto the desk. It was as if Nelson's ghost had found flesh and blood. All three eased into chairs.

"Playing music, were you, Christopher?" Mountbatten continued. "In some orchestra in New York?"

"A jazz quartet, sir."

Lord Louis arched his eyebrows. "I was in a jazz quartet once," he said. "At Cambridge. I played the drums until deposed by Claude Hulbert. A fine professional. That great composer Noel Gay also played in it . . ." He looked at Christopher and smiled. "And of course your father, who played every instrument known to man. Come to think of it, it was *his* group. Sometimes Jack Hulbert and Cicely Courteneidge joined in."

"I did hear about it, sir."

"Yes, well, quite. How *is* your father, Christopher?"

"Pretty fair, thank you, sir."

"Good. Good," answered Mountbatten as he surveyed Christopher with a long, critical gaze. Creighton was used to the Sea Lord's lightning fast none sequiturs and rapid-fire shifts of subject. But he wasn't ready for what followed. "Christopher." Mountbatten said, "I want you to take command of Desmond Morton's old intelligence section. M Section. Your old unit. With immediate effect."

Momentarily, Christopher was stunned. "Good God, sir. I've been on the Reserve List for three years. I don't know the first thing about current operations."

"Doesn't matter. I'm about to tell you all you need to know. I've a task to set before you. Something I cannot do myself. I must have a man whom I trust implicitly. No room for the Cantebrugian poufs and traitors who permeate our so-called Secret Intelligence Service." One of Mountbatten's long epicine fingers tapped slowly upon Nelson's desk. "Tell me honestly. Are you up to it?"

"If you think I am, sir. Yes," Creighton answered.

"Fine." For a moment Lord Louis' eyes twinkled mischievously and he appeared younger than he was. He continued to address Christopher. "Now. Second Officer James. I know you've just met her. But what do you think?"

"Sir, I hardly know her—"

"You'll have time to read her file. Meanwhile I'll save us some time. Here's what I think. She's a most

48

unusual and formidable young officer. Immensely talented, marvellous sense of humor, thoroughly and classically educated. Speakes four languages perfectly, five if you include American. Brave, selfless and enterprising. She's achieved a lot for her age, which is twenty-eight, in case you're wondering."

"Sir, I actually hadn't —"

"Like all the Wrens attached to the Section, she has a black belt in karate. Just like the men. She's the best woman I've ever seen with your martial arts. A true demon. Glad she's on our side."

"Yes, sir."

"Soviet expert, too. You probably know that. I'd say she's close to the best our section has on that score, too. Knows everything right off. Even has her own network of informants. Fancy that."

"Impressive again," Christopher said.

"Here are the drawbacks," Mountbatten continued. "She's driven too damned hard for success in the Royal Navy. Out to pick up where her disappointed father left off. See that bloody George Medal? Know how she earned it? Charged into a burning helicopter that crashed during exercises. Pulled out three officers before the damned machine blew up. Total disregard for her own safety. Could turn into a problem. Bears scrutiny. But the M Section also needs a second in command. Since this is to be a Russian operation, she would be perfect. Since you'll head the operation, Christopher, the choice will be yours. But if you were to recommend her, I would look upon it favorably."

"I'll bear that in mind, sir."

Mountbatten stared at him. Other officers would have accepted the pressure from the First Sea Lord at once and would have immediately made the recommendation. But not Christopher. Mountbatten would have been disappointed if he had. "Bear it quite firmly in mind, Christopher. Deputy Commander in the Section normally presupposes a First Officer's status, so there'd be a promotion involved."

"Yes, sir," Christopher acknowledged.

There was a silence. "All right. Wheel her in." Mountbatten said suddenly.

"Aye, aye, sir," said Christopher, getting up and opening the door.

Jemima James came in. She walked to the table and stood smartly to attention, her hat under her arm.

Mountbatten glanced at her impatiently. "You can belay all that rubbish, Miss James, and sit down. Both of you."

They both sat at Nelson's table.

"Miss James," said the First Sea Lord. "Commander Hamilton is now in command of M Section."

"Congratulations, sir," she said quietly to Christopher.

"All right then," Mountbatten said, forging ahead. "This is why you're here. Nikita Khrushchev is to be assassinated upon his arrival in England on April 18 next. We don't know yet how potent the threat is, or who is behind it. But we know it does exist and we know we must take it extremely seriously. Your job is to prevent it from happening. Clear?"

"Clear, sir" said Christopher. Jemima echoed the

words.

"Good. Now listen very carefully. Here's the general idea."

FOUR

Christopher would never have sat still for any part of the story had it come from anyone other than Mountbatten.

Lord Louis had been in Gibraltar a week earlier while Christopher was still tickling the ivories at Father John's. As First Sea Lord, Mountbatten had been charged with overseeing British participation in joint NATO maneuvers in the Mediterranean.

On his way back, he'd stopped in Paris, checking into a four-bedroom suite at the Crillon, overlooking the Place de la Concorde. "A view fit more for a lord than for a sailor," Mountbatten allowed. The visit to France was social, he said. He was visiting Bourbon cousins who'd resided there since Franco sent them on indefinite vacation.

"And that's what we're discussing today, young Christopher," said Mountbatten, beginning. "Relatives. But not Bourbons. Romanovs! Allow me to revise history for you."

Mountbatten had been returning to the hotel a few evenings previously, he recalled, when he took a walk up a side street, the Rue de Pont-Aven. It was a favorite shortcut past some old shops which sold bric-a-brac. When he had the time, Lord Louis loved to prowl here for hours on end. On more than one occasion he had purchased genuine relics of his own family, the Battenbergs and the Hesse-Darmstadts. He was ever hopeful of finding another. Yet on this evening as he ambled slowly back toward the Crillon, scanning the windows of the closed shops, he was suddenly conscious that something was wrong. It was not anything he saw or noted; it was something he felt.

He scanned the street. It was past 9 P.M. and there was no one to be seen on the block. Very few cars were parked on the old cobblestones and there was no immediate traffic. Yet he *knew* there was something. He made up his mind to walk briskly toward the hotel. Just then, he heard a voice.

"Admiral Mountbatten, my lord?"

Very slightly, Mountbatten felt himself jump. The voice was male, accented and very close. He turned and faced a sturdy, heavily built man who appeared to be about forty. The man was dark and jowly. A trench coat hung loosely around his shoulders, giving him a vaguely military appearance.

"Yes?" Mountbatten answered.

The man stood quietly for a moment. He had been

waiting for Mountbatten — knew him well enough to know the route he'd take — and had lurked in a doorway. Two other men, tall and Germanic, now appeared from the same spot. Mountbatten looked at them disdainfully, but wondered if the day had finally come when he would rue his stubborn refusal to travel with a Royal Navy bodyguard.

"We have come to escort you to a meeting," the leader said.

Mountbatten glared at them. "Who's so damned important that you have to hide in doorways to abduct me?'

"We would not force you to come with us or threaten you in any way, my lord," said the heavy-set man. "This is a request from a blood relative, a woman, who will be in peril if you do not come."

Mountbatten was eased by the absence of any spoken threat. And curiosity was upon him. Intrigues, dramas, and secret plots had always been part of his life. Fact was, he loved them.

"How do we get there?" he asked.

"We have a car."

Mountbatten walked with the first man back up the block. The other two proceeded ahead. Mountbatten and his escort stopped by a shuttered café. Moments later, a black Citroën appeared with the two men in it. They gave Mountbatten the passenger side of the front seat. They stressed the fact that he was free to get out at any time. Naturally, he remained.

There followed a brief ride through some of the

back streets of Paris. A light drizzle began. Eventually, the car turned at the southwest corner of the Bois de Boulogne and swung into the short driveway of a three-story house. Mountbatten tried to memorize the route, but failed. He noted that the house had no marking of any sort, diplomatic or otherwise.

The leader graciously escorted Mountbatten through a double-doored portico and through another large door across a hallway. The Sea Lord passed an enormous wood fire. Outside another door, two great bearded men — they appeared to be Cossacks — stood guard, arms folded before them. The leader nodded and one of the Cossacks opened the door. "Please enter," he said to Mountbatten.

Lord Louis went into a private chamber. The door closed silently behind him.

The room was large, beautiful and furnished mostly in the style of Louis XV. It had windows which overlooked a large illuminated garden which, in turn, bordered the Bois de Boulogne. Mountbatten gave it a quick look.

A small door opened in a wall where no door appeared to be. A slight, bearded old man appeared. He was fancifully dressed, almost in the style of a nineteenth-century gentleman-at-court. Mountbatten's first instinct was to laugh. He was now convinced that someone was playing an elaborate joke.

"Lord Mountbatten," the man intoned with a curt bow. "I am Count Mikhail Petrovich Nesterov."

Mountbatten sighed at the Russian insistence on always giving all their names at once.

"Please tell me why I'm here," Mountbatten answered kindly.

"My mistress would prefer to tell your yourself," the old Russian said.

"And who would that be?"

Nesterov fell silent, then gave way. A slight sound made Mountbatten look up. A woman in a cowled robe, her face obscured, had followed the old man into the room. She stopped a few feet away from the First Sea Lord. She stood quietly.

"I think this joke is bloody well close to its end," Mountbatten said. "Come on. Let's see you."

The woman began to tremble slightly, as if ill. Then Mountbatten realized that she was laughing. Mountbatten would have been angered, but a disturbing sense of recognition was upon him. It deepened when the woman spoke.

"I'm sorry, Dickie," she said in lightly accented English. "I couldn't stop myself. You know I always laugh when I become emotional."

Her easy familiarity gripped him. But it was the strange, intimate way she addressed him that chilled him. He took a step closer. "Who are you?" he asked, very serious now. "What do you want?"

She squared her shoulders and the laughter was gone. "I greet you, noble blood brother, on behalf of your imperial relations. May God be in your head and on your lips and in your heart."

It had been forty years since he had heard the traditional Romanov greeting for an intimate member of the family. It settled uneasily upon him.

"Anyone could have learned those words," he said.

"Yes, dear cousin. But I am not anyone."

"I suppose you're one of the many imposters who claim to be a daughter of the last Czar. And that you survived the family's execution at Tsarskoe Selo."

"It was Ekatirinburg in the Urals. In the cellar of the Ipatiev house."

Mountbatten blinked, but countered, "Yes. And according to Sokolov's official inquiry, there were no survivors."

"And since when have you respected the official word? The young Dickie of Battenberg I knew was a confirmed rebel."

He drew close to her, annoyed. He reached for the hood that shadowed her face. "Who are you?" he snapped.

His hand came up quickly to move the hood aside, but her hand moved with astonishing speed. She held his wrist and stopped him.

"Long, long ago," she said patiently as she released her grip and moved away from him, "in August of 1908, you and your mother, my Aunt Vicky, were staying with us at our villa in the Alexandrine Park at Peterhof. You took me by the hand and led me into the conservatory. There you told me you loved me. You asked me to marry you when we grew up. I accepted happily. The betrothal was our secret."

Mountbatten was motionless. Over a lifetime, he'd

discussed his youthful engagement with no one — except his wife, Edwina. And to Edwina he'd never mentioned the conservatory.

The woman went on. "And then in 1913 at Schloss Heiligenberg, we renewed our promise. Don't you remember, Dickie? You wore a cutaway coat for the first time. Oh, but you were proud, feeling so grown up. You teased me that day about being an older woman. One year older than you." Mountbatten stood before the woman, speechless and motionless. Her voice bubbled with amusement. "We never saw each other again. Because of the World War. The Revolution. But I sent you my photograph. And you wrote back, saying you would always keep it near you."

Mountbatten vividly recalled the truth of everything she said. Even the photograph. It still rested on the mantelpiece of his bedroom at Broadlands, his estate in Hampshire, a reminder of what might have been. He'd had every intention of marrying his first love as soon as the World War ended.

Mountbatten walked to her and gently pulled back her hood, revealing her graying hair. For a moment he averted his gaze, not knowing what he hoped to see. Then he looked into her deep blue eyes — cornflower eyes, the family used to call them — and instantly he knew.

"Marie," he said gently.

"Yes," she answered.

"But *how?*" Incredulous, he couldn't restrain himself. He kissed both cheeks of the woman he hadn't seen for forty years. He embraced her. He was suddenly lost in another world, not a doubt in his mind that the woman in his arms was the third child of the last Czar. Her Imperial Highness, the Grand Duchess Marie. After several moments he broke away. "Why did you never contact us? We heard a rumor about your marrying in Romania. But I didn't believe it."

Marie put a finger to his lips. "I'll tell you everything when I can. I promise," she said. It had already dawned on him that she might not be free to answer all his questions.

He held her by the shoulders and looked closely at her. "Are you all right?" he asked. "Why have you brought me here? Why today after all these years?"

For a moment she hesitated, as if alarmed. Her eyes went to Nesterov.

The old count cleared his throat. "With respect, Marie Nikolayevna," he said softly.

"You must forgive my tutor," Marie began quickly. "He reminds me that there is so little time. Some White Russians have conceived a terrible plan. For decades they have wished to avenge the murder of my father and my brothers by the Bolsheviks. And now, for the first time since 1918, they will have a real opportunity." Marie's voice was distinct and calm. "They intend to murder President Bulganin and Chairman Khrushchev this April. In Portsmouth harbor."

Mountbatten let it sink in for a moment, then replied calmly, "They're attempting the impossible, I'm

60

happy to say. The Soviet visit was scheduled by Prime Minister Eden several months ago. Security, as you might imagine, has been and will be extremely tight. The tightest, I'd venture, since the wartime meetings between Churchill, Roosevelt and Stalin. Three Soviet ships will be visiting, and no unauthorized person will get anywhere near them." He paused for a moment, thinking it through. "This is the first visit to any Western democracy by any Soviet head of state since the Revolution. It's Eden's diplomatic coup, you know. He'd be apoplectic if anyone even hinted at a cancellation."

Marie was steadfast. "The assassination could be accomplished if you helped."

Mountbatten was stupefied. "What?"

"As head of the Royal Navy, you could arrange an adequate security gap."

"They are *mad* to even suggest it, much less believe that I would!" He was suddenly furious. "Is that what they sent you here to suggest?"

She nodded. "They know only too well that my mother, Alexandra, the Empress, was your mother's sister. Khrushchev has publicly praised the murder of the imperial family. So has Bulganin."

"And so these White Russian crackpots consider the Soviet heads of state appropriate targets? Even though they could set off a world war?"

"That's correct. They've traveled the world raising money in my name. They've hired mercenaries. Irish and German. They may not succeed, Dickie, but they will attack with great force."

"And they *forced* you to come here to solicit my help?"

"That's correct."

"How do they know you'll return?"

"They maintain a very close surveillance upon my grandson, Alexis. My father's only legitimate male heir. They located his family's home in Cannes at the same time they came to Mégève." Marie blew out a long sigh. "They've also asked me to tell you this: if you do not help them, or if they do not succeed, they promise to kill you, your wife Edwina, and your daughters Patricia and Pamela, as well as Alexis and me."

"The bloody thugs!' Threatening women and children, are they? Well, you can damn well tell them—"

"I will tell them only one thing, Dickie!" she interrupted. "I will tell them that you wished to think the matter through. While they think you are searching for a security gap they desire, you can be preparing your means of striking back. I know you, Dickie. That's exactly how you are thinking."

Mountbatten folded his arms and for a moment his gaze drifted from the woman before him. He turned in thought and walked to the window that faced the garden. He suddenly understood the illumination round the house. No one could approach from any direction without being seen. He was in the center of an enemy fortress.

He turned back to Marie and nodded gently. "As

you suggest," he concluded. Marie smiled. Her eyes spoke volumes.

She nodded. "I also might be able to help in a small way," she said.

On the desk was a small leather folio. From it she pulled a formal note card. Her own. On it was the pencil sketch of a man's face.

"I drew it from memory earlier this evening," she said. "It's a fair likeness of a man I've seen several times. I believe him to be their leader."

Mountbatten nodded and studied the face. This man, Marie said, had called upon her once since she'd been taken prisoner two weeks earlier. He'd been shown great deference by her guards. If this whole operation wasn't his idea, then he was high up in it. That was enough to prompt her to make a sketch, she explained.

"He's about six feet tall," Marie said. "Very proper, very calm, very polite. Prussian, I'm certain. And a fanatical anti-Communist, I'm sure. I know one when I see one, Dickie."

Mountbatten studied the face. It meant nothing to him. In the space of three seconds he searched through decades of public life trying to fix the man at some remote moment. He failed.

"Keep it," she said. "You'll find someone who knows him."

"I'll put it through the files," he said. He pocketed the drawing.

"Marie," Mountbatten finally said, "tell me one

other thing."

"Anything I can."

"Eldest male heirs did not necessarily inherit the imperial throne. It was always the Czar's duty to appoint a successor from a family if the Imperial Council was unable to assemble in a national crisis."

"I knew you'd ask," she said.

"Before your father died, did he make an order of succession?"

Marie nodded.

"Whom did he name?"

Marie slowly held up her left hand. One the fourth finger was the ring of Peter and Catherine the Great — the symbol of the sovereign ruler of All the Russias. Astounded, Mountbatten took her hand. It was a supreme moment for him, loving protocol as he did. He would kiss the ring, step back a pace, bow his head and say, "Your Imperial Majesty!"

But she stopped him short, raising the hand away from him and shaking her head. "No, Dickie," she said. "Remember all those knobbly-kneed courtiers we used to laugh at?" She took his hand. "Well, between you and me — there is no way."

She smiled again and Moutbatten nodded. Then he hugged her. He kissed her on both cheeks. As he recalled it, he was gone a few minutes later, driven back to the Crillon in the same car that had transported him to Marie.

At the head of Nelson's table, Mountbatten steepled

his fingers. "I took the next plane back to London," he said, "getting angrier all the time. A bunch of White Russian crackpots cook up a scheme like this and they drop it in our backyard. I went to see the Prime Minister immediately. I was absolutely right: he was furious. Apoplectic!"

Eden's disbelief preceded his anger, Mountbatten said. Disbelief that a Romanov grand duchess, the Empress of all the Russias in exile, could be alive. Disbelief that a Prince Alexis could exist, much less be held by a faction of militant anti-Communists in France. Disbelief even that his First Sea Lord could have arrived at 10 Downing Street in full admiral's uniform at six A.M. to tell such a monstrous tale.

But then Eden's disbelief had dissolved into fear: specifically, fear that the Soviet state visit could be jeopardized. As Eden listened to Mountbatten, a thin line of sweat beaded along the Prime Minister's temples. His face reddened. Finally, Mountbatten raised Eden briskly to his feet by offering his resignation.

"Your *what?*" Eden roared.

"Well, how would it look if an attempt on the life of Khrushchev and Bulganin *were* made?" Mountbatten asked. "Here I am, head of the Royal Navy, the nephew of the last Czar. Imagine —"

"Preposterous!" said Eden, waving away Mountbatten's suggestion with a curt stroke of his right arm. "And if you offer your resignation directly to the Queen, I'll recommend that she refuse you, too. Cousin or not."

Mountbatten's eyes twinkled as he recounted the moment to Christopher and Jemima. The wolfish grin returned. Creighton knew how greatly pleased Lord Louis must have been if his resignation was refused.

"Which brings us back to you, Christopher," Mountbatten said. "You and Second Officer James."

They waited, both of them.

"You now know the situation you are facing. As you may also know, I have long-standing engagements to inspect the Commonwealth navies in the Far East. Austrialia, New Zealand, India and so on. This will take me out of the country from March 11 until April 27. During the last ten days of this period, Bulganin and Khrushchev will come and go. That moves this problem onto your shoulders. The decisions will be yours. You'll be able to contact me by cypher, of course, but you'll have to make your own moves."

"Yes, sir. Of course," was all Creighton could say.

"What is your initial impression?"

Christopher thought quietly for almost a full minute. Jemima made no effort to interject. "Mostly a big blank slate," Creighton finally answered. "But the capture of Her Imperial Highness does show that they can act boldly. And with some efficiency."

"Taking a woman prisoner isn't quite the same as getting at the Soviet leaders," Jemima said.

"No, but it does confirm that these people do exist. The question is, can they really launch an operation of this scale?" Christopher thought again for a moment. "I know they won't succeed. But we can't have even an attempt. Not in England. And particularly not in Portsmouth. I assume, sir, that the Russians and their ships will be under Royal Navy protection?"

"You assume correctly."

"Coordinating security with the Soviets will be a nightmare," Christopher said.

"I expect it will," replied Mountbatten. "But that is our Jemima's business. She'll charm the 'nyets' out of our Soviet friends." He thought for a moment, then added, "Well, maybe this'll help." He put his hand into his uniform jacket and pulled out a small ivory envelope. He tossed it across the table to Creighton, who reached for it. "What do you make of that?" asked Mountbatten.

Both Christopher and Jemima recognized it from Mountbatten's account of his meeting with Marie. It contained the sketch that she had made.

"That is the mercenary leader," said Mountbatten.

Christopher took out the drawing from the envelope. Jemima looked over his shoulder. But both their eyes fell upon the sketch with no recognition.

Suddenly Jemima picked it up and put it back in the envelope. "I'll run it through our files," she said. "And those of our European subsections. Also, I have a contact in S.D.E.C.E., the French Secret Service. I'll try it there as well."

Mountbatten nodded and rose, bringing the meeting to a conclusion. "I'll make two suggestions," he said. "You might look up your old mentor, Desmond

Morton. He can give you some background on current intelligence situations. It might help. Similarly, you might call upon some of Jemima's favorite informants. Miss James, anything in progress on that score?"

"Roger Garin, sir."

Mountbatten thought for only an instant. "Yes. Of course."

"Strangely enough," Jemima said, "I already received a signal directly from him. Unusual. So he must have something for us."

"When do you meet?"

"Three evenings from now, I think," said Jemima. "Maybe four. He's not the easiest, you know."

"Who's Roger Garin?" asked Christopher.

She explained. "He's my best double agent," she said. "A sly old Russian. Lives in London under a pseudonym. Displaced person after the war, spent time in some of the camps. He's a Jew but nonpracticing, so Moscow trusts him."

"He's also an old lecher. In love with our Jemima," Mountbatten said, needling.

"Trust him to do what?" asked Christopher, staying with the point.

"Soviet intelligence, the MVD set him up as agent in place for Great Britain after the war," she answered. "Medium-level stuff. Started reporting back to them in 1947. We turned him right away, though, and he's been ours without question since the following year. He's my best source on Soviet operations against the West. My own window into their new KGB, as they now call their state security apparatus."

"Marvellous," said the Sea Lord, standing. "You're on your way already." Mountbatten retrieved his cap from the desk and, seconds later, found the door just as easily.

On a day twenty degrees below zero in Red Square, General Ivan Alexandrovich Serov's shirt was soaked with sweat. Serov threw off his sealskin greatcoat, fur cap and scarves in the Kremlin cloakroom at the south entrance and hurriedly climbed the last of four flights of steps. Nikita Khrushchev's private office was a large corner one which had once been Stalin's favorite. It was from there that the First Secretary of the Communist party of the Soviet Union now presided over the Party, the government and All the Russias. So summoning Serov, the director of the KGB, from lunch had posed little problem.

To give the invitation its proper emphasis, and to make certain that Serov came directly and without contacting anyone else, Khrushchev had sent along a pair of Red Army majors. One was Russian. The other was a Tatar, a huge strapping thug of an army officer. As Serov arrived on Khrushchev floor, the majors walked stolidly behind him. They had much more spring in their steps than the fifty-year-old intelligence chief.

Serov was a burly, rugged man with piercing blue-gray eyes, closely cropped hair and an uneven skull. He was an enigma to the West, but totally plausible within internecine Soviet politics. Once, in his native Ukraine, he'd been a Red Army artillery officer until transferring into Beria's NKVD in 1938. There followed a swift rise within the Soviet intelligence community. In Kiev he first worked beside Khrushchev sniffing out — and liquidating — enemies of Stalin and the state in 1939. By the end of that year, he was head of the Ukrainian NKVD.

Throughout his career he had been a killer, but a businesslike one rather than an enthusiastic one. He was a Party man, though, detached and cynical, a man who approved executions during the day, then emerged as a droll, grinning witty guest at social occasions in the evening. When the MVD, the Ministry of State Security, was reorganized into the KGB following Stalin's death, Khrushchev, trusting Serov, appointed him the KGB's first director, thus creating a KGB distinctly loyal to himself. But loyalties in the Kremlin were transient, and as Serov arrived at the door to Khrushchev's office, he fully expected the worst.

He was there, he reasoned, to hear charges that were to be lodged against him. His arrest would follow, as would execution or imprisonment.

Serov turned to the two majors as they stood before the door. "What is the Party Secretary's mood today?" he asked nervously.

The majors stared humorlessly at Serov for a few

moments. The Tatar finally responded. "Just as it always it," he said. "Excellent and fair-minded."

Serov gave a weak nod. Then all three stood in silence for twenty seconds. Finally, the Russian major reached to the door and knocked loudly five times with a clenched fist. Khrushchev shouted something unintelligible from within. The major opened the door and gently shoved Serov into Khrushchev's chamber.

Serov stepped in the direction he'd been pushed. The door closed behind him; the soldiers remained in the corridor outside. The KGB director stared at a large oval table and found himself looking at the most recognizable living man in the Soviet Union. He said nothing.

Khrushchev was seated at the table, reading what appeared to be agricultural reports. The First Secretary of the Party sat with his reading glasses across his nose, wearing a wine-colored regimental tie and his blue serge suit. Khrushchev owned three other suits, two gray and one brown. The blue one was Italian and was his favorite — the three others were Russian. Today his suit was bedecked with his Order of Lenin on the right breast and three Orders of the Soviet Union on the left.

The office was spacious and, like the outer corridor that led to it, was painted a uniform light green. The three windows were shielded with heavy beige screens and all illumination came from a pair of big white globes on the ceiling, topped with shades and concealing bulbs that burned with the harsh light of flares. On the First Secretary's desk was an array of six telephones, all black.

Khrushchev finally looked up. He was a portly, balding figure, almost comical as his large stomach and stocky arms kept him at an awkward distance from the writing surface of his desk. But his brown eyes were keen with concentration and his brow was wrinkled. His thick fingers were wrapped clumsily around a fountain pen, which he set down as he began to speak.

"So. Comrade General Ivan Alexandrovish Serov?" he said slowly. Khrushchev was a master at making uncomfortable those called before him. He used those moments as a way of assessing a man's calm, seeing if a visitor had something to be nervous about. He was often given to addressing even those whom he knew well by their given and family names.

Serov knew the procedure and remained silent.

"Did you hear the latest joke that some of the Red Army officers are telling?" Khrushchev asked. "A journalist from *Izvestia* prints a story about Beria. He says that Beria was a syphilitic moron and was executed for the decay of his brains. The journalist draws twenty-five years at a labor camp. One year for telling the truth and twenty-four years for giving away a state secret."

Khrushchev's lips parted. He grinned like a gargoyle then laughed indulgently, his strong yellowing teeth dominating his smile. Serov managed a nervous chuckle.

"So then, Comrade Ivan Serov," Khrushchev said next. "What do you think about our trip to Great Britain in April?" Khrushchev asked the question as if he almost cared about Serov's opinion. Again, Khrushchev was trying to ferret out disloyal thoughts.

"I think it is an excellent idea," said Serov, knowing it was Khrushchev's initiative.

"So do I," the First Secretary agreed.

Serov glanced around the room. Two portraits had formerly presided on the wall behind Khrushchev's head, one of Stalin and one of Lenin. Stalin's was gone. So was the old portrait of Lenin. In their place hung a much larger portrait of Lenin, which occupied the same space. The grim, serious Lenin of the previous portrait had given way to a Lenin who was slightly—almost imperceptibly—grinning. Lenin the Godhead replaced by Lenin the beatific old man. This, too, made Serov nervous. Khrushchev sat beneath the grin, as if the grand old Bolshevik were watching in approval.

Other things had changed, too, Serov noticed. Stalin's hand-carved ornamental chair had been pushed into a corner where no human hand fell upon it. Khrushchev might dare to occupy Stalin's office, but for all his bombast and cockiness he dared not sit in Stalin's chair. There were still some devout Stalinists around, Khrushchev must have reckoned, who might be galvanized into some sort of action by such a heretical sight. So Khrushchev hadn't actually gotten rid of the chair, but he wasn't using it either. It reminded Serov of the sly way Khrushchev handled the matter of official cars. Stalin had kept an entourage of six automobiles: five Zil limousines and an old American Packard. He always moved in a convoy, sitting each time in a different car. This way no one ever knew exactly where he was. Lenin himself had decreed shortly after the Revolution that the political elite should be recompensed more than ordinary workers. And Lenin himself had owned a Rolls-Royce roadster. Serov recalled Khrushchev making an acerbic remark or two about all of the deceased Stalin's cars. Yet Khrushchev, now in power, had kept four of the cars, including the Packard, and moved about Moscow in a similar convoy. To Serov, all of this had an echo. They'd removed Stalin, but then again they hadn't.

Serov's eyes moved back to Khrushchev, who was gently chewing on the eraser end of a pencil. Mercifully, the First Secretary moved quickly to the issue at hand.

"I'm appointing you, Comrade General Ivan Alexandrovich Serov," Khrushchev said, "to take charge of all the security arrangements for the trip to England. Rear Admiral Kotov will be in charge of our warships, including on-board security in Portsmouth harbor. You will coordinate land security, both with our Navy and with the British."

Serov blinked in disbelief. Instead of being arrested, he was being placed in charge of the most significant protective arrangements since Yalta. He was so nonplussed that he merely nodded. He said nothing.

"You will have my complete backing and confidence, Ivan," Khrushchev concluded. "I will support any reasonable action you take."

Serov nodded again. Khrushchev looked back down to the papers before him. There seemed to be agricultural charts beneath a handwritten draft of some sprawling document. Serov supposed it was a speech, as Khrushchev loved to harangue any captive audience. The KGB director took his cue to leave. Another of Khrushchev's icy mannerisms: he never ended a conversation. He merely stopped talking.

When Serov left Khrushchev's chamber, the two Red Army majors were gone. Serov found his coat, fur cap and scarves in the lobby vestibule, wrapped himself tightly in them and left the Kremlin. His own driver jumped out of the black Chaika which had brought him and the two majors to see Khrushchev, but Serov waved the driver away. Despite the howling cold wind, he preferred to walk back to KGB headquarters two long blocks away. Serov often felt claustrophobic in Moscow, particularly when some political crisis was at hand. Fresh air permitted him to think.

Protect Khrushchev, Serov ruminated. Protect Bulganin. He tried to comprehend how he could even begin to make such arrangements. The trip was unprecedented. As he walked the direct route across Red Square to the "Center," as Russians of all classes called 2 Dzerzhinski Square, a panoply of unpleasant thoughts was upon him. Worst among them were two. First, he would have to depend on English security agents, particularly after the three Soviet ships entered British territorial waters. And second, as head of Soviet security, he would probably have to make the trip himself. He was less than excited about what his ambitious subordinates might attempt in his absence.

Serov arrived at the Center, a complex of unmarked gray stone buildings, and passed through the front door without glancing at the two armed guards in the large sentry booth. Before the Revolution this structure belong to the All-Russia Insurance Company. After World War II, as the MVD expanded both in personnel and goals, a nine-story addition was constructed by political prisoners and captured German soldiers. The old section enclosed a courtyard, on one side of which—conveniently—was Lubyanka prison. Here hundreds of men famous in Soviet history had marched or been dragged to their execution. Included were three chiefs of the state security apparatus—Beria in 1953, Yagoda in 1936 and Yezhov in 1939—a historical footnote not lost upon Ivan Serov.

Serov walked up the stairs to his office, a large but stark room which straddled the passageway between the old and new sections. He locked the door behind him and stood perfectly still. What he was most aware of were the portraits of Lenin and Stalin on his wall. How soon, he wondered, would the latter's picture be replaced by a likeness of the beaming, beneficent, coarse, unlettered Ukrainian peasant who was now First Secretary?

He walked to the bathroom and unlocked the medicine cabinet with keys from his pocket. He took out a bottle of Johnny Walker whisky, the one with the red label. He poured himself a stiff measure in a glass and carefully locked the whiskey back in the cabinet. It spoke volumes about his own agency that he, the director of the KGB, was obliged to lock up his liquor in his own office. He returned to his desk.

I will support any action you take, Khrushchev had told him. As he sipped his scotch, Serov was deeply irritated that Khrushchev hadn't equipped him with the facts needed to go with that support. Who would be the English liaison officer, for example? How would Serov deal with him? From which branch of their intelligence services would the man come? How could he coordinate anything when —?

Suddenly the worst thought of the afternoon was upon Serov. Was failure what Khrushchev *wanted?* Serov had supported Khrushchev on every step of the latter's path to absolute power in the Soviet Union. But now Khrushchev was less an old friend than a boss who filled the KGB director with dread. There wasn't a man in the Soviet Union, Serov reasoned, whom Khrushchev would hesitate to turn against if it suited his purposes.

Serov glanced at the calendar on his wall. It was February 3. The visit to England was ten weeks away.

He calmed himself. There was time, he told himself, to provide for Khrushchev's security abroad even if he did have to learn everything from scratch. He made a mental note, as he savored more of the Johnny Walker, to talk to some of the diplomats who had spend significant time in the West. Molotov. Mikoyan, Gromyko.

He sipped the remainder of his whiskey and found himself entertaining a strange thought. He considered the era of Joseph Stalin. He was surprised to find himself longing for it just a trifle. Old Joe had what the Russian people called "broad shoulders," meaning that he could carry all of the Soviet Union upon them. And as for the terror of that era—the purge trials, the labor camps and the executions, all of which started with a sharp knock on the door in the middle of the night—well, Lenin himself had sanctioned it.

As a young officer candidate at the Frunze Military Academy, Serov had done the mandatory memorization:

Felix Dzerzhinski, founder of the Cheka, the Bolshevik secret political police: *We stand for organized terror . . . We are not a court . . . The Cheka is obliged to defend the Revolution.*

And Lenin: *The energy and mass nature of merciless terror must be encouraged. Only a few in the narrow-minded intelligentsia will sob and fuss when the sword of the state lands on the heads of a few innocents.*

The comforting thing about Stalin, Serov mused as he finished his scotch, was that his terror was predictable. With Khrushchev, who knew what would happen next? And Khrushchev's shoulders, as everyone could see, were fat and stooped, capable of carrying nothing other than his own mantle of self-aggrandizement.

This image gave way to a more immediate concern. Who would be his opposite number in England? Who would coordinate Anglo-Russian security? It was vital that Serov contact this man right away. His life might well depend on it.

FIVE

Sergei Popov, the Russian, was doing what he did best: waiting for the right moment. He checked his watch as he sat in Regent's Park. It was a few minutes past nine in the morning, which meant that Benjamin Kugelhof, the man he intended to kill, would soon pass by.

Popov was a tall, sturdy, fair-skinned man with thinning, sandy hair. He wore a dark overcoat in which a bulky Smith & Wesson .38 revolver sat clumsily in the left-hand pocket. And now that he'd entered the day-to-day orbit of his victim, he was anxious to get on with things.

Popov stayed on his bench, his face buried in the morning *Daily Express* as Kugelhof came into view, ambling along the walkway in his slow but deliberate manner. Pudgy and sixtyish, with untidy gray hair and a generous gut, Kugelhof was a man who normally wore an easy smile. The assassin who was waiting for him never had any smile at all.

Kugelhof passed a few feet in front of Popov, but the Russian never looked up. The older man's eyes settled upon the younger one for a few seconds, then continued on. A minute later, Popov rose and followed from a distance.

Benjamin Kugelhof, as he explained it to his new circle of friends within the world of London classical music, had come from Canada to England in 1950. Once, when he'd downed a liberal amount of claret, he'd muttered something about having spent time in a Nazi death camp in 1944. But he'd never spoken of it again. And if he bore psychological scars, they didn't show. He was a cheerful, easygoing man, liked by all who knew him. Now he was building himself something of an impressive musical career late in life. Friends were happy for him.

He could play a competent Rachmaninov on the piano and could do great justice to a Beethoven concerto on the violin. But upon the strings of a harp, Benjamin Kugelhof could play like a lost angel. "My fingers are celestial," he liked to tell anyone who'd listen, holding up ten gnarled, stubby little things. "My gift from a benevolent God." He could light matches from a matchbook with one hand and could make a deck of cards sing and dance. "I also could have become a great pickpocket," he'd brag to friends. "But unfortunately, I'm honest. So I play the harp."

And he played it with great success. At the end of the 1955 music season he auditioned for the London

Philharmonic, where he won a spot, replacing a much-loved woman in her forties who was cruelly beset with arthritis.

Each morning, as Popov now knew well, Kugelhof walked in a circuitous route from his home in St. John's Wood to a small office he kept in Wigmore Street. He was part-owner of a family import-export firm which did business in spices and lace between Hungary and Canada. He spent the morning at the office going through mail, keeping European accounts in order. Occasionally, he took time out to flirt outrageously with two women — one English, one American — who ran a prosperous literary agency across the corridor. Popov knew all that, because he'd been tracking Kugelhof for ten days and had broken into his office.

The old man was slow afoot, and it cost the Russian great effort to remain far behind him. But at least, Popov noted, Kugelhof was an unsuspecting soul, not given to quick reversals of direction. Fact was, this assignment looked painfully easy. The old man appeared a bit of a nonentity, with no protection at all. It wasn't the assassin's habit to question why his commanders wanted a certain person killed. But this mission struck even Popov as odd, to the extent that he wondered about anything at all.

The Russian knew that the crucial moment was coming. He had learned the old man's schedule. He followed him for a few minutes this morning and made the decision.

Kugelhof lived alone in a comfortable house. No

wife, no maid, no children. Occasionally he would pick up a young woman—the old man indulged an unquenchable appetite for leggy blondes in their mid-thirties—and take her home overnight. But these he apparently picked up after performances. He had just had one on Saturday, a nice Danish blonde at that. But this was Monday. The old man would invariably be at home alone for the next few nights.

As Kugelhof passed out of Regent's Park, Popov turned in another direction. An old Jew, he concluded, sleeping alone in a vulnerable house. An easy job. In a way, Popov felt mildly ashamed of himself. But orders were orders, he reminded himself. It was time to get on with the job.

Just being in London, after all, made him more than slightly nervous. It was time to finish business and go home.

At the same moment, not far away in the same city, Christopher Creighton pulled his navy greatcoat tightly to him. He was on his way from the Admiralty to the Palace of Westminster. He had left HMS *Victory* the previous afternoon and had bedded down at the old M Section apartment at Northways, at Swiss Cottage. He was finally rested.

The Royal Navy's landmark headquarters was buttressed on its western flank by the same concrete walls that had been thrown up during the last big war. The walls were among the city's finest eyesores. All polished Londoners, in particular the late Queen Mary, loved to hate them. Although the old Queen waged a lifelong battle against ivy, which she reckoned a pest, she had on occasion sent notes to various Sea Lords lauding the Navy's attempt to camouflage their edifice with the dreaded weed. The Queen, the widow of George V, had passed away peacefully three years earlier. On this afternoon, Christopher noted with a wry smile, she was probably rolling in her grave. In the harsh midwinter sun, the vines were bare. The concrete bunker was there in all its ugliness for the world to see.

Christopher walked from Admiralty Arch down Whitehall. He saw that some scattered wreaths still decorated the base of the Cenotaph, Britain's memorial to the dead of the two World Wars.

Other officers walked past without stopping. Creighton stepped off the pavement, faced the monument and saluted. He was not a fervently religious man, but in wartime too many he had known and loved had died. Some because of him. His superiors in M Section had been responsible only to King George VI and Prime Minister Churchill. They had sometimes deemed it in the national and Allied interest that certain of their own countrymen should perish. Young Christopher, upon occasion, had been the instrument of their destruction.

Now Mountbatten had conferred upon Christopher powers so comprehensive that now *he* could order a death in the national interest. He shuddered. This time the morality, and the guilt, were squarely his.

He read the epitaph chiseled upon the granite monument: LEST WE FORGET. He made the sign of the cross and continued on.

Beneath the pavement level of the City of London, Jemima James presided in a fifteen-by-twenty room with whitewashed walls, green ventilating conduits and red heating ducts. Half a dozen Wrens moved quickly about, putting the finishing touches on the place that had been designated as Section headquarters.

There were no windows. An enormous mahogany table that would have been E-shaped had its center bar not been removed dominated the chamber. Ranks of hard armless chairs faced the table's focal point — a large wooden armchair. On the floor beside the chair stood a fire bucket, once used primarily for snuffing cigars. Above the chair was a huge map of England and continental Europe. On a side table was a red dispatch box bearing the royal coat of arms and a twelve-by-six-inch card. The card, in bold block letters, bore the words Queen Victoria once uttered in retort to a suggestion, during the Boer War, that Great Britain was courting a bloody nose:

WE ARE NOT INTERESTED IN THE POSSIBILITIES OF DEFEAT. THEY DO
NOT EXIST.

Jemima James stood behind a pair of communications officers, Lieutenants Philip Dobbs and Peter

McGhie. They were installing equipment on frequencies and circuits that had been designated Most Secret. Included was a single red telephone which would sit at the command position on the table and work only on a microwave frequency rated Top Secret/Priority One. Communications, Jemima's specialty, was also Mountbatten's specialty. Any slipups in that department could cost her a career. But like Queen Victoria, Jemima James was not interested in the possibilities of defeat.

The selection of the old War Cabinet Room as Section headquarters had been her idea, quickly accepted by both Mountbatten and Christopher. Situated three stories deep below the Office of Works, the tourists and the traffic of Whitehall, the complex was known within the military and within the government as "The Hole in the Ground." Or, less flatteringly, simply as The Hole. Tight, compact and secure, these rooms remained untouched since 1945, just as Churchill had left them. It was said that a wet cough drop couldn't slip in or out unnoticed.

As Christopher came to the double safety doorways of the War Room, the depression he had been expecting came swiftly upon him. Memories filled him. He could have stood there for hours, conjuring up old friends and the things they had achieved together in the war years. Then through the doors, he observed Jemima James checking her communications and his mood had gone.

Jemima was facing away from him as the electrical officers waited for her approval of their work. She tested each line and completed test calls to the Admiralty, Broadlands and other key stations.

Christopher grinned. Even in uniform while giving orders or taking them, she was inordinately pretty — tall, puckish, perfectly authoritative in manner. He noticed her long legs again, her almost perfect figure, her hair pinned back and her slim arms. He caught himself thinking. She was exactly the type of woman that he could . . . But Jemima James was not for him, he reminded himself. There was serious business at hand. Personal feelings were always the first breakdown of discipline, as well as the most fatal.

Christopher walked into the room. Jemima turned and saw him. "Attention in the room!" she ordered. All the officers and Wrens snapped to. Then Jemima walked to Christopher and stood smartly before him.

"M Section communication room, sir! All equipment installed, tested and operational. Duty signals staff closed up, sir!"

"Thank you, Miss James. Signals watch may carry on."

"Aye, aye, sir." She turned to her staff. "Carry on, please!"

"Aye, aye, ma'am," said the senior Wren.

Christopher flung his cap on an adjacent table. He caught Jemima smiling as she turned away. It was just as Mountbatten had done on the *Victory*. They both noticed. "All right, Miss James!" he snapped. In a voice consciously imitating Charlemagne's, he used Mountbatten's favorite terminology. "Wheel them in," he said.

"Aye, aye, sir." She turned to her senior Wren officer, Angela Lawson, a brunette with dark eyes and a round face, almost heavy, but still pretty. "Subsection commanders, Angela," Jemima ordered. "Security Rating 1-A. And clear the room, please."

Angela shepherded her Wrens out of the room. They'd no sooner gone than four Royal Marine officers entered, followed by a Royal Navy officer. The five men formed a line before Christopher, who remained standing.

The four Royal Marines were dressed in khaki with green berets that supported gold crowns and globes. At their shoulders were the navy blue badges with ROYAL MARINE COMMANDO in red. All four were over six feet tall and powerfully built. Two were captains; one was a major. The last wore the crown and single star of a lieutenant colonel.

"Colonel Sainthill reporting, sir!" the man said. He saluted Christopher crisply. Then the two men shook hands. He and Creighton were old friends.

"Good to have you aboard, Timothy," Creighton said.

Sainthill was exactly Christophers's idea of an officer. At age thirty-seven, he was rugged, intelligent and dedicated, a veteran of the toughest fighting of the World War and a man who understood that all orders were to be executed perfectly, whether given or received.

"Thank you, sir." Sainthill answered. He then introduced Christopher to the three other marine officers.

The other man present wore the two-and-a-half

stripes of a Royal Navy lieutenant commander. He needed no introduction and did not elicit anything resembling a warm response from Christopher. His name was John Trott. He was even larger than the marines, with a neat red beard and small intense eyes. Jemima cringed when she saw him. He was the current commander of a subsection under Royal Navy cover simply called "The Squad." Christopher, once a member, remembered Trott all too well from the war years.

The Squad consisted of sixty-eight highly trained men and women. Their expertise comprised all fields from languages to electronics, but their focus was operations which were — in Mountbatten's words uttered that very morning — "not to be played by the Marquess of Queensberry rules." They could do practically anything, and did. No questions were ever asked; officially they did not exist. Many enemies of the United Kingdom — some lying in unmarked graves around the world — might have wished they didn't.

"Please, everyone sit down," Jemima said. "You'll find your places marked with your code names."

As seven civilians, five naval officers, Trott, Jemima and Christopher occupied places around Churchill's conference table, Christopher picked up Winston's old armchair. He turned it to the wall and sat next to it.

"Before briefing all of you," he said, "I should tell you that we still don't know exactly who or how potent our adversaries are. Threats are made to heads of state all the time, as you are aware. Some are much more serious than others. All have to be dealt with. Let's hope we can run this one down quickly and that it turns out to be no more than a few crackpots. But if it's more than that, we have to be ready."

There were nods around the room. Then, for two hours, Christopher generously doled out responsibility to the subsection commanders before him.

SIX

It was 5:47 in the afternoon when Jemima and Christopher left The Hole together. They walked to her automobile, an improbable MG-TD parked on Horseguards Parade. It was bright red, and when Christopher first saw it he refused to get in.

"In that case," she said jauntily, "I'll be driving and you'll be walking. All the bloody way to Chiswick."

He stepped into the car and she drove.

They took the Great West Road and headed south toward Kew Bridge. For several minutes, he refused to speak. The car was much too young for him. It irritated him. There were not that many years between Christopher and Jemima, but the car pointed up their difference. It was the war, he finally decided, that created a chasm. He had been in it and she had not. Thereby hung the definition of a generation. Finally she spoke. "Who exactly are we going to visit, sir?"

"My favorite bachelor uncle."

"Why with me?"

"Wait and bloody see," he answered.

"Charming."

On the outskirts of London, they hit some open road. Her foot fell heavily upon the accelerator. She was a fast and aggressive driver, but a good one, not inhibited by normal bounds of speed.

"I'd venture a guess that we're not actually driving," he suggested. "We're about to take off."

She smiled. It was dark out and the only lights were the dim ones from the dashboard and the headlights of cars passing in the opposite direction. But he could see her quite well. They'd changed to civilian clothing. In an aquamarine suit and matching beret, she was very attractive. Then he looked back to where the road rapidly unfurled before their windshield.

"I don't believe in wasting time," she said. "And in case you're wondering, I've never so much as scratched paint on any vehicle I've ever driven."

"I'm so glad to hear that."

They they took a corner through some mist and the tires wailed like a banshee. But the MG moved as if it were on water and Jemima shifted gears with the easy flowing movements of an undergraduate woman skulling on the Cam. Christopher tried to relax. "But why tomato red?" he asked, gently teasing.

"I will tell you why, sir!" she said. "The car is red because when I found it at the garage is *was* red. This one had the least dents in the body and the fewest quirks under the hood. It was also the one I could afford. So red it was and red it has stayed." She flashed her lights at an oncoming driver who'd forgotten his high beams. The other beams lowered. "Like the bloody Bolshevik revolution, *sir*, if you don't mind the analogy. The difference is, the car I like."

There was a long silence. "I see," he finally said. They both laughed.

They rode in silence until they reached Kew Green, a well-manicured stretch of England surrounded by lawns, dormant flower beds, bare trees and the Thames. Opulent detached houses of various types of architecture formed a large square by the address Christopher sought. Finally he pointed. "Right there," he said. He indicated a Queen Anne house. Jemima pulled the MG to the curb.

Moments later, a man answered the bell when they rang. He was in his mid-sixties and very tall. His eyes were an electric blue while his hair and mustache were a deep black, flecked with only the tiniest specks of gray. He wore charcoal slacks, a tie and a patched maroon cardigan. His face was blank for a moment, then incandescent when he recognized his caller.

"Christopher! I've been expecting you! How are you, my boy?"

"Well. Very well, thank you, Uncle Desmond."

The two men embraced with unabashed affection. Jemima stood awkwardly to one side. Major Sir Desmond Morton, founder and first commander of the M Section, was the last person Jemima had expected to meet that evening.

Morton turned toward her. "Ah, our Jemima," he

said. "Our code name, 'Kanga.' Do come in, my dear," he said, taking her arm and leading her.

Jemima James knew all the legends about Morton, many of which were pale in contrast with the truth. Now, as he led her to a divan in the living room of his home, she tried to make some sense of the stories. She tried to peg them to the lean, austere man—code-named "Owl"—before her.

In the spring of 1917, she knew, Morton had been a major in the Royal Field Artillery at Arras, commanding the most advanced field battery. There he took a bullet that lodged against his heart. The doctors were afraid to remove it, the wound was closed and Major Morton lived to receive his Military Cross. By the bredth of a hair, the bullet changed his life instead of ending it.

The wound brought him to the attention of Winston Churchill, with whom he had served under Field Marshall Haig. The friendship between the two men flourished in the twenties and thirties. In 1934, when the government ignored the threats from Nazi Germany, Morton and Churchill—with authority and financing from George V—formed the clandestine M Section. The Section began covert operations in Germany, returning to Churchill complete information on the Luftwaffe, German rearmament and plans for a European war. Churchill confronted the Baldwin and Chamberlain government in Parliament and presented the information to the Sovereign.

Both Edward VIII and George VI continued the money and authority until more sensible heads prevailed within the government. By that time, May 1940, Churchill had become Prime Minister and Morton had become the new P.M.'s secret chief. Thereupon, Morton secretly founded the SOE — the Special Operations Executive — and organized his own section, the appropriately named "M" Section — for particularly dirty work. Then finally, he coordinated all British security services, from the Foreign Office and SIS, then MI 5 to the Special Branch. Next came all Army and Navy units. Morton outranked even Intrepid and reported only to the King and the Prime Minister. Only in this way could M Section be completely secure.

As for Christopher, the reunions with Morton had grown all the more infrequent with the passing of his adult years. But he couldn't step into the man's house without his own memories cascading back.

Desmond Morton wasn't his real uncle, of course, but it had been the fashion of the 1930s to so address the close male friends of one's parents. Morton had been a very close friend, indeed. When Christopher's parents had separated, his father had remained in his family house and urological practice in Harley Street. His mother, who'd grown up with Morton, had used Desmond's influence to rent a cottage on Winston Churchill's estate in Kent. They'd occupied it for two years. During his school vacations, Christopher had become close not only to "Uncle" Desmond but also to the voluable, cantankerous retired politico who sat day after day with his oil paints at Chartwell Manor, quietly seething over the state of world affairs. So great had been Morton's influence on the Creightons, that he was largely responsible for young Christopher's conversion to Catholicism in 1937.

"I trust you got to mass this morning," Morton said as Christopher eased onto a sofa.

Christopher was taken off guard. Morton, who stood next to his dry sink, a line of decanters at arm's length, turned and frowned when Christopher did not reply.

"I didn't actually," Christopher fumbled. "We were a bit busy in London. It never crossed my mind." In truth, it had. Christopher had noted in the *Times* that it was the Feast of St. Paul. And he knew that Morton would ask that evening. "It's not a holy day of obligation, it it?"

"Surely you learned at Ampleforth College, Christopher. It is a day when the *instructed* Christian is naturally impelled to attend." He shook his head in exaggerated disappointment, making a tisking sound with his tongue. "Miss James," he continued, turning to her, "perhaps if I ply you with alcohol you'll do your commander the future service of reminding him of his spiritual obligations." He motioned toward the decanters.

"A sherry," she said. "Fino."

He produced a crystal sherry glass and filled it halfway. Without asking Christopher, Morton opened a bottle of ale and handed it to him, followed by a glass. "Pour it yourself, my dear young lad," he said.

"I know how fussy you Navy buggers—pardon me, Miss James, a lapse—are about your filthy Worthingtons."

It was a vintage performance which Christopher had seen many times before. But he always enjoyed it. Morton then reached beneath the sink to a cabinet and produced an elixir for himself.

"I think this would be appropriate for this evening," he said. It was vodka—Russian, and a bottle not intended for export. Red label, red star and Cyrillic lettering. "Cheers," Morton said, hoisting a double shot of it in a brandy glass. "A toast to M Section and my successor. To both of you, my dears, good luck!"

Christopher's hand stopped in midair. Jemima sipped her Fino and Morton threw down half the snifter of vodka in one dramatic gulp.

After tasting the ale, Creighton set his glass aside. Morton sat down.

"I had no idea that ex-commanders knew so much," Creighton said.

"Normally they don't. But M Section isn't 'normal.' Mountbatten telephoned me the same morning he went to see Eden."

"Then you know everything?"

"Enough to know that I wouldn't want the Krushchev problem myself. Not at my present bloody age. So they asked me to recommend someone."

Christopher sighed. Jemima smiled.

"Well, come, Christopher," Morton said sharply. "Who in God's name did you think suggested you for the job? What was I to do? Leave you in New York playing banjo—"

"Piano."

"—playing banjo with negroes in a homosexual beer joint? Did I convert you to the True Church of Rome for *that?*"

"It happens to be one of the finest jazz clubs in America," Creighton said. Morton made a sour expression and gave a contemptuous dismissing wave of his hand. "And our quartet was—"

"You were bored silly, Christopher, and you ought to admit it. Further, who else to lead the M Section? Trott? Sainthill?" Creighton's eyebrows raised at the invocation of the other officers' names. "They wouldn't do. It's you, fella-me-lad, and if you were honest, you'd admit that you're damned well flattered."

Christopher took a long draw on the ale. He looked at Jemima, who kept a perfectly straight face. Yet he knew how she was enjoying seeing the old commander drag him over the coals.

"So I'm flattered," Creighton finally said.

"See! There!" Morton looked to Jemima for approval and she laughed. "He's just proven he's insane enough for this job."

"Then why don't you tell us what you can," Christopher said, angling the conversation in its inevitable direction, "before we go out to confront Ivan Ruskie."

"So I shall, Christopher. So I shall." Another double vodka and Morton was ready. "The White Russians' motivation is easy enough to understand," Sir Desmond began. "They're still fighting the war they

100

lost forty years ago. It's understandable in its stubbornly Russian way. Did you know there are some Japanese units still fighting in the Philippines? Well, same thing, Christopher. Some people never surrender." Morton's expression was as usual impenetrable. The phone rang. He picked up the receiver from a table next to him. Not a muscle stirred on his face. "Morton," he said. Then, after a moment, "It's for you, Miss James," he said.

Jemima took the phone.

"Second Officer James," she said. "Yes. Yes, Angela. Go to code V-5 group cluster."

Jemima opened her bag and pulled out a stenographer's notebook and pencil. "Ready, Angela."

The two men watched as Jemima wrote fourteen groups of cypher into her notebook. Morton winked at Christopher.

"Thank you, Angela," said Jemima, putting down the phone. She took out a small book and flicked through the pages, found the one she wanted and started to write again in the book. Morton got up and refilled Christopher's and his own glass. As he sat down, Jemima came to life.

"Signal from our cypher office, sir. Top Secret, Priority One," she reported to Christopher. "Christopher Robin from Ann Vergamo, Chief of our French Subsection. Message reads: Sketch positively identified by SDECE, French Secret Service. Subject is Baron Wilhelm von Ostenberg. Full description to follow. Still on SDECE wanted war criminals file."

Morton's eyes glistened. "ObergruppenFührer von

Ostenberg," he said with some relish. "Among other things, the 'Butcher of Cherbourg.' " He looked at Jemima and Christopher. "Would you credit it, I was at his wedding, in 1935. To the Baroness Tania. A beautiful woman. The Russians raped and murdered her in Berlin in 1945. I recall that Hermann Göring was at the wedding. Baron Wilhelm is an enemy of long standing."

Christopher and Jemima reacted in amazement. "And what is von Ostenberg doing in this affair?" Christopher asked.

Morton rubbed his hands together as if against a chill. "That's the most troubling part." He edged forward in his chair, getting into the game. "What is a former SS officer doing with White Russians? From the political point of view it makes sense. Passionate anti-Communism. All right, but is that enough? I'm not sure and I can't offer any advice. But von Ostenberg is most likely a hired gun as Marie suggested. Let's face it. The White Russians are not professional soldiers. They knew that. So they went out and bought themselves a commanding officer, one whose anti-Communist sympathies couldn't be questioned."

"Plausible," Christopher admitted. He took another long drink of ale. Morton steepled his fingers, then broke them apart.

"Doesn't make your job any easier, lad," Sir Desmond said in grieved, lower tones. "Try outguessing an SS officer. Impossible. But you remember yourself."

"Too well."

Morton turned toward Jemima as if to instruct her. "During the war it was easy enough to make assessments when dealing with the Wehrmacht," he said. "Regular, and dare I say it, decent German army. They acted upon sense and tactics. The SS formations, however, did whatever came into their heads. Their commanders? Fanatical, tactically ignorant and usually unbalanced. Therefore totally unpredictable."

She was nodding. The tone of levity left Sir Desmond's voice.

"And that's what you have in von Ostenberg," Sir Desmond said. "In professional behavior—never mind personal behavior—he's a textbook example of an SS officer." He paused. "As I said, I shouldn't like this on my plate, Christopher. The fact is there's little decisive action that even can be taken by the Section until von Ostenberg is located. And, I hasten to add, captured."

Christopher thought for a moment, then advanced the subject. "I know the Soviet visit would never be canceled," he said. "But what about the agenda? Could it be changed? Or held flexible?"

Morton cocked his head back and chortled. "Not bloodly likely! Change the agenda now and the Soviets could interpret it as a snub. Then they'd cancel. You have to understand Anthony Eden, Christopher. His political fortunes now hinge on a successful Soviet visit. It gives him instant credibility as a 'statesman' prime minister. When he was very young in the late thirties, he achieved that sort of respect as a foreign minister. He hungers for it again as P.M. Not that he's a bad fellow," Sir Desmond sang out, his voice rising in inflection. "And not that he doesn't deserve it. But it gives him what he doesn't have now: a seat at the top table. A viable position between the Americans and the Russians. That also brings us to why Khrushchev must be protected at virtually any cost."

Creighton waited. So did Jemima.

"Khrushchev's an upstart, to be sure. God knows how he ever wrestled his way to power, but it's damned well certain he was helped by everyone underestimating him. I think we do, too. Churchill agrees with me, by the way. The Americans see Khrushchev as a loud little man in an ill-fitting suit who by chance became a world leader during the Atomic Age. Give him more credit. To be sure, at one moment he swaggers about with his army, and the next moment he holds out an olive branch. He tells the Americans he'll bury them, then coins the phrase 'peaceful coexistence.' How do you measure that? I'll tell you how. You look at what he's actually done. Sure, he came to power in the only manner possible in the Soviet Union. Through the CPSU and through execution. But he's also liberalized their society. Not much. But enough. Do you remember the uprising in East Berlin in 1953?" Here both Christopher and Jemima nodded like rapt university students taking their tutorial. "One million East Germans in the streets, all shouting—what was that slogan . . . ?"

" *'Butter, nicht ein Volksarmee,'* " Jemima said concisely. Then, translating: " 'Butter, not a people's army.' "

Both men looked at her with surprise.

"That was it," Morton said. "There were no consumer goods to be found in the entire Eastern sector. The local Communist leaders got shouted off the pedestals and, in some cases, stoned. So Khrushchev sent in the Red Army two months after Stalin's death. The East Germans buckled and went back to their jobs. But the message wasn't lost, particularly when a third of a million Eastern Germans, the entire professional classes included, headed west each year. So Khrushchev started making concessions. Reduced quotas from local industries. Lower taxes for farmers. More imported consumer goods. State loans for small businesses. Christopher, these are major, major concessions for a card-carrying Marxist. And they followed in Romania, Hungary, Bulgaria and Poland, also. So you see what I'm saying? Like it or not, that fat little Ukrainian is the West's best chance to avoid an atomic war someday. Without Khrushchev, we're back to the Stalinists: Malenkov. Molotov. Kaganovich. God knows who else. So I think you see what I mean. Khrushchev is possibly the most liberalizing force in Soviet politics since Lenin. We may not like his table manners, but it's jolly well in all our best interests to protect the fat Red bastard. Pardon me again, Miss James. Another lapse."

In the moment that Sir Desmond's voice tailed off, Christopher sensed a tiny air of relaxation go around the room. But Morton had saved the best for last.

"There's something else," he said. "Not good,

either. This past Christmas, our Soviet friends exploded a new nuclear device. Not out in the ocean and not underground in Siberia. They blew it in the atmosphere. There's only one conclusion: they have a transportable hydrogen bomb and they have a way of delivering it. Our intelligence reports — obtained at deep cover and with considerable risk, I might add, Christopher — tell us that they could have an atomic warhead in New York in seventy-nine minutes and London in twenty-six." Morton gave it a suitable pause for emphasis. "Now," he finished, "suppose some maniac got to Khrushchev or his warships in Portsmouth. And suppose, back in the Kremlin, someone decided to retaliate against the West." Morton carefully eyed his two callers. "Not that it matters," he said, "but theirs is more powerful than anything we or the Americans have to throw back. So, I suspect we'll be wishing Comrade Khrushchev a safe journey until he's happily home again. Won't we?"

Much later that same evening, Jemima James wore nothing but a sleeping kimono — pink and light blue printed silk from Liberty's — as she sat on the cushioned bench in the bay window of her London bedroom. She gazed down upon Abbotsbury Road three flights below. Up the block a bit, just beyond where her red MG was parked overnight, she could see the corner of Holland Park.

It was 3:15 A.M. She remained at the window, the curtain pushed slightly aside by her finger. It was an hour when the street was usually free from any activity. On the many other nights when sleeplessness had gripped her, she'd watched the sidewalk from this same perch. The street was normally empty. No cars. No cyclists. No drunks or illicit lovers wending their way home. Not even a taxi whining its tires as it hit the curb in an empty street.

She thought about Christopher. She knew he was attracted to her. She could tell by the way he looked at her. Well, it had been a long time since she'd had a lover. Not that she hadn't had her chances. It was just that, well, as a woman she had to be more careful.

For seven long years she'd labored in Royal Navy Intelligence, a department carved out by men, operated by men and controlled by men. A few women were allowed to tag along and hope for some pickings of responsibility and command. Well, she'd paid her dues. She'd holed up in garrets monitoring the phone calls of Russian and Polish hoods and, during field maneuvers, she'd been decorated for bravery. Her record was exemplary and she was just starting to see the responsibility and command to which she was entitled. She wasn't about to throw it away by having an affair.

For a moment she was angry. Any male officer, pouf or otherwise, could have an affair. But if she did, she'd be out. Out unfairly, like her father. Well, she wasn't going to let them do that.

Not that the Royal Navy hadn't been good to her. If the Navy hadn't commissioned her during her last year at Cambridge and paid the fees as well, she might have had to leave. Certainly her mother couldn't have carried the tuition.

Jemima scanned Abbotsbury road again. First there had been a man sleeping on a bench. Then a couple of teenagers had sat on some steps down the block in the other direction, sharing a bottle of liquid lightning. One of them had lurched to a coin box, made a call, and a few minutes later—as the teenagers departed—a Daimler had rolled to a halt behind her MG.

What bothered Jemima was that the events were consecutive, like the changing of a watch aboard a ship. Mountbatten's people? Christopher's? Or Russians—Red or White—who'd already picked up the scent of opposition?

Or had she simply seen a vagrant, two indolent teenagers and man doing Heaven-knew-what with or without a partner in the private, friendly confines of his car?

Then again, she couldn't ever recall seeing a man sleeping outside on a bench in February. There were shelters. Steam grates. The train depots.

A final fatigue came upon her and she slept. Fitfully.

The next evening she spent differently.

It was shortly after eleven P.M. when Jemima turned the corner onto the block where Roger Garin had a maisonette. His door was fifty paces down the street. She kept track of such things. There appeared to be two men leaving just as she came around the corner.

Or were they? They were a pair of tall, rugged men, she noted, and they seemed to have just stepped down from Roger's doorstep. More than likely, she reasoned, old friends or new business contacts. But likelier still, if they'd rung Roger's bell unannounced at this hour, he might very well have not answered. It was the time of night when some sweet little Danish or American thing had probably been charmed off her feet and out of her clothes by the wily old Russian.

Well, no matter, Jemima reasoned. Roger had long ago given her a coded system of ringing his doorbell. three rings, then one, then two. Jemima's ring. The sweet young blonde—if there was one—could perfume herself a second time in the bath, Jemima reasoned with a grin. She had to talk business with Roger. Section business.

She arrived on his doorstep and rang his bell. From the corner of her eye she saw something. The two men who'd passed her had turned to watch her. Their eyes met hers. She turned away. Men watching her was nothing new. The men continued on. Jemima smiled to herself. They probably assumed *she* was Roger's lover, she concluded. Or *one* of Roger's lovers. She shook her head and tried to dismiss such thoughts. Roger was too damned old for her. She'd told him so herself, though he denied it.

Then she noticed that the door was open.

She put her hand on the knob and pushed it forward. A moment later she was inside, closing the door behind her.

"Roger?" she called.

There was no answer. Oh, God, but he was getting careless. That or his friends were, She stood in his living room and looked up the stairs. The radio was playing in his bedroom. That door too was ajar. The BBC evening concert. Her mind ran away again: this time Roger had seduced a young music student.

She called louder. "Roger? It's Jemima! Can you come out? Should I wait?"

There was no answer at all. The awkwardness of the moment ceased to amuse her. Now she was concerned. Roger didn't answer, and she didn't have much more time. She was not about to report to Section HQ the next morning and explain that her informant's rapacious sexual reputation stopped her from making contact.

"Damn," she said. She started up the stairs to the first-floor landing, walking as loudly as possible. At the top of the stairs she stood a few feet from his bedroom. The music was louder. She called a final time. "Roger?"

Seconds later she pushed the door open.

Roger Garin was alone. But he hadn't been for long. She knew, because the blood was still pouring from the obscene open wound in the back of his head.

"Oh, my God!" she gasped. She held a hand to her mouth, fought back her revulsion, and rushed to him. He was fully clothed and face down on his bed, his neck angled impossibly to one side. A bullet, or more

110

than one bullet, had been fired at close range into his brain. The music must have masked the shot.

She reached to his wrist and felt for a pulse. There was none. And the wrist was still warm.

She felt as though she would throw up. But she didn't. She reached to his bedside telephone, picked it up and dialed the Section's unlisted number. She waited for a voice from the old war cabinet room.

She began. "Angela, Kanga here. Residence Garin. Priority One. Ambulance, Doctor. And the Squad."

She set the telephone down. She stared at the body. "Poor old boy," she said. She wished he *had* gotten lucky with some leggy young music student that night. Maybe he would have gone to the girl's place, instead. Maybe—

Jemima sighed. She slipped quietly out of the room, closing the door behind her. She stood at the first-floor landing at the top of the stairs. Her gaze wandered and then her heart thumped wildly.

"You saw our faces," the man said.

There were two of them. They were the same two whom she'd passed outside. They were Roger Garin's killers and they'd returned for her. The man who spoke had a guttural mid-European accent.

She was rooted to her spot as the first man came to the steps and slowly started upward. He drew a Walther automatic from a coat pocket. She could see the silencer. All she knew was that she was terrified— and that she had to control herself.

He came up one step at a time. For all he knew, she reasoned quickly, Jemima was one of Roger's lovers, a simple girl easily seduced, even by an old man. Royal Navy? Black belts in jujitsu and karate? They could have no idea. Surprise, she knew, would be her only weapon.

The man with the gun was halfway up the steps. The other man moved to the bottom step, thoroughly blocking her escape. Her mind raced. *An armed opponent*. She measured the man's height, weight and strength, then calculated the angle, distance and bearing. She would have to hit him hard. She would have to hit the fulcrum point; otherwise she could never throw a man so much bigger than she.

He came within four steps. "Move," he said to her. "Back into bedroom with your friend."

"Please," she begged, "let me go."

The man grinned. He eased, sensing her fright. It was what she wanted. Images of all the unarmed combat exercises flashed before her. Only this was no exercise. This was kill or be killed.

The man raised the automatic to her heart. He prodded her in the breast. She started to turn away, then struck.

Both of her hands cut downward across the man's wrist. The gun flew from the weakened grip. Jemima ignored it. As the man groped for his weapon, Jemima swung around and grasped the banister. Both of her legs came up and she kicked the man in the pit of the stomach, summoning up all her strength with the blow.

The man groaned fiercely and doubled up. With one arm he held his stomach. With the other hand, he

112

lunged for his pistol. Jemima brought a knee into his face, then pushed him backward.

The second man tried to mount the steps, but he was blocked by the first. Jemima grabbed the pistol and shot the nearest man in the top of the head. The bullet smashed sickeningly into the skull. She fired a second time and saw the skull shatter. The gun was unsteady within her own grip.

The slain man fell over backwards. His partner lost balance and fell with him. Jemima felt a sharp pain in her hand and knew she'd torn a tendon or pulled a muscle. She brandished the pistol, but her grip on it was shaky. She fumbled with it. The second man turned, however. Stumbling into furniture and scrambling for his own balance, he went for the door.

She grabbed the weapon with her left hand and raised it to fire. She pulled the trigger once, then twice again. The shots launched with a low hissing sound as they burst from the silencer. They crashed against the wall near the door. But they missed the intended target as the assassin escaped.

Jemima pulled herself down the steps and leaped over the fallen body. She went to the door and looked out. The second killer was already gone. The street was empty. She closed the door and locked it.

She went to the man she'd shot. She knelt beside him and felt for a pulse. For a second it flickered. Then it stopped as she held his wrist. He was dead. There was a dark red pool of blood beneath his shattered skull.

Jemima was sickened. In exercises there was never a

real body, never real blood. Tears of hysteria came, but she fought them back. A man was dead and she had killed him. As her nerves settled, her head throbbed. She thought again of Roger Garin's body upstairs.

The room was strangely quiet. As she looked around, she saw a drinks cabinet. *Don't be ridiculous*, she told herself. *You're a professional. You're on duty.* She glanced at the body again, then back to the liquor.

A scotch, she decided, would be medicinal, not a crutch. She poured herself a stiff one. Then she took a position halfway up the stairs and halfway down, midway between the two dead men. She waited. Trott arrived in seventeen minutes. A section doctor was with him.

Jemima was fully in control when she spoke.

"You'll find a second body upstairs, John," she said. "his name was Garin. Lived under the alias of Kugelhof. He was one of my best informants. Trouble is, the opposition got here first."

Trott nodded. The doctor confirmed that both men were dead. The second assassin, Sergei Popov, was already far away by the time Jemima was relating the full story.

SEVEN

At seven-thirty, three evenings later, Jemima and Christopher drove through Romsey, in the county of Hampshire. They drove in the direction of the former estate of the departed St. Barbe family. Christopher had grown used to the MG by now and refrained from comment throughout the trip from London all the way to the perimeter of Broadlands, Mountbatten's sprawling six-thousand-acre estate.

Lord Louis adored every aspect of the place, from the woods and fields where he exercised his horses, to the walled garden planted with mulberries by King James I, to the two hundred trees planted by visiting dignitaries from Nehru to the current Queen. In daytime as well as nighttime, the visions of the eighteenth-century landscape artist Lancelot "capability" Brown still dazzled the eye. It had been Brown, under the direction of the first Lord Palmerston, who had exploited the "Capabilities" of the earlier Tudor and

Jacobean manor house, thus transforming Broadlands into a mid-Georgian masterpiece.

On this particular evening, a clear moon struck an eerie silver from the rippling trout-filled waters of the River Test. The river was at flood level, swelling against its banks from the melting snows and rain of the previous day. Old Capability had loved those moonlit waters and had landscaped accordingly.

As Jemima's pranger entered the driveway, Christopher distinctly recognized the figure of Mountbatten on the lawn, not far from the main entrance. The First Sea Lord was standing very still, half in darkness, half in the reflected illumination from house lights and headlamps from the MG. Christopher had the eerie sense of seeing a living statue, one of flesh, one wearing clothing, but definitely not of a living man. Then Mountbatten welcomed them loudly, beckoned them inside to dinner, and the sensation was gone.

Two and a half hours later, after a dazzling meal of roast lamb, Christopher, Jemima and their host had found their way into Mountbatten's private library in the east wing of Broadlands. No fewer than a thousand books lined three of the walls. The fourth wall was dominated by two large windows which, in the daytime, caught the morning sun and overlooked a meadow. Between the windows hung a portrait of Prince Louis of Battenberg in full dress admiral's uniform. On Mountbatten's desk were a collection of old photographs.

"Now take your time and have a good look," Mountbatten said. He sat in an ornate chair with ivory arms, a gift from Nehru. "The photographs are from my Russian period. Quality's not so keen on some of them. About 1908 to 1916. Do handle them gently."

Jemima and Christopher leaned over the desk and examined a complete photographic history of Mountbatten's aunt and uncle, Czar Nicholas and Czarina Alexandra, and their children: Tatiana, Olga, Marie, Anastasia and little Alexis. There were pictures of friends, officers, guards, associates and most of the nobility of the House of Romanov. There were even several close-up studies of Rasputin, with the Czarina's arm through his and the Czar brooding the background.

Mountbatten smiled as Jemima picked up a sepia print of the Czar's immediate family. Christopher looked over her shoulder.

"Now look at those daughters," Mountbatten said. "Tell me which is the most beautiful."

Jemima was quick to answer. "This one," she said.

"The third one along." Christopher nodded.

"Marie Nikolayevna Romanova," Lord Louis said.

Christopher stared at the flawless young face, a face of innocence and kindness, the latter inherited from her father.

"What a beautiful young woman," Jemima said, almost with envy.

Mountbatten drew a small silver-framed black-and-white photograph from a desk drawer. It was a stunningly clear picture of the same Marie, sixteen years old, in an ornate white dress. Marie was even more delicate and beautiful in this portrait. Her cornflower eyes stared out from across five decades.

"How did she ever escape?" Creighton asked, looking from the photograph back to Mountbatten.

"You want to know, do you?"

"Yes, I would."

"Then that will be part of your challenge, young Christopher. Find her, rescue her and ask her yourself."

"Aye, aye, sir," he said.

"That's the point of these photographs, after all," Mountbatten said. "I want you to stare at them. Memorize those faces. Etch Marie in your mind, then touch her hair with gray, add some lines, but hold fast on those eyes and that Romanov spirit. That way you'll know her instantly when you see her."

Christopher was nodding. Jemima arranged the pictures on Mountbatten's desk.

"Ditto the unfortunate little boy," Lord Louis said. "My cousin Alexis. The Czarevitch. Picture a teenage boy with those features. Then you have the current Alexis. Which brings to mind: I leave for Singapore on Sunday, March 11. Why, Jemima James, have you suddenly decided to demonstrate your proficiency in unarmed combat?"

"I didn't have much choice, sir," she answered.

"No," said Mountbatten, suddenly turning very serious. "That's what troubles me."

118

"We've put Garin's body on ice," said Christopher. "MI 5 came to inquire what we'd done with it. Didn't tell those fools, of course."

"Who was the man I killed?" she asked, looking at Mountbatten.

"How do I know?" Mountbatten answered. "But I suppose we can safely assume that it's the first sign of an active opposition."

"Roger Garin had something important to tell me," Jemima said. "That's why I went there."

"And that's why they killed him. To protect their conspiracy against Khrushchev. Is that a safe assumption?" Mountbatten looked from one to the other.

"It's the only logical explanation at this point," Christopher said. "Somehow the White Russians knew about Garin. For all we know, they didn't know he was a double agent. Thought he was a Red. There are a number of explanations, but only one conclusion; those who want Khrushchev dead had to silence Garin first. To obstruct us."

There was agreement around the room. Mountbatten nodded. "What else?" he asked.

"Communications systems are fully established aboard *Victory* and in the war cabinet room, sir," Jemima said. "We've established *Victory* as subsection HQ."

"I was going to suggest that," Mountbatten said. "Very good. From her yard arm, *Victory* will provide a first-class view of the Russian warships, as well as a comprehensive line of sight over the entire harbor."

"And we're putting Birdham into full commission

again as the main section command, sir," said Christopher. "It's going to be the operations and training base for all ranks and ratings of special parties. Royal Navy, Royal Marine SAS and Wrens."

Birdham was a small village only eight miles from Pompey harbor at Portsmouth. But M Section had occupied the manor house there off and on since 1938. It was a huge old building with many large barns and additional outside structures. It stood on about thirty acres of fields and forest land. Up until two days earlier, it had only a skeleton RN holding crew. Now HMS Birdham bustled with activity.

"I am very pleased about it, sir," said Christopher. "I was starting to get a bit concerned that we might get forced aboard Victory III, or possibly Eastney. The large amount of our personnel about would be bound to elicit comment."

"I entirely agree with you," said Mountbatten.

"To sum up, sir," Jemima piped in, "the Hole in London stands as the section's HQ for organization and communication, *Victory* as a subsection for the section control of Portsmouth and Birdham as the Section home, main operational training base and Section command. All three to be linked in direct communication, and each possessing its own Priority One/Top Secret worldwide linkups."

Mountbatten leaned back in his chair, greatly pleased. "Excellent," he said. "What else?"

"Once I've met as many of the Section as possible," Creighton said, "I'll detail separate naval parties. One to try to pin down von Ostenberg and his thugs. The second, and the most highly trained, to rescue Marie if possible. The third will be a roving one to take immediate counteroffensives against any conspirators we might find. In addition, I am allocating Subsection C, in cooperation with the Squad, to establish our own special security for Khrushchev and Bulganin. This will be separate from all the official security services."

"Protecting Khrushchev and Bulganin remains our first priority," Mountbatten said evenly, his eyes lowered upon the photographs. "Don't forget that."

"Certainly not, sir."

"But you're correct. Have your naval parties set to go. If you could secure Marie and Alexis, I'm certain you might take hostages at the same time. That could be most useful."

There was an uneasy silence for a moment. Mountbatten gathered the photographs and set them aside. Then he drew a sheet of paper from the top drawer of his desk. "Here," he said at length. "Something for you to get busy with. The Russians are coming on April 17. They wish to start coordinating security arrangements with us now. With official security services and with you, Christopher." Mountbatten tore off the sheet and handed it to the younger man. "This is whom you'll be dealing with, a Comrade General Ivan Serov. He's their man in charge. Know anything about him?"

Christopher shook his head, "No."

"Foreign Office could give you a background, but I prefer that they don't even see you. Jemima?"

"Comrade General Ivan Alexandrovish Serov," she said, "was former deputy Minister of the MVD. The *Ministerstvo Vnutrennikh Del,* or Ministry of Internal Affairs. Since 1954 Comrade General Serov has been the First Chairman of the new KGB. The *Komitet Gosudarstvennoy Bezopasnosti,* the Committee of State Security." Jemima looked from Christopher to Mountbatten. "For some reason, they are trying to keep the formation of this KGB secret."

"Why are they trying to do that?" Mountbatten asked.

"My opinion, sir?" she asked.

"Yes."

"One, it's a secret organization. Two, I suspect they're trying to conceal its scope. The new KGB is both the political and federal police agency, as well as the intelligence and counterintelligence unit within the U.S.S.R. It's additionally responsible for supervision of frontier troups, enforcement of security regulations and the protection of CPSU leaders. The last being paramount."

"Very good, Miss James," said Mountbatten appreciatively, "and very comprehensive. And very frightening."

Christopher looked at the piece of paper and read Serov's name again. Then he folded the paper and tucked it inside his jacket.

"How did we get Serov's name as contact?" he asked.

"Ambassador Litvinov contacted Eden directly," Lord Louis answered. "Interesting protocol, isn't it?

All of which reminds me, I had the occasion to talk to Anthony Eden myself this evening before you arrived. He's about to leave for Canada." Mountbatten drew a breath. "He's informed all of the police and intelligence sections — and *us,* most of all—that there is to be no snooping around the Soviet ships when they arrive."

Christopher shrugged. "Who's planning to snoop?" he asked.

"I hope to God, no one. But when the Soviet cruiser *Sverdlov* was in Portsmouth last October, SIS sent a diver down to examine the hull."

Christopher managed a smile. "What bad boys they were. Who went down?"

"Crabb," said Mountbatten.

Now Christopher could barely conceal his amusement. Commander Lionel Crabb was an old friend, a onetime instructor and an early mentor. They'd served together during the war and afterward. But over the last few years, Christopher had barely seen Crabb. Only since returning to England in January had he learned that Crabb had fallen upon difficult times. He'd retired from active duty four years earlier, not by choice.

"How *is* Crabbie?" Creighton asked. "I've heard—"

"Whatever you've heard is true," said Mountbatten. "The worst part of it is that the man now sits around the pubs in Kensington and tells anyone who'll buy him a drink how he snooped on the Russian ship. He's got a pathological hatred of the Soviets, you know."

Christopher nodded. He turned to Jemima, mildly amused. "Crabb's so fervently right wing," he said, "that I remember him once trying to sue a man who'd sent him a letter with the British stamp upside down. Disrespect for the Queen." Creighton rolled his eyes. Jemima smiled.

"In any case," warned Mountbatten, "the stories are getting around. Crabb won't shut up. Eden knows and is furious. So he doesn't want any repeat performance by any divers around those ships. He wants, in short, *no one* anywhere close to those ships. No incidents, Christopher. No divers and no assassinations." And with a laugh, "No bloody *attempts* either."

Creighton shook his head. "How the hell can we protect the Soviet ships without divers?"

"That's *your* problem!" snapped Mountbatten. "Further, the Russians are not to be told anything about the threats to their leaders."

A moment passed. "How do we protect them if we can't even tell their own security people that—"

"It's a direct order to *you* from the Prime Minister," Mountbatten said softly. "You'll have to work within that directive." Mountbatten's dark blue eyes bored into Christopher's. "And furthermore, there is to be *no* pool of information between M Section and MI 5, the Secret Intelligence Service and Special Branch. The Prime Minister wants no risk of irresponsible rumors and no risk of the Russian visit being canceled. He forbids you even to make contact with our other security services."

"How will I find Serov? What's our means of communication?" Christopher asked at length.

"That's the very best part," Mountbatten said. "You meet him in person to make the preparations. The Soviet Navy plans to smuggle him into England." Mountbatten treated both Jemima and Christopher to a broad wink. "With a little help from ours!"

Christopher smiled at Jemima. "And Eden knows all about this?" he asked.

Mountbatten laughed. "Lord, no!" he exclaimed. "The Foreign Office, the Home Office, all the intelligence agencies et cetera, are violently opposed to it. However, *I* am for it. Therefore, he's coming. Wednesday, February 29. Hour and venue to be arranged."

"Good God," Christopher responded. "Where?"

"Portsmouth, of course," Mountbatten answered. "Treat him well, Christopher. He's to be your guest."

"And what about his safety?"

"Entirely your responsibility," Mountbatten said. "It's on you completely."

EIGHT

A few hours after Mountbatten spoke, it was dawn in Moscow. A United States national named John Carter sat in the basement of Lubyanka Prison, bound hand and foot and strapped into a straight-back wooden chair. He was in a cell which he shared with another American named Tom Sinden.

Sinden and Carter were soldiers of fortune. They had always recognized the possibility of spending time in an American prison. But never had they envisioned a Soviet one. Somehow this seemed worse. Sinden and Carter were also professional smugglers. And their most recent undertaking had gone badly awry.

They'd begun in San Francisco two weeks earlier with a nighttime burglary from a munitions factory. They'd taken their haul by truck to the Finnish Consulate. When local police in California traced their cargo, however, they found it protected by diplomatic cover. Sinden and Carter, meanwhile, were already in Vancouver.

From there they traveled to Montreal, with the next stop Helsinki. In the Finnish capital, they were reunited with their heavy stash: four dozen limpet mines of American manufacture. Soon, Sinden and Carter reckoned, they would be rich. So to complete their job, they purchased an old Volvo truck.

They had passed through customs at the Finnish-Soviet border with little more than a cursory glance. Then, fifty miles along the frozen highway to Leningrad, local police stopped them and seized their truck. They spent two days in a Leningrad jail before being brought in an armored van to Moscow. They'd arrived at Lubyanka the previous evening, demanding to see the highest-ranking intelligence officer available. Sinden, hotheaded as always, had become violent, resulting in both men being bound hand and foot.

There were footsteps along the stone passageway to the basement cell. Carter looked anxiously in that direction. If only they could find a high-enough KGB officer, he'd ranted all night, they'd be freed and rewarded. But he needed someone high in Soviet intelligence. He was working for them, he maintained, and could explain only to someone in the upper echelons.

Sinden had no such high hopes. He already guessed they were to be executed. But the whole argument had been lost on the nightime guards: none spoke English.

The footsteps came closer.

Carter called out, "Hey! Hey, over here, man! You speak English?"

There appeared a man in his early fifties, brutal looking with a high forehead and piercing blue-gray eyes. He wore a gray suit and stared at the prisoners.

Then he turned to two guards and spoke with them in Russian.

"See?" Carter said to Sinden. "We're going to get out of here." Even Sinden looked hopeful for a moment.

The two guards departed. The older man held something that looked like a rolled-up canvas cover beneath his arm. He reached into his left trouser pocket and withdrew a ring of keys. He opened the cell and entered.

"Speak English, right?" Carter blurted. "Russian intelligence and you speak English?"

The man looked them up and down, taking special note of the efficiency with which they'd been tied. He nodded slowly. "Yes. Speak English," he said. "Soviet State Security."

"God damn it, man!" Carter blurted. "Would you get us untied?"

The Russian looked at them blankly.

"You know why we drove into Russia, don't you?" he said. "You know what we were delivering to Leningrad?"

The Russian appeared distressed. "I know you were arrested. Your truck seized. Have you revealed purpose of trip to anyone?"

"No!" snapped Carter. "I'm an American. I don't talk to my captors."

"Honest to Jesus," Sinden added as the Russian's gaze flicked to him. "We didn't tell a soul. We demanded to talk to a KGB officer, but that's all."

"Your contraband was American-made, wasn't it?" the intelligence officer said.

The Americans paused. "Yes. Damn right it was,"

Carter said.

"Who did you tell that you were smuggling into the Soviet Union?" the Russian asked. "Who before you left America?"

"No one!" snapped Carter.

"That's the God's honest truth, mister," Sinden added. "We didn't tell no one. You have to take our word."

The Russian looked back and forth between the two of them, apparently trying to make a decision.

"Not a friend? A wife? A brother, maybe . . . ?"

Sinden was silent. "No one!" snapped Carter. "Now deal with these fucking ropes."

"We're telling you the truth!" Sinden said again.

"Yes," the Russian said thoughtfully. "I suppose I am inclined to believe you. Americans, I have heard, can be very stubborn, very silent."

Both Carter and Sinden initially took the remark as a compliment and assumed they were to be freed. But the Russian instead unfolded the strip of plastic beneath his arm. Then he started to pull it across his chest. It was a butcher's apron.

Carter didn't understand it all until a simple logical process took place. Butchers, he realized, wore aprons like that to keep from spattering their clothing with blood. His eyes went wide with terror when he saw the Russian draw a pistol from within his coat. Then the sound in his ears was the same as was in his throat: a scream. A scream straight up from hell itself.

The man pushed the pistol into Carter's face. The American revolved his head to avoid the blast and as a result the bullet blew off the side of his head instead

130

of entering more neatly through the eye socket. Carter's body was propelled backward by the force of the shot, spasmed and crashed onto the floor, dragging the chair with it.

A warrior to the end, Sinden tried to get to his feet, though he was bound to the chair. He made an effort to move toward his killer, though he was screaming "No! No!" as loud as he could. The Russian was an old hand at this, however, a veteran of Russian prison camps during the war as well as the executions of convenience in the Stalin and Khrushchev eras in this very prison.

He grabbed Sinden by his hair. He held him with one hand and with the other hand jammed the pistol into the American's right eye. He pulled the trigger twice.

Sinden's body convulsed but went slack almost instantly. The Russian pushed the man to one side and Sinden fell, taking the chair with him as Carter had done. For a moment, the Russian stared at them, deciding whether or not to administer a coup de grace. By the particles of skull and the quarts of blood flowing on the floor, however, he judged that such a coup was unnecessary. For a moment, he stood and admired his work. Close-in slaying like this always excited him sexually. He would want a woman this evening.

He removed his apron and tossed it onto the nearer of the bodies. He unlocked the cell door, pushed the pistol back to within his jacket and clapped his hands.

The two guards reappeared. Ivan Alexandrovich Serov switched back to Russian.

"Have the bodies incinerated," he said. "The apron,

too. Keep them tied to the chairs, the wood will make the flesh cook faster." His eyes glimmered.

The expression didn't waver on the face of either Russian. They'd attended to this basement many times before. Even glancing at the two foreigners lying in the cell—half of one skull blown to red pulp, a flood of blood coming from the eye of the other—there were no surprises, no new horrors.

They opened the cell to take away the bodies. They mumbled quietly to themselves. The only real sound was that of Ivan Serov's footsteps, slowly receding in the same direction as which he'd come.

NINE

Jemima James arrived at the Section London Headquarters in the former war cabinet room deep under Whitehall at seven in the morning. She surprised Christopher, who, looking tired and strained, was sitting at the great E-shaped table. In front of him were a pair of H. M. Stationery Office coiled notebooks, a number of handwritten notes, and a half-finished pot of black coffee.

Jemima glanced at the notes in front of him. She saw a series of names, many of them in Russian. "I started off at the Foreign Office at about ten last night," he said. "Then I was at Special Branch at about two A.M.. I have old chums in both places. They let me have access to some of their more sensitive records. Unofficial, of course." He looked up at her. "I didn't find bloody anything."

Christopher sighed and sipped the paper cup of coffee. The coffee was cold and tasted like plastic. He had now been awake for twenty-four hours.

Jemima took away his cup and the coffee pot. She walked across the room to make a fresh brew. "So all right, we know that Ostenberg and his mercenaries are holding Marie," he said. "But that doesn't mean they're planning to kill Khrushchev themselves. And if they're not? Who is? And are they in Great Britain yet? If not, can we keep them out?"

"I don't think that potential assassins are in England yet," answered Jemima. "Why should they risk premature discovery?"

Christopher nodded and sighed with fatigue. "If it *is* von Ostenberg, he won't even get past immigration," he said. "Special Branch know him. They'll be scanning for him more meticulously than ever."

"I doubt if any potential assassins will even try to come through immigration," Jemima said. "I suspect at least some of them will try the 'back door.' Yacht or glider across the channel."

"Which means we may need the help of Sûreté Nationale," Christopher muttered. "Or the Police Judiciaire. They each have extensive files."

"Right," she said.

"You can see the problem," he continued, thinking aloud. "M Section doesn't officially exist. We're forbidden to communicate with any police agency or security service. So how do we proceed? Just wait for von Ostenberg to make a move? Impossible."

"Actually, sir, the Prime Minister only forbade us from contacting domestic security services. He made no mention of us contacting the French or the Germans."

"Even so," Christopher answered, "how much help could we expect? It's a British problem and the French are . . . French, after all."

Jemima eyed him squarely. "Not all of them, sir."

"Explain," he said sharply.

Jemima moved to the table. She put a hand on the back of one of the chairs and thought for a moment. It was Sir Desmond's chair during the war, Christopher recalled. Jemima slid into it and looked up at him.

"We have twelve members in our Anglo-French subsection," she said. "The subsection chief is a woman. She's also held a position for eight years with the Frog secret service, the SDECE." She rolled it off her tongue like a language teacher: "Le Service de Documentation Extérieure et de Contre-Espionnage. She serves both Bureaux R2 and R3, the departments for Eastern and Western Europe. She's American born."

Christopher responded suddenly. "Good Lord. What's her name?"

"Captain Ann Vergamo."

He began to smile.

"Know her?" Jemima asked.

"Yes. From the war." He thought for a moment. "Yes, you're right. She can be of great help to us if she holds that position. Can you put things in motion?"

"I already have, sir. All available SDECE personnel in Europe have their eyes peeled for von Ostenberg. That is their primary objective. But they are also trying to locate Marie. Alexis is in Cannes under the surveillance of Ann Vergamo's subsection. If anyone tries to touch him . . ."

"Very impressive," he said. "You seem to be firmly in command of the ship. Almost like a Deputy Commander."

Jemima clicked her teeth. "Hardly eligible for that sort of appointment," she said. "Much too junior."

"I admit, it does present a problem for you."

"That's for sure," she agreed, with a despondent sigh.

Christopher scratched his head, appearing very ill at ease with subject. "The appointment of my deputy has had some discussion. Admiral Mountbatten, Director Wrens and, indeed, the Board feel that the job should go to a First Officer. I've given it a lot of thought, and I have to agree with them."

Jemima nodded, hiding her deep disappointment. *So she was out,* she supposed. Quickly, suddenly and unfairly, like her father. An anger started to simmer within her, but she kept it in check.

"I see," she said. "I suppose it doesn't matter that we don't have a First Officer with Section experience!"

"Ah, but we do," he said provocatively. "We just got one this morning."

"Who?"

Christopher picked up a signal from the table and handed it to her. Her anger gave way to shock. It read:

FOR INFORMATION OF ALL
SUBSECTION COMMANDERS:

Second Officer Jemima James (née Jablonowski)

George Medal WRNS, promoted to acting First Officer and appointed Deputy Commander M Section with effect this date.

Jemima bit her lip. "I don't know what to say or do," she said quietly.

"If I were you," he said, rising and stretching, "I wouldn't say anything. I'd go and sew in a half stripe, chop-chop. That way at least you'll *look* like a First Officer. And maybe *feel* like one, too."

She could no longer suppress the girlish smile that had been bottled within her. "Aye, aye, sir," she said.

"I'm going to get some sleep." Christopher closed his notebooks, slipping the written notes inside. "There's nothing more I can do now. I've got to get a clear head. You finish here as quick as you can. Then get down to the Section main HQ at Birdham and take over the ship. There's one hell of a lot of work to be done there."

"Aye, aye, sir," said Jemima.

"I'll be aboard by tomorrow evening." He walked to the door, then turned back. "Goodbye, Number One."

"Goodbye, sir," she acknowledged as Christopher went out.

Jemima smiled. Christopher had called her *Number One*. The expression always used by a captain to his first lieutenant. And she was glad.

Enraged, Prime Minister Anthony Eden slammed down the telephone. He cursed violently. Two advisors cowered at a safe distance behind him in the British Ambassador's office in the Ottawa Embassy. Eden turned.

"Get me out of this damned colony and back to England immediately," he said. The news over the telephone had been less than euphoric. Problems in Parliament concerning the proposed budget; an intelligence report suggesting an impending problem with Nasser over the Suez; the transportation unions suggesting that a nationwide strike might teach the new government a little respect; and then there were all the unsettled arrangements concerning the Khrushchev visit.

So much for travel plans that had been made five months in advance. Eden canceled plans to return to England on the RMS *Queen Elizabeth* and instead rushed a British military plane into service. Aloft, however, the aircraft developed a disturbing mechanical knock and set down at Gander for eight hours of repairs. The Prime Minister was livid.

He was still seething at noon on February 9, when he finally arrived in London. He summoned a helicopter to fly him from Heathrow Airport to Horseguards Parade behind Downing Street. But incredibly, a clerk in the Department of the Environment refused to authorize the helicopter to land on a public thoroughfare. The craft returned to the airport and Eden went to his residence by motorcade.

Mountbatten was waiting in Eden's study when the Prime Minister finally arrived. Eden entered in a rage, cursing bureaucracy and all its work and pointedly, profanely carping about "Labour people in their petty department rolls."

"How was your journey otherwise, Anthony?" Mountbatten inquired.

"Tell me about your Section," Eden shot back. "What's been accomplished?"

Mountbatten provided a soothing progress report, citing security precautions already in effect, a plan to closely monitor all immigration between then and April and the establishment of communications procedures.

For the time being, the Prime Minister was mollified, though not entirely overwhelmed either.

Two evenings later, on the eleventh of February, an Englishman stood in the drizzle in a different part of London. He was a world away from Whitehall and the Admiralty on a cold Saturday evening in Kensington. He stood outside a public house called the Nag's Head, peered through the doorway from the outside and pulled his rumpled black mackintosh close to him against the rain. On his head was a battered old trilby. The brim was turned up all the way around, but the hat was sloped downward over his eyes. An acquaintance passing close by would probably not have recognized him.

The man had killed many times in his life. Now, on

this inclement evening, he steadied his gaze on a rosy-cheeked barmaid in a white blouse who served tables in the busy pub. Her name was Julia. She was a nicely proportioned brunette with an easy smile and freckles. The man who stood in the rain watched for several extra seconds. He flexed his fingers. He felt his muscles tighten: women excited him.

The man moved slowly into the doorway, still lurking beyond the view of the barmaid or anyone else in the Nag's Head. He was a powerful little man, the shadowy figure in the mac. He had a large, almost hooked nose, bushy eyebrows and sideburns. He carried a walking stick — which could instantly be a lethal weapon — and had a choppy gate, as if he'd once injured a leg and the injury had never completely healed. He was forty-six years old, but alternately felt twenty-six and eighty-six.

Julia left the bar with plates in both hands. She served a table, then took an order from another. She moved closer to the doorway. The man's predatory instincts were up. Julia would be such an easy target. Sneaking up on a pretty young woman like Julia excited him so.

She took another step toward him and the man positioned himself to strike. He held the walking stick under his arm. Julia would be easy, he told himself. Very easy. She wouldn't know what hit her until he was upon her.

She turned to walk to the bar and the little man in the trilby was in motion. He struck.

He moved with astonishing speed for a man of his

140

age and condition. One of his arms was swiftly around her waist. The other hand came up in a flash, the walking stick left behind against the door. The hand covered her mouth and perfectly muffled her shriek. Her entire body stiffened in shock as he pulled her closely to him.

Then slowly her body relaxed. Her wide eyes returned to normal. The man kissed her on the back of the neck.

"Good evening, gorgeous," he said.

He released the hand over her mouth. The hand joined the other and he hugged her affectionately.

"You're a bad boy, Crabbie!" she said to him. She leaned over her own shoulder and gave him a peck on the cheek. "Flirt with all the girls, then go home to your main lady."

"I know," said Commander Lionel Crabb. "We all know it. That's the cross we have to bear, isn't it?"

He released her. He snuck a pat on her backside and she playfully pushed his hand away. From behind the bar, Jeffrey, the bartender, looked up and grinned. He liked Crabb and tolerated much worse in his establishment on other occasions. And he knew Julia was quite sweet on the retired commander.

Crabb made the rounds of tables. Friends. Acquaintances. Drinking partners. The Nag's Head was a second home to Crabb. He vastly preferred it to all his other haunts. It was hidden away in Kinnertown Street, not far from his flat. The clientele was amusing and predictable, not too trendy, not too many stuffy young executives. There were few foreigners.

The Nag's Head allowed an old Navy man like Crabb to drown his sorrows — and by February of 1956 there were many — and spend a comfortable evening among friends and lurch home unharmed. A gin and tonic was waiting for him by the time he eased onto his usual bar stool. No wonder the Nag's Head was Crabb's favorite watering hole. But then again, Lionel Crabb knew all about water and its varied uses: from mixing with whiskey to the draft levels of battle cruisers.

As a national hero, which he was, Crabb was an unlikely figure. But since the coronation of Queen Elizabeth II three years earlier, Britons had been hoping for a revival of the traditional English spirit and the appearance of the "New Elizabethans." The brave, flamboyant, gregarious Crabb, a man of good spirit, ruthless energy, total dedication to his unusual trade, was just such a link to the Englishmen of the day of Elizabeth I. He was also a professional frogman, the archetype for all those who served in the secret sections and private armies of World War II, the special units formed by men like Mountbatten or Desmond Morton to meet the unforeseen requirements of an expanding conflict. Crabb and those like him fought on the fringes of the war and were disdained by the "book" generals and admirals who looked down upon them as undisciplined irregulars. But men like Crabb were tolerated for one simple reason: the war could not have been won without them.

Crabb emerged as a hero in the early days of the war. The Navy needed divers who would search the hulls of their own ships for mines, attack enemy ships with similar mines and find and disarm mines left in harbors. Crabb's assignments were mostly in the Mediterranean, where the Italian Navy had made a specialty of all three types of work.

By the end of the war, at age thirty-five, Crabb had been promoted all the way to commander and had his own unit: a Royal Navy clearance diving team. As the British Eighth Army advanced in Italy, Crabb's unit followed it in a truck which flew the white ensign of the Royal Navy. When the army paraded through a liberated city, Crabb would cajole his grumbling irregulars into uniform and march them behind the troups. Then when the Army moved northward, Crabb and his men stayed behind to deal with whatever terminal surprises the Germans or Italians had left in a harbor. Their missions took courage and an incalculable steadiness of nerve. Crabb had both qualities in excess: once in an Italian harbor it was observed that Crabb was uncharacteristically slow detonating a mine. Later, he admitted that he'd been suffering from jaundice for two weeks. But he'd never removed himself from action.

Even his enemies admired him. The Italians, who were among the best at underwater work, often made their way to Crabb to personally surrender in the closing days of the war. When an enemy frogman was killed, Crabb always laid a wreath at sea and saw to it there was a funeral. When the war was over, he possessed the George Medal and the Order of the British Empire. But peacetime hung heavily upon him.

There were some jobs, and from time to time he surfaced again as a hero. He was the first diver to reach the British submarine *Truculent,* nestled in the mud at the bottom of the Thames. Not long afterward, he barely escaped death recovering some of the Admiralty's top-secret equipment in St. Anstell Bay. But younger divers were coming along, and soon Crabb was pushed aside. The best jobs went to younger men with more orthodox approaches to both diving and conditioning. He fell into a depression. Alcohol helped. Then a marriage failed. Middle age crept in. Crabb turned to more alcohol, and even the Navy had no further use for him.

Retired, he took a job as a salesman of equipment for coffee bars. He rented a cheap flat in Kensington and in the evening made the rounds of the local pubs. This was one such evening.

"What's new, Jeffrey?" Crabb asked.

The bartender, a slight, graying man in a black vest and white apron, shrugged. "Nothing more or less than usual," he said.

From down the bar a man in his early thirties nodded to Crabb. Crabb nodded back. Crabb knew him but had forgotten his name. He was an American and had been in the Nag's Head every evening for the last two weeks. Some sort of businessman, he'd explained a few sodden evenings earlier. Crabb had amused him with war stories. Jeffrey moved to the television mounted above and behind the bar. He flicked it on. A black-and-white picture slowly blurred into view.

Foster. That was it, Crabb recalled. He sipped his drink. The American's name was Bernard Foster. He was a Texan who worked for an oil company. He'd chatted with Crabb on several occasions and had confessed to being a former soldier himself. Crabb could take the man or leave him. Foster said he'd grown up on Tarzan movies and insisted upon calling Crabb by his other nickname, the one Crabb hated: Buster.

"What's on the TV today, Crabbie?" Jeffrey asked, motioning toward the television. "Football tonight, don't you know? Want to see some news first?"

"I make a point to avoid the news, actually," Crabb said. "News is about politicians, and politicians piss me off."

"That right?" Jeffrey asked.

Crabb nodded. He raised his eyes and saw the television screen. The image of a BBC announcer came into focus. The man's voice was barely audible above the jazz from the record player across the pub.

"Better be sure to avoid it today," Jeffrey said. "You'll be furious."

That was enough to intrigue Crabb. He gazed at the set, then immediately recognized the pictures of two Englishmen who were shown on screen.

Guy Burgess. Donald Maclean.

On that morning, two English journalists in Moscow had been summoned by Tass to Room 101 of the old National Hotel across the street from the Kremlin. There Guy Burgess and Donald Maclean, missing from Britain's Foreign Office since 1951, were seen for the first time in five years. Maclean, the BBC reported, was his usual quiet, surly self. Burgess, who'd once elevated his grating, homosexual brand of obnoxiousness to a fine art while stationed in Washington, was in his usual form. The bottom line of the story was clear: as had long been rumored, a horrible breach of security had occurred in the Foreign Office. And now the press asked the obvious questions.

How many more were involved? How long had the Soviets had their agents within British intelligence? How high did the scandal go?

Crabb sat at the bar and seethed. Bernard Foster moved a few seats in Crabb's direction so that he could better see the television. Foster looked quizzically at the screen, as if he didn't completely understand the story and its implications.

"Who are Maclean and Burgess?" Foster finally asked.

Crabb's eyes were small, narrowed and dancing with rage. He stared at the television set until the next story was on. Then he virtually inhaled a second gin and tonic before silencing the Nag's Head with his response.

"Traitors!" Crabb shouted. "They ought to be fucking shot!"

Sunday promised to be a quiet day both upon the streets of London and three stories below Whitehall as well. Accordingly, Jemima and Christopher made plans. It had been her suggestion.

She met him with the red MG at ten o'clock in the

morning. At a quarter hour before noon, they drove through the quiet village of Abingdon, near Oxford. Christopher marvelled how well she drove and, for that matter, how nicely the car handled. Christopher had officially pronounced the car Section transport, allowing Trott's mechanical group to take it apart, overhaul the engine, put it back together—fixing even the minor dents and knicks along the way—and then apply two coats of bright red paint. Jemima had been in heaven.

The car found its way to the driveway of an exquisite country cottage. Jemima cut the engine and coasted the car to a rest, parking by a pair of old stables that had been converted to garaging.

"Know where we are?" she asked.

"Somewhere in Oxfordshire."

"More specific than that."

"I could venture a guess, Jemima."

"Do, then."

"I suspect *this*," he said, "is your county scat?"

"Right-o," she said with a grin. "My ancestral home in the country. Come on then. Meet my most immediate ancestor."

They stepped out of the car. Jemima led the way across a flagstone path. "We're here, Mother!" she called out.

A voice resounded from within the cottage. "Coming, darling!" a woman answered. Then Mrs. James appeared from the front doorway. "Hello, darling," she said. And she embraced her daughter as Christopher stood to the side.

147

"Hello, Mother," Jemima said. And then, "Christopher, this is my Mum."

Mrs. James was an older version of Jemima. Same shape, face and voice. Her hair was dark, but flecked with gray. Her eyes, too, were the same.

"Hello, Mrs. James," said Christopher, extending his hand.

"Hello, Christopher," she said to the commander.

Lunch was roast Scottish beef, Yorkshire pudding, gravy, horseradish sauce and a young claret. There followed brandysnaps and thick cream, fruit, cheese and coffee. Mrs. James entertained throughout, telling gently reproachful stories about her daughter as a young girl, then turning serious and describing her husband's career in first the Free Polish Air Brigade, then the RAF. She asked Christopher many questions, but never touched upon their current operation.

Christopher loved her.

At about three, Mrs. James announced that she had to visit a sick friend on the other side of Oxford. She said she'd be back about seven or eight. Christopher and Jemima watched her walk to her Triumph.

"Look after the girl, Christopher," she commanded as she put the car in gear.

"I shall," he agreed. "I shall."

Jemima and Christopher watched the auto disappear. "Come on, then," Jemima finally said.

They walked down the road about a quarter of a mile until they came to a stable. There were a half dozen horses there, plus a stableboy who broke into a wide grin when he saw Jemima.

"Back home from the service, are you?" he asked.

"Sadly, only for the day," she told him. He was a fifteen-year-old named Lenny. He quickly saddled two mounts. A few moments later, Jemima led Christopher and the two horses through a copse of beech trees and into a vast clearing at the foot of the hills.

She knew the best bridle paths. The two riders were more than happy to let the horses amble at their own pace. It was meant to be a leisurely day and even a trot would have been too brisk for their mood.

Jemima led them to the summit of the highest hill, and there they reined in the horses. "We stop here," she said. "We sit on our mounts and we take deep breaths. It's like breathing in new life."

It was. Christopher could see for scores of miles in every direction. There was a wind, but it was mild and seasonable, like that of a late autumn day rather than mid-February. Far off in the distance, he could see Oxford, the spires of the university buildings appearing like little needles on the horizon.

"Bracing, isn't it?" she asked.

He could only nod. The peacefulness made him wonder about other ways of living his life, rather than continuing an existence that revolved around violence and the defense of the kingdom. He didn't question anything he'd done in the name of duty. Rather, he wondered if anyone could blame a man who might opt for some peace and tranquility in his middle years.

"How often do you come up here?" Christopher finally asked.

"As often as I can," she said. "And whenever I feel the need to recharge myself."

He struggled with the next question. Before he asked it, he wondered how it would sound. He phrased it carefully.

"Do you bring all your friends up here?"

She suddenly wore a cagey smile. She turned away from the view and looked at him. "Friends? Lovers, you mean? Is that what you're asking me?"

"Yes."

She shook her head. "This is Jemima's private spot," she said. "I've never brought anyone else here."

"Then why me?"

"When I saw you last Sunday," she said, "all tired and haggard after being up all night, I thought you *needed* a day like this."

"You were right."

"It's part of my humanitarian work," she said.

"I appreciate it. I used to go to Devon when I was a boy. Not all the time, but for a week here and there. It reminds me a lot of that."

"Back in the late 1930s?" she said, intrigued.

"That's right. When the family lived in Kent. After my parents' divorce."

"Different world, wasn't it? Before and after the war."

"More than you could imagine." He could have told her all the ways, but chose not to. Think of how one death changes the lives it touches, he felt like saying. Then imagine how twenty-five million deaths change a planet. Imagine spending years learning how to hate, only to then spend a lifetime learning how to forgive.

The sun touched the horizon in the direction of the West Country. "Time to start back," she said. She reined her horse to the left and started to move. "You're invited to come back here on another day in the future," she said. "I promise."

"I accept," he said quickly.

The horses meandered for several minutes. Neither Jemima nor Christopher spoke. Creighton noticed that the horses knew the trail back. At length, he spoke before he actually knew what he was saying.

"Tell me one thing," he said.

She waited.

"Is there a man in your life? A man whom you like?"

She watched the trail before her for several long moments before she replied. "I'm having trouble with that question myself, Christopher," she said. Another few beats, and, "Maybe you'd better not ask me. Not just yet."

"Then I'll withdraw the question."

"Truth is," Jemima said, "I think I already answered."

"Did you?"

"I said we'd come back here another day, didn't I? Well, that must mean something."

"It does," he said. "That you don't have a man."

"No," she countered gently. "It means that I do."

As the horses fell into stride together, Jemima leaned to Christopher and kissed him on the cheek.

"I've enjoyed today," she said. "I really have. I dread going back to London."

He reached to her. His free hand took hers. They rode together in silence for several minutes.

"Poor Roger Garin," she finally said. "He had something to tell me, but they got to him first."

Christopher nodded. "We're not the only ones with a good intelligence system," he said.

She thought of the old musician shot dead in his bathrobe. She saw again the face of the man she had killed, still fighting, she assumed, for a cause lost forty years ago. Then she thought of the other assassin, the one who'd escaped. Somehow the threat before them now seemed all the more real and terrible than it had been before, particularly when contrasted to the peaceful hills of Oxfordshire at sundown. The day faded into evening, and with it her joy to anxiety.

The BOAC 707 that returned the Queen from Nigeria taxied to a landing on a secluded Heathrow runway at fourteen minutes after noon the following Friday, the seventeenth. Prime Minister Eden stood in an overcoat and Homburg on the Tarmac, waiting to greet Her Majesty.

His attendance there, however, was only a traditional courtesy. He brought Elizabeth II up to date on the Khrushchev visit—and the conspiracy that M Section now struggled to thwart—on Monday, the twentieth, as part of his regular weekly audience with the Sovereign.

She had been on the throne for only four years, but Eden had quickly discovered what Churchill before him had learned. Young—the Queen was not yet thirty years old—she was nevertheless tough as an old combat boot. She kept secrets well, yet never appeared secretive. She could range from insightful questions to pithy comments within a single breath. "The country," Sir Winston had once said, "is getting a good deal."

Eden passed along the information that Mountbatten had given him. Elizabeth II listened quietly and had only one observation.

"I do hope," Lord Louis' niece said, "that the Russians visit without incident. Don't you?"

Eden responded that he, too, fervently held that wish.

TEN

Birdham Manor was half a mile south of Birdham village on the old Portsmouth Road. The house stood a mile back from the main entrance, at the end of a gravel driveway. It was also completely hidden among the trees.

Barbed-wire fencing ran around the entire perimeter of the thirty-acre estate. The wire was supported by RG surveillance lights. These lights were invisible to the naked eye, but in the Section control room in the manor house, intruders would show up in a green haze upon a monitoring screen. Christopher liked the system. He had it in mind to use the same RG system underwater around the Soviet ships in Portsmouth.

At 0555 on the dark early morning of February 21, Colonel Timothy Sainthill's voice echoed down the tonnoy system within the manor.

"Do you hear there? Do you hear there? Right,

then. Let's have you. All of you!" As sleepy Section members bounded from their cots, Sainthill's voice resounded from every direction. "Let's have you all on parade outside. Number twelves. In four minutes."

The M Section commando refresher training course had commenced. Number twelves were thin cotton shorts and T-shirts. A freezing drizzle had pelted Birdham and the surrounding countryside south of Hampshire since midnight. It had abated only a few minutes before Sainthill's wake-up summons.

"I'll warn you all once," Sainthill concluded. "Anyone who's adrift won't use his backside for sitting tonight. Wrens included."

By 0559, the entire Section serving at Birdham was assembled outside in the cold. The drizzle recommenced.

The refresher course began that morning and each morning thereafter with a five-mile run. There followed unarmed combat, karate and jujitsu. Lunch was taken in the field for half an hour. Afternoons brought weapons training and calisthenics. Evenings saw dinner and virtual collapse. The next two nights were spent out in the rough—clad only in number twelves—where warmth was provided only by whatever each commando could find in the wild.

Colonel Timothy Sainthill was the toughest of all the Royal Marine SAS Commando. He and his three marine sergeants put the Section through training that would kill most mortals. One reason that Section members survived was that all Section officers led from the front. The sergeants, who did the bullying, shoving, prodding and cajoling, brought up the sides and the rear. They were softer, gentler souls than their devoted colonel.

And as for the bamboo swagger canes that they carried, the metal tips were removed. In the tradition of their forebears, however, they did not hesitate to award "stripes" to the backside of any Section member, officers and females included. In the service, this "encouragement" historically had pushed Section members to heights of fitness beyond what might otherwise have been possible. And fitness saved lives.

"Bloody hell," Jemima said a few moments after the torture began with Tuesday morning's run. "Bloody hell," she repeated a hundred times more over the next hours and days. She might have begged off on seniority grounds, and so could have Christopher. But it was an unwritten bylaw of the Section that the commander and his deputy partake in all training. If they wanted to lead the toughest unit in the British armed services, they would have to prove they were the toughest officers.

On Friday, a third of the Section broke away from Sainthill's command. Christopher led this subsection back to Gosport, where at 11 A.M. they stood side by side on Fort Blockhouse, ruminating on their aches and pains.

"Know what that is?" Christopher finally asked. He pointed to the huge one-hundred-foot gray submarine training tank: the DSEA (standing for Davis Submarine Escape Apparatus) tank. Within the tank, naval divers practiced the nearly impossible maneuvers to escape a sinking, foundering submarine.

"I've heard all the stories," she said, "including the stories about drowned trainees."

"No turning back now," he said. "Go get changed. Take some small consolation: the water's heated."

"Thank God," she said.

The strange thing was, Christopher's association with the DSEA tank now conjured up different memories than when he'd passed Gosport on his return in January. Mountbatten had put the name of Lionel Crabb in the air. As Creighton waited to reorient Section members who might be required to dive during the Khrushchev visit, he thought of his own training.

Crabbie had been the tutor to some of the wartime M Section.

During the war, Christopher had been sent to Gibraltar with two other members of the special unit. There he'd met Lieutenant Commander Lionel Crabb for the first time. Crabb, thirteen years older than Creighton, was already an extensively decorated hero. He was the master diver of the Royal Navy; he drew only the up-and-coming pupils . . . such as young Christopher.

"Right, then," Crabb had said by way of introduction on the first day. "You're about to learn just enough to get yourselves killed. Or to save your lives. It can go either bloody way and I don't care which. So pay attention."

Then Crabb had taught them everything. After three weeks, Crabb sent them one by one below the surface of the Mediterranean to remove what he described as dummy limpet mines from the hull of a mothballed British ship. Limpets had long been the aristocracy of the naval mine: they could be planted on a hull and detonated later, sometimes *days* later.

Christopher spent forty minutes below the surface. When he brought up three mines to Crabb, the instructor handed them to his petty officer.

"Give these things a full de-activation test," Crabb ordered.

"What?" asked Christopher, aghast. "They're *live?"*

"Of course they are," Crabb answered. "No point teaching you virgins how to dive without getting on with the job."

Christopher's mouth hung open. "They could have detonated."

"Damned right," Crabb said. "Look. How the hell else do I know whether you removed them properly? If they'd detonated, there would have been a blast. I would have known immediately that you'd fucked it up."

"I would have been killed."

"That's right. And you would have been replaced by another recruit. One who did the job better."

"Well, I was bloody lucky, wasn't I?" Creighton snapped angrily.

"No!" Crabb retorted in even harsher tones. "And that's just the point! You weren't lucky. You were good! They only send me the best. I've never lost one. But if you'd known those mines were live you would have blown yourself and the ship to kingdom come. So the lesson is simple: it's all in the mind; it's all self-confidence. Always tell yourself it's just an exercise. Then you can relax and get on with it."

"Yes," Christopher said slowly. "I suppose so."

"What?" ranted Crabb.

"Yes, *sir!*" Christopher corrected himself.

Jemima James reappeared in swimsuit and Davis Submarine Escape diving gear, which included face mask and small oxygen cylinder.

As Christopher clipped up his own gear, he noticed that his section trainees and the chief petty officer instructors were scrupulously pretending not to look at Jemima. Immediately, Christopher knew why. He turned toward her.

Across her bare shoulders, the burns and scars from the helicopter rescue were still mottled and scarlet across her skin. They would always be there, a badge of courage that she would wear as long as she wore the George Medal.

She saw Christopher looking at her. There was nothing either could say, but Christopher felt his

160

admiration for her grow, knowing how she'd stayed with the rescue even as the flames burned the uniform from her flesh.

A chief petty officer stepped into the awkward silence. He spoke to Jemima.

"Right now, ma'am," he said. "You'll receive a complete retraining in your equipment. A lot of it has changed in the last two years."

Christopher spoke next, an eye on the training tank. "When you feel comfortable with your apparatus, you'll dive," he said. "Don't be intimidated. It's all in the mind. It's all self-confidence. Tell yourself it's just an exercise. Then you can relax and get on with it."

Her first dive was that same afternoon, and it scared her stiff. But like all Section members, she survived. The second dive came easier and by the third she was over her fear. By 6 P.M. Saturday, she could dive as well as any man in the Section. Truth was, she was better than most.

Half a continent away, Nikita Khrushchev was scorching the Kremlin wallpaper. At ten in the evening, Friday, February 24, he had already been on the podium for three-and-a-half hours before a carefully selected audience of Party members. In the Great Hall of Lenin, he was less than halfway through his speech to the Twentieth Party Congress.

The subject was Stalin, and the cult of the individual.

Khrushchev, a portly figure in his gray suit bedecked with his medals, leaned over the podium, ranted, bellowed, raged, stabbed the air with a stout forefinger and point by point denounced Stalin as the greatest criminal in Soviet history. Sweat poured off Khrushchev. But it also poured off his fourteen hundred spectators. The speech had a nightmarish quality to it; the indictment against Stalin was sweeping. And if Stalin was guilty, weren't those in the audience who'd supported Stalin also guilty? Khrushchev's voice rumbled through the hall like Siberian thunder. His softest words were like growls from a hungry timber wolf.

On into the night the indictment went. *Four hours. Five hours. Six hours.* Certain phrases recurred with distressing regularity: *Brutal violence against everyone who opposed him. A reign of cruel and despotic oppression. The liquidation of seventy percent of the Party's Central Committee. Mass repression. Deviation from Leninism. Causing tremendous harm to socialist advancement. Not preparing the country for the German invasion. Belief in himself as "the great leader."* And finally, most damning of all: *indulging in self-glorification — naming cities, prizes and collective farms for himself, even erecting statues to himself.*

Here Khrushchev broke from his prepared text to take the blood pressure of his audience. He grinned. "The statues," he said to the Party members, "were the best erections Stalin ever made."

The laughter came slowly and was nervous. Good, Khrushchev reasoned. His audience was just the way he wanted it—terror-stricken.

Seven hours into the morning, Nikita Khrushchev ranted. There was tirade after tirade of *sua culpa,* and not one word of *mea culpa,* though everyone recalled the aspiring Khrushchev's fawning devotion to Stalin during the former's political ascent in the Ukraine. Khrushchev chose not to invoke for his audience the image of failed Ukrainian agriculture after Stalin had chosen him to be its administrator. Nor did he recall the time in 1944 when he had induced thirteen Ukrainian poets to author a collective work. *To The Great Stalin from the Ukrainian People,* it had been called. The text was delivered personally to Stalin in Red Square, along with what purported to be more than nine million signatures.

Eight hours. With a wide, self-satisfied smile, Khrushchev concluded his denunciation of Stalin at a few minutes after two in the morning, February 25. As applause began, he gathered his one-hun-dred-twenty-seven handwritten pages and shoved them together.

The applause grew. Then it filled the great assembly hall. High Party leaders—Molotov, Malenkov, Kaganovich, Serov—rose and joined. Khrushchev refused to relinquish the podium. He stood with his hands above his head in a victorious clasp, striking a heroic pose. He nodded jerkily and self-confidently

163

to the other Party leaders, his yellowed teeth dominating a preposterously wicked grin.

The history of Stalin had been exploded. So had the legend. But what sent paroxysms of fear through those who had heard the speech was a simple dreadful realization, apparent to everyone as soon as Khrushchev began the attack on Stalin: if Khrushchev was strong enough to denounce Joseph Stalin, who could dare utter a syllable against Khrushchev? In the West, reports of the speech filtered out within a day. Witnesses said that many of those in attendance left the Grand Hall of Lenin dazed, stony-faced and soaked with perspiration.

But it had not been heat that had caused the sweat. Nor had it been fatigue. Purely and simply, it had been fear, the particularly Russian type of fear that wallowed in the soul, grew like a cancer and fed itself upon knocks on residential doorways at midnight, or army execution squads patrolling streets in the towns of rural Russia.

Khrushchev, the popular hero. Khrushchev, the reformer. Khrushchev, the supreme ruler of the Soviet Union, from the Caucasus to the ice of Siberia, from the barbed-wire border with Finland down through Mongolia to Vladivostok and the Pacific border with China. Khrushchev.

The next day Stalin's name began to disappear from public places in the countryside. Statues were pulled down overnight by obedient Party members, smashed or thrown into rivers. At the same time,

Ivan Alexandrovich Serov departed by submarine for Great Britain. He left behind a nation riddled with a fear unknown since the death of Joseph Stalin himself in April of 1953.

ELEVEN

At the Nag's Head in Kensington, Khrushchev's speech was received with a gigantic yawn. The BBC gave it thirty-eight seconds, their number-three story. Crabb was already parked in front of a gin and tonic when the news came on. He was used to turning his head away at any mention of Communists, then looking quickly back if there was word of football or the Royal Navy.

Tonight he had another distraction. Bernard Foster, the American, had sidled up again and was enjoying anew the details of how Crabbie had inspected the hull of the *Sverdlov.*

"They needed someone outside the Service," Crabb bragged. "So they came to me. Hell, I'm better than any diver in the navy. I'm damned well *the best* inside *or* outside the Service."

"I don't doubt it, Buster," said Foster.

Crabb turned to the American. "Listen here, Foster," he said. "Buster Crabbe is an actor. Same name, but with an 'e' on the end. He played Tarzan. He's also a swimmer. I can't stand him. He's a puffed-up ignoramus propelled through the water by gaseous bullshit fired through a questionably enlarged arsehole. A good male crabb is a Crabb. A pouf is a 'Crabbe' with the 'e' on his ass."

Foster blinked.

"So don't call me 'Buster'!" Crabb roared.

"Sure thing, Crabbie," said Foster.

Jeffrey reappeared. "Crabbie, you're going to talk about those Russian boats until the story has gray whiskers on it."

"Well, why the hell not?" huffed Crabb. "You know what's going to happen to this kingdom, Jeffrey? We'll get Labour coming back into Downing Street. They'll turn us all into Bolsheviks and you won't see any British ships in English harbors. You'll see nothing but hammers and sickles."

"What's the bottom of that ship look like?" Foster asked. "The *Sverdlov.*"

Crabb gave him a knowing smile. "I know," Crabb said. "But I'll never tell. Follow?"

"I follow."

"Come on, Crabbie," Jeffrey said. "Let's have a *vintage* story this time. Maybe something ten to twelve years old."

"Got plenty of those," Crabb said.

"Sure you do," Jeffrey said good-naturedly. "Trouble is, we know them all."

Crabb took the reproach more seriously than it

had been intended. He looked at Jeffrey with growing anger, which allowed Bernard Foster the moment he'd been waiting for.

"What you need," Foster said, "is some new stories. Maybe we ought to speak privately."

Crabb's restless gaze flicked up and down, then settled upon Foster's face. The American made a gentle gesture toward one of the tables in the corner, far away from anyone else. Crabb picked up his drink and followed.

"I suppose I should tell you," Foster said, "that I do more than trot around the globe for the Mobil Oil Company."

"I suppose," Crabb answered, "I should tell *you:* I've never met an oil executive yet who had four weeks to follow me from bar to bar."

Foster leaned back slightly, grinning. "So you know I have some other purpose? And you don't mind my watching you for a few days before making the pitch?"

"Mister," said Crabb, "you've been paying for the drinks since late January. Why should I complain? If you were me, would you want this bloody alcoholic miracle to come to an end?"

From the corner of his eye, Crabb caught Julia looking his way. She smiled. Crabb tapped the edge of his glass and the barmaid went to the counter to find him a refill. Foster was drinking pale ale and had barely touched the one he had before him.

"I can make you a very good offer," Foster said. "To do some work."

"I don't suppose it has to do with making a dive somewhere, does it?" Crabb said with a malicious grin.

Foster measured Crabb carefully. Julia arrived with Crabb's gin and Foster laid a pound note on the table. He signaled that he didn't want the change.

"Oh, for Christ's sake, man!" Crabb snapped. "Tell me what you want me to do! Don't keep me in your bloody suspense!" Crabb's voice boomed, which made Foster nervous.

"Something similar to what you did in October," said Foster.

"Russians again, eh?"

"Yes. And for God's sake, keep it quiet."

Crabb recoiled slightly. "I wouldn't make a peep to anyone," he said.

The American continued indulgently. There would be three boats in Portsmouth harbor in April, he said. Three Soviet ships. A battle cruiser and two destroyers escorting Bulganin and Khrushchev to London. Crabb hated the whole idea of the Soviet visit. The Red bastards themselves, he said, calling on Churchill, scheduled for an audience with the Queen. "God-awful disgrace," Crabb growled.

"I agree," Bernard Foster purred. "But some good can come of it."

"Such as?" Crabb asked. The ice cubes clinked in his glass as he sipped.

"We want you to look at the hulls of all three ships," Foster said. "That would give us an excellent idea of how the Russians are equipping their vessels."

"Your story doesn't wash," Crabb answered. Foster waited. "I already took a look at the *Sverdlov*. And you know that. One of those Russian tubs is the same class as the *Sverdlov*. So what else am I going to be doing under those ships?"

"You'll find out just before you go down, Crabbie."

"Whose money am I taking?" Crabb asked suspiciously. "And how much of it?"

"Five hundred pounds." Almost imperceptibly Crabb's eyes widened. "And the instigation behind this comes from SIS. The Admiralty wants it done and so do the Americans."

"I suppose that's where you came in," Crabb said. "They sent a Yank out to hire me so that it can never be traced back to Whitehall."

"That's pretty close to it." There was a pause. Crabb considered it, then noticed that his glass was empty. He looked for Julia again.

Foster fell silent until the barmaid had been summoned and had refilled Crabb's bottomless glass.

"We need a good diver," Foster said in a confessional tone. "The *best*. And for obvious reasons we can't use anyone still in the Royal Navy or the American Navy. You're perfect. You know the harbor and will understand the operation. You're also the best."

Crabb's gaze restlessly prowled the room, then settled back upon Foster. "And I'm not actively in anyone's navy," he said. "So that if something should happen . . ."

"Nothing will."

"Americans in it, too, are they?" Crabb asked. Foster nodded.

"Then it'll cost one thousand pounds."

"Oh, Crabbie, come on . . ."

But Crabb was suddenly furious, leaning forward and pointing a finger into Foster's face. "Now, you listen to me!" Crabb snapped. "You want the best diver, you pay for him! I got fifty bloody pounds last time I went down there and I spent most of the time waiting for those Kalashnikov bullets to start raking the water. I got bills to pay, too, see, Mr. Foster, and if you want this dive done right, you have to make it worthwhile." Crabb drained his glass. "Clear?" he asked.

"Clear," said Foster without hesitation.

Crabb took a long cold look at him. Foster's expression never wavered. Neither wished to be the next to speak.

"Well, then?" Crabb finally asked.

"Well what?"

"When will you know? Will you pay me or not?"

"One thousand pounds," Foster said. "No question about it. You have a deal."

Slowly a smile crept across Crabb's tired, lined face.

"In that case, mister," the Englishman said, "you just hired yourself a frogman. Portsmouth harbor? Sometime in April, no?"

Foster nodded. That was the time and place, he said. The eighteenth of that month. He extended a

172

hand and Crabb accepted it. Yes indeed, Foster said, as he ordered another round of drinks for both of them, he'd just hired a frogman.

A damn good frogman. The best, as Crabb himself still liked to think, in the business.

TWELVE

The Keppel's Head Inn lay between Portsmouth Royal Navy Dockyard and the HMS Vernon, the joint shore establishment for mine, torpedo and diving training. All three were adjacent to the harbor. The inn had been there longer than anyone could remember. British naval officers had gambled away their pay or celebrated their promotions in the inn's smoky long rooms since before the Napoleonic Wars. Legend had it that Nelson himself, newly promoted to vice admiral, spent a memorable night at Keppel's Head with his dearest Emma before embarking for sea, finally to make landfall off Cape Trafalgar. But in 1956, the Nut Bar downstairs at the Keppel's Head gained a new distinction: it was the venue chosen by Comrade General Ivan Alexandrovich Serov for his meeting with Commander Peter Hamilton.

Both Christopher and Jemima had been there many times. They condemned it as the worst possible sort of place to rendezvous with Serov. It was always crowded. Private exchanges, let alone secret exchanges, would be impossible.

"Suppose," Jemima said aloud as she and Christopher drove in her MG on the A3 south to Portsmouth from London, "suppose some right-wing sailor recognizes our Bolshevik friend? Suppose someone takes a swipe at him? Or worse?"

He thought about it for several seconds as she drove in her usual fashion: white knuckles on the steering wheel, the little vehicle feeling as if it were seconds away from becoming airborne.

"If that should happen," he answered evenly, "I'm counting on Desmond Morton to throw us a damned fine retirement party from the Royal Navy."

She stared straight ahead, but bit her lip to keep from grinning. Then she elbowed him sharply in the ribs. "What a damned fine sense of humor."

"Well, we simply have to make the best of the location," he said. "The Russians wouldn't change it. Did Mountbatten tell you why?"

"No," she said, eyes on the road.

"Serov has some friends in the Soviet Navy who liked to go drinking and skirt chasing there during the war. So the Comrade General wants to see what all the fuss was about."

Jemima shook her head. She continued to drive.

They arrived in Portsmouth and moved slowly through the local streets to the inn. Christopher looked to spot any of the security arrangements he'd set in place the previous morning. Lieutenant Commander Trott had drifted into Portsmouth with about ten officers and ten petty officers from the Squad. They'd covered every entrance and exit from the inn. Additionally, any approach from the harbor was covered by Lieutenants Wilmot and Campbell, sitting in civilian clothing on the deck of a small yacht. Other than M Section and their commanders, no one knew that in the cockpit locker in baskets rested two Thompson submachine guns, loaded and ready. Trott took great glee in the security measures. He had stationed himself on a frigate in the harbor. Creighton had inquired about the ship's firepower.

"Of the first rate, sir," Trott had answered joyfully. "Could blow the Keppel's Head clean over Southsea and Langstone Harbor onto Hayling Island, if we wish to. I'd enjoy it enormously, sir, but it won't do much for you if you're still inside with the Red."

Even Christopher had to suppress a smile. He'd never met a man so spoiling for action as Trott. He would have made an excellent mercenary if he hadn't loved the Royal Navy so dearly.

Jemima parked her car in the dockyard, fifty meters from the Keppel's Head. It was one minute after noon.

Christopher and Jemima walked down the stairs to the Nut Bar at exactly five minutes after twelve. She was wearing a smart, well-tailored, light gray wool suit with a matching roll-neck sweater. At her lapel was a small emerald cluster which had once been her mother's. Christopher wore an ordinary blue blazer, dark gray slacks, white shirt and a maroon tie. As they entered, a few heads turned toward them. He was conscious of how they looked like a couple. He led her immediately to a small table by a window close to the harbor.

A waiter appeared. Without asking, Christopher ordered a fino for her and a Worthington for himself. Without speaking to each other, they scanned the room, she looking behind him, he covering the area behind her. A few minutes later the waiter delivered the drinks.

"And what if our Soviet friends don't show up?" she asked at length.

"They'll be here," he said. "Count on it." Another ten minutes passed. They sipped their drinks slowly. They'd already agreed: as little alcohol consumed as possible. Christopher's gaze drifted out across Portsmouth harbor, through the cold February mist, to the great bastion of Fort Blockhouse, better known as HMS Dolphin, the base of the Fifth Submarine Flotilla. He glanced back to her, easily reading her thoughts—which he took to be the same as his own.

"Seven weeks from now," he said softly, "Krushchev and Bulganin and half the other heavyweights in the Soviet government will come steaming into that harbor, Jemima." She looked back to him. "They'll be sitting aboard a cruiser, with two destroyers moored alongside. And somewhere, some group of misguided fools is planning to take a serious shot at them. Seven weeks. And to date, we

178

haven't caught or immobilized anyone."

"Commander Hamilton? Sir?"

Christopher's distraction ended. He and Jemima turned to see a man of about forty standing respectfully beside them. He was a big bear of a man, round with large thick arms and a bright red beard. His suit bore the marks of the finest Soviet tailoring: ill-fitting and of cheap, shiny gray cloth. "I am Comrade Major Sergei Lepovitch Dimitroff," he said in passable English. He held out a diplomatic identity card of the Soviet Union.

Christopher kept his hands on the table. Jemima took the card, assessed it wordlessly and handed it back to the Russian. She took him to be Ukrainian, which fit better than his suit. The Russian power elite was top-heavy with Ukrainians since the ascension of Khrushchev. Even the Navy. Jemima gave Christopher a slight nod.

"So what do you want with me, mate?" Christopher asked, leaning back in his chair. "And why do you think my name is Hamilton?"

"Oh, you have been reliably identified, sir," Dimitroff replied instantly. "By my superior."

"What superior?"

"By the man you've come here to meet. A man who will soon be your trusted friend."

Christopher looked around the room. "All I see is a bunch of sailors. I don't see any future trusted friends."

"If you would both come with me, sir, I will lead the way." When neither Christopher nor Jemima moved, Dimitroff added, "Upstairs." Christopher and Jemima looked at each other, then rose to follow. A thought flew through Christopher's mind: at that very moment, that crazy bastard Trott probably had the inn lined up in the site of a 9-mm gun.

The Russian escorted them across the bar and up the stairs to the first floor. Neither of them had ever been there. At the end of a corridor, Dimitroff opened some double doors which led to a private room, obviously rented for the occasion. Dimitroff bowed and let Jemima and Christopher enter before him.

It was an astonishingly pleasant room, with an atmosphere far different from the sailors' watering hole down below. There was a large, blazing wood fire in an expansive hearth. The walls were oak, as was a large single table in the center of the room. Standing on either side of the door as they entered were two young men, sturdy, clean-shaven, blond and high-cheekboned, whom Christopher took to be KGB guards. Dimitroff made no attempt to introduce them. By the window, Christopher next noticed a large table stocked with alcohol. By this stood an older man in a white apron.

"So where's Comrade Serov?" Christopher asked.

"You will meet him presently." The Russian's English improved by the minute. "If you will make yourselves comfortable . . ." Dimitroff motioned to the table, which was set for four. He indicated that the Englishman and woman were to take the two better seats, armchairs close to the fire.

Dimitroff turned and clapped twice to the man in the apron. The man bowed and brought over trays of caviar and smoked salmon. He laid them lavishly on all four plates. "What will you drink, Madam Comrade?" he asked in Russian. "There is vodka and schnapps. Wine, champagne and—"

"He asks," said the bearded major, "what you will—"

"I understand him, Comrade Dimitroff," Jemima answered in Russian. The major blinked. "I suspect vodka goes best with everything. Vodka for the commander and myself."

Jemima James speaking Russian was a sight for Christopher to behold. She was masterful. He felt a surge of pride for her and couldn't tell if it was personal or professional. Then again, he had only the vaguest idea what she was saying until a full glass of Russian vodka was set before him.

The waiter filled four glasses in all and picked up the fourth one himself. When Christopher raised an eyebrow, Dimitroff explained, "In Russia, everyone is equal."

"But some are more equal than others," Christopher found himself thinking. He noticed the expensive shoes the waiter wore. Italian, he guessed.

The waiter raised his glass in a toast. *"Nasdorovie!"* he said. A gold cuff link glittered on his wrist. Jemima saw it at the same time.

"Spasibo!" she replied to his toast. She and Christopher raised their glasses in unison. All four drank. Creighton assessed the waiter's age as early fifties.

Jemima was catching on, too. She inquired of the waiter as to the type of vodka served. When the older man completed a concise explanation, she switched back to English.

"We're so honored, Christopher," she said, "to be served by not one but two men from the Ukraine. The same Soviet republic as Chairman Khrushchev."

Dimitroff and the other man bowed gently. Christopher turned to the waiter. The man's eyes danced with amusement.

"I would ask," Christopher said in English, "when we would have the honor of meeting Comrade Serov. Except the question now is useless. I do believe that Comrade Serov, who spent three years with the Kiev State Theater as a young man, has already made our acquaintance."

The waiter stared blankly but with good humor, as if waiting for a translation.

"And I also recall, from our somewhat plump dossier on Comrade Serov, that during the war he was an outstanding liaison officer between Soviet troops and English and American troops. Hence, he speaks English quite adequately."

The waiter nodded very slightly, then reached to his apron. He untied it from the back. "They say all Churchill's handpicked officers are gentlemen," he said to Creighton with remarkable clarity. "Also filled with intelligence. Lady sailors, too."

Christopher smiled. "Together, Comrade," Creighton reminded him, "we demolished the Germans."

Serov's face illuminated. "Ah. Being true. But some demolishing more than others." He laughed. He set aside his glass of vodka and poured himself some scotch whiskey. "Another toast, my friend," Serov said. "To renewing old friendship."

They had a marvelous meal which Serov insisted on serving for his English guests. Borscht. Roast pleasant and venison, wild rice with salad. Fruit followed for dessert. All this was accompanied by red wines from the Ukraine, Russian champagne and caviar.

"All flew this morning on diplomatic pouch from Moscow," Serov explained with evident pride. "I predict this menu personally."

"Excellent," remarked Christopher. Two-and-a-half hours had passed. He wondered how Jemima was handling the massive amounts of alcohol served. If it affected her, she wasn't showing it.

Christopher stole a glance at his watch. It was almost three o'clock. Not one word had been mentioned about security and the impending Krushchev visit. He envisioned Trott growing edgy at the ignition end of his firepower.

"Now," Serov finally remarked. Christopher was hopeful. "Brandy," he said. "Czechoslovakian — finest in the world!" Serov virtually caressed the bottle.

"Perhaps," said Christopher, "we might move to the subject of —"

"Brandy," said Serov again. He set up four glasses. Christopher's patience dwindled. For a moment a horrifying notion was upon him: Serov was a raging alcoholic who would turn this entire meeting into a sodden misadventure, a waste of everyone's time. Christopher reached across the table and turned Jemima's brandy snifter upside down. He placed his hand over his.

Serov looked crestfallen. He poured brandy for Dimitroff. "Brandy from the Orlik region of Czechoslovakia. Gift from Czech government."

"Out of gratitude, I suppose," Christopher answered, "for helping protect them from the Czech people."

Serov gave Christopher a long offended look, but still poured brandy for himself. He made a tisking sound with his tongue.

"Now is time for bullshit expiring!" announced the KGB chairman.

Christopher nodded. "Yes, if you please!"

The Russian filled his glass. "Then we will now see if we can understand each other." Serov stood and held his glass aloft. Christopher wondered if it was too late, if the Russian was already sloshed. He cursed himself and recalled every Sunday *Telegraph* story he'd ever read about drunkenness in the Soviet workers' paradise.

"Great pleasure," Serov announced, "it gives me to drink to the Queen, Her Majesty Queen Elizabeth II." He stood to attention and clicked his heels. He bolted down the brandy. Christopher had the impression that Serov was coming to the conclusion of a well-planned act. Then Serov dramatically launched the crystal snifter through the air and into the raging fireplace. The glass shattered against the bricks and the fire surged and snarled from the remaining drops of alcohol.

For a moment Serov ruminated, staring at the fire. "Best I ever saw," he then announced, "throwing of brandy glasses into fire was woman. Marie Nikolayevna Romanova. Empress of All Russias. In exile, of course."

Serov glanced innocently at Christopher. Creighton's face was as still as a mask.

"Come!" Serov said exuberantly. "Now. Show your Portsmouth!"

Fifteen minutes later, accompanied by one of Trott's mail-fisted teams, Christopher and Jemima escorted the two Russians through the gates of Her Majesty's dockyard at Portsmouth. When Serov saw HMS *Victory* Nelson's flagship herself, he requested to inspect her. Led to the quarterdeck, he took Christopher by the arm and stood with him at the spot—marked by a bronze plaque—where Nelson fell at Trafalgar.

"Here, Comrade Hamilton," Serov said, "you and me defend Russian warships. As days of Admiral Nelson."

"Your grasp of history," Christopher said with some surprise, "is excellent, Comrade Serov." Serov beamed, as did Dimitroff. Rehearsed or not, Serov's allusion was accurate. The Russia of Czar Alexander I had been an ally of the British in their fight against Bonaparte.

"Of course," Serov added to the delight of all English ears within hearing distance, "the French aren't much as sailors, are they?"

It was a different Serov who inspected HMS *Victory*. His eyes were keen, his intellect just as sharp. Christopher was surprised again. The man was civil, perceptive and calm. He had expected a coarse, ill-mannered Bolshevik peasant. Serov was smooth, more diplomatic than the Russian diplomats he'd known. Creighton wondered if it had something to do with survival within Soviet politics. He would liked to have asked, but didn't.

Outside again, Christopher showed Serov the various mooring possibilities within the dockyard. Creighton offered to take a small boat through the harbor for Serov, but the Russian was content to stand on the jetty and scan the harbor with binoculars.

The positions were numerous. The South Camber, Watering Island and the South Railway Jetty; Bird Lime Point, Boat House and Pitch House jetties. There were also Mid Slip and North Corner jetties, as well as other jetties in Fountain Lake.

A long, technical discussion followed. Jemima stood by and Serov, to make himself clear, spoke in Russian, which Jemima translated. After more than half an hour Serov announced that he would recommend to Soviet authorities that the three visiting Soviet vessels use the South Railway Jetty on Watering Island.

Christopher agreed entirely. It was, from all strategic points of the harbor, the easiest jetty to see and keep under constant surveillance. It was also the easiest to protect from the dockyard and it afforded Christopher's Section many tactical advantages. Their subsection HQ was just three hundred yards away. The late afternoon wind whipped in from the channel. Christopher invited the Russians back aboard *Victory* for tea.

They sat in Nelson's great cabin, with Trott's detail on guard around the ship. Christopher and Serov discussed every aspect of the Khrushchev visit. They promised each other they would keep in close touch over the impending seven weeks. Again, it was the civil, intelligent Serov who faced Christopher. Creighton found himself starting to like the man, even respect him.

Concluding, Serov took Christopher by the arm and walked with him up to the poop deck. Jemima stayed behind with Dimitroff. Serov looked over the harbor and again spoke English.

"In seven weeks," Serov said, "Khrushchev and Bulganin coming out there." He nodded toward Watering Island. "Nothing happening to them, Comrade Hamilton?"

Christopher nodded. "Nothing will," he said.

There was a long pause, which Serov finally broke. "You knowing, Comrade Hamilton," he said, "my KGB and also MVD controlling all files in Soviet Union. My agents are being most fine. They pinching these files and squeezing out truth. Additional, I have friends with associates. Some having connections of White Russian émigrés."

Serov held a silence. Christopher looked him squarely in the eye for several seconds, certain now that he knew where this conversation was leading. He wondered, however, if his face would not give him away if he were forced to tell a lie.

"My friend, Comrade Peter Hamilton, I am in position necessary for trusting you. We both share responsibilities for lives of Soviet leaders. I assure you, far worse fate awaiting me in Russia than await on you if catastrophe is arriving."

Christopher nodded. "Exactly what are you leading to, Comrade Ivan?"

Serov blew out a long pensive breath. "I knowing without doubt, many years, that Grand Duchess Marie Nikolayevna Romanova escaped from Russia in 1918, and married Prince Nicholas Dolgorouky, January 21, 1919, in Bucharest. This going fine. And wishing her nothing of harm, as will be seeing, you not believing like half-wit Americans that because I was vice-chairman MVD and now director KGB, am also being bloodthirsty like ridiculously American horror movie."

"Please continue," Christopher urged.

"Émigrés holding Marie Nikolayevna, calling her Empress of Russia—in the exile, of course. That is her right. But since announcement our leaders visiting your queendom, Marie Nikolayevna's name being used raising money for avenging deaths of imperial family. Chiefly, her father the Czar. Not

188

knowing what form this vengeance taking, but making guess."

Serov's eyes were suddenly transformed. They became something deeper and bore in on Christopher's. "What say you to that, Comrade Commander Christopher Creighton?"

Christopher felt as if the weight of All the Russias had suddenly fallen upon his shoulders. Serov had manipulated him into this spot, then thrown his ace. He realized he would have to work with Serov. Only the truth could now suffice.

His own proper name was still ringing in Christopher's ears when he began to answer. "Comrade Ivan Alexandrovich Serov," Creighton said. "You say that you have reason to trust me. Then that trust will now be put to a test, because I cannot comment on anything you have said. But I promise you this: everything is being done to guarantee the safety of your leaders when they arrive here. And on the first day that I am able to speak freely with you, I shall discuss everything."

Serov nodded slightly, apparently mollified. "Late Czar's nephew, Admiral Mountbatten, your chief! Where will be?"

"On a Commonwealth tour. Far out of the country."

"Possible securing this harbor completely?"

"The harbor and everything contiguous to it will be absolutely secure. I promise you."

"You doing this for me? Without fail?"

"Yes," Christopher promised.

"Then I am returning favour, Commander," Serov said. "Courtesy of my KGB and information we obtaining." Brisk and blank. Time to do business, said Serov's tone, fractured grammar notwithstanding. "Town is south of France near Nice. Jourdanville. Believing you find it strong protected by mercenaries. French paras. Germans. OSS soldiers." He paused, his eyes narrowing. "Also you finding Marie Nikolayevna. Acting on these informations is your affair. Not mine."

THIRTEEN

On the day of Serov's arrival, the temperature turned radically colder through the south of England. By the evening, an unusually heavy snow swept down from Ireland, across Wales and the West Country. It crossed East Anglia until it slid out to the North Sea. The snow blanketed London.

On March first, the morning after Serov's departure, the sun magically reappeared toward 10 A.M. But there was no thaw. London began digging out. Children in the park threw snowballs, bus and motorcar traffic was hopelessly snarled and many small shops failed to open. It was both picturesque and a damned nuisance.

Christopher's thoughts wandered in several directions. An image of Serov remained with him: the cordial, shrewd diplomat who presided over the most savage police agency since the SS. Then there was the village of Jourdanville, near Nice. Jemima had signaled Serov's information to Ann Vergamo, head of the French subsection.

Christopher wondered: was Serov leading them astray or directing them along the right path? From long experience, Creighton remained ready for anything. Yet he could not imagine that Serov would prove intentionally unreliable. The Russian's own life might hinge on a successful operation.

But as Big Ben tolled the three-quarter hour that morning, Christopher's thoughts turned inward. He and Jemima were among a steady stream of visitors who made their way into the old Benedictine Abbey of Westminster. Both Christopher and Jemima wore greatcoats over their uniforms. Most of those in attendance wore black. They were at a memorial service.

Christopher was very pleased to be able to be present. Mountbatten had personally added Jemima's name to the list of the invited. Recently deceased, and already interred in a private ceremony, was A. A. Milne, a longtime friend of Desmond Morton as well as Churchill. Christopher felt a particular loss, though he'd only met Milne on two occasions. He'd grown up, like millions of other English and American children, on *Winnie-the-Pooh* and *The House at Pooh Corner*.

But in particular, there had been Christopher Robin, Christopher's code name. Desmond Morton had with much reluctance been Owl. Then there'd been Tigger, Christopher's old mentor from Chartwell Manor, the one man in the world he revered most of all. Sir Winston was eighty-two years old now and his flesh was failing. Christopher had hoped to catch sight of him, perhaps being helped to

192

a front pew. Christopher looked closely. The beloved old fat man wasn't there. Creighton was saddened a second time.

In fact, few old friends were there. He saw old General "Pug" Ismay, who'd been Heffalump. And Sir Desmond was there, sitting in a rear corner, obviously in a very secretive and cantankerous mood; Christopher gave him a nod, but Morton would only wink one eye without moving his head. Others were absent. Some, Christopher knew, were already dead. He had the sense of remorse that is normally the province of men much older, the surge of sadness that follows the loss of one's own generation. The old soldiers were passing.

An usher guided Christopher and Jemima to seats midway back on the left side. From a military family, Jemima was no stranger to these ceremonies. Christopher could read her expression. Stoic, but hiding her own set of personal memories. The loss of her father before his fiftieth birthday. Uncles, perhaps. The collective anguish of all Eastern European people who'd endured first the Nazi onslaught and then the Soviets. For a moment, Christopher grew very angry at Ivan Serov. But then he took Jemima's hand beneath the pew. He held it as a brother would. Yet the courage he rallied was his own as well as hers.

She smiled to him and let him keep her hand.

Then there was a slight buzz in the congregation. Heads turned in front of them. When Christopher looked over his shoulder, he saw Mountbatten. The admiral—resplendent in his uniform, cap under his

left arm, its gold braid with a patina like a halo —
was at the east door being greeted by the dean.
When Mountbatten took his seat, the service began.

Creighton turned forward again. His thoughts
were many. But his eyes must have been far away
because Jemima gave him a nudge, returning him to
the thirty-five minute service for the departed Milne.

After the benediction, on an icy sidewalk outside
Westminster, Jemima and Christopher saluted as
Mountbatten strode to them.

Mountbatten returned the salute without breaking
stride. "Right. Come on then or we'll be late."

They knew better than to ask where. The walk
took five minutes to the back entrance of 10 Downing Street. Private secretaries of Prime Minister
Eden welcomed them, took their coats and caps and
led them into the Cabinet Room. Eden was already
there.

The Prime Minister remained seated. Mountbatten introduced Christopher and Jemima. Eden's gaze
flickered back and forth among the three arrivals,
settled curiously upon Jemima's George Medal ribbon, then flitted away again. She looked the Prime
Minister squarely in the eye, which seemed to add to
his discomfort.

"Well, then," Eden finally said. "Won't you all sit
down?" He motioned to the other end of the Cabinet table across from where he sat. He spoke as if
greatly agitated. Before him were a series of papers
which appeared to be some sort of report. His hands

suddenly folded, though one forefinger continued to drum. His left eye had an occasional tick.

"Now. Now, Commander Hamilton. You, you and Miss James. You've met with Serov. I've read Admiral Mountbatten's report. I've read your reports. At the bottom, under recommendations, you say that this butcher Serov should be made aware of the White Russian threat against Khrushchev. You suggest you can act in conjunction with the Soviets to counteract it. Is that correct?"

"Absolutely, Prime Minister."

"And you know"—his voice was rising shrilly—"that my orders are absolutely to the contrary."

"Yes, sir."

"How do you equate the two? Tell me that!" Sharply, with the finger tapping angrily, "Explain that, please!"

Mountbatten gave Christopher a warning glance which Christopher caught from the corner of his eye. Eden's private tantrums were legendary.

"In two ways, sir," Christopher replied. "If we do not advise him of the danger and the Soviets discover that the information was withheld on your direction, you will lose much more than you will ever gain diplomatically from this visit. Second, the Soviets are coming because they wish to come. Khrushchev won't cancel. So sharing information with General Serov will only enhance our ability to work with the Soviets. It will enable us to make the visit as safe as possible."

Eden remained silent, daring Christopher to keep talking. Even the finger held still.

"That's all, sir," Christopher said.

Eden shifted his gaze to Jemima. "What about you, First Officer? You met General Serov? Your impression?"

"He surprised me and impressed me. I don't doubt that he's ruthless, but within the context in which we're dealing, he may also be honest. I'd recommend bringing him fully into the picture."

Eden was steaming. His fists were clenched. His face was pink.

"And what about you, Admiral?"

Mountbatten knew all the danger signs: Eden normally called him Dickie.

"I stand by the assessment of my two officers," Mountbatten answered.

Eden sat very quietly. All ten fingers drummed on the Cabinet table. His breathing was unnaturally fast. Somewhere there was a fuse burning.

Creighton sought to cool him down. "If I might add a word, sir?" The Prime Minister's eyes shot from Mountbatten to Creighton. Aside from the fingers, the eyes were his only bodily movement.

"The key objective of this entire operation, sir," Creighton said, "is to protect the Russians. Can we do that? Yes. But we can do it most efficiently if we share information with them."

"Do you estimate, Commander, that a plot against the Russians could succeed?"

"Assassinations have succeeded from the time of Caesar to the time of Gandhi. Six years ago, President Truman was nearly killed."

Eden was furious. "But these are crackpots!" he

retorted acidly. "White Russian *crackpots*, do you understand? Arrayed against our best intelligence services and you tell me they could *succeed*."

Eden's normally listless eyes sparkled with antagonism. Mountbatten had never seen him so angry.

"Begging your pardon," Mountbatten tried, "but you've forbidden us to share sources with even our own intelligence services. Which brings up that point. Perhaps you could authorize a pool of information with cover. That is, anything coming to MI5 or SIS could then go on to Room 39, to be redirected to—"

"And set off a host of rumors? Positively not!" Eden came back, his voice rising. "Don't be obtuse, Admiral. I might just as well pool information with the *Mirror* and *Evening News*."

"Prime Minister, we need to tell the Russians," Christopher tried again. "If we do not, then I cannot guarantee the success of M Section's operations."

Eden seemed to take root in his chair. For several seconds an awkward silence prevailed. Christopher had never seen anyone so angry sit so still. Finally Eden blew out a long breath through his pursed lips "We're all geniuses here, is that it?" he asked belligerently. "Three career sailors, and you all know diplomacy better than the Queen's own P.M.? The answer is No. A thousand times, No! One solicitation of information from one of our other services and I'll see you relieved of your commands. One word—no, one syllable—to the Soviets and I'll have the two of you court-martialed. The very bloody nerve!"

He shoved back his chair and bolted to his feet. His hands were unsteady as he pushed the reports before him into their folder. Then he turned and stalked from the room, leaving a silence behind him for several seconds.

Mountbatten was the first to speak. "He's rapidly becoming a megalomaniac," he said softly. "In less than a year, the pressure's got to him. He's gone quite mad."

Christopher glanced to a side table where a small calendar stood in a silver frame. He noticed it was March. A new surge of anxiety overwhelmed him.

Captain Ann Vergamo, chief of the French subsection, signaled from Nice that afternoon. One of their agents, an Englishman traveling under the name of Dunne, had passed through Jourdanville at the same hour as the service for Milne. Laden with hiking gear, he'd spent the afternoon in a local café. He noticed the little things: two cars with some heavy-set types who never moved from the single road leading from Jourdanville toward the Hamlet of Ybor-les-Pins. Christopher immediately dispatched four more Squad members—two couples— by air from London to Nice, to assist Captain Vergamo.

"Eden's quite wrong, you know," Creighton complained to Mountbatten that evening over dinner. "Our position is completely untenable without *some* help from other services."

"Of course, I know," Mountbatten answered. "But what do we do about it? Think of something. Maybe we just have to pray that Labour suddenly forms a government."

If it was meant as a joke by the longtime Socialist Mountbatten, it failed under the circumstances.

"We have no alternatives," Christopher said, "short of court-martial."

"Find an alternative and we'll do it," said Lord Louis. "And don't worry about the Prime Minister. He can't order a court-martial. He only *thinks* he can." The Sea Lord banged his chest with his thumb. "Only Muggins here can order one."

Christopher returned to his flat at Northways, Jemima to hers in Abbotsbury Road. But sleep eluded him. He agonized, tried a brandy to settle his nerves, yet found himself wide awake. He went out again. London was as icy as it was quiet. It was past two in the morning and he walked in any direction he saw fit, hoping the frigid air would lend him inspiration.

Eventually, he stopped on Westminster Bridge, standing, staring and thinking. There was ice everywhere, even upon the Thames, which was silent. His mind recoiled and he saw London under opposite circumstances, beneath the devastating nighttime fires of the blitz, bombs falling, sirens screaming, people moaning and dying.

He looked at Parliament. He thought of the War Cabinet room, three stories beneath the city: the spiral stairs, now gone, which Churchill said reminded him of submarines.

But, sir, submarines don't have spiral stairs, Christopher had replied.

Then they ought to, young Christopher!

Creighton managed the slightest smile. His eyes were heavy, burning with fatigue. The headache abated slightly. Still there was the conundrum: how could he lead when shackled by his leader? . . . *one word—no, one syllable—and I'll have the two of you court-martialed . . .*

Three A.M. The coldest, darkest, loneliest London morning he'd ever endured. He shivered, but not from the rawness of the climate—rather, from the vision in his mind's eye:

A cataclysmic, searing light burst across the horizon, transforming the dirty murk of Old Father Thames into a radiating torrent of liquid silver. An immeasurable tornado surged violently upward, forming a frenzied umbrella over the metropolis as the atoms of uranium 235 detonated from their precarious half-lives into the supporting elements of radium. The ensuing black umbrella embraced everything; it hung like a monstrous, beastly blanket over the Mother of Parliaments, the birthplace of democracy since the coming of Christ.

Christopher was sweating. He made the sign of the cross as the frigid London morning returned to him. He shivered a final time, only this time the tremor was in his soul.

He knew what he had to do. He was freezing as he walked to Northways, but he considered only one option: he would have to take it.

He slept fitfully for four hours, rose and sat

gloomily in a chair in his apartment for another four. Then he picked up his telephone. It was 11:30 A.M. Moments later he was out on the street. He found a taxi and prayed that what followed would not cost two officers their careers.

The taxi turned from the morning traffic near Hyde Park Gate and rolled to a halt before a house halfway down. Christopher paid at the driver's window, feeling the man's eyes upon him the entire time. Too many people in London seemed to recognize this address.

Christopher went to the front door and rang the bell. A butler opened the door and threw him a very critical glare.

"I'm Commander Hamilton," Christopher said.

The butler's expression wavered only slightly. "Very good. Come in, sir." Christopher entered. The butler took his coat, then led him across the hall. "Will you go in, please?"

The butler held open a door, though Christopher knew the way. He had been here once before, in 1947. The door to a study closed behind him. There was a grunt from a chair facing the logs burning in the fireplace. Christopher could smell the familiar cigar.

Then a small, old, rotund figure gathered itself from the massive armchair and struggled to its feet. The man held a blanket from his lap and squinted slightly, enshrouded by the smoke from the cigar protruding from his mouth. The black coat, striped trousers and bow tie were gone. Today the man wore a rumpled linen romper suit. Then his expression changed and his eyes came alive.

"Christopher! My dear, dear boy!" Creighton smiled and felt his own heart step up a pace. He walked to Winston Churchill and the two men grasped each other's hands tightly. "And you're a commander today," Churchill remarked with ill-concealed pleasure. "Well, well, well. First class. How are you?"

"Pretty good, thank you, sir. All the better for being here."

"Can we get you something?"

"No, thank you, sir."

"They didn't tell me you were coming until a quarter hour ago. Naturally, I told them to send you in when you arrived. Were you waiting long?"

"Not at all."

"Do sit down." Churchill motioned to a second chair not far from his own. Christopher sat. He glanced at Churchill as discreetly as possible. He was again saddened. The former Prime Minister had grown terribly old. Distressing lines and jowls had formed on the lower contours of his cheeks. But Christopher loved him dearly however he looked. And he always would.

Churchill looked back to Christopher, assessing him in the same manner. "Out of office again!" Sir Winston said after a long moment.

"Yes, sir."

"It's bloody boring, you know. Retirement will probably prove fatal before the year is out."

"You've been retired before, sir."

"Not at age eighty-two, I haven't. I'm an old man and I hate every minute of it."

"I imagine you do."

"So cheer me up. Give me some news. What are you doing? Regale me with some anecdotes."

Christopher hesitated. In the days before the war, when Churchill was much younger and in his first retirement, Desmond Morton had been authorized by King George VI to tell him everything. But things were different now, and damned if the old man didn't know it.

"Oh," Sir Winston said sulkily, "so they've even got to my Christopher Robin, have they? Told you not to talk to your old Tigger, eh? I'm supposed to sit here with my extract of malt, nod toward the fire and enjoy my slow death. Is that it?"

"It's not you in particular, sir," Creighton answered. "Just everyone who's not concerned with the current operations."

"What bloody impertinence!" roared the old man. "Will you really not tell me? You who in the old days never kept *anything* from me?" He glanced quizzically at Christopher. "Well, not much, anyway."

Christopher looked away. The old man leaned forward. His cigar fumed like a smokestack now and his hands were upon the carved handle of a cane.

"Would you keep secrets from a Knight of the Garter? From a Privy Councillor?" The old man turned sadly toward the fireplace. Christopher thought he was going to cry. "From an old friend?"

he asked softly.

Christopher looked down. He preferred not to look at the man who appeared lugubrious and failing.

"What harm could there be?" Churchill asked. "How can you not share a few secret thoughts with an old playmate at Chartwell?" He held a long pause and fumbled with a folded handkerchief. "Do you remember that fine lift we constructed, you and I? At the manor? I wonder what little boy rides in it now? Young Christopher, look at me."

Creighton looked.

"I am a bitter, broken old man, Christopher," said Churchill. "I'm seen as a hero, but my own countrymen turned me out of office when victory had been won. And this time I was too old; I had to give way. I spend my time writing books again, and I know not one person in twenty million will read any single volume in its entirety. And my dreams? The visions that sustained me through forties and fifties, and indeed, my sixties? Forcing the Dardanelles; reaching Berlin before the Russians; tearing down their damnable wall; peace with justice. Everything is shattered, Christopher. Very few of my dreams ever became reality. Perhaps you'd better be on your way. Tears do not become a former Prime Minister."

Creighton's resistance was gone. "Damn it, sir, this is expressly against my orders." Churchill swung toward him. "But I've come here for your advice. I've come here to share something with you that I'm under orders not to reveal to anyone."

Churchill's eyes narrowed. He puffed triumphantly on the cigar. "The Russian visit, is it, my dear boy?" A cloud of smoke rose. "You need to know how to handle it."

"Yes. Yes, that's it," Christopher answered at length, not really surprised.

"I already knew why you came," said Churchill. "I merely thought I'd take the burden of speaking from you."

"You old bastard!" Christopher said affectionately.

"Dispense with the compliments, young man. Tell me what the problem is. Before the bloody empire collapses completely."

Christopher found himself smiling, then telling Sir Winston about the Russians.

That afternoon, Christopher presented himself at Mountbatten's office in the Admiralty. Mountbatten kept him waiting for twenty minutes in an anteroom, then admitted him.

"This bloody Commonwealth trip," Mountbatten growled as Christopher sat down. "I wouldn't even be going if we weren't having our Soviet visitors. So Lenin and his cutthroats butchered my family forty years ago. Does any rational person think I'd compromise world peace over *that?*"

Christopher was quite taken aback by the comment. Mountbatten was in a mood of considerable irritation, one in which Christopher had rarely seen him.

"In exactly one week from Sunday, Christopher,"

Mountbatten continued, "March 11, I'm off on this bloody trip. I won't return until April 27. And preparations aren't even complete. Why are you here?"

"We have an alternative," Christopher said. "On the Khrushchev visit."

Mountbatten looked at him sharply. "What is it?" he asked.

Christopher tried his best. "We have a historical precedent, sir. M Section was set up by Sir Desmond back in the 1930s not only without the permission of Prime Ministers MacDonald, Baldwin and Chamberlain, but also without their knowledge. It was financed in direct continuity by three sovereigns: George V, Edward VIII and George VI. This was done, if you recall, sir, because all those concerned were troubled by the stupid and shortsighted actions of the Prime Ministers. Particularly Baldwin and Chamberlain, who, our sovereigns felt, were leaving us vulnerable to the Nazis."

Mountbatten set aside his pen. His gaze settled firmly upon Christopher. Normally when a history lesson was being given, Mountbatten was not on the receiving end.

"The authority for M Section lies in the Constitution. The Sovereign is the head of state and the Prime Minister derives his powers from the Sovereign by the Seals of Office. This is the key point, sir: if the King, or in our case the Queen, believes the safety of the realm is imperiled by the Prime Minister's actions, he or she may recall the Seals. Or, he or she may take any action deemed prudent over the head of the Prime Minister. There are many historical precedents to this, sir," said Christopher, "dating all the way back to Elizabeth I."

Mountbatten stifled a yawn. "Christopher, I did not have you recalled to the Active List to be my tutor in constitutional history. So please get to the bloody point."

"I submit," said Christopher, "that you see the Queen. Explain to her that under existing orders we cannot seek, exchange or compare information with anyone. Not the police, not the various intelligence services, not even the RAF or other departments of our own Navy. Obtain her authority as Lord High Admiral to overrule Eden's directives. Then we can follow your orders. And tell her that if anything happens to Comrade Khrushchev, the safety of her realm very well *may* be imperiled."

Mountbatten reacted slowly, his shrewd eyes drifting away from Christopher, then back again. "Go over Eden's head? Is that what you're suggesting?"

"Yes, sir."

"Ha! Anthony would have one sweet fit, wouldn't he? We'd be well amused by that!"

"It's a serious submission, sir."

"I know it is, Christopher." Mountbatten eased back in his chair. "Tell me: where have you been since I saw you last? Where did you take this crash degree in history and constitutional law?"

"I'd rather not say, sir."

"But you've already disobeyed one of Eden's most insistent orders. You spoke to someone outside the Section about our problem."

Christopher was silent. Mountbatten waited for a

response.

"Yes, sir, I did," Christopher finally said. "I felt it was perhaps not in my best interest, but definitely in the interest of Eng—"

Mountbatten's hand came up sharply, silencing the younger man. "Oh, cut out the bloody melodrama!" he said abruptly. "I came to the same conclusion as you this morning—*without* the aid of old Winston!"

Christopher, astonished, barely drew a breath.

"Oh, yes, young Christopher Robin," said the First Sea Lord. "Don't imagine that I don't know where you go."

Christopher had run out of words. He could only stare at Charlemagne.

"I'm already set on precisely that course of action," Mountbatten said. "I decided this morning at about 5 A.M., while you were tucked like a teddy bear into your bunk at Northways. I am seeing the Queen this evening." His grin was suddenly crisp and mischievous. "I shall enjoy the visit as usual. And I think she will give us what we want."

Christopher replied heatedly, "If you'd already decided, why didn't you tell us? I've agonized all day."

"Well, for God's sake!" Mountbatten snorted. "You and First Officer James are a pair of bright young things. I hoped you'd come up with another idea and get me off the hook. Christ Almighty, Christopher. Getting subordinates to conjure up brilliant ideas is what leadership is all about!"

"Yes, sir," responded Christopher lamely.

"And there's another thing you don't know," said

Mountbatten. "I'll be inspecting you tomorrow morning at five bells in the forenoon watch precisely."

That same morning, under a Canadian passport bearing the name of John Katrinien, Popov flew from Geneva to Orly. He was rested and clean. Using the cover of a linen salesman, complete with samples and a book of accounts in four different countries, he took his lunch in Paris and traveled to Calais by train in the evening. If stopped at customs, if questioned, he could say he spent one afternoon of business in Paris before continuing on to the United Kingdom.

He stood in the Salle d'Attente smoking a cigarette. He heard the boarding announcement for the ferry from Calais to Dover. He fingered his ticket, then passed through the line. The few French customs or security people present were busy chatting among themselves. They paid no attention to the professional assassin.

Popov looked at the security people as he passed them. There was one major difference between them and him, he mused. They didn't use a weapon for a living. Plus they were complacent, content with their jobs and the established political-social order.

Then he looked at his own reflection in a mirrored passageway. He looked himself up and down. Yes, he easily could pass for a Canadian. His English was excellent. He'd spent time in Toronto and had a perfectly memorized cover story. This job, he told himself as he boarded the ferry, would conclude more smoothly than the last.

He found a seat alone. Across an aisle he eyed a very pretty blond woman in her mid-thirties. He listened and determined from her speech that she was American. He wondered if he should go through the ritual of striking up a conversation as a prelude to a seduction. Women found him handsome, he knew. In his travels across the globe, more than one attractive female had found herself straying unexpectedly with him into a seashore hotel. Then Popov saw that the woman was traveling with a small child, a boy between three or four, he reckoned. The assassin turned his attention out the window and saw the shoreline of France begin to pull away.

As was his custom, Popov did not know why his next victims were to die. He only knew that it had to do with ideology. That, and it had to do with the grander schemes of things. Repercussions from the execution of the Czar. Didn't everything follow that?

His victims' names were Peter Hamilton and Jemima James. Royal Navy Intelligence. He'd seen a photograph of the man. He'd seen the woman all too well in person. No matter. With the execution of these two, the eradication of Khrushchev could proceed much more readily.

So Popov would simply do his job. He had an address in London, that of a twenty-three-year-old university student named Jimmy McClintock who'd served two years of National Service in the Royal Engineers. Now he augmented his income by making things that exploded. Popov like the idea of working with a bomb. He could could be far away, he reckoned, by the time the damned thing went off.

FOURTEEN

On March 3, 1956, a Royal Navy helicopter touched down on the lawn at the rear of HMS Birdham. Precisely as it landed, the fifth bell struck in the forenoon watch. A civilian chronometer would have shown 10:30 A.M.

Eight of Jemima's operational Wrens and eight Marine Commandos formed a guard of honor. The Wrens wore their khaki battledress with ROYAL NAVY COMMANDO on the shoulder patches. Like the male commandos, they wore navy blue berets. Mountbatten, when he emerged from the landed helicopter, was dressed in the same rig — just as he usually had when he'd been Chief of Combined Operations and Supreme Allied Commander in Southeast Asia.

Mountbatten began an inspection of the premises immediately, nothing human or inanimate escaping his eye. To the fury of Colonel Sainthill, Mountbatten found one Royal Marine with one green sock and one red. Christopher's steward, Jilly Ludd, felt her face go deep crimson with embarrassment when Lord Louis found a strip of dust beneath her second-best coffeepot. And Angela had been mortified when Mountbatten crawled beneath her main control board and held up two loose wires for all to see. Surprisingly, when he finished, he nodded benignly. "Very good," he'd said. "A few things amiss, but all in all very good."

But when it came to the inspection of the specialized communications, Mountbatten had been at his most demanding. Jemima presented the setup. Dobbs and McGhie had installed an entire radio station under a bed. Mountbatten marveled at it, his mind awash in fiendish ideas for future operations. Then he subjected the apparatus to a detailed examination, including practical contact with far reaches of the globe. Angela and Jemima provided answers to his technical questions. When he was satisfied, he smiled broadly.

"This is excellent," he said. "Your unit is to be congratulated. When I leave England, I'm to be kept fully informed of everything, no matter how trivial. All this should make that possible."

The system was based on a relay procedure of transmitting encoded and/or scrambled messages from one secure radio post to the next. Specifically, the network over which Jemima and Angela now presided crisscrossed Asia and Australia, the locations where Mountbatten could be found during the most critical junctures of the Soviet visit. By relaying signals, then decoding them, Mountbatten would never be more than few minutes away from any decision. Command tactical judgments, however, remained with Christopher.

The current code names—an update of the wartime system—were confirmed and expanded. Christopher was Christopher Robin. Desmond Morton was Owl. Jemima was Kanga and Mountbatten was Charlemagne. The Sovereign, in this case Queen Elizabeth II, was the Author. The Russians continued the sly ursine motif: Bulganin was designated Bear One and Khrushchev was Bear Two. After much discussion, Marie became Alice and Serov became Ivan the Terrible.

Mountbatten's mood changed at lunchtime. He became gregarious and jolly, expending a great deal of energy meeting Section members he hadn't met previously. He laughed and joked with his men and women, treating them as equals. In the mess hall, all ranks and ratings ate together.

Then at teatime in the library, the Sea Lord sat down with Christopher and Jemima. Lord Louis was in a somber and serious mood again. He drank his tea in silence. At last he unburdened himself.

"We obtained the authority we wanted from the First Lord High Admiral," he said. Christopher and Jemima knew better than to speak or even show the faintest sign of glee. The permission from the Queen, the authority to supersede the orders of the Prime Minister, was an awesome responsibility. "This isn't any carte blanche," Mountbatten continued, "although constitutionally it is." He picked up his cup and sipped again. "What I have to say to you two is this: I have given you full powers, but only on the understanding that you never use them unless you absolutely have to. I see no point in rushing off and telling the KGB everything right away. Let's wait. See how we progress. And then, tell them only what is vital." He paused. "Of course, if the safety of the Russian leaders, and therefore the realm, rests in the balance, then all must be told. And Christopher, that decision will rest with you."

"Yes, sir," Creighton said. He couldn't think of anything else.

"And only in the direst of emergencies are you to tell the P.M. of your authority. It that clear?"

"Very, sir."

"Otherwise, we shall have a full-blown constitutional crisis on our hands." He stuck out his cup. Jemima instinctively filled it with tea from a white china pot. "Eight days and I'm gone," Mountbatten said. "So this is our last real chance to talk." He took the cup back from Jemima and sipped. "God Almighty," he said loudly. "You forgot the sugar."

"Sor-ry," she said. She reached to the small sugar bowl, took two lumps and dropped them in his tea.

"So I should jolly well think," he said to them both. "Did you manage to get your subsection chiefs together?"

"Yes, sir," Jemima answered. "Other than the overseas ones. They're waiting in the main office."

"Wheel them in."

"Aye, aye, sir," she said. She went out to find them.

In three minutes, they all sat around the table: Colonel Sainthill, Commander Trott, Angela and five others. Each reported on his or her particular sphere of activity. In one hour, all reports were complete. Then, since it hadn't been specifically stated during the reports, Jemima turned toward Mountbatten and added, "We're not forgetting the most crucial detail, sir. If a Soviet warship is attacked while under our protection, even if the attack misses and fails, the Soviets might consider it just as much an act of war as the assassination of one of their leaders."

"We'll have their ships under constant watch from all aspects the moment they enter our territorial waters," Trott said. "When they're tied up in Portsmouth harbor, we shall guard the hulls on a twenty-four-hour basis. Not only against attack, but also to prevent any repetition of the *Sverdlov* fiasco last October with Crabbie. I mean, Commander Crabb, sir."

Mention of Crabb seemed to suddenly spark the First Sea Lord. His eyes became sharp. "I have given strict instructions at the Admiralty," Mountbatten said abruptly, "that there are to be no, I repeat *no, I Say again, no!* examinations of the Russian hulls by Crabb or anyone else. Service or nonservice." His voice was hot, impassioned. "Is that abundantly clear?"

Everyone around the table nodded. Christopher

sought to defuse the topic. "I'm glad this was mentioned, sir," Creighton said. "I want a round-the-clock watch on Commander Crabb personally. Trott, I think that would be for you and your personnel. Report in everything, whether you think it's important or not."

"Aye, aye, sir," Trott answered.

"Let's move on," Christopher said, suddenly standing. "Put up the chart of Pompey harbor."

Jemima and Angela were on their feet just as quickly. They unrolled an Admiralty chart of the entire area around Portsmouth and its harbor. The chart had been enlarged to about six by eight feet. They pinned it to the wall.

"The Soviets will be protected," Christopher began, "by a 'ring of steel' as soon as their ships have safely arrived. Impenetrable electronic steel. The protection will stretch from here," he said as he placed his finger on the spot where the Russian ships had been sketched in alongside Watering Island, "to here." His hand swept around the extremities of the harbor, through Gosport and Portsmouth, in a gigantic circle. "In this area nothing will move above or below the surface without our knowing about it. First, we have our normal visual watch, supported by our Royal Marine Special Boat Service, all armed. Second, on every point of the compass will be skilled divers, ready to strike. Third, at the perimeter of the no-go exclusion zone will be the most up-to-date and sensitive electronic alarm systems. Not just one, which could go wrong, but *twenty*, all independently wired. If tripped, the alarm will be given not only aboard *Victory*, but at ten other subsection posts." Christopher faced Mountbatten squarely. "Finally, sir, our top-secret RG protection lights, practically the most secret equipment we possess, pioneered for us by you in 1943, when you were Chief of Combined Operations. These lights, invisible to the naked eye, will show us everything—man, machine or fish—that enters our protection zone. Above or below water, day or night, in any weather. That is our ring of steel, sir." Christopher sat down.

Mountbatten watched him closely. He contented himself with a nod.

"And now security, sir," said Jemima walking across from the chart, "Your daughters, Pamela and Patricia, and Lady Mountbatten are as secure as we can make them. A twenty-four-hour watch on each one. And your nieces, too, sir."

Mountbatten looked up sharply. *"What?"* he snapped. He thought she meant the Queen and Princess Margaret.

"Prince Philip's *sisters,* sir," Jemima quickly clarified. "They are also under constant surveillance. Our German opposite numbers have been most helpful and efficient. Everything else in that line also seems on the ball."

Mountbatten snapped again. "How could it be 'on the ball'? You still haven't located Marie."

Jemima sighed, then drew a deep breath. "We're on a tightrope at the moment, sir. Two hundred men and women are scouring Europe—mostly southern

France—for von Ostenberg, and the Grand Duchess Marie. Through our subsection, we have the full cooperation of the SDECE, the French Secret Service. German intelligence has also cooperated fully with us since the beginning." She sternly eyed Mountbatten. "It's like trying to find the *Bismarck* in the Denmark Strait. Or the *Kelly* in the waters off Crete. Both were found eventually by patience and tenacity."

There was nothing better than Jemima could have said. Mountbatten had been the *Kelly's* Captain. "I take your point, Miss James," he said after a moment of reflection. "Naval history is something to which I'm not a complete stranger." His eyes sparkled for a moment. Christopher caught two subsection commanders stifling schoolboy grins.

"We believe," Jemima concluded, "that the Grand Duchess is of particularly vital importance. There is her personal relationship to you. But also we feel she is the link that will allow us to root out and destroy the threat to Khrushchev and Bulganin *before* any strike can be made."

Mountbatten was quick to reply. "So if my cousin had no such vital link, you would leave her and Alexis to an almost certain death?"

"Yes, sir," said Jemima.

Agreeing, Christopher came to her support. "You have made that much very clear, sir," Christopher said. "All of us have accepted it fully. No one's rescue can imperil the overall objective of the Section: the successful protection of the Russian leaders

220

and their ships. To that end, I would sacrifice not only every member of this Section, including all of us, but also our families. And that includes you, sir."

Mountbatten studied him for a long moment. "Christopher," Mountbatten said at length, "sometimes your ruthlessness frightens me."

"With respect, sir, that's what they say about you."

The Sea Lord continued to gaze at Christopher. For several seconds, he looked as if he would take issue with Creighton. Then he eased back into his seat. Mountbatten was first and foremost an objective, honest man. "Yes," he said finally, "that frightens me as well."

And the meeting was over. Mountbatten heaved himself up. "Well, that's bloody that," he said.

At 1900 hours, the RN helicopter rumbled on the lawn of HMS Birdham. The rotors spun and the aircraft lifted off the ground, carrying aloft the First Seaman of the Royal Navy. The send-off was boisterous, with more waves than salutes. Mountbatten, as always, had engendered that sort of response from those under his command.

Christopher watched quietly, standing alone not far from the chopper. Just before boarding, Mountbatten had taken Christopher aside. "I know you've got a devil of a task cut out for you, Christopher," Lord Louis had said. "So I've arranged things to make your exercise of command a little easier."

"Thank you, sir." The men shook hands.

"Carry on, please," Mountbatten had said.

But there was no further explanation. The Sea Lord's promise was elusive at best. And as Mountbatten's helicopter disappeared from view, Christopher felt the responsibility of command slip ponderously onto his shoulders.

It was a feeling that was confirmed eight days later when the First Sea Lord departed for his tour of the Commonwealth. It was Sunday 11 March. Mountbatten would not return until April 27, just as the Soviets were leaving British waters. Up until this point, Mountbatten's physical presence and command had provided a powerful support to Christopher. But now, at the most critical of moments, he had whisked himself away. The burden was now fully upon Christopher.

At six that evening, Christopher sat alone in the Birdham library. Two dim lamps furnished the only light in the room. Depression was wafting in upon him, crawling upon him like a black beast, and he was helpless before it.

In his mind's eye, he was on the edge of Portsmouth harbor, watching the strong hands of British seamen as they pulled bodies from the water. Two appeared right before him, their lifeless, bloodied faces vibrantly clear. *Bulganin. Khrushchev.*

The sweat rolled off Christopher's forehead. Those terrible visions would not leave him alone. He saw the flattened remains of Dolphin and Vernon,

Hornet and the RN hospital at Haslar. Further round, he could see no sign at all of the Russian ships, and in the dockyard itself just a pile of charred wood was all that remained of Nelson's *Victory*.

Christopher had failed. The most important operation of his career. And he had failed.

Christopher knew these morbid projections had to stop. But he also knew they were inevitable. So he had to see them through this evening. Vanquish them. Give them their due, then rally his courage. To this end, he had decided to skip dinner. He had left an order that no one was to disturb him. Better to battle one's demons alone. But he had forgotten about Jilly Ludd, his Wren steward.

Traditionally, even if others were barred from the presence of the commanding officer, his steward still had the right of entry — to busy about, fold up his clothes and generally carry out the details of housekeeping quietly and unobtrusively. And so, dead on the stroke of six thirty, Jilly bustled in.

For the first few seconds, Christopher was unaware of her presence, so dark was his mood. Then she spoke. "Could I have your uniform jacket, please, sir?" she asked.

Christopher looked up with a start. "What the bloody hell are you doing here?" he snapped.

"I've come to do my evening duties as usual, sir," she said. Jilly was used to dealing with unpredictably moody seniors. "So if I might have the jacket?"

It took a moment to sink in. "Yes. Of course," he

said at length. "Excuse me, Jilly, I was half asleep."

He slipped out of his jacket and threw it to her. Jilly caught it and placed it on a hanger in the closet. Christopher noticed that the door to the library had been left ajar, but it didn't register. His eyes drifted back to Jilly as she held up one of his battle-dress tops. Something was wrong with it, but Christopher was unable to find the irregularity. Yet his eye knew: something was different. She handed it to him. He put it on, buttoned it up and stood before a full-length mirror. Then he saw it.

At first it was just an unusually bright glint from the gold braid on his epaulets. But as he looked closer, he saw that the three stripes of a commander had been increased to four. The insignia of a captain.

He swung round on Jilly. "All right! Who's idea of a joke is this?"

Another woman's voice spoke. "No joke, Captain, sir. It's for real."

Christopher swung toward the doorway, where Jemima James stood.

"Don't be ridiculous!" he retorted, not a little angry. "I'm not a captain."

"The *London Gazette* thinks you are."

She held out the journal, the official court and government publication. Among other things, it listed all daily service promotions, appointments and decorations. Combined with *The Navy List,* it was the bible of naval officers.

Christopher read his name and his promotion.

224

Now he knew what Mountbatten had meant: *I've arranged things to make your exercise of command a little easier.*

Of course, Mountbatten had known about the self-doubts and depressions. And once again Lord Louis had contrived with his Section to rekindle his self-confidence and refurbish him into a human being. And a leader.

FIFTEEN

At 0700, Sunday morning, March 18, a mist lifted and the sun burned off the daily haze. Jemima skidded her red pranger off the B3035 and left onto the A34 to Winchester. Then she drove northward to Oxford and Abingdon. The journey would be no more than fifty miles.

Jemima wore a white polo-neck sweater and jeans. Christopher, sitting next to her, was casually dressed, too. Jeans with a medium blue flannel shirt beneath a navy blue cashmere sweater. The casual clothing was a relief, a tangible break from the pressures of duty. He enjoyed the drive. And when he looked at Jemima, far away from the life and death realities of Portsmouth, he again wondered what it would be like to live life the way other men did—with family and domestic responsibilities, and the privilege of waking up each morning next to the woman he loved.

They had decided on this trip late the previous evening. Neither had had a day off for some time. A

227

quick call to Jemima's mother had arranged everything. When they arrived in Abingdon after a two-hour drive, she had breakfast ready in a wink. Coffee, eggs, toast, bacon and all the trimmings. She had also prepared a light farmer's lunch and packed it in a haversack with a bottle of claret and a corkscrew. By 10:30, Jemima and Christopher were at the stables, where Lenny again greeted them. He'd already saddled the same two hunters as the previous time.

"Our itinerary today is slightly different from last time," Jemima announced as they turned their horses away from the stable.

"Today you're the commander in chief," he answered. She grinned mischievously in response. "Lead the way," he said.

She did. She led the two horses across a bridle path that traversed two neighboring farms. The trail climbed one of the moors, then led through a path in the forest. When they came to a clearing, they were upon yet another farm. They rode to the stables, where a man in his sixties smiled when he saw Jemima. She and Christopher dismounted.

"May we leave our mounts here for an hour or two?" she asked him.

"For my girl?" the man asked. "Of course."

Jemima introduced the man as Charles Wood; he'd known her father. He was a sturdy graying man who had worked the same farm every day of his life.

In the stable were a pair of sturdy sticks for hiking. Jemima suggested Christopher take one. She took one, too. He carried the haversack. They walked through a pasture, then the land became wooded again.

Jemima knew every inch of her county. The forest path led to the north side of a large rock formation which overlooked another stretch of moors. It was almost eleven now. She unfolded a thin cotton blanket and sat down. He joined her.

She drew a deep breath. For several minutes neither of them spoke. They took in the breathtaking view southward across the English countryside.

"Sometimes," she said, "I think this is the real me. Sometimes I think I've no business being in the Royal Navy."

He was surprised. "Why? You're doing very well. And you were just promoted."

She shrugged. "So were you. But there are other things in life, you know."

He turned to her. "Oh. I see," he said. "Home. Family. Children. All the usual jazz."

"It's crossed my mind more than once."

Christopher grinned. "And so?"

"I'm twenty-eight. If I complete this appointment, I won't be out of the Navy until I'm thirty-two. A woman has to think ahead. Time works differently for women than for men."

He nodded. She pulled the cheese and bread from the picnic basket. He opened the wine.

"If you married, you could leave the Navy right away," he said.

"I know," she answered, and gazed out toward the south, looking very thoughtful. "Oh, in the end I'll probably marry. But the Service has been good to me, I admit. It's been fun, a challenge, an education and an adventure."

"It's all of that," Christopher agreed, thinking back over his own sixteen years.

After they ate, Jemima gathered together what remained of the bread, cheese and wine. She crouched over the basket and packed it. The sunlight gently touched her and Christopher watched her carefully. She had no need to be concerned about aging, he thought to himself — not like other women. She was so trim and youthful in her sweater and jeans — not much younger than he was, yet he felt much older. She looked up and caught him watching her.

"And just what would you be studying so intently?" she asked playfully.

"You."

She motioned to the view. "With everything else to see up here, you're looking at an old first officer?"

He grinned. "Yes," he admitted. Several seconds passed, then he spoke again. "There's something I've been meaning to ask," he said. "None of my business, but I'm going to ask anyway."

"Shoot," she said, standing. He stood with her.

"What happened to your regular man?" he asked.

Jemima hesitated slightly before answering. "I haven't had a regular man since Cambridge," she said. "In my job it isn't exactly sensible."

"Yes. Of course," he replied quietly.

They hiked back to where they'd left the horses. It was about two o'clock when they returned to the stables. They handed their mounts back to Lenny and turned toward the house. As they reached the side of the barn on Mrs. James' property, Jemima stopped and pointed up above the stable.

"That's me," she said. "Up there."

"What? The hayloft?" Christopher asked in surprise.

"My mom gave it to me when I matriculated," she said. "When I was seventeen." She stopped and looked at him. "I bring only my special friends up there."

She led him up the creaky wooden steps. Reaching the top, she took a key from a nail in a hidden niche. She opened the door and ushered him in. "It's mine," she said. " 'Jemima's place.' I love it and it's home."

Two thirds of the loft had been converted to a spacious open plan for living, eating and cooking. The other third, she showed him, was arranged for sleeping, dressing and bath. On the floor was a thick, plush green carpet, a dark rich green to which the entire loft was tastefully and restfully coordinated. The rafters and beams had been renovated to their natural wood and thoroughly polished. The furniture matched, as did the cupboards. The fittings were burnished brass and in the middle of it all was a solid fuel fire which was alight.

"Go on. Make yourself at home," she said. "I'll get you a drink." She crossed the room to a liquor cabinet. "Brandy okay?"

"That would be excellent."

Jemima produced a bottle of aged Delamin and poured two drinks. She brought one to him. She kissed him lightly on the cheek. "I've enjoyed today," she said. "Or rather, I *am* enjoying today very much."

"There are still a few hours left," he said.

She sipped her brandy. "Yes." she said. "There are."

Jemima walked away and warmed her hands at the fire. She spoke to him without turning. "Christopher, you know I've done quite well. Mostly because I'm a planner. I make a plan and I stick to it."

She turned to him. "Then you must have a plan now," he said.

"I have two. But they contradict each other."

He shook his head and admonished her gently. "No good," he said.

She walked back to him and sat down. She set aside her brandy and took his hands. "My plan was to avoid having an affair within the Royal Navy," she said. "It won't work for a woman with career plans." She paused. "My other idea was for us to make love. Here. Today. I know how you feel about me. I feel the same toward you."

"So which one wins?" he asked.

She looked at him and stared calmly into his eyes. "As if you don't know," she said.

"Then that's your plan?" he asked, poker-faced.

"If you send me up, Christopher-fucking-Robin, I'll kill you," she threatened loudly.

But he put his arms round her, looked into Jemima's green eyes, and whispered. "Your plan approved for immediate execution."

Christopher would have spoken again, but they

were lost in the urgent kiss and embrace that followed. They gently started to undress each other. As he pulled off her jumper, he saw again across her shoulders the scarred remnants of her injuries sustained while saving the navy aircrew from the blazing helicopter. He'd seen her disfigurement before, when they had dived together at Dolphin. For a moment, he'd forgotten. He gently took her shoulders and kissed her.

Jemima could not restrain the tears. They embraced tenderly and then passionately. She did nothing to restrain him. It was instead a high pitched beeping sound which made him jump and stayed his hand.

"Damn," she said. She pulled away. When the beeping repeated, she went to a shelf across the room and removed a large wooden owl. She unscrewed its head and pulled out a red scrambler telephone. "Kanga," she said. Her voice was now prim and efficient. The voice of a Wren officer.

It was the Section calling. "Yes," she said to the caller. "Yes, Angela. Affirmative. We can be there in about two hours." There was a pause as she listened further. "Goodbye," she concluded.

She returned the telephone to the owl and reunited the bird's head with its body. She returned to the sofa and looked down. She sighed, her sweater in one hand.

"I'm afraid our beautiful moment is gone," she said.

"What happened?"

"The Section has located Marie," she said. "South

of France, as expected."

It took a second, then he asked coldly. "Dead or alive?"

"Alive," she answered. "Looks like you're going to Nice to see for yourself."

SIXTEEN

His passport was British and made out in the name of Peter Hamilton, but there was no mention of rank. Christopher wore civilian clothing when he stepped from the Air France Caravelle in Nice at 11:30 A.M. the next morning. The weather in the south of France was balmy and warm, more suggestive of late May than March, but Christopher happily took his sunshine where he could find it.

He hired a Renault at the airport, and shortly after one o'clock he rolled into the center of Cannes, the changing azure sea on one side, the low row of hotels, restaurants and tourist shops on the other. He parked along the Croisette. As he stepped from his Renault, a small blue convertible—a car the color of a robin's egg—came to a halt right next to him, then backed slowly and tentatively into the parking place behind his. The car was American, a Thunderbird if Christopher had any recollection of American automobiles. It reflected its driver: young,

American and brash. Christopher knew because, as the car parked, the young man at the wheel was arguing noisily with a pretty dark-haired girl seated next to him. She looked no more than nineteen. When the car was still, she jumped out, slammed the door and stalked off.

Christopher turned and walked toward his prearranged contact point, the Majestic Hotel. It was a convenient location. He was hungry for a good lunch.

It was the same as any other beautiful day along the French Mediterranean coast. But Christopher hadn't been here since the war, so he took in much of it with new eyes. Even in March there were the lithe brown girls strolling along the beaches. Their tiny bathing suits clung to them in defiance of gravity. Imported Cadillacs from the United States and Maserattis from Italy purred and snarled along the Croisette, their male drivers scanning the beaches and cafés for whatever females seemed young, bronzed and—for the moment, at least—unescorted. The sun washed everything and in the sea, on the opposite side of the boulevard, bathers splashed and laughed.

God, the sybaritic lives people lived in this glittery part of the world, Christopher thought. What had happened to the Roman Catholic morality he had learned as a boy?

He found her on the front terrace of the hotel. She was thirtyish and very pretty with long brown hair. Her name was Ann Vergamo and her cover was that of a real estate agent catering to wealthy foreigners. She was Anglo-French though she'd been married to an Italian for several weeks in 1954 and had kept his name. She was chief of the M subsection (France) and was also one of the best surveillance photographers in Europe. She was also the only person to be employed simultaneously by The Section and SDECE, the French Secret Service.

Ann Vergamo spotted Christopher immediately and waved him to her table, one set well away from all the others. Ann got up and they embraced warmly.

"Good afternoon, sir," she said, with a touch of irony. "Or can I still call my new chief, *Christopher?*"

Christopher smiled as they sat down. Ann had been in the section since 1945, when as a very young girl, she had been one of Christopher's subsection in Berlin. She had proved a very avid and successful hunter of Nazi War Criminals.

"I hope you're going to be happy with my work again," she said.

Christopher was. Her surveillance team, backed by units of the SDECE, had pinpointed a manor house ten kilometers north of Cannes. The building was beyond the town of Jourdanville and technically at least, was situated on a road just past the hamlet of Ybor-les-Pins.

"They've got Marie Nikolayevna in there," Ann said. "We know because they let her come out and walk in the courtyard for about fifteen minutes a day, usually in the morning."

Ann Vergamo opened a packet of enlarged photographs shot with a telephoto lens and, Christopher presumed, at some peril. On the top were shots of Marie. Christopher nodded. "That's her," he said.

"They've quite a bit of muscle around the place," Ann said softly. "If this is a snatch operation, you're going to have your hands full."

"I already do," said Christopher. "What are the details?"

Ann took out a piece of paper. Upon it she had sketched a map with remarkable clarity. "One road, right here," she said, indicating the access to the house. "From what we've seen there's no electronic surveillance. Don't need it. There's usually three to six men out there, day and night, with automatic weapons." She indicated a slight rise above the road that led to the manor. "In the grounds at the back, there is another patrol of at least six men. They all change position from time to time, and sometimes there's more than the usual numbers. You'd need a battalion to outgun them. Going round them won't be much easier either."

"Why?" asked Christopher.

As an explanation, she produced more photographs. The site had many natural advantages for a defender, Christopher learned. Behind the manor was a cliff with a straight drop of seventy feet. The summit of it had been reinforced with two double rolls of barbed wire, tightly bunched. The wire continued all the way around the manor grounds, forming an outer perimeter with considerable teeth. The cliffs were effectively unscalable. Christopher scanned the photographs and determined that all sides were under surveillance at any given moment. "It's floodlit at night," Ann Vergamo added. She produced another photograph to make her point.

"How many mercenaries are in the place?" Christopher asked.

"We've identified thirty-five of them," she said. And then there was another sheaf of photos, all long range. She went meticulously through them, identifying each member of the security force by a number. Finally she came to Number Three and held up a photo.

"This one is the leader," she said. "Baron Wilhelm von Ostenberg."

"We have to take him alive," Christopher said, after staring at the photo for several seconds. "It's essential we interrogate him. Thoroughly." He glanced back to her. "As usual, Ann, you've outdone yourself. I suppose you have a layout of the manor's interior, also?"

Yes, she said, with the help of two other SDECE agents, she'd attended to that, too. Being in the real estate business, she'd recalled which agent had tried to sell the estate two years earlier. She had dropped by the agent's office one night about seven hours after closing time. The SDECE agents broke in and let Ann through after them. They stood guard while she went to work with a subminiature camera and photographed the complete records.

"Not too much to it," she concluded modestly. Christopher studied the layout.

"I know what you're thinking," she said.

He raised his eyes. "What's that?" he asked.

"You're trying to figure how to get in, effect a rescue and take one specific prisoner," she said. "I can give you a lead on that."

He waited.

"For the past six months the house has been a center for financial contributions to the operation against the Soviet leaders," she said. "It's not unusual for some dotty White Russian to appear at any hour of the day or night to contribute cash, jewelry or a check. Does that give you any ideas?"

"Some," he said. He began to assemble the photographs and return them to an envelope. "I'll particularly need to know how many men are on guard at any given time," he said. "Can your people maintain surveillance and keep careful track of that?"

"Of course. We've already established the points from which the perimeter of the grounds are watched."

"Perfect," he said.

"Now I've one final present for you," she said. From a leather carry-all beside the table, she took out another packet of photos. "The dining room is on the ground floor at the back. Every evening at eight, dinner is served to the Grand Duchess, Nesterov and his sister. Baron von Ostenberg invariably joins them."

Christopher accepted the pictures from her. They

were grainy, but the dining table was clear. The exact positions of the four diners were shown. "That's the key time," he said, thinking aloud. "The four principles are together and separate from the guards."

"Exactly," she said.

He looked up. "Why did you say the cliff behind the manor is unscalable?" he asked.

"A river," she said. "A tributary of the Isère. At this time of year it's one of the fastest and most dangerous in the world, flooded by ice and melting snow from the Alpes Maritimes."

"White water rapids?" he asked.

"White water starts at thirteen knots. Beneath these cliffs, I'd say it's closer to sixteen or seventeen."

"Do you have any binoculars?" he asked.

"Yes. Why?"

"Let's go have a look."

The drive took thirty minutes from Nice. Ann Vergamo first led Christopher to the Château Nicole, a vacant, deserted old domaine which she'd obtained for her subdivision of the SDECE. Château Nichole was situated three quarters of the way up the Chamboire Hills. Below, on the other side of the village at a distance of five hundred meters, was the Manor of Ybor-les-Pins.

Next Ann led Christopher to a higher vantage point which looked down upon the cliffs and the river. Scanning with binoculars, he could see the violent, white twists and turns of the water as it ripped by the base of the cliffs. The access to the manor which held Marie and von Ostenberg was guarded least at this point. Assault from the cliffs was an impossibility. Yet Christopher already knew that the operation would have to begin from this angle. Every other route in was guarded too well.

At ten A.M. the next morning he sat on a simple wooden chair at the kitchen table in Château Nicole's old kitchen. He was alone. Meticulously, he planned the raid that would have to happen within forty-eight hours. But some of his thoughts turned against him.

This was the first time since the war that his section had taken part in an operation in France. Inevitably, he thought of the last times he'd himself been involved. He recalled two agents he'd known well: Violette Szabo, code name "Louise" and Noor Inayat Khan, code name "Madeleine." Both had been officers in the F.A.N.Y. as well as the Women's Royal Air Force. Both had earned the George Cross. And both had died terrible deaths at the hands of the SS when their final operations had ended in failure.

Christopher walked to the window and looked far down the hill at the manor on the other side of the village. He had a plan, one which hinged on an officer from his Section entering the enemy camp first and alone. Like Madeleine and Louise, the officer had to be a woman. She had to speak fluent Russian and French. Christopher wondered: would she suffer the same sort of brutal death when things went wrong?

He spoke aloud in the empty room. "I'm sorry, Jemima," he said. "It's you. It has to be you. You're the only one who's qualified."

Not for the first time, Nikita Khrushchev was pleased with himself. Serov had made a successful contact with the English. The visit to Portsmouth was definitely proceeding without the slightest wrinkle. Even the agenda was now confirmed. No changes.

Khrushchev sat alone at a sturdy oak table in the living room of his Moscow residence. He drank tea and smoked a yellow-skinned cigarette. His surroundings were quiet, unusual in the Soviet Union by anyone's admission. His wife was away at some meaningless function for CPSU wives. His son was at the university, studying engineering. It was 2 P.M. Moscow time. Idly, he wondered where Molotov and Bulganin were and concluded that wherever they were, they'd probably be plotting against him. If they dared.

Unlike the United States, which has the White House, France which as the Élysée Palace, or Great Britain, which has 10 Downing Street, the Soviet Union has no official residence for its head of state, much in the same way that it has no official line of succession. Soviet leaders from the time of Stalin onward have always put greater emphasis upon their country dachas—usually by the Black Sea—than upon their Moscow addresses. Nonetheless, Khrushchev lived comfortably in the capital. The residence that he shared with his wife was an entire floor of a tall, clean yellow brick apartment house on Lenin Hills, overlooking the downtown part of the city—Red Square and the turrets of the Kremlin—from across the Moscow River. The building itself was an in-town ghetto for the political elite. Upstairs, for example, lived Nikolai Shvernik, the head of the Soviet trade unions. Downstairs lived an influential major in Serov's KGB, Yuri Andropov.

Khrushchev's apartment was dazzlingly opulent by Moscow standards: two bedrooms, a living room, a study, a dining room and two baths. There was also a kitchen, with built-in cabinets and Formica countertops from Italy as well as a Kuppersbusch stove specially imported from West Germany. And unlike the leaden, heavy styles which marked many Russian living quarters, Khrushchev's living room was tastefully appointed in Finnish modern furniture—again specially imported. The room seemed even brighter than it really was, thanks to the bay window that dominated the central area of the residence. Despite the poverty of his youth, and the peasant Ukrainian upbringing that set the tone of his entire life, Khrushchev felt at home and at ease in these surroundings. It pleased him considerably to withdraw here in the afternoon, just as it pleased him that his visit to England was now going forward so smoothly.

Khrushchev had long regarded Anthony Eden as a man he could deal with. Eden was a much more reasonable man than those damned pseudo−left wing Labourities in Great Britain. It had been Eden who, in 1938, had resigned as foreign minister when the fool Chamberlain rejected an Anglo-Russian defense pact and tried to cut his own deal with Hitler. Now it was Eden who would again help the Soviet Union. Reaching agreements with Eden would allow Khrushchev to undercut the position of the Americans in the Western Alliance. The English could be reasonable. The Americans preferred not to be.

The Americans! Khrushchev snuffed out his cigarette and lit another. His tea was luke-warm now, but he finished his glass and refilled it. The Americans made him damned angry. Nothing, in fact, enraged him the way the Americans conducted themselves.

Just the previous week that maniac John Foster Dulles, speaking for the old, confused broken-down general in the White House and his lackey vice president, had uttered another pack of provocative lies about the Soviet Union. Dulles had called the Kremlin leadership "imperialist, warmongering and expansionist." The nerve!

At the end of World War II, the Americans had occupied a vital strip of Germany, every strategic island in the Pacific−including Hawaii−a canal in Central America on land that another North American bandit named Roosevelt had stolen from the government of Colombia and all of Alaska, which Czar Alexander II had foolishly peddled to finance his profligate life-style.

In contrast, the Soviet Union had been victimized by the West for decades. No sooner had the Revolution of 1917 been successful than the Germans attacked and penetrated from the Ukraine to Kiev. The French attacked in the south, the English in the Murmansk region and the Japanese and the Americans in the eastern territory. Churchill and Roosevelt had conspired even at Casablanca to delay the invasion of Europe as long as possible, wearing down Soviet defenses for an extra two years. Then, at the end of a world war that the Soviets were said to have won, the republic was surrounded by enemies: by Western military bases in Europe and Asia Minor and by hostile Western fleets in the Mediterranean, the Pacific and the Indian Ocean. Not a Soviet ship could leave port without being tracked by the West. And the imperialist Americans had the gumption to blame their so-called "cold war" on the Soviet Union. They'd done one better on the "big-lie" concept of Hitlerite Germany. But Leninist-Stalinist history was quite clear who was to blame for the frigid international condition.

Khrushchev started another cigarette and looked over his agenda in the United Kingdom. He would have some pleasant talks with Eden and he would attempt to avoid the meddlesome Labourities altogether. And as for the Americans, well, there were some surprises in store for them, too. Top Soviet scientists were almost ready to launch a small man-made moon around the earth. How the Americans would enjoy *that!* And as for those damnable high-altitude spy missions Dulles insisted upon flying over Soviet territory, well, Khrushchev would keep quiet on those. He would pretend he didn't even know they existed. But pretty soon he would have the missile technology to blow one out of the sky. And the Americans called *him* a warmonger!

Old Stalin, who had never cared much for Khrushchev, would have been stunned at the way things were proceeding. For a moment, Khrushchev mused on the old man.

He remembered Stalin's friendless, lonely final days. Khrushchev, Bulganin, Beria and Molotov would be invited to dinner at Stalin's and the old man's favorite dishes were always prepared. But the meals followed a routine.

"Look. Salted herring!" Stalin would say. Then he would give it to Khrushchev to taste before he ate it. Molotov would have to taste the next course. And another diner would taste the wine. He was the most feared and powerful man in the Soviet Union and he didn't even trust the food from his own kitchen. Only Beria was exempt from being a taster. "Seaweed face," Stalin called him. Beria, the mass murderer, was a vegetarian and never ate the same meals as Stalin.

"Here's your seaweed. Here's your grass," Stalin used to mock, inevitably producing a bowl of boiled greens when Beria dined at Stalin's dacha. Beria would stuff the greens into his mouth with his fingers, every now and again fumbling with a fork.

Stalin loved to ridicule his MVD chief. Maybe he felt impervious to Beria. He had, after all, executed both of Beria's predecessors. Or maybe Stalin was whistling in the dark. Then again, Beria had had the last laugh. When the old man died on the night of March 4-5,1953, Beria had been the first to arrive and view the corpse. Then he spat on it and was the first to leave. He was a frightful man, Beria. Khrushchev had been pleased to rid the Soviet Union of him. Some reports in the West had it that Khrushchev had gone over to Lubyanka prison to personally fire the bullet into Beria's head. That report always puzzled Khrushchev. There had been no one else present other than trusted guards. How had the true account ever filtered out of the Soviet Union?

Stalin: Khrushchev remembered him the way he had been at the end: a sick, paranoid, half-sodden old man who feared the inevitable ambush by friends around him. In early 1953, drunk one evening in the Kremlin, Stalin described a film which was repeatedly shown in the cinema archive. The film had no title frames and had apparently been taken from British troops during the war. It was an adventure story about an English pirate captain who was returning a treasure from India to London. Along the way, the captain began to rid himself of his crew one by one in order to avoid a mutiny. He had a method. He would post a picture in his quarters of the next man close to him to be thrown overboard, just to keep track of the proper order.

This way, his authority upon the ship remained supreme.

Khrushchev, as drunk as Stalin on this evening, made the mistake of opening his mouth. "Comrade Stalin," the pudgy Ukrainian blurted, "in the Socialist paradise aren't the enemies of the state being eliminated in much the same manner?"

Stalin grinned. He turned full face to Khrushchev and gave the widest, craziest smile Khrushchev had ever seen in his life. Fortunately for everyone, one month later Stalin was dead.

Khrushchev finished the tea in his apartment. He went into the bedroom, where he would take his two-hour afternoon nap. He thought back on that final bizarre incident involving his predecessor. Stalin had been a great teacher, but Khrushchev wasn't sure what lesson was to be taken from that incident. Was it, Rule the Soviet Union and you will end up old, alone and frightened? Or was it, Keep an eye on your enemies, destroy them as you go along and you will live to die in your seventies?

Stalin had ruled the Soviet Union for almost three decades after the passing of Lenin. So far, Khrushchev had held power for three years, and had struggled for part of that. He came to a conclusion on that strange incident based on the British pirate: he would keep an eye on everyone. Molotov in particular. Kaganovich and Bulganin bore watching, too.

Khrushchev lay down, still wearing his suit. He closed his eyes; then they came open again. *Serov,* he decided. *Of course, Serov!* Anyone who was head of the KGB deserved close scrutiny, too.

He closed his eyes again and soon dreamed of English pirates.

SEVENTEEN

In civilian clothing, the special Royal Navy raiding party filtered into Ybor-les-Pins two by two on Tuesday, March 20. They proceeded to Château Nicole. Christopher briefed them that evening, then thoroughly explained the impending operation, using enlarged photographs and charts, in Château Nicole's drafty old salon the next morning. Section members ate toast, sipped coffee and tea and listened carefully.

The party comprised thirteen men and women: Christopher, Jemima and Tim Sainthill. Eight Royal Marine Commandos, four SAS and four officers from the Special Boat Service, the so-called Cockleshell Heroes. Finally there were Second Officers Angela Lawson and Joan Prewitt of the Operational Wren Unit. Thirteen of them, Christopher noted again. An unlucky number up against three times that many trained mercenaries.

Elsewhere another M Section special Party had moved into Nice. They had located von Ostenberg's mercenaries who stood guard around the Palais des Dunes. Simultaneous to Christopher's raid at Ybor-les-Pins, the Nice team would move in on Alexis, Marie's grandson. They would destroy the mercenaries who guarded him and take him into close protection.

They would do all that, Christopher reminded himself, if everything went properly. He concluded his briefing toward three in the afternoon.

"Questions?" he asked.

There were several. When he'd answered them all, the raiding party went their separate assigned ways. It was a time to prepare mentally, to be alone with one's thoughts and to concentrate.

Christopher and Jemima found themselves alone at the kitchen table. They went over the plan for the final time. Jemima made some tea. She brought it to the table and poured out two cups from an enormous painted tea pot. They drank in silence. Then their eyes met over the rim of the cups.

"So it's *me!*" said Jemima in mock protest.

Christopher sighed. "Well, you volunteered," he said, his voice gentle.

"Blimey," she responded. "Into the valley of death — and all that jazz!" She smiled, but Christopher saw that it didn't disguise her fear.

"Somehow you've got to ensure that they are all together in the dining room at eight P.M. this evening. Marie, von Ostenberg, Nesterov and his sister. And if possible, you too."

She looked at him for a long moment. "So now I'm supposed to be a bloody magician, too," she

252

answered rudely. She finished her tea and walked away.

Christopher lay on his stomach at the perimeter of the Royal Navy Commando position above the manor occupied by von Ostenberg and his mercenaries. It was 1857 hours. Christopher scanned the front guard position through binoculars.

Colonel Tim Sainthill, Angela and Joan lay a few meters away. All three were dressed in Marine Commando camouflage combat gear with no badges of identification. Christopher wore a navy blue beret, as did the Wrens. All had blackened faces for dusk and night raiding. The men carried Colt .45 revolvers and the Wrens Smith and Wesson .38's. Slung across their backs were Thompson submachine guns, and razor sharp fighting knives at their belts.

They waited. Christopher's heart pounded. His tongue was dry. Despite the cool night, sweat rolled off him.

He glanced again at his watch. 1903 hours. *Where is Jemima?* he muttered. *Where in God's name is she?*

Sainthill glanced at him. The old structure was lit up with floodlights. A cat couldn't cross the entrance unobserved. There were six mercenaries on guard, and another fifteen patrolling the grounds.

All around, the barbed wire was still in place, huge rolls of it, tightly bound together. The old manor was as impregnable as a medieval city. Surely the first member of the party who tried to penetrate would die.

Then it should be me, not Jemima, Christopher thought to himself. *I'm a coward. I should have gone in first. What kind of craven commander sits safely at the rear?*

His fingers tapped the earth. He had the worst sense of catastrophe that he'd ever known. He looked at his watch again. Hours seemed to have passed, yet the minute hand had barely crawled along. 1904 hours. *Where was Jemima? She was late.*

"Where *is* she?" he asked aloud.

"Any second, sir," Sainthill replied comfortingly, barely speaking above a whisper. "It's coming along nicely. Everything is in place and on schedule."

Christopher put his sleeve to his brow and, in a most nonnaval gesture, mopped the sweat off his forehead. His arm came in front of his eyes for a second. When he moved it, he saw the red MG-TD come into the access road.

The red pranger! Jemima's, with her at the wheel. He mentally rechecked his weapons, a check he'd already made a thousand times. *Here goes,* he thought.

He watched the beams of the little red car shine up the access road to the first guard post. The red English sports car was thoroughly improbable for this sort of operation: It was A1 cover. No one with hostile intent could possibly drive such a car. For good measure, Jemima had stuck on the back an "S" — for Sweden, another country with right-hand drive.

254

The MG came to the guard position and slowed. Christopher watched, his hands soaking upon his binoculars. One of the six guards stood and motioned the car to stop. Two others, both with automatic rifles, stood back, one to each side. The remaining three stood hidden in a clump of trees.

Christopher didn't look at his watch, but it was 1905.

"Angela," he said suddenly.

"Sir," she replied, rolling over to him.

"Make to Charlemagne, via Birdham relay, repeat The Author. Priority One, Most Secret 'Operation Cut Out has commenced.' Time it please."

"Aye, aye, sir," she whispered and flicked on her transceiver.

One hundred meters away, the first guard shone a hand-held torch in Jemima's face. "Who are you? What do you want?" he asked her in heavily accented French. He could see that there was only a single young woman in the car.

The man came around to her window. She looked at him critically. "I've come to see the lady of the house," she said in French.

The guard looked to his back-up, a tall Prussian with cropped hair. "There is no lady here," he said, amused more than suspicious.

"There is a very special lady here," Jemima insisted. She spoke the classical French of the Imperial Court. "I am Countess Natasha Olga Alexandrova Pouravich," she said grandly. "I have come from

Sweden to contribute to the cause. Do you admit me or do I turn my car around this instant?"

The first guard looked uncertain and therefore dangerous.

"I would suggest that you find a room in the village, Countess," the second guard said. "There is no one to receive you. You are not expected. Return in the morning and arrangements may be made to have you admitted."

"You Bavarian peasant!" Jemima snapped, switching to fluent German. "I don't drive the length of Europe to be told to return in the morning!" She angrily opened her purse and pulled from it a bearer's check made out to ten thousand pounds sterling. She rudely waved it in the faces of the two guards. "This," she said, "is what the Countess Irena Petrovich will *not* be receiving!"

She stuffed it back in her bag and reached for the gear lever. She revved the car as if about to turn it around. A long arm reached through the window and stopped her.

"Please wait," said the first guard in German.

He drew his pistol and entered Jemima's car, holding the weapon across his lap. He slid into the seat next to her.

"I want to assure the Countess," he said, "that she will arrive safely into the company of the Countess Irene Petrovich." He grinned.

"And why shouldn't I?" she snapped in Russian.

He shrugged. Then he nodded to the other guards. They slung their automatic rifles across their backs. Jemima's red pranger revved and drove onto the driveway of the manor and up to the front entrance.

An old man opened the front door of the manor and led Jemima into the grand hallway. Then he seated her in a large wooden chair and disappeared.

On the edge of the established perimeter, Sainthill, Christopher and the two operational Wrens lay very still as they intently watched the scene below. Angela's radio brought in Jemima's voice clearly. A small transceiver had been taped to the inside of her thigh with an extension wire leading to a miniature microphone attached just under her breasts.

Christopher watched. His face was void of expression. "Angela," he whispered.

"Sir."

"Away SBS," he ordered.

"Aye, aye, sir," she responded and clicked on her transceiver. "SBS — Sierra Bravo Sierra — commence, commence, commence."

Within moments her transceiver came to life again.

"Cut Out Control. This is SBS — Roger," The Special Boat Service Commandos acknowledged nonchalantly. Their lives too would soon be up for grabs.

Christopher looked back to the manor and sighed. The red pranger stood empty in the driveway. Jemima was nowhere to be seen. *How many other people's lives am I to put at risk this day?* he wondered.

* * *

High up in the ravine, four Royal Marine SBS Commandos watched the bucking, frothing torrent as it tore and smashed its way down below the cliffs at the rear of the manor. They were two teams: Captain Peter Johnson and Sergeant John Terry, and Sergeants Bill Tebb and Bob Pritchard. Close to their feet was a small backwater which would allow them to get aboard and set off. After that it would be a maelstrom all the way.

"Now listen again, you lads," said Captain Johnson. "Getting your grappling hooks to engage is the first priority. Sod the boats. They're expendable. *Hook* on and *hold* on."

They all knew this inside out. They'd done it a hundred times.

All four men wore crash helmets with special flotation and survival gear. They carried underwater Colt .45's and plastic type-60 grenades. Their fighting knives had serrated edges. Around their waists and shoulders were slung cliff-scaling lines and two grapnel hooks.

"Okay, John," said the captain. "Let's get stuck in."

The other two sergeants held the kyaks as they boarded. Safely in, they fastened their oars into two double bladed rapid slashers.

"Now!" said Peter Johnson, and their kyak launched into the swirling overfalls.

It did not seem even remotely possible that they would survive the deafening rush of white water.

Twice they were overwhelmed and capsized, only to right themselves well within the four seconds allowed in training sessions.

The third time, the lead kyak did not right itself. But after seven seconds, both commandos emerged, free of their boat, and hurtled past the base of the cliffs by the manor. A grappling hook on a line appeared from below and whirled around once, and shot toward the rocky bank. It slipped and ran. Then with a jerk, it made fast. The men let the line slip through their hands to avoid too much purchase. Then they held on. The line took the strain. The grapnel was fast. The fulcrum balancing against the murderous current swung them to the bank. In the back eddy, they pulled themselves up and close into the cliffs. They were ashore.

Johnson looked up. Terry coiled his line, and swung the grapnel once again. He let it go and caught a small cliff overhang at about twenty feet. He tested. After a scuffle or two, it held. Three like that, and they'd be at the summit.

Captain Johnson started to climb, while the sergeant swung his second line. Neither looked back. The first team had to make the heights no matter what happened to the second.

In the great hallway of the manor, after what seemed an age to Jemima, the old man reappeared. "Please come this way, Countess."

He escorted her into a large study and closed the door behind her.

259

Nesterov was at his desk and rose as she entered. "Countess Natasha," he said, in French. "I welcome you on behalf of my sister, the Countess Irena. At the moment, she is engaged and I trust I may be of service instead."

Count Nesterov circled around the desk and stood in front of her. Jemima held out her hand. Nesterov kissed it. "Charmed, my dear count," she said.

"And how may I serve you, Countess?" asked Nesterov. He indicated a chair for her. When she sat, he did the same.

"I've brought a donation for your special fund. From my father and mother," she said. Jemima withdrew a different check than she'd shown the guards and handed it to him. "Please examine it carefully," she said. "My parents would not like any mistakes."

"Thank you, Countess." He took it and looked at it. He controlled his surprise when he read. Upon it there were no pounds, shillings, or pence, simply a message:

I must get to Marie Nikolayevna immediately.
It is imperative that I be invited to dinner with her and the baron.
I'm in Royal Naval Intelligence and an emissary of Lord Mountbatten.

"This is most generous, Countess," said Nesterov. "I will write a receipt." He wrote one and handed it to her. It read: "I fully understand."

At that moment, a door opened at the other side

of the room. Marie entered. Nesterov turned to her. "Madam," he said, bowing, "may I present Countess Natasha Pouravich."

"Enchanted," said Marie, holding out her hand.

"Ma'am," said Jemima. She curtsied and kissed the ring of Catherine the Great.

"The countess has brought us a most generous contribution," said Nesterov. He handed Marie the check.

Marie turned out to be the best actor in the group. She read the note and responded gently, "My dear Countess Natasha. This is really most generous. We are most grateful. Tell me, can you stay for dinner?"

"I would love to, Ma'am," said Jemima.

She crumpled the note and tossed it in the hearth. She replaced the check with the one made out to sterling. Nesterov turned and poured brandy for the three of them.

The time was 1951 hours. Christopher, Sainthill and the two operational Wrens lay at the same position they'd held when Jemima had entered the manor.

Angela's RT clicked to life. Then she whispered, "SBS reports, sir. Both crews atop and through. East lateral breach four minutes."

Christopher shook his head in admiration. "Perfect," he said. All four SBS commandos had survived the river, scaled the cliff and breached the treble rolls of barbed wire behind the manor grounds. In four minutes they would breach the wire at the east side of the manor's rear gardens. They would leave the way open for Christopher and two other commando units.

"Angela! Tell all units to rendezvous as prearranged."

"Aye, aye, sir."

Christopher looked down. This was the critical phase. If they could make a silent approach and neutralize the guards without firing a shot, then they had an even chance of reaching the dining room undetected. Even, but no more than even.

The commandos had Christopher's orders. Unarmed combat, fighting knives, garottes and the butts of their Colt .45's were the prescribed tools. But no shooting unless under direct orders. Tommy guns were in reserve.

"All right, Tim," said Christopher, "I'm going in now. You take temporary command."

"Very good, sir," acknowledged the colonel.

Christopher made a quick final check of his gear as Angela joined him. "Follow me," he said to her.

In the darkness, Angela gave Tim Sainthill a little wave. Then she followed her chief down the edge of the wood, moving as silently as he did.

EIGHTEEN

On the first floor at the back of the manor at Ybor-les-Pins, candles and electricity illuminated the huge chandeliers. A twenty-five-foot rosewood table filled the center of the dining hall which lay beneath the vast gallery on the east side.

Upon the table were large bowls of fresh flowers as well as five place settings of the finest antique linens, crystal goblets and silver tableware, each piece bearing the crest of the Russian Imperial family. The servants who prepared to wait on them also wore the motif of the Romanovs.

Maric entered on Nesterov's arm, wearing a simple but elegant white dinner dress that contrasted superbly with the diamonds and emeralds of her tiara, necklace and earrings. Nesterov wore a plain but elegant uniform of royal blue. Behind came Countess Irena. She was a tall, skinny woman, who appeared much older than her brother. She too wore white, but with only small items of jewelry.

Jemima found herself still dressed up like something out of a jumble sale. Both Marie and Countess Irena had offered other clothes to her, but nothing had come within inches of fitting. Marie was too short and round and Countess Irena too tall and thin. So they had all decided she had better remain as she was. "You're so pretty, my dear," Marie had told her. "You don't need to dress up like we do." Jemima had agreed reluctantly.

The sound of a double door opening made Jemima turn. From across the dining hall, she recognized Baron Wilhelm von Ostenberg. Ten mercenaries escorted him, then distributed themselves around the great hall. It was apparent from varied disproportionate bulges that they were all comprehensively armed.

Von Ostenberg walked to Marie. He clicked his heels, Prussian style, and bowed his head. Marie did not give him her hand.

"Good evening, Herr Baron," she said stiffly.

"Good evening, your Imperial Majesty," he responded.

Mercenaries held their chairs as they sat at the table. Marie was at the head and von Ostenberg far away at the other end. On Marie's right was Nesterov and his sister, and on her left was Jemima.

"Tasha, my dear," said Marie. "This is turtle soup. Just the same as you had as a child by the Volga. See if you agree?"

Jemima picked up her spoon and sampled it. "Absolutely delicious," said Jemima. "And how, Marie, is one able to get such a flavor so far from the Peterhof?"

264

Marie put out her hand and held Jemima's. But to further reassure herself, Jemima ran her fingers over a French 7.65-mm Bubi automatic that nested in a leather holster strapped to her right thigh. It was her favorite weapon, loaded with dum-dum bullets carved with deep crosses upon their tips. They would blast to pieces on impact, incapacitating any human target.

Jemima glanced at her watch. It was 1953 hours. Attached to her thigh, the silent receiver would pulse with a slight electrical shock when the commandos entered the manor. She felt the sweat seeping around the holster and the transmitter, looked around, and realized that she, Marie, and Marie's entourage were right within the line of fire of the ten guards.

The four commandos of the Special Boat Service swiftly breached the east wire close in under the shadow of a spreading oak tree. Two SAS commando units passed the six foot breach in the wire directly behind them. One minute later, Christopher and Angela approached the breach in a crocodile crawl, flat on their stomachs, safely in the lee of the floodlights.

Nearby in the darkness something moved. They heard voices. They froze. A patrol of six mercenaries was making a guard sweep of the wire. They came within four yards of Christopher and Angela, and within one foot of the breach in the wire. They saw nothing and continued back toward the house. Christopher watched. He wasn't surprised that they hadn't seen the severed barbed wire. He couldn't see it himself. But he knew exactly where it was.

The breach was not a cut in the wire, but a disconnection of it from its steel peg anchorage. Underneath were three wooden levers balanced on pivots. Angela and Christopher pushed down on them and the loosened wire slowly rose upward, allowing about three inches clearance for their crawling bodies. They slowly came through. Then Christopher turned and released the pivots. The wire fell back into its set position.

Christopher looked about him. He glanced at his watch: 1956 hours. He gave Angela a nod and she clicked on her transceiver. "All units," she whispered, "search and destroy."

The four commandos of the Special Boat Service acknowledged just as the six patrolling guards came abreast of them at the west side of the building. The commandos struck instantly. The butts of their pistols smashed down on the skulls of the last two mercenaries. In the darkness they then killed the first four with their fighting knives. It only took sixteen seconds.

The SBS units then ran toward the front of the manor. There they consolidated with the SAS commandos from the east wing.

Christopher and Angela arrived at a small window at the back of the manor on its ground level. Christopher looked up at the window above him. It was the dining hall. Its lights gently shined out onto the garden.

He tapped Angela on the shoulder. "Move!" he

ordered sharply. They both ran along the base of the building and pulled up close to an entrance to a flight of cellar steps. The door was unlocked.

From around the corner, a SAS commando arrived to make a report. They had killed twenty-one of the mercenary guards and were still searching.

Christopher acknowledged. Then he and Angela entered the manor.

Three minutes later, by virtue of the accuracy of Ann Vergamo's plans of the manor, Christopher and Angela stood on the gallery above the great dining hall, their backs against the wall. Gradually Christopher edged forward. He could see the five diners. He could hear their voices. But his main concern was the exact number of the enemy. Ten were below him. Twenty-one had been killed outside. Were there really such another four? He didn't know. But the time had come to strike.

It was 2000 hours.

He nodded to Angela. She extended the aerial of her transceiver and pressed a blue button three times.

On the ledge outside the main windows of the hall, a blue light flashed on the transceiver of a Royal Marine Commando. He nodded to his companion and they both crept forward.

At the table below, Jemima tensed as she felt the vibration from her silent receiver. She had ten seconds before the strike. She raised her glass. "It is now," Jemima said in Russian.

Marie understood and raised her glass in reply. Jemima set down her glass, put her hand under her dress and pulled her automatic from its holster.

Neither Christopher nor the other commandos hesitated. On the beat of the tenth second, they opened fire. Bullets crashed into the bodies of the mercenaries. The guards screamed, cursed and grappled for their own sidearms as the barrage of gunfire cut them down.

At exactly the same moment, Jemima kicked away Marie's chair, landed the Grand Duchess on the floor. Without pausing, Jemima hurtled across the table and pushed Nesterov and his sister downward. Von Ostenberg then drew his pistol.

He raised it to kill her. But she turned and kicked at his hand the second before he fired. The shot blasted upward past her head, but missed. Her second karate kick caught him off balance, turning him over backward. She leaped after him, knocked his gun away, and jammed her automatic against his head. "One move, Herr Baron," she breathed in German, "and I'll kill you."

The shooting had stopped. Ten mercenaries lay scattered around the room, their blood spilling onto the floor. For a moment the room was strangely silent as no one moved. Then the Marines came in. Captain Peter Johnson and Sergeant Eric Fletcher doubled over to Jemima and relieved her of von Ostenberg. They placed him under arrest.

Christopher lowered himself down from the gallery. Angela followed. Christopher looked to Jemima. "Number One!" he said. "To this moment, we've killed thirty-one."

"That leaves four on the roam then, sir," she said, too anxiety-ridden to be sickened by the carnage.

"Let's hope Sainthill's got them," Christopher said. "Angela?"

"Sir?" Angela answered.

"Stop first phase and commence second," ordered Christopher. "And warn of four possible strays."

"Aye, aye, sir," acknowledged Angela, clicking on her transceiver.

Christopher glanced around the great dining hall, distracted only for an instant. He thought of the many old passages, hidden stairways and overhanging galleries that were peculiar to this old house.

Then it happened, the instant which changes lifetimes. From the corner of his eye he saw movement from the small gallery above. He knew by the colour of the two figures that they were not his own. And he knew how vulnerable he was.

He turned, but the shooting had already begun.

"Christopher!"

It was Jemima's voice. Clear and penetrating. Incredibly, she had seen them first.

She launched herself from the safe cover of the stairway and into the hail of bullets. Shielding Christopher with her body, she turned and blasted with her Bubi automatic. She hit one man in the centre of the chest. The automatic weapon in his hands sprayed upward for a moment, then flew into the air as he fell. She hit the second man in the face and shoulders. The dum-dum bullets blasted his head and the skull flew apart. His shots smashed into the floor at Christopher's feet. Angela fired. Christopher fired. But there were no more of them. The Deputy Commander had hit them first and had saved both their lives.

Jemima avoided Christopher's eyes and went to Marie who was still lying obediently on the floor under the table. "Are you all right, ma'am?"

Marie's smile answered the question. Jemima helped her up. Marie squeezed the Wren officer's hand and said: "Thanks to you and your friends. Yes." She glanced to see that Nesterov and his sister were rising to their feet, shaken but unscathed.

Colonel Sainthill arrived with Joan and two Commandos. With some relief he observed that his captain and the rest of the party were safe. "Everything fully secure, sir. We've picked up the last two strays," he said to Christopher. "And no casualties to the party."

"Thank you, Tim."

The two men were standing at the far end of the dining room. Christopher was still holding his Tommy gun. He handed it to a Marine and walked across the hall, coming to a smart attention before Marie. He saluted and bowed his head in the Coburg bow. "Ma'am, I am Captain Hamilton of her Britannic Majesty's Royal Navy."

Marie came a pace forward and looked at Christopher intently. Then she smiled. "What else could you possible be but the Royal Navy of Admiral Mountbatten?"

Marie moved closer, embraced him, and kissed him on both cheeks.

"Ma'am," said Christopher, straightening himself and standing back at attention, "I am ordered by Admiral Mountbatten to escort you to a place of safety. I have the honor to ask your permission to carry out these orders."

Marie smiled at Christopher and the men and women who were under his command. "It is *I* who am honored," she answered.

Marie took Christopher's arm. But as they crossed the great dining hall, she stopped at the body of a fallen mercenary. She knelt on the floor beside him. Marie made the Russian Orthodox sign of the Cross, bowed her head and whispered a prayer.

"Angela," said Christopher when Marie finally rose. "Before you leave, Make to Charlemagne by Birdham relay. Repeat to The Author and the Prime Minister."

"Sir," said Angela, pulling out her signal pad.

"From Christopher Robin. Operation Cut-Out completed as planned. No casualties in section. Thirty-three mercenaries killed, two prisoners plus leader. 'Alice' safe."

"Aye, aye, sir," Angela acknowledged. She switched on her transceiver. But before she could send, a red light upon it flashed. "Signal coming in, sir," she said.

"Give it to me direct, please."

Christopher waited as Angela took it.

"To Christopher Robin from B subsection Cannes," she said. "Opposition guards destroyed. Alexis safe and under first-grade protection."

A cheer went around the room. Marie clapped but

was unable to restrain herself any further. Emotion welled up inside her and tears flowed. Jemima put out her arms and held her closely. Angela and Joan came to help, too. Presently the three operational Wrens gently escorted Marie Nikolayevna, Empress of All the Russias in Exile, from the manor of Ybor-les-Pins.

Shortly past dawn, the dead mercenaries were placed aboard two refrigerated trucks and spirited away by the SDECE, the French Secret Service. The two surviving mercenaries plus von Ostenberg were placed aboard an RN aircraft. They would be transported back to Birdham Manor, via HMS Daedalus, the Royal Navy Air Station at Lee-on-Solent. Jemima and the rest of the party and their equipment would return on two other RN aircraft from the French military base just outside Cannes. Marie went with them, together with Nesterov and his sister. Christopher stayed behind.

Before they left, all the Royal Naval Party plus about twenty SDECE agents, took off their jackets, rolled up their sleeves and pulled the manor apart. Then they put it together again. When they'd finished, no one could have known of the vital and bloody operation that had taken place the night before — nor of the men who had died there.

But Christopher knew. He stood halfway up a rock path that looked down on the swirling river and the manor beyond. His operation had been a sensational success. In his heart he knew it might easily have been the opposite. A bloody defeat with Jemima shot to pieces, half the commandos, and probably him, too. Marie could have been assassinated by the spiteful Prussians. And then, God knew what else.

At the top of the hill, an ancient Roman Catholic chapel stood alone. Christopher had noticed it the day he had arrived in Ybor-les-Pins. Today, when he went to it, the door opened at his touch.

Inside, the chapel was empty, dim and cold. Little light filtered through the stained glass. The wood of the beams was dark and riddled with worm holes. The pews were musty and bare with no cushions.

Christopher went to the altar and knelt down, crossing himself, much in the same manner as he'd done in his youth. He thought back to the great Benedictine Abbey at Ampleforth. He tried to pray but couldn't. He asked himself when he'd last been in a house of worship and recalled that then, too, had been an occasion of death: the memorial service for A. A. Milne.

Christopher thought of the dreadful number of men who had been killed by *his* section under his orders. He mumbled a prayer that he knew by heart, but it had no meaning under these circumstances. He tried to say a prayer for his own soul, but that would have been hypocrisy. So he said one for Jemima and thanked God for sparing her life.

Then he felt better and other prayers came tumbling out, just as they had at school, at the Royal Naval College at Dartmouth and at so many other times since.

Now, as then, a thought came to him. His only real purpose for being here was to ask God's forgiveness for breaking at least half of the Ten Commandments.

This he did on behalf of his entire section. Then, before he left, he asked for forgiveness too on behalf of Lord Louis. It was just, Christopher reasoned, for good measure.

NINETEEN

With the arrival of Marie, daily routine at HMS Birdham changed dramatically. She asked to be of help in whatever way possible. Peggy Scott, the Section's chief Wren paymaster in charge of housekeeping and victualing, took to Marie right away and invited her into the galley. Marie responded with enthusiasm. Within the day the Section began to enjoy recipes from Serbia and the Steppes, the Baltic and the Ukraine—dishes that had once graced the imperial table of her father, the last Czar. Simultaneously, Joan found a sweet, dark Russian wine in a small shop in Cosham. The Section ordered several cases, along with a liberal supply of vodka. Marie's only royal decree was that she was to be addressed by her code name—Alice—and that no special courtesies would be tolerated. On her part, she learned the Christian names of as many of Birdham's company as she could and used them.

Jemima detailed guards to von Ostenberg and held him incommunicado on the second floor. Two senior officers with Thompson submachine guns were on duty around the clock. "Von Ostenberg is to be accorded the status of a general officer prisoner of war," Christopher had told his section. Then he dictated signals to Angela, reporting the situation at Birdham. The signals went out on the cypher immediately, first to Mountbatten in Australia, then repeated to the Prime Minister and Lord High Admiral.

The raid on Ybor-les-Pins had been a smashing success, but now a more complicated problem loomed. How was von Ostenberg to be interrogated? Trott and his professional inquisitors, Christopher quickly decided, were to be kept away. Nor did Christopher consider himself capable of the job. Any small miscalculation could throw a pall of silence over von Ostenberg. The approach would have to be subtle and sophisticated. And it would have to succeed. Christopher desperately needed certain specific answers:

What was the scope of the attack on the Soviet leaders? Who would do it? When? Where? What preparations were already in place? Was a team of assassins already in England or could entry be closed to them?

Christopher agonized. In the afternoon, after an hour's discussion with his senior officers, he still had no satisfactory solution. Inside, he burned. He began to understand the solitude of command. Decisions which would affect or cost lives were clearly his. It was said that during the war, Roosevelt and Churchill never lost a night's sleep due to worry. He wondered how. He felt a depression creeping upon him, one that would last for days if not checked. He sat alone in his office and simmered.

An hour later, there was a knock on the door followed by the even more welcome appearance of Jemima James. She carried two cups of coffee.

"Hello, grumps," she said.

Christopher looked at her and did not answer. The third finger of his left hand tapped slowly and nervously on the desk.

"I thought you would like some refreshment and it's too early for vodka. Coffee will have to do."

He accepted a cup. She sat down in a leather armchair, just where she'd sat silently throughout the morning meeting. He sipped the coffee twice, then set aside his cup and saucer.

"So what do we do?" he asked at length.

"You mean it's not obvious?" she asked.

The pressure, the frustration, the incipient depression: he looked up in exasperation, on the verge of losing his temper. "You have an idea? And you've just sat there like a bump on a log?"

She looked at him over the rim of her coffee cup and nodded. "Then bloody well tell me what it is!" he shouted.

"It's called 'Owl,'" she shouted back. "And he has to be requisitioned."

He stared at her for a moment as she smiled very

slightly. Then he shoved his coffee aside with a clatter, spilling some of it. "Bloody God Almighty!" he said. "Of course! Angela!" he bellowed. *"Angela!"*

Outside his study, Angela's footsteps were heavy as they descended the staircase. The answer had been so simple, Christopher told himself, that it had been in the back of his mind all along. Jemima neatly set aside her coffee cup as Angela threw open the door and burst into the library.

"Yes, sir?" she responded, breathless.

"Angela," ordered Christopher, "all past Top Priority Secret signals are to be repeated for Owl and delivered to him with an armed escort."

"Aye, aye, sir."

"Lay on a helicopter. Liase with London Welsh Rugby Club at their ground at Old Deer Park. It's very close to Kew Green. Have our London subsection order a car to stand by for you there." He paused as she wrote hurriedly. "How long will that take?"

"With all girls closed up to duty, one hour, sir. And a further hour to get to Kew."

"Good girl," said Christopher. "And one signal from me to Owl. Most Secret and the usual guff: 'Christopher Robin needs his wise old Owl.' "

She looked up.

"That's all," Christopher said. He gave her a wink and she departed.

Four hours later, a Royal Navy helicopter set

down on the rear lawn at HMS Birdham. Christopher and Jemima welcomed Desmond Morton. The two men embraced as they always did. Jemima received a warm handshake that turned into a kiss on the cheek. For Desmond Morton, a man in his sixties plainly bored with retirement, arrival was like a homecoming. HMS Birdham *had* been his virtual home from 1936 into the 1950's, the years he had commanded the M Section.

They entered the manor and crossed the great hallway. Two marines carried Morton's gear. Angela showed Morton his room. Then he returned downstairs to the library, where Jemima joined them for a private dinner. Christopher began briefing Morton during the meal. It was not until coffee was served much later that Christopher moved toward a conclusion.

As Morton listened and concentrated, his blue eyes were cold, luminous and slightly frightening. His hair was sleek and polished, his mustache trimmed very severely. Christopher, as he covered the final details, recalled the chills Desmond Morton had given him as a boy, sitting on the edge of his bed telling him ghost stories. Back then, Morton's interest in children had always seemed slightly forced and Christopher had never entirely liked him. It was only as Christopher grew older and understood him better, and followed much the same life path, that the two men grew close, despite the generational gap.

When Christopher finished, Morton thought quietly for several minutes. Creighton knew he wanted time to form a reasoned response. When he answered, he spoke slowly, methodically, almost as if reading.

"I'm not usually as well briefed as this. I'm most grateful," he said. "Your most pressing question is von Ostenberg? How to proceed? How to interrogate him?"

Christopher nodded.

"It's my opinion," Morton said, "that at this delicate stage *none* of you should speak to him. He has the answers you want. But of course, he is prepared to die rather than give them to you. We're also not so naive as to think that the destruction of his section at Ybor-les-Pins marked the end of the threat."

Morton glanced at Jemima and Christopher. He saw that they agreed.

"*I* should talk to von Ostenberg," Morton said. "My appearance as his questioner will give away nothing of importance. He will know who I am and, most probably, quite a bit about me. We are of the same generation and I might be able to establish some trust. At this moment, pressuring him would be wrong. Rather, he should be led to the realization that his only hope lies in cooperation."

Morton finished his sixth cup of coffee.

"If he's prepared to die," Jemima asked, "why would he cooperate at all?"

"That, dear lady, is precisely our problem."

"What about Marie?" asked Christopher.

280

"She has a great deal of respect for you, Christopher. You led the party that rescued her and you are the commander of this section. In those circumstances, and in the absence of Dickie Mountbatten, you should be the gentleman to discuss her captivity with her. As for her dotty old manservant of hers . . ."

"Count Nesterov," Jemima said.

"I doubt if he knows much of anything. Detail one of your men to him. You have more important matters."

"When would you like to start with von Ostenberg?" Creighton asked.

"Tomorrow morning. Early. With your permission, of course, Christopher."

There was a timid knock on the door. It broke the mood in the room, irritating Christopher. "Come in!" he yelled.

The door opened hesitantly and Marie appeared. She wore a pair of black velvet trousers and a maroon knitted jumper. "I'm sorry. I'm interrupting," she said.

"Good gracious, no. You're not!" Christopher answered. He, Jemima and Sir Desmond were on their feet.

Marie joined them, but declined coffee or brandy. There was a momentary silence and they all looked expectantly at her.

"As I'm sure you realize," she said, "we've barely had time to talk since yesterday. At Ybor-les-Pins and in transit to England, it has been as impossible for me to talk as it was with Dickie in Paris. But there are some things I must tell you now. As a child in the Russian court, I learned much about eavesdropping."

She glanced at Morton, Jemima and Christopher. All three were riveted. Her eyes sparkled.

"I know you don't want to hear everything now. It would take too long. But I picked up snippets here and there at Ybor-les-Pins. One bit, I believe, is vital to you."

The three Section officers waited.

"Von Ostenberg and his mercenaries regarded the destruction of the Soviet ships to be equally important as the deaths of Bulganin and Khrushchev. To this end, they had secured a team of divers. The ships will be attacked underwater in Portsmouth harbor. Shortly after arrival."

There was a hush as the three officers exchanged glances. It was Christopher who finally spoke. "That's what you overheard?"

"Yes."

"And these 'divers,'" Morton quickly pressed. "They were not among the guards at Ybor-les-Pins?"

"No," she said. "What I heard was that a diving unit was waiting elsewhere. They were never to come to France."

"Were they in England already?" Creighton asked. But Marie didn't know.

"German? American? White Russian?" Morton asked.

282

"I'm sorry," she said. Again, she didn't know. Christopher leaned back, relaxing slightly, not skeptical but not entirely convinced either. He would have to be certain of everything, he reminded himself.

"Why are you so sure that the attack involved divers?" he asked.

Marie almost laughed. "Because I believe not only my ears but my eyes, also. I saw the equipment."

Half an hour after the meeting, Christopher lay in bed. He was exhausted from the last four days. But his rest was fitful; sleep would not come. Marie's words had confirmed his worst expectations.

Yet the Section was fortunate, he told himself. If the attack was to come underwater in Portsmouth, the conspirators would be assaulting the area over which the Section had most control. A ring of steel, the RG lights and their electronic sensors, could be established around the Soviet ships, just as one had been established around Birdham. The system was infallible and Colonel Sainthill was a master at installation—above water or below. Anybody moving without authorization beneath the Soviet ships would be destroyed. That much was definite.

What worried Christopher was anyone managing to get that close. He turned uncomfortably in his bed.

Then he heard something. It was a low, muffled noise from not far away. When he heard it a second time he realized that he'd been listening to it subliminally for several minutes. It was as if someone were heaving, or gasping for breath.

He lay still for only another two seconds. It was coming from the officer's quarters next to his. Jemima's cabin.

Christopher rose from bed, pulled on his dressing gown and stepped out into the gallery. That statutory Royal Marine Captain's guard outside his door snapped to attention. Christopher gave him a nod, stepped to Jemima's door and went in. He left the door ajar.

She was on the floor, huddled in a corner near a window. The light in the room was from a dim bedside lamp. She was sobbing and shaking, her knees up and her hands to her face.

"Jemima . . . ?" He spoke very gently, seeing that she was alone. "What's the matter?" He knelt by her on the floor and pulled her hands slowly away from her face.

"Oh, my God," she whispered. "Oh, my God."

Christopher got his arms underneath her and carried her to the bed. As he put her down, she turned on him sharply, almost hysterically. "It's all very well for *you,* isn't it?"

"Isn't it what?"

She looked at him, almost in contempt. "You've got so many scalps on your belt already, that a few more don't count. Is that *it?* Not to mention

284

notches on your gun!"

"Jemima . . ."

"Well, I'm just starting out," she said.

Christopher put his arm around her, but she pulled away.

"Jemima," he spoke softly, "please listen to me. Those men were professional killers. If you hadn't killed them, they would have—"

"It *doesn't matter!* Don't you understand that?" Her voice was breaking with sobs. "I've killed two human beings!"

It was almost two in the morning and Christopher was out of words. He put his arm on her shoulder, but she rejected it again, pushing him away. "It's as if I'm Joan of Arc," she rambled on, "or some murderous lout who enjoys her work and doesn't need a word of understanding. I should go back to Abingdon. This is not for Jemima."

She cried unabashedly and Christopher felt deeply ashamed. He personally had looked after all his operational personnel after the raid on Yhor-les-Pins. He had congratulated them and comforted them. He'd written out recommendations for medals. And yet he'd not said one damned thing to his second in command. Her first two kills—a moment of shattering psychological trauma in the life of any God-fearing human being—and he had said nothing. Not a single kind word, not a syllable of understanding. Now, in the darkness of night, the demons emerged from the darkest recesses of her mind and there was small wonder that she was torn apart.

Christopher heard a sound behind him. He turned. Marie stood in the doorway, a woolen dressing gown pulled over her pajamas. "May I come in?" she asked in a half whisper.

"Did you hear?" he asked.

Marie nodded. Her room was on the other side of Jemima's.

Christopher beckoned her in. She went at once to Jemima who was sitting on the bed. Her knees pulled up tight to her tummy—huddled in a ball. She was still talking. Her eyes glazed; her breathing was fast.

"Poor dear girl," said Marie, sitting down next to Jemima and putting out her arms.

Jemima looked up and collapsed into the embrace of the Czar's daughter. She cried while Marie stroked her hair and her back. Marie spoke to her in a soft, affectionate voice.

It went on for several minutes. Jemima gathered herself slowly and Christopher felt very out of place.

Marie caught his eye. "You must be very tired, Christopher," she said. "Go, I'll put her to bed."

"Would you like me to call Angela?"

"No," Marie answered.

"Thank you." He nodded. He was both grateful and helpless. He closed the door behind him as he left.

But he did not return to his cabin. Instead, he stood for a long time at the edge of the minstrels' gallery. He thought about Jemima. He told himself that he'd said nothing to her after the raid out of fear of underscoring the horrible implications of what had happened. Yet in that analysis, there was not one shred of honesty. And he knew it. The fact was, Christopher had simply forgotten. Jemima's first kills had been lost in the excitement and confusion of the moment.

He wandered further along the gallery, hearing his own footsteps. Not far from him was his guard, standing silently at attention, like something from a wax museum. Christopher looked at him.

"Stand easy," Creighton said softly.

"Sir," the Marine answered, relaxing. At ease, the guard seemed less a statue. Creighton hungered for human contact.

He looked down at the vast hallway below. Birdham was quiet as a tomb at this hour. No voices, no movement, no clatter of anticipation. On an old clock, Christopher could hear seconds tick off, bringing the Russian visit ever closer. It was two thirty a.m., March 23, 1956.

An attack underwater, Marie had said. *By whom? When, damn it, when?* The mere presence of such divers in England was threat enough. If they came within a thousand miles of Portsmouth it was too close. But the threat was real. It was human, as flesh and blood as Jemima's trauma or the mercenaries who had died at Ybor-les-Pins. And it would happen in three and a half weeks.

287

At exactly 0830 the next morning, two Royal Marine captains escorted Desmond Morton to von Ostenberg. They knocked on von Ostenberg's door. When it opened, Morton entered the second-floor room. Two more officers were within, keeping watch.

Morton nodded to them. They left, giving the Englishman and the German privacy. Von Ostenberg sat comfortably in an armchair. He looked at Morton, who returned the gaze.

"Baron von Ostenberg," Morton said in civil tones. "I am Sir Desmond Morton."

"I know," von Ostenberg answered. He stood, nodded and sat again. "I expected you would be called. We have met before."

"Nineteen thirty-six," said Morton, sitting and nodding. "In Hamburg in the old Kaiser's palace. Our host was Reichsmarshall Goering. He was in the process of forming the Gestapo at the time. I had the pleasure of meeting your late wife, Baroness Tatiana."

Von Ostenberg nodded and said nothing.

"I was very saddened to learn of her death in Berlin in 1945, at the hands of the barbaric Red Army," Morton said.

Von Ostenberg fixed him with a penetrating gaze, then relaxed slightly in his armchair. "Thank you, sir," he said softly.

"I suppose you know why I'm here," Morton said. "We know a great deal about what you and your followers were about. But we need to know more. You are our key prisoner. That means we will have to obtain the information we need from you."

Von Ostenberg was silent. Morton sat down on a small cot which was against the wall. "I understand how you feel about the Bolshevik government, Herr Baron," Morton continued. "But it's hardly a reason to start World War III, would you say? Not exactly the most fitting memorial to a woman like Tatiana." Morton's eyebrows were raised with the question.

"You are a Briton, sir," von Ostenberg answered. "I am a Prussian. We view things differently."

For the first time, Morton was face-to-face with the long road ahead. He sighed. "Yes," he allowed. "I suppose we do."

The session lasted ninety minutes. When it was finished, Morton came downstairs to the Section office. The interview had been fruitless, which came as no surprise. Christopher poured coffee for Sir Desmond.

"Well?" Creighton finally asked.

Morton sipped his coffee and thought about it for several seconds. "He's going to be just about impossible," Morton finally answered. "I can try my methods. I'll do everything I can. But it could take several days. Maybe a week or two. And even then, I might fail."

Creighton felt like something stronger than coffee. "We have a little bit of time. But not much. Proceed the way you want to do it."

Morton nodded.

"What if you *can't* break him?" Christopher asked.

Obviously, Morton had already considered the possibility. He was ready with the answer.

"Have you ever heard of Surgeon-Commander Robert Rawlins?" Morton asked.

"I don't think I have."

"I had to recommend him in some very dodgy Section cases in both India and Egypt over the last few years. A very unpleasant man. Not personally. Just his methods."

"Then let's haul him in," Creighton said. "Von Ostenberg needs to have something unpleasant happen to him."

Morton nodded.

"But let's only use him," Morton suggested softly, "if it's unavoidable."

TWENTY

McClintock's flat, a red brick building of little distinction with an entrance flanked by a curry parlor and a news agent, was in Notting Hill. As Popov stood before it he double-checked the address that he'd cribbed inside a matchbook, found it to be correct, then entered. When he rang a doorbell at street level, a buzzer admitted him. There was no intercom.

Popov climbed to the third flight on a set of stairs that cried out to be swept, then painted. On one floor he heard a loud argument in Welsh. From another apartment he heard a noisy Victrola and from a third he heard someone — possibly a child — practicing a violin very poorly. From the apartment of Jimmy McClintock, he heard nothing.

The assassin knocked. A quarter minute passed and the door, held by a chain, opened a few inches.

Popov was surprised to be looking into the face of a young woman. She had very white skin and eyes completely devoid of any animation. They were brown, focused and set like a terrier's.

Behind her, the frame of a tall, lanky youth glided in and out of view. The young man spoke. "It's all right, Nicole," he said. "I'm expecting a visitor." He was Ulster; his hard distinctive accent said so.

The door shut and opened quickly. The young man, Jimmy McClintock, drew the Russian into the flat and closed the door again. Popov found himself in a mirrored hallway. He was welcomed not so much by one McClintock as by a whole legion of them.

Jimmy was taller than Sergei Popov by half a head. His eyes glittered, presumably from complicated university-level thoughts, and his arms were long and gangly. His shoulders stooped slightly, as if to reduce his abnormal height to something that could pass more readily through the average doorway. "Come on along, mister," he said, sweeping a shaggy forelock from his eyes. "I don't know your name and I don't want to know it. I know only why you're here."

The woman wore an Icelandic print dress — woolen and wrinkled — and, like McClintock, was beanpole thin. She was about twenty-five, Popov reckoned, a handful of years older than McClintock. But at her temples, the black hair was streaked with gray. She never spoke. Popov guessed that she might be a philosophy student, or maybe a classicist, engaged in some doctoral level study. To Popov that's how she looked. He later discovered, in conversation with McClintock, that she was a telephone operator.

She fetched two bottles of lager from a cabinet in the kitchen, opened them and brought them to the men. She was so obedient and silent that Popov assumed McClintock cherished those qualities in a woman.

"So," the student said as he and his guest settled in on well-worn living room furniture, "talk to me." The room's wallpaper was atrocious: brown, with large green flowers.

The Russian waited until the woman had returned to the kitchen. When she left the door slightly ajar, the assassin looked at it critically.

McClintock didn't take the hint.

"That's my little Nicole," he said. "My most re-cent sexual miracle. See, you and she have sort of come into my life together. It was only a day or two ago that I picked her up at the greengrocer's. Been a hot time ever since, let me tell you."

Popov grunted. "In this line of work I didn't know coincidences existed," he said.

McClintock looked blankly at him for a moment until he got Popov's message. "Well, I'm not about to kick her out, if that's your suggestion," McClintock said with undue bellicosity. "Things like this don't just come to pass every day. What do you want? A time bomb, is it? With or without a remote?"

The Russian's eyes were hard and censorious. They both heard Nicole flick on the kitchen radio. She cruised the dial until she found Elvis Presley. Popov glared at the partially open door, then looked daggers at McClintock. He said nothing.

McClintock stared back, then finally relented. "Bloody hell!" he snapped. He rose brusquely and strode to the kitchen. He pushed the door wide open. "Nicole, dumpling," he said.

She was silent, but came to him.

"This man wants to chat. Private business," he said. McClintock dug into his trousers pocket and came up with a pair of rumpled pound notes. "How'd you like to run around the corner like a good girl and get us a good dago wine for dinner?"

McClintock gave her a swat on the buttocks, then came back to the living room. He sat on a tattered armchair, facing Popov who was on a sofa. "Completely unnecessary," McClintock said in lowered tones.

"Listen, you young featherhead," the assassin answered. "I'm a good bit older than you. If you want to make it to my age, you'll take a few basic precautions."

"It's all bullshit, man," McClintock said.

Popov's fingers fidgeted impatiently along a frayed section of upholstery upon the sofa's arm.

The assassin studied the boy very coldly, as if deciding whether to take him outside and give him a good thrashing. Or maybe he'd just stay inside and administer it. McClintock must have read his thoughts because his attitude swiftly changed. He turned to the kitchen and was opening his mouth to hurry Nicole along. But then she appeared in a coat and was out the door, leaving them alone, except for Elvis on the radio.

"Now what is it you wanted?" McClintock asked, turning back.

"Apparently you already know. And so will half of London if you don't shut your face."

"I can have it for you in four days," McClintock said. "You pick it up from a garage in Lambeth. Do you know how to install a bomb?"

"Probably better than you do."

"The device will be in a package. You'll make the final wiring connections yourself. I don't leave anything set to go. What's today's date?"

It was Tuesday, March 27, they decided after consulting with that morning's *Daily Mirror*.

"I'll give you an address," McClintock concluded. "Go there Saturday when they open. Ask for Mr. Flint. Say your name is Signor de Valera. From Spain."

Popov cocked his head. "De Valera?"

"That's my little joke," said McClintock, regaining his impudence. "That's how I work. My signature, call it. Tell me, can you do a funny accent when you call?"

"Only yours," said Popov who rose and, with great self-discipline, left quietly.

On the last evening in March, Marie retired to her chamber quite early after dinner. By prearrangement, Christopher followed her a few minutes later.

Marie's room was large and comfortable, with a four-poster bed and timbered walls. French windows opened onto a balcony. Christopher saw a very light snow beginning to fall. Not a howling arctic snow as in the Soviet Union, he found himself thinking, but a civilized, gentle English snow. A fire blazed in a sixteenth-century grate.

"Tea?" Marie asked. "Or brandy?"

"Tea, to start with," Christopher answered, settling into a Queen Anne chair.

Over the fire, Marie had a kettle on an old iron grid. She poured boiling water into a pair of sturdy Russian glasses, brewed tea and settled into a chair across from Christopher. "I suppose there is a lot you want to know," she said.

"Not such a lot, Alice," he said. "Just what will be useful." Her code name still felt strange upon his lips. But she insisted.

"When you're a woman of my years," she answered, "being useful is life's greatest challenge."

"Then you're meeting the challenge very successfully," Christopher countered, amazed at his own sense of diplomacy. Then she began.

Her memory was encyclopedic. She recounted her abduction by the Prussian mercenaries as well as every significant moment of her waking hours in captivity. She had made mental notes the entire time and was ready with them. She had observed and listened, her mind trained for the small detail. Christopher listened for about an hour and three cups of tea. Yet in the end, von Ostenberg and his captors had revealed little to Marie. Their only apparent slip had been to let her see diving equipment and overhear a few phrases in reference to an attack in Portsmouth harbor.

In the end, Creighton was very quiet. He asked a few questions out of a sense of obligation, but they led nowhere. Then there was an awkward moment when Christopher stared into Marie's eyes for several seconds, yet could bring himself to say nothing.

A slight smile came to her lips. She set aside her tea glass, then looked back to him. "I am reading your thoughts, Christopher," she warned.

"Are you?"

"You are not entirely convinced that I am who I say I am. So, logically, you are wondering how I could possibly have escaped from Russia. And from the Bolsheviks."

"Yes, ma'am," he affirmed with unshakable courtesy.

"Of course." She nodded. She shifted herself slightly in her chair and began. "The two sisters,

Dickie's mother and my mother, the Empress, were both grandchildren of Queen Victoria. So was the German Emperor Wilhelm II, better known as the Kaiser of World War I. Despite the war with Russia, cousin Willie was determined to bring our family to safety."

She drew a breath to steady herself. "In July of 1918, my family was imprisoned together in the Ipatiev house in Ekaterinburg. On a very warm night, the sixteenth-seventeenth I've always thought it was, we were separated for the first time."

For a moment, Marie's hand trembled. Christopher took it and held it tightly. She looked up and smiled. "In the cupboard there you'll find some brandy. If you care to bring it. And two glasses."

Christopher went to the cupboard. When he turned back, Marie was sitting on the hearth before the fire, half huddled against the brickwork. He poured two glasses and handed one to her.

"Thank you," she said.

He sat on the thick carpet near her. For a moment she held her glass to the fire to warm it. Christopher would no sooner have interrupted than he would have coughed during a great diva's finest aria.

"I was taken to Perm and held alone in a separate house. The conditions were hideous. Unsanitary lavatories. Crude, cartoonlike effigies on the walls, depicting my mother and Rasputin in filthy sexual embraces." She blinked her eyes fiercely. Her gaze

298

drifted to the decanter of brandy. "I tried to escape three times. I was always caught. The last time, the soldiers flogged me with a riding whip. They tried to rape me, but an officer pulled them away."

She motioned to the decanter and Christopher refreshed her glass. "Six weeks later," she continued, "in September 1918, two senior Bolshevik officers came to see me. They treated me with great courtesy and took me to Moscow. I asked about my sisters and my mother. They replied that they had orders to bring only me. In Moscow, I was taken to Georgy Chicherin, the Bolshevik commissar for foreign affairs. He protected me. Everyone suddenly treated me with great respect. I was given the best of everything. When I asked why I had been brought there and not my mother or my sisters, Chicherin said, 'Czar Nicholas is dead. You are the Empress of Russia. Before he died, your father named you as his successor.' He gave me a document, signed and sealed, he said, by my father He told me that Alexis had died with him. Both shot. Chicherin said he regretted it very much and that it had not been by his order."

Marie sipped her drink. Then, very suddenly, she moved to her feet. She stretched herself and walked to a cabinet, Christopher's eyes upon her the entire time. From a drawer she took a walnut case. She returned and sat down beside him.

"I don't know if you are aware," she said, "but in the Imperial Russian family it was not necessarily the eldest son or daughter who succeeded to the throne. It was whomever the Czar had nominated."

With a small gold key from around her neck, she opened the walnut case. From it, she took a rolled parchment and handed it to Christopher.

Against his best instincts, Creighton felt his flesh shiver as he examined the document. It appeared to be very old. It was in French, headed by the Great Seal of All the Russias. The signature purported to be that of Nicholas. The same handwriting named Marie Nikolayevna Empress.

"Thank you for letting me see it," Christopher finally said. He rolled up the parchment and placed it back in the walnut box. She relocked it, then slipped the key onto the chain around her neck.

"There's very little more," Marie said. "Under the name of Countess Czapska, I was taken to the Ukraine, which was an independent state. I was placed under the protection of the Volodar, the sovereign ruler, a White Russian named Prince Alexander Dolgorouky. I fell in love with his son, Prince Nicholas. We were married three months later in Bucharest. I used my proper name — Marie Nikolayevna Romanova — for the ceremony."

She sipped brandy again. "We had a child, a girl. Princess Olga Beata. She married Prince Don Basilio d'Anjou Durassow, head of the House of Naples. They had one child: Alexis. My grandson. The heir of Imperial Russia." She sighed. "My husband was killed at the end of the World War. What more is there?"

"A few things," he coaxed gently.

"Will you bleed my memories dry?" she asked softly. "You are a very curious, skeptical man, Captain Christopher."

He returned her gaze. "Forgive me," he said. "But I cannot serve you properly if I am not fully informed."

Marie calmed. "My sisters and mother escaped," she concluded. "My mother lived in Italy and died in a convent in 1946. Tatiana lived in Poland and disappeared when the war began. Olga is alive. She lived in Germany for a long time, protected by Prince Sigmund of Prussia, the Kaiser's nephew. Now she lives in Italy."

"And Anastasia?"

"She lives in America. In Chicago. Under the name of Anna Anderson."

"There's only one thing that doesn't logically follow," Christopher said. Marie waited. "With all due respect, I would have thought the Bolsheviks would have murdered the entire family immediately. Just as the world believed they did."

Again she smiled, this time broadly. "Never underestimate the slyness of a Russian, Red or White," Marie answered. "You make the same error that many Western politicians make."

"I'm sorry. I don't understand."

"Do you think Lenin was a foolish man? Do you believe him stupid?"

"Of course not."

"The deaths of my father and my brother destroyed the male lineage to the throne. But what would the deaths of a woman and a few girls accomplish? Nothing. We were ransomed, Captain Christopher. For gold bullion. The Kaiser had it and the new Bolshevik government needed it. A straight business deal," she said. "Remember that always when you deal with Russians. We are, above all, practical people." She let a moment pass and Christopher understood her final point. "And that's that, yes, Captain Christopher?"

He nodded. Marie started to push herself up. Christopher gave her his hand, helping her. "Again," he said, "I'm so very sorry to have intruded on—"

"Shhh," she said. She put her finger to his lips. "It's many years ago. Much of the pain is gone."

She raised her brandy glass. "To us, Captain Christopher. Long may we live to laugh together!"

They both drank. A mischievous glint came into Marie's eyes. She laughed, and the sound of her voice echoed very slightly across the timbers of the old room. Then she faced to the fire, lifted her glass and—

"Marie!" said Christopher sharply.

"Oh, Christopher!" she admonished, almost like a petulant child. "Be fair!"

He softened. "All right," he said. "Why not?" he stood beside her. They flung their crystal glasses over their shoulders and into the fire. There was a loud bang like a gunshot as the glasses exploded. The fire *whooshed* and raged for several seconds from the alcohol.

"Marvelous," she said, clapping her hands.

The door burst open. Angela stood in the doorway, concern all over her face. "Sir?" she said. "Are you both all right, sir?" Marie turned away, hiding a smile.

"It's all right, Angela," Christopher said.

Marie turned. "Angela, dear, I'm very sorry," Marie said. "We were having a toast. Somehow, some brandy landed in the fireplace, together with two glasses."

Angela looked at the fireplace anxiously, then at Christopher.

"Thank you for your concern, Angela. You were quite right to come and check."

But she held the door without closing it, ignoring her cue to depart.

"I was on my way, anyhow, sir," she said. "Signal for you. Urgent. No code name."

"No code? Who the hell else knows I'm here?"

"The Prime Minister, sir. He was on the telephone personally. Yelling at me." Angela looked shaken.

"What exactly did he yell?" Christopher asked, suddenly amused.

"You're to report to London right away, sir. Prime Minister's office. First thing tomorrow morning." The room was silent for a moment. The fire receded to its previous level. The walnut box sat on a side table. Then Angela concluded.

"He was furious, sir. Absoulutely furious."

Christopher inadvertently caught Marie's eye. Then, to Angela's astonishment, they burst out laughing.

TWENTY-ONE

"Did you enjoy yourself?"

"Sir?" Christopher asked.

"I said, Did you enjoy yourself?" Eden repeated. "I am referring here to the south of France."

It was three minutes past eleven o'clock on the morning of April 1. A perfect date, Christopher mused, to stand before the Prime Minister.

Eden sat at the large oval desk in the Cabinet Room. Christopher stood before him in uniform. "I'm not sure 'enjoy' is quite the word I'd use, sir."

Eden's temper was rising. "I have received reports, Hamilton, that someone other than SIS or MI6 engaged in an operation in France. There was bloodshed. The local police are furious, as is the government of Premier Guy Mollet." Eden paused angrily. "Naturally, I thought of your bloody section first. Am I correct?"

"You are, sir."

"Would you mind telling me exactly what the hell it was all about?"

"With respect, sir, you received a copy of my full report two weeks ago. Nothing has changed since then."

Eden's face twisted with menace. "Suppose you give me the report again. You. In person. Now."

Christopher explained again the rescue of Marie and Alexis, as well as the capture of Wilhelm von Ostenberg and two of his mercenaries. Then he told of Marie's report — still unconfirmed — of a potential attack by a diving unit. Here Eden was transfixed.

"And do your intelligence reports indicate that such an attack may be organized against the *Ordzhonikidze?*"

"The reports could be interpreted that way, sir."

"Oh, damn it! Yes or no?" he raged.

"Yes more than no, sir," Creighton answered.

Eden's face was crimson. "Good God, man!" he raged. "Can't you intelligence people ever act on something straightforward? Your sources indicate an attack on these ships when they come to Portsmouth and you're pissing around in France like a fairy!" His fists banged on the Cabinet table. "Your job is to make plans to guard those bloody Soviet hulls in English waters, not play cloak-and-dagger in France. Guard those hulls, damn you! Ring them! Don't let anything close to those hulls, and *don't you dare approach them yourself!* . . . Do . . . you . . . understand . . . that?"

Christopher could take very little more. "If I read

you correctly, sir, you are ordering me not to approach the Russian hulls, even though it may be necessary to defend them properly."

"You don't have to approach them to defend them, you bloody fool! Don't you understand simple military tactics? Form your defense in good army style *around* the ships. Don't go poking around under the hulls! That wouldn't defend a pussycat!"

Christopher considered reminding him that this was not a military operation, but a naval one — with intelligence considerations included. He restrained himself.

"And a final word to you, Captain Hamilton, and to your so-called 'elite' section. Again: not one word of these threats is to be given to the Russians or anyone else. Do you understand that?" He beat out the timing of his words on the desk before him. Clenched fists, both together. It was an absurd, frightening gesture. Christopher had seen it before: one of Adolph Hitler's favorite ways of emphasizing a point.

"And now this bloody interview is terminated," Eden said, his voice hoarse and barely above a whisper.

"Thank you, sir," replied Christopher. He rose, turned and walked across the room. His hand on the doorknob, he turned back. He eyed the tormented, pressured man at the desk and decided that yes, it was his responsibility to say exactly what was in his mind.

"When I joined secret intelligence, Prime Minister," he began as Eden's head shot up, "I took a solemn oath to do all in my power to protect the Sovereign and the United Kingdom. This included giving full advice and information to my superiors as appointed by the monarch. I give it to you now. If the Russians do not receive full information of these threats to their leaders and to their ships—and if I and my section are prohibited from approaching the Russian hulls in furtherance of protecting them—then the safety of the realm will hang upon a thread."

Eden was very still. Christopher waited ten seconds as it sank in. The time seemed like an eternity, and for part of it Christopher had no idea how Eden would respond. Then he saw. Eden's whole body began to shake. A visible sweat broke upon his forehead and poured off his temples. He leaped to his feet, his face incarnadine, and shook a frail fist at Creighton. "Get out of here!" he screamed at the top of his voice. "Get *out!*" It seemed to Christopher that the man was having a psychotic fit. At any moment he would jump over the Cabinet table and attack him.

But he didn't.

"No one's going to spoil this visit," Eden howled. "No one's going to get it canceled. Not you. Not anyone. It's the diplomatic coup of my life! Do . . . you . . . hear . . . me?" Saliva dribbled on the man's furious, quivering lips. Christopher stared at him in disbelief. "Now go on," Eden shrieked even

308

louder. "Fuck off out of here! Just fuck off!"

Figuratively, Christopher did just that, closing the door to the Cabinet Room quietly behind him.

Creighton was furious. He fumed all the way on the drive back to Birdham from London. Politicians and their petty vanity! Their arrogance! Their unquenchable thirst for self-aggrandizement! Why could they never listen to reason or let experts in the field carry out an operation?

He drove at a mad speed, using Jemima's car. Near Petersfield a strange sensation was upon him and he had the sense of being followed. He searched his rearview mirror and did in fact see a small brown Austin, which remained behind him for a stretch. But when Creighton slowed to allow the car to overtake him, it turned off and was gone.

Paranoia, he told himself. Another indication that all of his nerves were on edge, thanks largely to Eden's interference. He thought back to the American in Cannes who Christopher surely would have shot. He had to keep his nerves in check, he told himself again, and focus his suspicions upon the operation itself.

The bomb was at Waterloo Station. Popov had picked it up in Lambeth on Saturday morning. He'd packed it into a suitcase, stuffed with newspapers. There was the device itself, a long steel cylinder packed with TNT and with wires protruding from it like insect antennae. The timing device was a twenty-four hour clock, about half the size of a small transistor radio.

On Saturday evening, Popov reviewed the details he'd been given: the male officer used a flat in Northways. The female lived near Holland Park. She had a car, a red MG-TD.

Popov rented a brown Austin, paying two weeks' fee in advance. He prowled the areas of his two victims' living quarters, but didn't get lucky until Sunday morning. It was then, surveying the streets around Whitehall, that he happened to see a tall, fair-haired handsome man, with the clean-cut appearance of the Royal Navy, unlocking the MG and climbing in. Popov pulled his brown Austin to a halt. He let the MG pull away, then followed.

The red auto traveled to the A3 south toward Portsmouth, then steadily accelerated on the uncrowded road. It was just past noon on a cold Sunday. There were few cars.

Popov lurked about a half mile behind, dropping just back from sight whenever he pulled into view. Beyond Guildford, traffic increased. Popov felt himself much less conspicuous.

Again, he began to think. He recalled his victim's name: Peter Hamilton. He recalled his rank: captain R.N. He was concious of his pistol. Why not overtake the MG now, Popov thought. Get this over. Here was half the target. Alone. Vulnerable. More than likely unarmed.

Toward Petersfield, Popov drew closer. Yes, he told himself, that's what he would do. Force the MG from the road, shoot its occupant and be out of England within a few hours.

He fingered his weapon. It was loaded and ready. He closed in.

Then the MG drastically cut its speed. The brown Austin came within thirty feet. Then fifteen.

The MG had dropped its mph to less than twenty. Popov had to overtake it, which would have given the driver a perfect view of him. That, or he'd have to start shooting.

No, he told himself. His orders were to use the bomb.

Popov flicked on his left directional signal and veered away. The driver of the MG accelerated again and was gone.

Popov pulled the Austin to the side of the road. His shirt was soaked. So were his hands. He sat for a minute, breathing heavily, feeling his heart thump. Then he settled himself.

He backed the Austin and turned. He rejoined the A3 and pressed the accelerator. During one long stretch, he saw the MG again. Then, toward Cosham and Birdham, it suddenly disappeared from the road.

Popov followed the A3 to Portsmouth, gradually increasing his speed, but never seeing the MG again. He reasoned that wherever it had stopped, it was in the Birdham-Cosham area. Well, that wasn't such a bad bit of detective work for the day.

He returned to Cosham and checked into a bed and breakfast under the name on his forged passport, John Katrinien.

He settled into his room in the late afternoon. Conveniently, it overlooked the road.

TWENTY-TWO

One the evening of the same day, Christopher sat in the Birdham library with Jemima and Desmond Morton. After one hour of discussion, they were unanimous in their reaction. Christopher rang for Angela. She arrived with pad and pencil ready.

"Make to Charlemagne," said Christopher, "repeat to the Author. Do *not* repeat, I say again, do *not* repeat to the Prime Minister. Priority One. Most Secret, Immediate. Message reads . . ."

It was a long one. It recounted Eden's tirade and described his behavior. It recapped the situation at Birdham and took note of the advanced date. At the end, Christopher dictated a simple request. "Submit we take independent action," he said.

Angela departed. She put the signal on a transmission pattern that would take it around the globe. A heavy silence lingered in the room after she left. It was Desmond Morton who read Christopher's thoughts.

"That's what you had to do, Christopher," he finally said. "Don't be intimidated. You've done right by your job."

Christopher nodded. But it seemed almost ungodly to go above the Prime Minister's head.

The next morning, at 0832 hours, Angela brought in the reply. It read, in traditional naval terminology:

> *Yes, please. Charlemagne.*

Like most small towns, Cosham had its gossips. Popov tuned them in at a local pub. Down the road at Birdham, it seemed, some sort of Royal Navy secret intelligence unit had functioned during the war. According to a pair of men who held the bar up each evening, there'd been a significant amount of new activity there recently. Even an R.N. helicopter had choppity-chopped in a couple of times.

During daylight hours, Popov saw nothing to dispel those rumors. Every now and then a few young women in civilian clothing would appear at the local stores. They bought wine and provisions in quantities suited to something larger than the largest of families. Once they were accompanied by a woman in her fifties, which Popov couldn't figure out at all. He spent time in Portsmouth, only a few more miles down the A3, to try to catch another glimpse of either of his targets. But they were gone again, locked up, he assumed, at Birdham.

An hour before midnight on April 3, he returned to London. He retrieved his suitcase from Waterloo Station, then drove directly back to Cosham. He knew the end was near. Popov wanted to be ready.

In the days that followed, Christopher set a harsh routine. Interrogation increased upon von Ostenberg, often continuing into the night. Parallel to this, all units of the Section both in England and abroad tripled their tight surveillance and investigative duties. But no new developments came to light. And von Ostenberg proved a testy, recalcitrant witness.

Christopher broke away from Birdham and traveled to Portsmouth. There he supervised the setting of a defensive underwater ring around the eventual berthing positions of the Soviet ships. Section divers under the command of Lieutenant Commander Trott practiced laying their ring of steel in Portsmouth harbor. The ring could not actually be set in place until the Soviet ships had arrived, but Trott's divers could rehearse and make every preparation. Christopher kept an eye on Trott's men, dived with them several times and was pleased with Trott's command. Mountbatten,

Creighton decided, had probably been right about the man after all.

The ring of steel was an underwater version of the RG barrier that had earlier been set around HMS Birdham. The secret technology, which was currently in the hands of only the British and the Americans, had been refined considerably since the Second World War. Even underwater, the principle remained very simple.

RG lights, a form of infrared light invisible to the naked human eye, were strung out around the underwater area, linked to complementary sonar scanners. Any underwater movement, or any alien sound under the water, would be detected by the RG and sonar and trigger an electronic response at the control console. In this case, the console would be aboard *Victory* in the communications room. In the case of a defect, or in the case of tampering under the water, or an intruder trying to evade the "ring," the RG would trigger the signal without the sonar, and vice versa.

To put teeth behind the ring, Section divers stood by to plant underwater grenades which could be detonated at different depths by remote command. Christopher did not see how any diver could evade the ring. Experts from Vernon gave the ring's components every test over several days. Everything worked perfectly. Anyone approaching the Soviet hulls after the three ships had arrived and after the ring had been laid down would be easily detected and destroyed. Christopher could not imagine who would be foolish enough to even try.

Lionel Crabb raised the glass of gin and tonic to his lips, sipped and drew a deep breath. It was only lunchtime on Monday, April 9, but there was a large crowd at the Grove Tavern in Beauchamp Place, Knightsbridge. They were good listeners, this crowd. Crabb had regaled them with stories from the Sicilian campaign of 1943.

"But I'll tell you what's going to be the biggest yet," Crabb said. He spoke to the bartender and an assemblage of a half dozen strangers who found him entertaining. "This affair next Wednesday. With Krusch and Bulge visiting us from the Workers' Paradise. Well, I've got a little job to do that day they arrive. One thousand pounds. I'm going to get my feet wet. I'm going to take a little dekko underneath the *Ordzhonikidze*."

"Who for?" someone asked.

"CIA. The Admiralty. SIS," Crabb said, lowering his eyes modestly and booming the initials across the pub. "They're all working together on this. Need a top diver. Well, sir, Lionel Crabb is the *best* there is!"

"Who's Lionel Crabb?" asked one stranger, an American woman.

"I am!" Crabb raised his eyebrows. The barman laughed. Crabb banged his empty glass down on the counter. The barman filled it without charge. A few good characters like Crabb, he'd noticed, perked the place up at lunch. They brought people back. Who cared that he was half sloshed already and probably no one believed him?

"Last year I surveyed the hull of the *Sverdlov*," he started to tell the crowd. "Went looking for fancy new Russkie electronic equipment on the hull. Didn't find—"

Crabb stopped in midsentence and looked into the glare of Bernard Foster, the American.

"Crabbie, what in hell are you doing?" Foster spoke in a low voice. He was furious.

"Got to be quiet now," said Crabb to his new acquaintances. "This Yank friend of mine here is CIA. He's here to shut me up."

"Crabbie, let's go talk."

Foster took Crabb by the elbow and led him to an empty table. Two young women, both English, chatted at the only table close by. Foster checked them quickly. They didn't look like a threat.

"Crabbie, you're drunk."

"Yes, sir," Crabb said merrily. He lifted his glass to the American.

"You've got to stop popping off like this. The story's going to get around. It's not as if no one knows who you are, Crabbie."

"They *should* know who I am!" Crabb answered righteously. "Best diver in the world. Laid off by the Royal Navy."

"I want you to come with me," Foster said. "I want you to sober up. Then you have to look at some new equipment. You can use it for the dive."

"New diving gear?"

"Yes. And it will be yours to keep. It's got something new. An oxygen recycler so that there'll be no air bubbles."

Crabb grinned like a sodden gargoyle. He reached for his gin and tonic and finished it in one long gulp.

"I hope you enjoyed that," Foster said. "It will be your last for a while."

Crabb held the American in a long, critical glare. Foster was coy enough to defuse the moment. "Come on, Crabbie, you can do all the drinking you want once your assignment is finished. But for now you've got to learn your equipment. You're leaving for Portsmouth in a few days."

"Damn . . ." Crabb said, very drunk now.

"Come on," Foster said cordially. He helped his acquaintance up and pointed him toward the door. Crabb made it most of the way, but not without Foster's help.

The two Englishwomen sitting nearby paused for a moment. They watched the drunken war hero, then resumed their conversation. A pair of suburbanites in town for the evening, they appeared. Disdainful and slightly askance at the inebriated ex-sailor. Then Crabb was out the door.

Outside, in civilian clothes, two Royal Marine

lieutenants of Trott's squad covered Foster and Crabb until they disappeared back into the frogman's flat four blocks away. Simultaneously, the two Englishwomen, Wrens of the M Section, reported everything they had seen and heard to Communications HQ at Birdham. When they had finished, it was past midnight. The date was now April 10.

TWENTY-THREE

"So how does Crabb fit into all of this?" Jemima asked. She sat in the library at Birdham with Christopher, Angela, Morton and Trott. It was the evening of the eleventh.

Christopher turned to Sir Desmond. "He's been lurching all over Kensington telling people he has a job for one thousand pounds," Creighton said. Morton grimaced. "He thinks he's working for the CIA, the Admiralty and our Secret Intelligence Service."

"Good God," Morton snorted. "All at once?"

Christopher nodded. "He'll be disintegrated if he gets under those ships, of course," Creighton said.

"Could there be any element of truth to what Crabb thinks?"

Christopher nodded to Trott, who had the answer.

"In accordance with my orders yesterday," Trott said, "I checked with close personal contacts in SIS. Foster *is* in fact one of theirs. A new recruit from Trinity College, Oxford. He has degrees in both Russian and German. But they deny any knowledge of a diving operation."

"Well, someone is giving him money," Morton said. "I suppose that leaves the CIA. It's just the sort of half-wit stunt they'd try." He went to work on his pipe, squinted slightly and drew a bead on Christopher. "Did you quiz Charlemagne?" he inquired. "He has a direct line to Eisenhower. Plus, Foster is an American, after all."

"I just signalled to Mountbatten," Creighton answered. "But there's a problem."

"What?"

"You don't think Eisenhower knows every little game the CIA is playing, do you?"

Morton leaned back in his chair, plainly irritated. "No. Of course not," he said. "Eisenhower wouldn't know. And Allen Dulles doesn't like us, let alone trust us."

There was a long silence, which Christopher finally ended. "What about von Ostenberg?" he asked Morton. "Anything?"

Morton shook his head slowly. "He's softening," Sir Desmond said. "But he won't break. So there we are. Less than a week to go and we're nowhere."

***

On Friday morning the thirteenth at 1012 hours, Mountbatten's response from Washington was relayed to Birdham. Jemima brought it to Christopher, who was in the library. No: the White House knew of no operations by the CIA against the Soviet warships visiting England. Which proved, as the officers of the Section agreed, all of nothing.

Jemima sat for a moment with Christopher. Then there was a sharp rap on the door.

"Come in!" Christopher shouted.

Colonel Sainthill, returned from France, appeared in the doorway. He grinned joyously and carried a large bag on his shoulder.

Christopher and Jemima looked up abruptly. "Hullo, Tim," she said, eyeing the bag in surprise. "What's the swag?"

"Our solution, maybe," Sainthill said. He motioned to a chair. "May I?"

"You know bloody well you can sit down," answered Christopher. "What's in the bag?"

"We did some digging at Ybor-les-Pins," said Sainthill. "About a hundred yards from the house, we found these."

From the bag he pulled a diving suit and a limpet mine. "A present for you both on this Friday the thirteenth."

Christopher froze as he saw them. "British Sladen shallow water diving suit," he said.

"Yes," nodded Sainthill. "We uncovered six of them."

Christopher was looking at the mine. "And that's a United States Navy mine. No name yet, but it's coded CG2."

"We found seventeen of them, sir," reported Sainthill.

Christopher whistled.

"Here," said Sainthill. "It's defused."

Christopher took the mine respectfully and turned it in his hands. As Crabb had once taught him, he assumed any limpet mine was live until he saw for himself that it wasn't. As he examined it, many impulses rushed at him. Involuntarily, he saw Crabb many years ago, teaching him to dive, to disarm and to remove limpet mines from a ship's hull. Then, as suspicion raced up upon him, he saw Eden and recalled the Prime Minister's hysterical admonition.

Can't you intelligence people ever act on something straightforward! This was straightforward. Too much so.

Sainthill looked crestfallen. Somehow his commander didn't appear to share his enthusiasm for his discovery.

"Angela!" Christopher bellowed. His steward appeared. "Get Sir Desmond and Commander Trott in here right away." He turned to Sainthill. "Tim, you stay. You've done very well, but I think it's

324

time to look at this from an entirely different angle."

Quickly, within five minutes, Christopher's audience was assembled. He firmly held court. He reviewed all developments since the operation began, then ordered Angela to make a signal to Mountbatten reporting discovery of the limpets. Then Christopher changed gears.

"I'm starting to find everything a bit too convenient," Christopher said. "Everything points in the same direction: an attack on the Soviet vessels in Portsmouth harbor. There is not one dissenting whisper in any other direction. Marie warned Mountbatten of an attack. Later she 'happened' to see diving gear. Now we raid a mercenary camp in France and we find our mines. It's as if we're being cleverly manipulated," Creighton said. "But what if there is *not* to be an attack in Portsmouth harbor? What better way to have us chasing our own tail than to convince us of the former?"

Christopher scanned the four faces before him Sir Desmond looked particularly troubled. "We've been concentrating principal Section resources against one form of attack," said Christopher. "If the assassins have chosen another, we are presiding over one of the biggest screwups in intelligence history."

Hush reigned in the room. Finally Morton spoke. "What are you leading to, Christopher?"

"We have to know what we're up against. The

325

baron knows. We have to break him." Morton scowled very slightly, but obviously agreed. "What's that doctor's name?"

"Rawlins," Morton answered. "Robert Rawlins."

"What's his procedure?"

"It's called 'narcosis,'" Morton explained. "A psychiatric procedure. Not very pleasant. It involves a drug called Pentothal. Alternating doses of shock and pain. Physical and psychological."

"And it will make him talk?"

"If it doesn't kill him first. But Rawlins is good with it. I've seen him work."

"Call him," ordered Christopher. "We can't wait any longer."

There was a soft, familiar tap on the door. "Come in, Angela!" Creighton called. He was grateful for the interruption.

"A signal for you, sir," she said, entering.

"Read it, please."

"'Confirm arrival in U.K. Saturday, 14 April,'" she read. "'Reserving Monday April 16 for you. Meet at Keppel's Head, Portsmouth. Midday. Nasdorovie.' It's signed, 'Ivan Groznyi.'"

Jemima couldn't fight back a smile.

"Who?" asked Morton.

"'Ivan the Terrible,'" answered Jemima.

"In other words, bloody Serov," said Christopher.

***

326

Surgeon Commander Robert Rawlins injected Pentothal into a vein in von Ostenberg's left arm at 1513 that afternoon. The baron was held down by two sick-bay attendants. A Queen Alexandra Royal Navy nursing sister was also in attendance, as were Colonel Sainthill and Lieutenant Commander Trott as Section witnesses.

Von Ostenberg struggled very slightly. Then, in a matter of minutes, he fell into a deep coma.

"I gave him a relaxant as well," said Rawlins. "That's why he's gone off so quickly."

Rawlins was tall, youngish, with blond hair and a firm build. He had brown eyes and a quiet confidence. Christopher took some time to walk on the Birdham lawn with him after the Pentothal had been administered. He found Rawlins to have a thorough grasp of what he was doing.

"He's in a half sleep now," Rawlins explained. "It will last about five days. During that time, I'll handle the interrogation. I'll be looking for his secrets, his worries, his fears." Rawlins walked with his arms folded behind him. The grass was wet, and as they walked Christopher saw the cold moisture gathering from the grass onto their shoes.

"When can we start?" Christopher asked.

"Possibly this evening. But tomorrow morning would be better. Much depends on the skill with which the questions are posed. I want every bit of information you have on this man."

"Everything is in the library. You'll have to sign the Official Secrets form."

"Yes. Of course." Rawlins stopped walking long enough to pull out a pack of cigarettes and light one. "During the interrogation, another person might be able to assist. I'd suggest at least one officer present who speaks German. The patient will probably start rambling in his own tongue."

"First Officer James is fluent," said Christopher. "She'll stand by."

The doctor nodded. "The patient will be able to walk, wash and go to the head. I don't think he should be trusted with a razor, however. There's a potential for violence, or extreme depression."

They continued to walk. "I also know the interrogators usually get what they're looking for within the five days," Christopher said.

The men walked together for another few minutes, turning back toward the manor.

"Very few people have ever managed to resist this drug," Rawlins said. "Very few. In the hands of a skilled interrogator, it's virtually infallible."

"Sounds like you've been reasonably successful with it," Christopher allowed.

Rawlins took it as an affront. "Captain Hamilton," he said, "I've never failed yet."

At 0815 the next morning, Saturday the fourteenth, Surgeon Commander Rawlins began the interrogation of Wilhelm von Ostenberg. In the room were a nurse and Captain Peter Hawkins, a Royal Marine. Von Ostenberg sat in an armchair smoking a small cigar offered to him by Rawlins. Rawlins smoked also and everyone present sipped coffee.

Rawlins' methods were slow and unhurried. He spent two hours taking the baron through his early life, ages five to about twenty. There were no hesitations. At one point, von Ostenberg continued on for about forty-five minutes without stopping.

"I did my university at Heidelberg," von Ostenberg said. Then he smiled. "A Prussian in slobby, messy, backward Bavaria." He laughed. "I soon showed them." He lapsed into silence and stared at Rawlins, who looked up.

"How did you show them, Wilhelm?" Rawlins asked.

Proudly he answered, "I married their most beautiful woman, my Tania." Rawlins dwelt upon the silence and let von Ostenberg speak. "She preferred a Prussian to her undisciplined brethren from the south."

"I see," said Rawlins. Patiently, he continued on, hour after hour. Eventually they arrived at World War II and von Ostenberg's promotion to the SS. By then it was noon.

Four miles away, Comrade General Ivan Alexandrovich Serov arrived in Portsmouth via a fast RN patrol boat that had kept a rendezvous with a Soviet submarine. Serov brought with him a considerable and unexpected retinue. Among them, seven Moscow-trained hoods, his own weight-lifting team, it appeared. Trott and some of his sharpshooters, male and female, met Serov on Christopher's behalf. Trott was to protect the Russian, as well as keep a close watch on him. Anything Serov did or said was to be reported back.

Then Trott introduced Serov to Colonel William Burt, head of the Special Branch, and they all went together to the Chief Constable, Mr. A. C. West, in the Portsmouth Guildhall. Serov made a brief scene, refusing to drink a toast until full security arrangements for Wednesday had been explained. West obliged, detailing not only harbor security but also the actions to be taken by the Portsmouth police along the route the Soviet delegation would take to and from the railroad depot. They would travel to and from London by train.

Then they all went to lunch at the Keppel's Head. Trott was invited also and it soon fell to him to explain the ring of steel that was to be established around the Soviet ships when they were berthed in Portsmouth. Serov approved enthusiastically, insisting only that the ring be operational immediately after the Soviet ships arrived. That,

Trott assured him, was the plan.

By 1640 hours that same afternoon, Rawlins had brought von Ostenberg through to the present time. Von Ostenberg's voice was clinical, self-assured and unwavering. He behaved like a man in a very light trance.

He described the last days of Berlin, as well as the capture, rape and execution of his wife, Tania. This he related with no apparent feeling at all. He went on to describe his postwar life, leading up to the present operation. Here he asked for more coffee, which he was given, but refused to talk of the Grand Duchess or the visiting Russian ships.

There was a glass slit in the wall for observation. Christopher watched through it. A microphone in the corner of von Ostenberg's chamber carried his voice to both Christopher and a marine who manned a tape recorder. When Jemima joined Christopher, Rawlins saw them both. He waved to them, indicating that they could come in. Only Jemima did.

Jemima sat down on a straight-backed chair. Von Ostenberg's trance remained light. He could see that a young woman had entered the room, but until Dr. Rawlins gave permission, his senses would not fully confirm that she was there. Yet he continued to squint in her direction as he sat on

331

his bed.

Intrigued, Rawlins followed with the opportunity. "Has someone joined us, Baron von Ostenberg?" the doctor asked.

"A young woman," the German said. "In uniform."

"You may speak to her," said Rawlins.

The light was intentionally dim: Rawlins worked in twilights of all sorts. As Jemima leaned forward to pour coffee, von Ostenberg stared at her. "Why do you wear that strange uniform?" he asked, still speaking in German.

"It is a British uniform, Herr Baron," she answered.

"But *why?*" he pressed.

Von Ostenberg strained and stared at her. His disorientation was obvious. "You mean that you *escaped?*" he asked.

For a moment the entire room was frozen. Jemima looked at Rawlins. Then von Ostenberg broke the spell himself.

"No," he said, looking away, "I was mistaken. You are not my Tania. My Tania would come to me in pearls and her favorite black dress. You are not she."

"Baron . . ." Rawlins tried gently. But it was too late. The prisoner lapsed, lost consciousness and was gone.

***

Very distantly, Popov had a premonition of trouble when he saw the local constable's car roll to a halt in front of the bed and breakfast in Cosham. Popov sat where he often did, in the downstairs reading room. He favored one particular chair, which allowed him a view of both the entrance and the road.

As the local policeman walked to the front door, Popov was conscious of the loaded revolver beneath his coat. He saw that the policeman was unarmed. He was relieved, though he knew that if real trouble started, he would have to kill the constable and the innkeeper before leaving.

The policeman came to the front desk and rang a bell. He glanced at the reading room. His eyes met Popov's. Popov nodded and the policeman gave him a slight smile.

The innkeeper appeared from his own quarters. "Hello, Tom," he said to the constable. "What brings you around?"

Popov couldn't hear the conversation. A sweat began to break on his temples. The inn's owner, he recalled, had a wife in the back. Plus two children.

Popov looked back down into his book. His right hand was ready to move for the pistol. *And the wife?* he asked himself again. *And the children?* Yes, they would all die.

From the corner of his eye, Popov saw the policeman scanning the register. The owner spoke openly. "I've got only two guests right now," he said. "An American couple who are sightseeing, and Mr. Katrinien over there."

Popov's right hand was on the revolver. His finger slid onto the trigger. It would just take a few more seconds, he guessed.

The constable looked at Popov again. Popov hearing his alias said aloud, looked up also. For the second time, Popov's eyes met the policeman's.

The constable's eyes sparkled and he grinned. "Mr. Katrinien, sir," he said aloud. "Your name isn't really Meglov, is it? A man wanted for murder!"

The innkeeper chuckled.

"No. I'm afraid that's not me," Popov answered.

The constable looked back to the register, scanning previous days' guests. "Good thing for both of us," the cop concluded. He pushed the book back across the desk. "Well, I did my job. Nothing much ever happens out here anyway."

Popov looked back down to his book. The constable excused himself and returned to his car. The assassin was conscious of his palm, hard upon the revolver, soaking with sweat as the police car pulled away.

Four hours later, and two miles down the road,

Popov's designated victims concluded another fruitless interrogation session with Von Ostenberg. Even Rawlins was now conceding that the baron had proven to be difficult. The German's will-power was enormous. Rawlins could normally lead a narcosis subject around to any point of view he wished. The baron, however, still believed only what he wanted to believe.

It was late Saturday evening before the Russians' Wednesday morning arrival. The tension upon Christopher became palpable. He yearned to break it some way, and suddenly longed for the ornery musicians in his jazz quartet in New York. He wondered how they had adjusted to his disappearance. Just fine, probably, he concluded. But he would have loved a session with a piano. Anything to relieve the pressures of command.

It was Jemima who read his thoughts and came up with the solution. Sunday would be quiet, and von Ostenberg was now in Rawlins' hands. The Royal Navy Sailing Association kept two yachts in Portsmouth. Why not take a Sunday sail, she suggested. He could reconnoiter the harbor at the same time.

"Bloody wonderful idea," Christopher responded. Marie even offered to pack them a lunch.

There was only one final wrinkle, reported shortly before midnight.

Crabb had reappeared earlier in London to do

an evening of drinking and boasting that was heavy even by his standards. And all the time, the little frogman had been bragging about his impending trip to Portsmouth.

"Going to have me the dive of a lifetime," Crabbie had told anyone who'd listen, including several members of one of Trott's surveillance teams.

Angrily, Christopher doubled the surveillance on both Crabb and the elusive American, Foster. He could not conceive of Crabb actually sabotaging ships in an English harbor. He knew Crabb too well. So then, what *was* his role? Or what did the little diver *think* he was doing?

Christopher went to bed shortly before one. He had a genuinely lousy night's sleep.

TWENTY-FOUR

At 0800 the next morning, Jemima and Christopher left Birdham in the red MG. They parked the car in the dockyard, crossed to Dolphin in the Captain's barge, and walked to the submarine slips at Haslar Creek.

They arrived at a deserted piece of backwater. There were several yachts moored to stanchions. "So where is this bloody boat?" Christopher finally asked.

A moment later a female voice called out, "Hello, ma'am!" Christopher turned. Angela stood with Joan and Caroline, Jemima's Wren operational officers, aboard a fifty-three-foot Bermudan sloop.

"That's it there," she said. *Seabird.*"

"Bloody big dinghy."

"Come on," Jemima said, taking his hand and pulling him along. "If you dare."

Jemima and her Wrens soon had the *Seabird*

337

under way. As they emerged from Haslar Creek, they turned to port and slowly circled the harbor.

Christopher looked about him. He knew this harbor as well as any man alive—from the submarines, aboard which he had arrived and departed at Dolphin during the World War, to the steam gun and motor torpedo boats at Hornet, which had delivered him to Haslar Royal Navy Hospital, where doctors had removed his appendix. He had assisted in charting sections of the harbor for the hydrographer of the Navy. Finally, in early 1944, he'd learned a bucketful more about these waters when helping find temporary moorings for Churchill's "Mulberries," the great concrete hulks invented to be sunk into position off the beaches of Normandy, where they served as makeshift harbors. All this passed through his mind. It was familiar and reassuring. What bothered Christopher on a peaceful Sunday morning was the unpredictable.

Somewhere here very soon, assassins would launch themselves against Krushchev and the Soviet ships. They were looking for a gap in security. But where was it?

Seabird turned one-hundred-eighty degrees to starboard and sailed toward the harbor entrance. Jemima and her Wrends hoisted sail. The force-four breeze from the northwest filled the canvas and swept the yacht along at a good eight knots. The burgee of the Royal Naval Association flew at the masthead and the blue ensign flew at the stern.

338

Seabird cleared the harbor between Vernon and Fort Blockhouse.

They looked up at the great stone bastion. In fewer than seventy-two hours the Soviet cruiser *Ordzhonikidze* and her two escorting destroyers would enter Portsmouth harbor between these two distinctive marks, carrying Krushchev and Bulganin. Would the trip be a footnote to history, or one of the dark turning points?

The *Seabird* proceeded to sea. Caroline relieved Jemima at the helm. Christopher used a pair of powerful binoculars to scan the water, the shoreline and the other ships, searching for anything out of the ordinary. But he saw nothing that evoked the slightest suspicion.

He sat back comfortably in the yacht's cockpit. Jemima's conditions for taking him aboard the *Seabird* had been clear and concise. "You are to forgo rank, offer no nautical suggestions, mind your own business and shut up."

"Yes, ma'am," he'd gratefully concurred.

Now he turned his attention back to the Wrens. Why, he wondered, didn't the Royal Navy give more credit to their Wrens? The women were terrific sailors. Christopher would have stood up to any commodore or warrant office in any pub in the English-speaking world and proclaimed that belief. Better, Christopher decided as a bracing wind hit him in the face, women were naturally more gifted as sailors than men. They were quick and obedient;

339

they had a better respect for the ocean than men. They didn't fuss or panic, they were clear and concise with orders, both giving and receiving. They were fine navigators and seamen. And above all, he thought as he turned his binoculars back to the shoreline, they were women and usually fun.

The *Seabird* and its crew caused a sensation as they came alongside in Cowes in the lee of The Royal Yacht Squadron Building. Dressed all alike in matelot rig, the Wrens turned every male head. But when Christopher, Jemima and her crew came ashore, they remained together, heading for the Ram in Thicket, Angela's favourite pub, though this didn't stop some of the lusties from giving pursuit; on entering the pub, the girls were entirely surrounded. Christopher even lost Jemima to a frighteningly handsome Lieutenant, who must have been six years Christopher's junior.

Christopher sighed. He gave up trying to buy drinks for them and settled on getting one for himself — a pint of Worthington. He was just taking a big gulp as Jemima reappeared.

"How did you get away?" he asked her.

"Easy," she replied. "I told him I was a First Officer and thus too old and sexless for him. He didn't believe me, so I showed him my ID. He backed off, very worried."

"Oh," said Christopher, nonchalantly. "What are you having?"

"I've no idea what old First Officers have in

340

pubs."

"Old First Officers are not supposed to *be* in pubs. They're supposed to be in the old Wrens Home."

Jemima pinched him and he jumped. "I want a Worthington, too," she said. "And chop, chop."

Christopher caught the barman's eye. "Another Worthington, please — pint."

"Tons of fun," she announced, when she finally got her beer and drank half of it in one gulp. "Blimey," she said, when she got her breath back.

Angela and Caroline, meanwhile, had found male friends too. They returned to *Seabird*, where Angela and Caroline broke out the lunch prepared by Marie: cold roast beef, roast pork, salad, soup from thermos flasks, bread and butter, Stilton and Cheshire cheese and Marie's specialty, Malenkoff cake. Accidentally, Jemima revealed Christopher's rank, which inhibited conversation for at least a quarter hour.

"Oh bugger," Christopher finally said. "This is a bloody holiday. Anyone calling me 'sir' gets thrown overboard."

"*Yes, sir!*" cried out the three Wrens and two RN officers in unison. Then the boat rocked with laughter.

The two young officers joined the auxiliary crew to Yarmouth. As they set sail and glided away from the harbor, the wind was against them. But as they proceeded, the tide was setting westward and tack-

341

ing was speedy.

The trip was smooth. The *Seabird* sailed at an even, leisurely pace. Eventually, the tricky entrance to Yarmouth harbor loomed ahead.

"Why don't you enter on your auxiliary engine?" Christopher suggested.

"Why don't you," Jemima responded with unflinching courtesy, "break out a pint of bitter from down below and get snookered. We're sailing in."

"Aye, aye, ma'am," Christopher answered.

He stayed on the deck to watch. He vowed to keep his mouth firmly shut. Jemima set the approach perfectly. Then, at her quick order, the yacht swung swiftly around to port. It took a southeast course, cutting across the tide diagonally and setting on a broad reach. The sheets were quickly paid out. Christopher saw some luffing, but said nothing. It would probably have been the same had he been the skipper. She was now moving toward the harbor entrance, crab fashion, almost sideways. Jemima watched the flow of the sea. She had to decide when the eastern wall of the harbor broke the flow of the tide upon *Seabird's* hull. Angela took the wheel. Jemima stood on the gunwale and watched the waves striking her boat. She waited. If she missed the right moment, the yacht would gather too much speed and smash on the eastern promontory of the harbor.

She still waited. Christopher felt the wind and the speed of the ship. "Jesus Christ," he thought to himself. "Too fast! Much too fast!" He stood. A beautiful day was now certain to end in catastrophe. The ship increased speed even more.

"Hard-a-starboard," ordered Jemima suddenly.

"Hard-a-starboard," acknowledged Angela, and she swung the wheel hard over.

"Steady."

"Steady, ma'am," said Angela and reported the ship's head. "One seventy-five."

"Thank you," acknowledged Jemima. She heaved in on the headsail sheet as the wind came in tighter from starboard. The yacht fairly raced into Yarmouth harbor.

Jemima checked across both beams to ensure she was clear and then conned her boat to starboard, down the clear water between the mooring posts and dead into the wind.

"And strike," she said.

The mainsail swept down the mast. Joan and Caroline gathered it in. Jemima hauled down the headsail, and *Seabird* hove to in the gentle protected waters.

"Bloody marvelous," Christopher thought to himself, managing at the last moment to keep silent. He sat down. He refused to wreck the moment by congratulating anyone.

After tea, Jemima revealed the rest of the itinerary. Caroline and Angela had to be back at Section headquarters in Portsmouth by evening. Both were on duty. Their male friends had to return to Portsmouth also. But Jemima had seen to everything. She had already arranged for a navy pinnace to be waiting at Yarmouth to return the crew to *Victory*.

"And what about *Seabird?*" Christopher asked when they were alone.

"We," she said, "will bring it back when the tide changes."

"That's seven thirty-two this evening," he said.

"That's not the tide I had in mind."

He arched an eyebrow. "No?" he asked.

"We're due to meet Serov tomorrow at midday. There's no point going all the way to Birdham and back. We take the tide tomorrow morning at eight-o-five. We'll be in Portsmouth by nine-thirty. We can have breakfast and showers in Victory III."

"Nice scheme. But you forgot about our gear."

"Not at all. I had it sent to Victory."

He looked at her for several seconds. "So in other words, we're all alone tonight on the *Seabird*. No one's coming back and no one will bother us until tomorrow morning, when we set sail?"

"I knew you'd understand eventually," she said.

He thought about it and began to laugh. "Any wooden owls aboard? Concealing Section telephones?"

"None," she said.

"Marvelous." He took her in his arms and kissed her.

During the afternoon, using a fold-up telescope much like one Admiral Nelson had once used, Popov had kept *Seabird* in view from Portsmouth to Cowes. He drove along the road close to the coastline. The assassin had an easy time marking *Seabird's* course on to Yarmouth. It was late afternoon when he pulled into that town, himself.

Then it was just a matter of time. He left the bomb in his Austin and ensconced himself at The Mermaid pub at the edge of the harbor. From there he could see the R.N.S.A. yacht perfectly.

If Popov was nothing else, he was a patient man. And the death of Khrushchev was something well worth waiting for. Waiting, that meant, for just the right moment. With the deaths of Peter Hamilton and Jemima James, security around Khrushchev would suffer a fatal blow four days before the arrival of the Soviet vessels. Recovery would be impossible.

Popov couldn't help himself. At the bar of The Mermaid he ordered a vodka and silently toasted the death of the fat little Ukrainian dictator.

Jemima and Christopher went for dinner at The Bell in Yarmouth. They enjoyed lobster thermidor followed by jugged hare. They drank the best champagne the pub could provide, Dom Perignon '52. It was extravagant, yet was one of those moments in a relationship when only mad extravagance would do.

The day had been magnificent, a gorgeous Sunday of sailing and socializing. And upon the waters beyond Portsmouth, Christopher had seen nothing to contribute to his apprehensions. Maybe, a second voice within him began to say, maybe things *would* go smoothly. Maybe all danger to the Soviets *had* been averted.

After dinner, they walked hand in hand around the almost deserted yacht basin and looked across the Solent at the lights of Lymington. They walked back around the harbor to where they had left the dinghy. They stepped in gently, cast off and sculled back to *Seabird*. The yacht stood out in a gaunt silhouette before the fading light to westward.

They had brandy aboard. Jemima had stashed it below in the bilges against her thirsty Royal Navy boarders. Now she broke it out. She poured and Christopher leaned back against the seat cushions, facing each other athwart the main cabin. They said nothing, their hearts full.

Within minutes, they were together in the quarter berth, the only berth of any size in the boat. Even so, it was only thirty inches across. But they were happy, blissfully so, wound around each other with nothing to separate them. Their lovemaking was a strange, exotic mixture of friendship, romance, respect and outrageous eroticism. And then that night it was predominantly love. Beautiful, overwhelming and true.

For a short time afterward, Christopher dozed

off. Then he awoke and felt her breathing in the same cadence as he. But as his eyes became adjusted to the dark, he saw that she was awake, staring ahead. Her eyes were moist, as if with tears.

"Jemima," he said, placing a hand on one of hers. "Penny for your thoughts."

She turned to him and answered, holding back none of what she felt. "I love you," she said. When he didn't answer, she continued. "And I'm scared to death that one of us is going to be killed."

TWENTY-FIVE

Spring always came late to Leningrad.

The official Party line had it that winter was supposed to conclude by the tenth of April. But so far, the mornings had never been colder, the Gulf of Finland had never been darker and the sky had never held for so long such a clammy shade of gray. Three million people in the old capital city and, despite the commotion in the harbor, every one was in a miserable mood. There was a joke circulating: when Khrushchev and Bulganin arrived they would find the mood of the city to be distinctly anti-Leninist. All three million inhabitants would thus be packed into a single trans-Siberian freight car bound for Yakutsk. That wouldn't be so bad, the line went, except that there was a stop planned for Archangel, where another five-hundred-thousand prisoners would be picked up.

In the bars, in private apartments and among informal vodka troikas in the public parks on cold afternoons, the joke brought wry smiles to the lips of ordinary Russians. Then again, in the Baltic north, Ukrainians had always been perceived as thieves and murders. So what really could be expected of Khrushchev and Bulganin?

Maybe it was just the rumors that had set the city on edge. But word had it that something big was about to happen. Aside from the brief passing of Khrushchev and Bulganin through the city. The rumors had been traced to the Navy Yard, Kronstadt, where the first rebellions against the Czar took place. Kronstadt, after all, was the center of all activity.

On Friday the thirteenth of April there were still chunks of ice the size of petroleum cars floating in Leningrad harbor. But on Saturday the fourteenth a legion of Soviet sailors, much to the amusement of those watching from shore, had set about the chunks with small charges of dynamite, blowing them into small cubes. That cleared the harbor. Naval divers in wet suits appeared and apparently completed the underwater security arrangements. Then came Sunday.

Much of the city turned out that morning to see the two sleek, gleaming gray pearls of the Soviet Navy that glided into Leningrad harbor and took up a position at the entrance to the port. They were the two Petrov-class destroyers, the *Sovershenny* and the *Smotryashchi*. But then the army took up positions around the piers and the workers of the city were told to keep their distance. Small explosions continued to crackle for another day, however, as the ice in the harbor attempted to reform.

The cruiser *Ordzhonikidze* arrived Sunday afternoon just before dusk, fresh from the Baltic Sea east of Denmark, where the ice was less of a problem. That same evening, frogmen again entered the water. Their official orders were to search the hull of the *Ordzhonikidze* and the floor of the harbor. After three hours, they pronounced it secure. Floodlights now were aimed at the water around the *Ordzhonikidze* and smaller Soviet ships watched the harbor's entrance. Even though Serov's people were in charge of security. Khrushchev had given extra instructions: there was to be no chance of *anything* happening to these ships. The three Soviet vessels were to be impeccable when they glided into Portsmouth.

Khrushchev and his entourage had arrived by train at 1845 that evening, completing a long journey from Moscow, a thousand miles to the south. An armada of black Volga limousines guided the Soviet delegation to the piers. Most prominent, aside from Prime Minister Bulganin and First Secretary Khrushchev, was Igor Kurchatov, the father of the Soviet atomic weapons system, and Khrushchev's wife and son. The party spent the night of the fifteenth aboard the cruiser.

The next morning, Monday the sixteenth of April, Khrushchev and Bulganin appeared on the bridge of the ship. Miraculously, the weather had cleared. It was bitterly cold, but sunny. Bulganin was the taller of the two men, trim, silver-maned and neatly bearded. He looked like what he was: a career Soviet diplomat. By contrast, Khrushchev was half a head shorter than Bulganin when the two men stood side by side. Next to Bulganin, and in the midst of the uniformed Soviet naval officers, Khrushchev looked oafish and clumsy. He wore a traditional Russian fur cap, which rested upon his proletarian head like a cylindrical, black tea cozy. His leather greatcoat was brown and bulky. From the shore, he looked ridiculous compared to men of physically better stature. But anyone close enough would have known better than to draw such a foolish conclusion. Khrushchev was on the bridge to watch the departure as well as assure himself that the proper Army and Navy people had been in the positions he'd asked Serov to assign to them. A head of government could never be too careful, even in his own country. Khrushchev's eyes on this bright morning were squinting, with dark specks the color of Ukrainian coal peering through the slits.

At 0800, Captain Josep Zoltov, the commanding officer of the *Ordzhonikidze*, gave a signal to his chief navigational officer. The cruiser's horn blasted twice. Moments later the ship lurched from its berth, Khrushchev still on the bridge with Bulganin and six senior officers of the ship. Then the ship moved resolutely and the city of Leningrad seemed to slip away from it. Outside the harbor, the *Sovershenny* and the *Smotryashchi* allowed the *Ordzhonikidze* to settle on her westward course to the Baltic, and thence south and west and north to the Skagerrak, and finally, due southwest toward Portsmouth. The two destroyers followed, taking up station-five cables on each of the cruiser's quarters. An hour later, a force of sixteen Soviet warships completed the escort.

It was a heady experience for Khrushchev. Despite the bitterness of the Baltic wind, he emerged on the bridge again several times that morning, to watch his flotilla and marvel at the smooth movement of his vessel through the choppy water. He liked to think of himself as the most powerful man in the world, just as Stalin had been. And now this whole flotilla was for him! He was pleased with his safe departure from the Soviet Union, just as he was pleased with himself. He had enemies, he told himself, anti-State people who bedeviled every leader. But in April of 1956, he gloated, they were all on the run.

He confirmed again with Admiral Litvinov that they would rendezvous with ships of the British Royal Navy in another thirty hours in a position to the southwest of the Skagerrak, in the North Sea. Then Khrushchev sat down to breakfast.

Accompanied by his family, the other diplomats and guests in the delegation, Khrushchev fed indulgently on pressed duck, smoked salmon, caviar, fresh bread, beets, potatoes and vodka. It was a meal, the First Secretary of the Communist Party noted with amusement, fit for a Czar.

As the Soviet warships proceeded on their passage to England, Khrushchev glanced at his watch. It was 0825 hours.

At precisely that moment, another ship turned eastward and proceeded toward the same destination. Both ships headed together toward Portsmouth.

That other ship, the *Seabird*, flying the Blue Ensign of Her Majesty's Fleet, fairly hurtled up the Solent toward Portsmouth under mainsail and spinnaker. A fair wind persisted, at force 4 to 5 on the Beaufort scale, with the tide setting eastward at three knots. At times the yacht rose up on the waves, especially over the shallows, and started to surf. A cast of the log registered a speed through the water of some twelve to fourteen knots, an "effective speed" over the seabed of almost eighteen knots. It was an exhilarating passage. The weather held fair, with a bright sun in the early morning. Then, quite suddenly, the humidity rose, the glass fell and heavy clouds loomed.

Reaching the harbor approach buoy off Spithead, they turned north for Portsmouth harbor. As the sheets were hauled in, *Seabird* heeled over and settled on a broad port reach. It seemed they might escape the coming storm.

They came abreast the Portsmouth SW market buoy. A blinding sheet of lightning flashed across the clouds, illuminating the dark harbor. Then the rain began to lash the boat and they knew they wouldn't escape the storm.

Another bolt struck somewhere around them. It seemed to travel across the quarterdeck of *Victory,* standing high up in its dock at the naval base. A crash of thunder followed and it appeared as if *Victory* had fired a broadside. The storm increased. They were the only ship moving through the harbor. Lightning flared out across the water above Whale Island. Then the thunder crashed again. It was as if a great naval battle were being fought in the middle of Portsmouth harbor.

A terrible fear crept into Christopher. In his mind's eye he saw the three Russian vessels, and with the thunder and lightning it appeared that they, too, had opened fire.

At least four bolts of lightning cracked across the Royal Navy base, followed by thunder that nearly burst his eardrums. Then all was silent and still, except for the rain, which poured, poured and poured.

It soaked him to the skin. It soaked Jemima as thoroughly. Then they looked through the rain. *Victory* was still there, proud and unscathed amid the violent storm.

Jemima took his arm and squeezed for a moment. The rain poured down like a monsoon. Then it happened.

There was another flash and a roll of thunder more devastating than any before. Their entire world blew apart.

Christopher was aware of standing next to Jemima, and the next thing he knew he was in the air, then in the freezing water. *Seabird,* in the center of the electric storm, had been hit directly. The ship had been blown apart.

It happened with a speed that had no measurement in time, for the next thing Christopher knew, the ship didn't exist. There were pieces of it in every direction, tossed through the water like so much flotsam, and he suffered a ferocious ringing in his ears as well as a throbbing in the center of his skull. It was all he could do to get his arms to move and stay afloat. He saw entire chunks of the

Seabird going down.

Then he thought of her, *Jemima*. He called out, but she was nowhere. Unconscious, he quickly assumed, knocked out by the force of the lightning or perhaps pinned to a beam from the ship, on her way under.

Her words echoed back . . . *one of us is going to be killed*. He struggled through the water. "Jemima!" he yelled. "Jemima!" But his own strength was already compromised as he fought against pieces of the ship shoved against him by the force of the storm-tossed water. There was another flash of lightning and more thunder. All he could hear was storm. No Jemima.

He swam fifty yards in one direction, then crisscrossed fifty yards in the other. He lost the feeling in his hands and his feet. Once, a main beam from *Seabird* struck him across the head as he swam, but he pulled himself over it and swam some more. He knew boats would come out from *Dolphin* within minutes. But an unconscious human can drown within seconds.

"Jemima!" he called again. He swam more. Then there were two launches. One came to the side of him, but he refused to come aboard. Somehow, leaving the water meant he was leaving her there. He looked all around him. But the rain was so torrential that he could barely see fifteen yards. And the sea kept splashing him in the face.

"Jemima!" he called a final time.

From the launch, two seamen in life jackets reached down and lifted him from under the shoulders. The fight left him, and he allowed them to help him climb aboard. The sea water stung in his eyes. He wiped it away and it was red from the cut on his temple.

He turned to the rescue party. "There's a Wren officer in the water," he said.

"No one else, sir," said one of them.

"I'm telling you. A Wren First Officer!" he insisted.

"No, sir," the young man said again. "All crew has been recovered."

Christopher looked blankly at the man. The man nodded toward the second rescue launch. Nearby Christopher could see its crew. They were pulling another body from the water. Jemima's. She was motionless. He stared.

Her words again . . . *one of us is going to be—*

But as they held her body, she moved. Then she was upright and on her feet. Christopher saw her clearly. She was unsteady, but she had turned her head and was looking at him. She was conscious, alive and standing.

"Thank God," he said.

He allowed himself to relax. His knees buckled and he collapsed onto the deck. There was another flash of lightning, a deafening roll of thunder, and then the launch turned in the water, and up Haslar Creek toward Dolphin right nearby.

TWENTY-SIX

"You'll live," said Jemima James. "I don't know what more you could ask for."

Jemima and Christopher sat in the office of Surgeon Lieutenant Commander Richard Pearce at HMS Dolphin. They wore fresh, dry uniforms. Two hours had passed since *Seabird* had been blown to pieces.

"How's your head feel?" Pearce asked Christopher. There was a bandange on the side of his forehead. He'd had five stitches.

"I'm grateful that my head is still attached to the rest of me," he said. He looked at Jemima. Like Christopher, she was still shaken. They had both escaped any serious injury, despite the fact that *Seabird* had collapsed beneath their feet. She smiled slightly.

"Am I cleared for duty?" Creighton asked Pearce.

"No reason why not, as I stated," he said. "In the

future, however, please be aware of the health risks of swimming in the entrance to Pompey harbor." Pearce lit a cigarette and inhaled deeply. "I'd advise against it."

"Of course," Christopher said.

Five minutes later, Christopher and Jemima were outside again. The rain had stopped. The sky was gray, but brightening. "Captain Hamilton," said a voice.

Christopher stopped and turned. He saw a stout bearded man walking toward him. He was John Turner, the Engineer-Commander of the base. Turner saluted Christopher and the two men shook hands. Christopher introduced Jemima and Turner saluted again.

"I wonder if you two would care to have a pow-wow with me," Turner suggested. "I've some things to tell you."

Christopher still had a few preparations before his noon rendezvous with Serov. "Can it wait?" he asked.

"No."

Two minutes later they all sat in Turner's small office in the engineering department of the base. A Wren brought coffee. Eventually Turner spoke.

"You're both lucky to be alive. You know that, don't you?"

Christopher nodded. "We were both together in the aft section of the sailboat," Creighton said. "The lightning must have hit the foreward section."

"Lightning never touched you," said Turner.

362

Christopher and Jemima stared at him blankly.

"While the doctors were looking at you, my divers went down and looked at the *Seabird* wreckage. They recovered a morsel or two. You were hit by gelignite. Within a pound, I'd estimate the explosive at about twenty pounds. I'd guess someone tucked a surprise for you aboard ship, probably in the focs'le locker where you wouldn't see it."

Christopher and Jemima looked at him in shock. Neither could speak. Turner looked them back and forth.

"Any idea who'd want to ruin your sailing party like that?" Turner asked.

Christopher answered neither yes nor no. "Turner," he said slowly, "I'm sorry to spoil your fun, but all this comes under Section 1 of the Official Secrets Act."

Turner smiled. "Of course, sir. I might have known. That's standard routine at Dolphin. But I'll inform Captain Submarines."

As Christopher and Jemima crossed Portsmouth harbor for the dockyard, his mind raced. There was little question now that the opposition remained both strong and effective. He had to assume that the threat to Khrushchev hadn't been defused at all by the raid at Ybor-les-Pins. Worse, Christopher had allowed his own security to lapse. *Seabird* had been left completely unguarded.

But he'd only been out for a sail, he told himself over and over. How could this faceless opposition have drawn such a close bead on them? How could they have even known who he was? He shuddered. Was there a lapse within his own Section? Impossible! Within Serov's tightly disciplined KGB? Unlikely. Within Eden's office at 10 Downing Street or within Mountbatten's at the Admiralty? Out of the question. So why then had he and Jemima come within a few feet of being blown to death?

At noon of the same day, Christopher and Jemima entered the Nut Bar at the Keppel's Head. Dimitroff saw them and led them upstairs to the first floor chamber, where they'd met Serov on the last day of February.

The KGB chief was seated at a table. He looked almost surprised when he saw them, then rose and smiled. He produced a bottle of Pimms Number One and proceeded to mix four drinks.

"Pimms?" Christopher asked, amazed.

"Your Constable Chief Portsmouth and Scotland Yard Special Branch," said Serov, "have given me Pimms Saturday. Fine British invention."

Christopher managed a smile. Serov took time out from his drink to give Jemima a bear hug, Russian style. When he refused to let go, she pushed him away, responding with some of her more colloquial Russian epithets. He was vastly amused and returned to the drinks. He mixed two rounds liberally.

"Has it occurred to you, Captain Christopher," said Serov, "that peacetime, Soviets and West are

364

enemies? In wartime, allies."

"Many things have occurred to me, Ivan," Creighton answered.

Serov's eyes narrowed slightly, but he lifted his glass. "To friendship," he said.

Jemima and Christopher responded in unison. "To friendship," they said. For a man charged with protecting his nation's leaders during a perilous visit, Christopher observed, Serov was remarkably calm. But then, Serov might have made the same observation about him. Maybe, Creighton concluded, a quiet calm pervaded both of their exteriors. It was only inwardly that their teeth rattled.

When Serov mixed a third round of drinks, Christopher moved to the window. Several of the Russian's KBG henchmen were in the room now. Serov spoke to them in Russian and poured scotch whiskey for them. A half-dozen bottles of vodka remained untouched on the serving table.

Jemima made small talk with them as Christopher surveyed the harbor. Christopher's eyes were as steady as a hawk's. He saw some of his own men in civilian clothing, making rounds. He inspected every detail of the English ships and he looked at the shore emplacements where Trott's men would be.

From where would the attack come? How would it come? he wondered. *What were the chances that it — ?*

"You holding things on the mind, Captain Christopher?" It was Serov, looming beside Creighton.

The Russian had moved very quietly to him and arrived unannounced, seeming almost to peer into Creighton's thoughts.

Christopher considered the question. Then he nodded slowly.

"Things which I should to be knowing?" Serov asked.

Creighton nodded again and turned toward his Soviet counterpart.

Serov's gray eyes had the icy intensity of a Siberian timber wolf. Gone was the jovial playacting. The drink was set aside. The facade of carefree irresponsibility had been just that. A mask. Several KGB assistants had Jemima surrounded and Creighton knew in an instant that Serov had the drop on him. Jemima had been intentionally cut off so that Serov could speak to him in private. Three rounds of drinks had even been part of the gambit.

"Are you to tell me your thoughts?" Serov asked.

Creighton had the sense of Serov being inside his mind already. Christopher looked back toward the harbor.

"Comrade Ivan," Christopher said, "as much as I feel it is my duty to tell you everything in order to protect your masters, I cannot."

"Someone has forbidding you?"

"You may conclude that if you wish."

There was a fearful silence. Creighton was torn apart by his dilemma. He had the authority from the Sovereign to override Eden's directives. But if he did? And if it ever reached Parliament that a section that was supposed to not exist had shared intelligence on authority from the Queen? Christopher shuddered.

"But you will not be saying?" Serov asked.

"No, comrade. I cannot."

"Then, my friend Captain Christopher, I try to make situation easier. As I told you at first meeting, my KGB has taken over files of MVD and NKVD. Throughout the world, we have agents. Informers. Everywhere. Every nation." He looked directly at Christopher, his face expressionless. "There is not much we do not discover. So to be easing your mind, tell me if your information recalls mine. Originally hear that White Russians emigrés, fanatics with much money, employ mercenaries — some German — to attack *Ordzhonikidze* as she lies there."

The Russian pointed out of the window to the Royal Navy dockyard and Watering Island.

"There, in Royal Navy base under your protection," said Serov. Christopher stared at him. "Insane people wish to trigger hostilities, even warfare, between English and Soviet Union. Better to advance their own cause, they think."

Creighton was riveted. Jemima joined them, but did not know what had been said.

"Perhaps these things you find difficult to tell me, my friend?"

Christopher's heart lifted. *Serov had told him! He could not be accused of telling Serov anything.*

Very slowly Christopher answered. "You may

conclude that if you wish," he said again.

Serov nodded resolutely, "Understood," he said, and quietly played his ace. "I am being sorry that this morning your navy yacht is blowing up! What calling it? Ah, yes, *Seabird!*"

Christopher could not control his reaction. Serov watched his discomfort. "Not to be concerning, Captain Christopher," he said. "I am seeing you in water from this very room."

Christopher glanced to the window and across Portsmouth harbor to Blockhouse. "Oh, yes," he said lamely. He gathered himself.

"Much needs to be done, Comrade Ivan," Christopher said. "And there is very little time. I've arranged for you to come to our headquarters just outside Portsmouth. Ask as few questions as possible. I will tell you as much as I can. Together, we will ensure the safety of your leaders."

"Very obliging," said Serov. "And then you can introducing me to your prisoner, Baron Wilhelm von Ostenberg."

Christopher stared at him.

Serov grinned, then laughed. "You think you can raid south of France and KGB not know?" His smile was toothy and merry, like one of Khrushchev's.

"No, comrade. Of course not," said Jemima. "Tell me. Is there *anything* you and your KGB do not know?"

Serov shrugged, the playful facade returning. "Well, Lady Jemima, if I know what I do not know,

I would know it," he said.

Christopher smiled. There was no way to refute Ukrainian logic.

Two hours later, Ivan Serov sat comfortably in the library at Birdham. With him were Christopher and the usual senior group. Serov had left Dimitroff behind but had brought with him the four Moscow-trained hoods. Without doubt, KGB officers. Two of them stayed at the main gate, and two in the entrance hallway. All refused to budge. Or talk.

During the afternoon, Christopher carefully briefed his Soviet guest on aspects of the impending security arrangements. Christopher explained the ring of steel that would be set beneath Portsmouth harbor around the Soviet ships. Serov responded with great enthusiasm, immensely pleased that nothing could approach the submerged hulls of the Russian vessels. Christopher carefully made no mention of the RG beam.

Just past 1630 hours there was a knock on the door. Jilly and Marie came into the library carrying large trays of tea and Malenkoff cake.

Christopher's eyes widened. Desmond Morton sat up from his usual slouching position, all of his senses keen and alert. Christopher and Morton exchanged a glance, and Jemima looked back and forth to each of them. The Empress of Russia in-exile walked directly toward the director of the

KGB.

Marie and Jilly set down the trays and tea on the table. Marie picked up a pot, looked directly at Serov and poured a cup. Christopher felt his heart beating faster. Idly, he wondered if he should intercept the cup or seize the pot. But no, he wouldn't. Marie wouldn't poison a man. He was sure. Rather, he reassured himself.

Marie placed the cup on the table next to Serov. She spoke to him in Russian. "Would you care for some Malenkoff cake?" she inquired. "My specialty."

The room froze. For the first time, Christopher saw an expression of surprise on Serov's face.

Serov nodded. "You are Russian?" he asked.

Marie nodded.

"Russian servants in England?" He looked to Jemima, who nodded. "What do they call you?" Serov asked the woman as he accepted the cake.

"Marie," Marie answered.

"Very nice. And your family name?"

"I am the daughter of my father, Comrade Serov," Marie said. "Marie Nikolayevna Romanova."

Serov paled, then looked at Christopher in astonishment. Christopher gave him a very slight nod as if to affirm Marie's words. Secretly, Christopher was pleased. At last there was something that Serov hadn't known.

But it was Jemima's opportunity for protocol. She came to her feet and spoke in the classical French of the Imperial Court. "Your Imperial Majesty," she said to Marie, "May I present Comrade General Ivan Alexandrovich Serov, first Director of the Komitet Gosudarstvennoy Bezepasnosti."

Serov slowly walked around the table and stood in front of Marie. A shattering silence possessed the room. The Pretender to the Imperial Throne surveyed the man whose predecessors had murdered her father and brother. They seemed to stare at each other for an eternity.

Then Marie held out her hand. Serov took it, knelt at her feet and kissed the ring of Catherine the Great. As he started to stand again, Marie helped him to his feet.

"You are most welcome to England, Ivan Alexandrovich," she said, "I am delighted to meet you."

"And I, most honored. Delighting," Serov said. He kissed her hand again. Christopher, Jemima and Desmond Morton stared on, savoring the moment.

Serov and his bodyguards departed at 2300, leaving Desmond Morton sitting in the library with Christopher. The rest of Birdham secured for the night watches.

In many ways the visit had unnerved Christopher. He found the Russians, Serov in particular, an enigma. Serov may have been an ally, working for the protection of Khrushchev side by side with Christopher, but that still didn't mean that Creighton understood him.

Sir Desmond attempted to put things in order.

"It's all quite understandable, really," said Morton. He was clad in ascot and smoking jacket, lounging in a leather armchair and stuffing his final pipe of the day. "What perplexes you, Christopher, is the Bolshevik mind. You must work on understanding it."

"How does a Bolshevik kiss the ring of the Imperial family?" Creighton asked cynically.

The pipe was lit and Sir Desmond sat in a cloud of his own smoke. "Russians are romantics, young Christopher. They love music and the arts, wine and food. The monarchy ceased to rule in Russia almost forty years ago. Since then, the average Russian has witnessed some of the worst barbarism perpetrated in the history of this planet. Far worse than anything ever allowed under the czars. So deep in the Russian psyche is a longing, a nostalgia you might call it, for a simpler day under the imperial family." Morton hunched his shoulders and puffed. "To meet the living head of that family evokes for the average Russian a feeling of devout respect and honor."

"And what about politics?" Christopher asked.

"We're talking about romanticism, Christopher. Politics don't enter in. Serov is a man of some power, but he is also a man from the peasant classes. You gave him the thrill of his lifetime introducing him to our Marie."

Christopher's eyes were tired. He blew out a long breath and felt sleep creeping up on him. Yet, the image of the head of the KGB kissing the ring of the Czar's daughter rankled in him. There was something wrong.

"What about these White Russians?" he asked Morton. "How would Serov know so much about them?"

"His Committee for State Security seems to function with a certain efficiency," Morton answered. "So I can believe that he'd hear about such a plot if it existed. My problem, I suspect, Christopher, is the same as yours. Who would really involve themselves in something like that?"

"Exactly," Christopher answered. He thought for a moment. So did Morton, drawing deeply on his pipe. "Of course, we have a dead Roger Garin to point to. As well as the two thugs who attacked Jemima. Plus a bomb meant to kill both of you."

Several more minutes passed in silence. Morton finished his smoke, then tapped the pipe noisily into an ashtray. "You know," he concluded, "when Brother Serov exchanged greetings with Marie earlier this evening, I was watching them very closely. Know who I was thinking about, Christopher?"

"Who?"

"Winston," said Morton. "I remember his attitude so well. All through the thirties. During the war. 'Don't trust Stalin. Don't trust Beria. Don't trust Molotov.' If a Russian diplomat came into a room in a raincoat, soaking wet, shaking out an umbrella, Winston would have looked out the window to make sure it was raining."

Christopher smiled.

"Never trust a Russian," said Morton. "That's what Winston always said. And that's what I was thinking when Marie greeted Serov."

"The trouble is," concluded Creighton, "They're *both* Russians."

"Exactly what I was thinking, Christopher. Exactly."

TWENTY-SEVEN

Less than two hours later, at 0155 on the morning of April 17, Christopher was in a deep sleep. He did not immediately hear the buzzer over his head. It sounded for almost three seconds before he bolted upright in his bunk.

His eyes flickered. He was exhausted but awake. He groped for the telephone at his bedside. "Captain," he said.

"Control, sir," said Caroline, identifying herself: "Images on RG. Almost simultaneously: perimeter and positions K, L, P, J, R."

Christopher was suddenly conscious of his own heartbeat. "Not Royal Marine patrols?" he asked.

"No, sir. Negative on patrols."

"Actions stations," said Christopher. "Silent and dark."

"Action stations, sir. Silent and dark," Caroline acknowledged.

Christopher shot out of the bunk and pulled on his navy blue battle dress. He scooped up his belt with fighting knife and Smith & Wesson .38. He hurtled out of his cabin. The night-vision lights and the flashing alarm lights had come on. He sprung up the stairs three at a time and into the control room.

Tim Sainthill had arrived first. He reported to Christopher. "Duty Royal Marines at the 'still,' sir," he said.

"Thank you, Tim. What do you reckon?"

Sainthill shook his head. "It's a strange pattern. Cumbersome. Not much attempt at cover. It's obvious they don't know about our RG."

Christopher was straightening his belt as he listened. Jemima came in behind him, followed by Angela and Joan.

"What about Serov's people coming back?" Sainthill asked.

"Not very likely. They'd identify themselves."

"Do you want the RG monitor?" Angela asked.

"Yes, please. Roll it now."

"Aye, aye, sir." She turned a switch on a sixteen-millimeter film camera close to the console. The section had adapted BBC-TV's Cinescope to its own use. Now they recorded the RG live action on the monitor.

"Royal Marines at action stations, sir," said Sainthill, setting down a telephone and standing at attention.

Jemima set down a second telephone. "All naval

units and Wrens at action stations, sir," she added.

Christopher opened his mouth to speak, but never said a word. A tremendous explosion rocked the manor. The force of it rattled the walls, floors and all their equipment. They groped and grabbed for their balance as the entire manor shook.

"Jesus!" Christopher cursed. The telephone flashed. Jemima picked it up.

"Deputy Commander!" she said. Then, turning to Christopher, "Explosion located in east wing. First and second floors," she said.

"Tim!" ordered Christopher. "K Marines to east wing and von Ostenberg." He turned to Jemima. "Number One, 'Alice' is yours. Go get her."

"Yes, sir."

"All units to attack. Search and destroy. No challenges. Find and kill," Christopher ordered.

"Aye, aye, sir," Jemima and Sainthill acknowledged in unison. They took one step in the respective direction of their orders when they were staggered again. The manor shook violently a second time from a second explosion. It was more powerful than the first, and Christopher guessed it came from the same direction, the east wing.

The telephone flashed again and Christopher received another report. The manor had been hit twice and was on fire. The initial assessment suggested an attack by mortars. Some marines and Wrens had been hit. The east wing, where von Ostenberg was housed and where Marie had slept, was in flames.

Jemima led three Wrens with her. They each took a Sten gun and a haversack of spare magazines, then raced toward the east wing and Marie. Junior Wren officers took over communications. Christopher ordered fire units to the same wing, then looked to Sainthill.

"Take over, Tim," Creighton said. "I'll be at the east wing."

"Very good, sir," Sainthill answered. His boots cracked down at attention.

Christopher raced from the command station and hit the second floor. He ran in the same direction as the Wrens, but one floor above them. Flat out up the corridor, he wove right at the end and came upon the Marine Commando Unit he had detailed to attend von Ostenberg. The devastation of the baron's quarters was almost total. It appeared to be the work of two medium mortars.

Christopher sent one of the marines back at the double to Sainthill to report fully on the situation in the wing. Then he went into the quarters. A sergeant and four marine commandos struggled to bring von Ostenberg out, assisted by Surgeon Commander Rawlins. Von Ostenberg lay on a stretcher. His eyes were closed and his pajamas were soaked with blood.

Rawlins saw Christopher. "Touch and go," Rawlins said. "We're getting him to another room away from here."

"Thank you, Doc," said Christopher. He wheeled around on a marine sergeant. "Keep your eyes peeled, Burrows. They're about here somewhere. Shoot to kill."

"Yes, sir," said Burrows.

Christopher turned back into the room. Two marines — a captain and a corporal — lay on the deck. Christopher knelt and looked at them.

"Doctor Rawlins says they're not too bad, sir," reported a marine captain who stood with them. "We've been detailed to set up a casualty station in the library."

Christopher nodded. "Thank you, John. But keep your eyes wide," he said, "and report everything."

"Sir!" the marine affirmed. Christopher stood and departed at full speed.

He charged down the steps, turned right and ran down the corridor toward Marie's room. At the end of the corridor, thick black smoke billowed toward him. Already, it burned his eyes and threatened to choke him. He could hear voices — women's voices — and the sound of deep, hacking coughs. As he turned a final corner, he could see flames as well as hear them. His heart pounded. As he feared, Marie's room had been hit.

Jemima and her Wrens were there. They had the fire hose off the wall and had just connected it to the wall hydrant. Jemima saw Christopher. She shouted. "The marine fire unit is on its way, sir!" she yelled. "But there's no time."

"Is Alice trapped in there?"

"If she's alive," Jemima yelled back.

Angela turned on the hydrant and water shot out

of the hose, which Caroline held. Jemima turned toward Christopher from the fire. For an instant, Christopher shared her fear. It was a replay of the helicopter which she'd charged into at Cudrose, the inferno which had burned the uniform and flesh from her back as she rescued three naval airmen — and from which she'd been lucky to escape alive. Then a second image was upon him, that of the two of them, lying next to each other only a day and a half earlier, and Jemima reflecting that one of them might be killed.

Somehow he feared this was that moment.

"On me, Caroline!" Jemima yelled.

Caroline held the nozzle and drove a stream of water into Marie's room. Jemima stepped forward and nearly walked into the flames. But she kept her balance, coughed violently and pushed forward. The force of the water helped clear the way. And Caroline, holding the hose, disappeared into the smoke with her.

Then Christopher heard the sound of gunfire and he knew that his worst prophecy was fulfilled. Yes, the manor was under assault. But by how many? Ten? A hundred?

And who were they, damn it? Who? Who in God's name were they?

The gunfire seemed to come from outside the manor. Creighton drew his Smith & Wesson .38. He looked for a window but when he found one it showed nothing. He drew a breath and gathered himself. Yet, in a flash, he knew that he'd barely led at all. He'd given orders, but others had seen combat. *Lead from the front,* he'd always told himself. Yet Jemima and her Wrens had charged into the fire, others had taken hits from the enemy and others had moved in to engage.

He turned from the window. No units had yet checked out the third floor. Christopher ran toward the stairs that led to the top floor of the manor. He turned a final corner at full speed and something that felt like a freight train cracked into his face. He reeled. For a moment he thought he'd been shot. A red blindness was upon him as blood trickled from his forehead into his eyes. Then something else hard hit him in the stomach. He doubled over, but remained standing.

A kick took the gun from Christopher's hand and sent it across the floor. Then he was aware that an automatic pistol had been pressed against his head.

He blinked. He used a forearm to push the blood from his eyes. He was still partially doubled over as he looked up. He expected to be executed.

He saw a man in an unidentifiable gray uniform. Battle dress with no marking, not even rank. And the man's face: high forehead with cold dark eyes.

"You give us von Ostenberg," the man said sharply. "Or we kill you."

The accent was strange. A low mid-European sludge. Everything about these invaders was gray and indecipherable. Everything about the operation, in fact, was that way.

The man poked the nose of the pistol against

Christopher's skull for what was undoubtedly the final time before pulling the trigger.

So this is how it will end, Christopher thought. *My brains blown out before Khrushchev even arrives.* A strange anger was upon him as he thought of not surviving this operation.

Slowly, he nodded. "All right," Creighton said, gathering himself. "You'll have von Ostenberg. He has been wounded by your own mortars, but you can have him."

The man nodded. For a tenth of a second he relaxed — a tenth of a second too much.

Christopher came up inside the man's guard. He smashed down viciously with his left hand across the man's gun arm, paralyzing the muscle. The gun fell as Christopher's palm came up neatly under the invader's chin. The man reeled backward, but Christopher held him. Two outstretched fingers, balancing their aim with the palm on the chin, shoved with sickening force into the screaming man's eyes. Christopher drove in with full force. The man twisted in anguish and brought his hands to the two bloody holes where his eyes had been.

It was instinctive now. Long ago, at the Royal Naval College at Dartmouth, in the field and on section training, he'd learned never to stop in pity until the job was done. Christopher seized the man's cheeks and forced his fingers into the man's mouth. He ripped sideways, splitting the man's face from mouth to ear. Blood poured from the strips of flesh. Then Christopher smashed a knee into the man's testicles, doubling him.

Without pause, Christopher wrapped one arm around the front of the man's neck and interlocked it with his other, the hand behind the man's neck. Both arms rotated together. There was a sharp crack.

The body went limp and quiet. Christopher released him and the dead man's body slid to the floor.

Yet Christopher had no time even to stare at what he'd done. There were footsteps in every direction now. Christopher picked up his gun and looked for a spot to take cover.

There was none. He crouched in a corner as gray uniforms surged along the corridor. He knew he could still die here. These men had automatic weapons. He had only six bullets. All he could do was stop as many as he could before they got him.

He fired. He hit one man in the stomach. The body reeled backward and jarred the rifle of the second man. Bullets crashed in Christopher's direction, but the invader couldn't locate Christopher's position. Creighton cut him down with two more bullets. But still there were gray uniforms. Two more men pushed forward — aggressive and relentless. Christopher fired three times more, and still they couldn't find his position. They sprayed their fire in his direction. Christopher emptied his pistol until it clicked on empty chambers.

Then they heard the clicks. They stepped out. There were two of them, and Christopher knew he had little chance. But they were fighting by the night-vision lights and the semidarkness remained Christopher's ally. He drew his knife and crouched down, ready to spring.

Then there were more bullets. His heart leaped and he was certain he was dead. He thought he felt the bullets rip into his chest, but then he knew he didn't, and the bullets were coming from another direction. It was a merciless barrage that cut the final two raiders in half, sent them spinning back toward the stairs and dropped them in a heap.

Creighton turned. He saw Caroline and Jemima, poised and unafraid, holding their Sten guns no more than fifteen feet away. Then, for what seemed like a very long time, everything was quiet.

"Five of them made it to the roof," Jemima said.

"We have all five," Christopher answered. A check of pulses showed that all were dead.

"What about your fire? And Marie?" Christopher asked.

Both Wrens were dripping wet. Their faces were black from the blaze.

"The fire we put out," said Jemima nonchalantly. "And Marie is fine. Maybe a little wet. Her night-clothes caught fire, so Caroline put her out too."

Christopher nodded, a wry smile creeping across his face. "With what? The hose?"

"Yes, sir."

"What about von Ostenberg?"

"Hurt. But Commander Rawlins says he'll survive."

Creighton nodded again. Then he realized that the Wrens were staring at him. He looked back. "What's the matter?" he asked.

Then he saw what they were looking at. He was soaked with blood. It was all over his hands, face and clothing. It was dripping off his sleeves and wrists.

"Not mine," he said, brushing some of it away. He motioned to the man nearest him. *"His."*

Minutes later, Birdham was reported secure. Christopher stood down action stations. The lights went on. Four marines and three Wrens had been wounded, although not seriously, but they were evacuated to the R.N. hospital at Haslar. Eight raiders had been killed. They were placed in body bags and Trott's Squad moved them to a makeshift mortuary later in the morning.

During the day, however, the postmortem continued. How had the raiders gained entrance? How many had escaped? How had they known von Ostenberg's location? Had it been him they'd been after, or was it Marie? Had they been the same people who'd blown up *Seabird?*

The questions persisted. There were no answers. Christopher knew only that the threat to Khrushchev was as real as the automatic weapon that had been held to his head. And he was left to conclude that the raiders had wished to silence von Ostenberg before the Section could uncover his secrets.

Christopher sent a long signal to Mountbatten, giving details of the raid. Then, as a final touch, he tripled the defenses and armaments at Portsmouth harbor.

An unknown enemy, he had long been aware, was the most dangerous of all. And that was exactly what he was facing.

TWENTY-EIGHT

Two minutes ahead of schedule, at 0658 hours, Wednesday, April 18, the prow of the Soviet cruiser *Ordzhonikidze* slid smoothly out of the gray waters of the English Channel and into Portsmouth harbor. The *Smotryashchi* and the *Sovershenny* remained behind the *Ordzhonikidze*. They seemed to sit still in the water as the cruiser carrying the Soviet head of state passed through the drizzle and haze.

As the cruiser came abeam of Fort Blockhouse, the crash of the first gun of a twenty-one gun salute sounded. It echoed through Portsmouth harbor. Christopher, standing with Jemima at the yardarm of *Victory*, jumped slightly when he heard the shot, though he'd fully expected it. Jemima was aware of his movement. She glanced at him and said nothing. She was every bit as apprehensive as he was.

"Well, so far," she said to break the tension, "so

good." The *Ordzhonikidze* had been in the harbor for at least ten seconds.

Christopher managed a smile. "It strikes me that firing guns today in this harbor is one hell of a bad omen," Christopher answered.

He glanced to the docks and to the perimeters of the harbor. For reassurance, he sought out Sainthill, spotted him and scanned the long line of Royal Marines deployed in every direction. Christopher looked the other way and saw Trott—for once probably *not* looking for a fight—standing precisely at the best vantage point.

Portsmouth harbor is secure, Christopher told himself. *A hundred times secure. I've seen to it myself.*

As the Royal Navy tugs softly butted up to the Soviet warship and guided her alongside Watering Island, Christopher had his first good view of the visitor. He scanned the armaments on the gray deck, fore and aft, displayed proudly before the Soviet ensign. Seeing *Ordzhonikidze* from *Victory* gave Christopher a better perspective on the Soviet ship. She was impressive. A seagoing bulldog. It casually occurred to him, as she came alongside, that *Ordzhonikidze* could reduce Portsmouth to rubble within a few seconds. Not that he in any way feared it. But it was a day for rambling, idle, terrifying thoughts. This was only one of many.

The berthing was interminable, as usual. Angela emerged from the cabin behind Christopher, where the communications subsection was located. She climbed to the yard and watched quietly beside Jemima as the Royal marine guards stood stiffly at the intended point of disembarkation. Close by, the naval, marine and Portsmouth civil police looked carefully about them. When the gangway was secured, Christopher glanced at his watch. It was seven minutes after eight. Lord Cilcennin, the First Lord of the admiralty, stood at the head of a reception committee that moved to the right of the gangway.

Christopher gave Jemima a nod. "Let's go," he said softly. Together, they left *Victory*, walked across to the marine guard and stood about four yards behind the reception group.

For several minutes, the gangway was empty. Christopher turned and scanned rooftops and windows. He looked for something—*anything*—out of place. Again, he saw nothing to alarm him. But this unbanishable sense of dread was upon him. *Something will happen*, he thought. He could almost taste it. He wondered if his black depressions, which he seemed to have finally defeated, were now to be replaced by fits of anxiety.

Then he heard voices. He turned his attention back to the *Ordzhonikidze*. Some Russians were collecting on the deck, preparing to disembark.

A pair of KGB agents stood at the top, hands clasped before them, looking downward and surveying the jetty beneath them. They looked, Christopher noted, like security men anywhere: frowning, high cheekboned, mean, with slicked hair. Six-cylinder Moscow hoods, Mountbatten liked to call them. Christopher suppressed a smile.

Across from him, the Soviet reception committee stood in place. He glanced at Serov at exactly the same time the Russian looked Christopher's way. Serov gave Christopher a slight nod of recognition. Then Khrushchev and Bulganin appeared. They started down, the dapper, neatly manicured Bulganin preceding the roly-poly Khrushchev. As Bulganin's feet touched British soil, followed closely by Khrushchev's, the Royal marine guard presented arms. Bulganin nodded. Khrushchev, clearly enjoying himself, grinned widely and gestured with his hands clasped above his head. Then the Marine band broke into "The Internationale. Fortunately, they played the shortened version, and as the rain picked up everyone other than band members stood perfectly still for three-and-a-half minutes.

A captain of the Royal Marines, ignoring the rain, invited the Russians to inspect the guard of honor. Bulganin, as head of state, followed, leaving Khrushchev standing awkwardly alone. Creighton watched carefully to see what would happen. The First Secretary of the CPSU suddenly looked very vulnerable alone on the rainy jetty in a foreign country. Serov moved quickly to Khrushchev's side, however, and held him in a whispered private discussion. Serov appeared to be explaining something intensely. Khrushchev was nodding and not smiling.

Bulganin returned. Then he and Khrushchev were motioned to a private car, a black Daimler, which had rolled into place to Christopher's left. The Russians eagerly climbed in. Christopher palpably relaxed as the car moved away.

The Russians were bound for Portsmouth station now, where a special train would take them to London. There the representatives of the Workers' Paradise would be comfortably ensconced in a second-floor suite at Claridge's. But for Christopher, at least the two main diplomatic targets were off his patch. He could now turn his full concern toward their ships.

He walked back to the quarterdeck of *Victory* and entered the communications room. Angela looked up as he entered. "Switch on the ring," he said.

Across the harbor, Webb was waiting for just that command. His section had methodically laid out an electronic defensive barrier that no human could possibly slip past undetected. It was the tightest ring that Webb had ever devised, with RG beams and sonar devices at ten-meter intervals. In the communications room aboard *Victory,* Christopher watched as the monitoring lights from the ring began to illuminate. He waited until all were operational then went aboard the *Ordzhonikidze,* where he met again with Captain Zoltov as well as the captains of the two escort vessels. Christopher sat in the captain's cabin, and, with Jemima acting as interpreter, discussed all matters of harbor security.

Then Zoltov asked a question in Russian. The two other Soviet officers never took their eyes off Christopher as Jemima relayed the question.

"He wants to know," Jemina said, "what's protecting their ships by an attack of divers against the hull."

"A combination of lights and sonar equipment, all around his ships," Christopher said in response.

Zoltov seemed to understand, because he asked his next question without waiting for a translation.

"He says that he has full confidence in the British security and defense systems," Jemima added. "But he wants to be reassured. Precisely what sort of lights equipment?"

Christopher looked carefully at the Russians. Then he spent another three quarters of an hour explaining the ring of steel, but carefully omitting details of the RG beams.

Afterward, they returned to *Victory*. Angela told them that Lieutenant Wilmot had reported that Crabb had left London early that morning and had arrived in Portsmouth before eleven. He had registered under an assumed name at the Sallyport Hotel, where Bernard Foster had joined him.

"Why don't we go get him?" Jemima suggested.

Christopher shook his head. "Not yet," he said. "I want to see if they have other divers or other sources of equipment. Move too quickly and we give ourselves away. Crabbie's no danger till he starts heading for water. And he'll never get that far."

Jemima nodded. "Sad," she said. "His whole situation." Jemima turned to Angela. "Any reports on von Ostenberg?"

"No change, ma'am," replied Angela. "Resting comfortably, but still touch and go."

"Has he said anything?"

Angela shook her head. "No."

"Thank you," said Jemima. "You may carry on."

"Yes, ma'am," said Angela. She bustled off to her communications room.

When there was nothing more to do, toward one in the afternoon, Christopher paced up and down the dockyard and on and off *Victory* like a caged beast. He declined Jemima's suggestion that they have lunch. He did not want to take his eyes off the Soviet ships. Toward one thirty, Jemima finally managed to settle Christopher by falsely claiming that Flag Officer Portsmouth wanted a working lunch with him. By the time he arrived in the wardroom and she admitted her deception, it was too late. She'd already ordered his lunch and he decided not to protest in front of the other officers.

That evening, following an unexpectedly quiet afternoon, Jemima and Christopher shared a light dinner aboard *Victory*. The harbor was secure. Khrushchev and Bulganin had remained in their suites at Claridge's the entire time since arrival, the

393

only incidents being the crowd of curious Londoners that had assembled down Brook Street, hoping to catch a glimpse of the Russians.

Christopher had even allowed himself to relax slightly. If the first twelve hours of the Soviet visit had proceeded without a hitch, well, he reasoned, there was no reason why the next nine days couldn't also.

Jemima looked radiant that evening, Christopher began to notice. It may have been due to the excitement of the day. Sometimes exhilaration of events can enhance a woman's beauty, he'd heard somewhere.

At 2200, Angela came in. "We've got a little problem, sir," she said.

Christopher waited.

"Commander Crabb's gone on an absolute alcoholic run ashore. He was royally sloshed at Monck's bar and blabbing his mouth all over Portsea about a spy dive against the *Ordzhonikidze* tomorrow morning. And it seems he's got his diving gear."

"Oh, bloody God," Christopher said.

"And Foster's slipped his cover," Angela continued. "All available Squad members are searching for him."

Christopher controlled his anger. "Where's Crabb now? Who's watching him?"

"Commander Trott has Lieutenant Wilmot and three officers with him, sir." Angela said. "They're at the Queen's Hotel. Wilmot is keeping him there."

"Forcibly?"

"They're providing him an audience, so he won't leave so readily, sir," she explained. "But he's getting increasingly drunk and unpredictable. They request permission to bring him in."

Christopher shook his head in exasperation as Jemima looked steadily at him. What a tremendous scene Crabb must have been making, he thought angrily: a drunken World War II hero in the Queen's Hotel, regaling members of the drinking public at large with details of an impending, forbidden, top-secret dive. All they needed now, Creighton concluded, was some reporter to pick up the story and plaster it all over the *Daily Mail* for the next week — D notices notwithstanding.

"Christ," he said aloud. And to Angela, "Where's Crabb's diving gear?"

"In the Sallyport Hotel, sir."

"Have it picked up."

"Aye, aye, sir," said Angela. "And what about Commander Crabb?"

"We'll bring him in," Christopher said. "And then lock him up, shut him up, keep him out of trouble, avoid a war with the sodding Russians and save the poor old bastard's life, all at once." He paused. "I'm going for him myself."

"Very good, sir," said Angela. She turned back toward the communications room. Jemima was on her feet and followed Christopher off *Victory* onto the dockyard.

The Queen's Hotel was two miles away. By unspoken arrangement they got into an unmarked Royal Navy car and drove off.

At length, she spoke. "Poor old Crabbie," she said.

"Yes," he answered, beset with the memories of Gibraltar, where Lieutenant Commander Lionel Crabb, the ace diver of the Royal Navy, had trained him. "Poor old Crabbie indeed."

TWENTY-NINE

The Queen's Hotel occupied a prime location in Southsea. A rambling, white Victorian building, it was perched back from the harbor, yet gave its guests a view of the sea. In the summer, with the esplanade and gardens of Southsea Commons nearby, it was a fashionable place to stay. In the winter, it had long been a favorite of naval officers; more than one would have designated the Queen's Hotel bar as one of his favorite watering holes in the world.

Christopher and Jemima entered the hotel through the narrow rear entrance in Osborne Road. Christopher knew the hotel well. He led Jemima up the short flight of steps to the main lobby, turned right and proceeded into the bar.

He saw Crabb. He hadn't seen the man for twelve years, but now recognized him instantly. The squat frame. The wide, muscular shoulders. The slightly bowed legs. Had there been any question, Christopher also would have recognized Crabb's voice, which boomed through the bar.

"Bloody cowards, that's what they are!" Crabb raged. "Royal Navy doesn't have a single diver who'll go into that harbor with me. Those Russian bastards sit out there and nobody's man enough to even take a dip under their ships."

Jemima, watching Christopher, saw anger settle over his face. It had been one thing to hear about this scene at the Queen's Hotel bar, quite another to walk into the crowded bar and hear Crabb's voice echo above all others. Around Crabb, keeping the retired diver cornered at the far end of the bar, were two men and two women.

Creighton glanced around the bar to see what other faces he could pick out. He wasn't even certain what he was looking for, other than trouble. A reporter. A Russian. Bernard Foster. SIS or CIA. Christopher's instincts were to keep a lid on the matter as firmly as possible. Removing Crabb was only part of the problem. Keeping loose tongues from wagging was the other part.

When he saw no one he recognized, he led Jemima to Crabb's end of the bar. Now Crabb was regaling his listeners with his exploits beneath the cruiser *Sverdlov* some eight months earlier. For a moment, Crabb broke off and slopped down the remainder of a gin and tonic. He slapped a five-pound note onto the counter and ordered a refill. He returned a thick roll of bills to his pocket. As a few seconds passed, Christopher was overcome with sadness. Crabbie was so rarely flush with money, that he was royally enjoying his few moments of glory, not to mention the thrill of having a roll of cash in his pocket. A strange emotion afflicted Christopher, a desire to leave Crabb as he was, lest he ruin the fun, lest he lure Crabb to a worse fate than his present one.

But Crabb's voice boomed again. Christopher was certain it could be heard in the corridor outside the bar.

"Know what I need?" Crabb asked, jumping away from the *Sverdlov* story as another gin and tonic arrived. "I need another diver to come with me tomorrow morning. Any takers here? Is there a navy man in this house?" A pause as he gulped more liquor, then, "Oh, hell. They all say no one could possibly get through to that Bolshevik cruiser. But what does anyone know?"

"I know you ought to stop shooting your mouth off, Crabbie," Christopher said, easing against the bar behind Crabb. He spoke quietly, almost with resignation, and he waited for Crabb to turn around.

Crabb turned immediately, almost slipping from his bar stool as he moved. Creighton looked directly at the little man. Crabb's eyes narrowed as he sensed recognition. At the same time, Creighton dutifully fought off a second wave of remorse. He observed the drawn, haggard look in Crabb's face, the unkempt hairs protruding from the little man's scimitar of a nose. The hair on his head was matted and dirty; the sideburns were uneven and the hair he grew just under his cheekbones was straggly. Even his hands were dirty.

And this had once been one of the country's great divers and war heroes, Christopher found himself thinking.

"Who the fuck are you?" Crabb asked indulgently, not even noticing Christopher's uniform.

Christopher surprised even himself. He started very gently. "Crabbie," he said. "This dive of yours tomorrow. It's not on."

"The hell it's not!" Crabb shot back aggressively. Now he noticed the uniform, but was undeterred. "You have no authority to stop me. I'm doing it for the Admiralty."

"Someone's using you, old friend."

"Damn right!" snapped Crabb proudly. "SIS and the Americans, as well as the Admiralty. I'm taking a leisurely swim, sailor boy. They're all using me 'cause they need a good diver. And no other diver in this failing socialist kingdom has the balls to—" Crabb broke into his own sentence. "I know you, don't I?" he asked.

"Peter Hamilton," said Creighton. "You taught me diving and mine disarmament."

"Gibraltar, 1943," Crabb said, suddenly lucid. "Or was it 1944?"

"Forty-three. You were right the first time."

Crabb shrugged. "Well, nice to know you didn't get yourself killed by the Jerries. What are you doing now? Last time I saw you—"

Crabb caught sight of the four stripes on Christopher's sleeve.

"Holy shit," Crabb said, breaking into his own thought once again. "You're a captain. You were a two-striper last time I saw you."

Christopher nodded. He lowered his voice and tried to reason with Crabb.

"Lionel, listen to me," he said. "I command M Section." Christopher saw the flicker of recognition in the drunken man's eyes. "You know what that is, damn it, because you taught most of us to dive. Do you remember that?"

Crabb sipped more gin. "Suppose I do?" he asked.

"As of this minute," Christopher continued, "I'm in charge of who dives and who doesn't. No one else. If you had authorization to dive, I'd know about it. You don't. And if you try this dive, you'll be killed."

"Killed how?"

"Either by a bullet or by an underwater grenade."

Crabb's expression darkened. He clinked the ice cubes in his empty glass and appeared thoughtful. Then he grinned. "I want to call the Admiralty and check this out," he said.

"They'll only refer it to me."

"Know what I think?" Crabb asked. He slid off his bar stool. There was a belligerent ring to his voice, though he was still smiling.

"What do you think?"

"I think you're a bullshit artist," Crabb said. "I'm going for a swim tomorrow morning. Right under the asses of those Bolshevik bastards. And you're not going to stop me."

Crabb took one step to get past, but Christopher barred his way. The two men were suddenly eye to eye.

"We've already got your diving gear from the Sallyport," said Christopher.

"I don't believe you. So let me past, God damn it," Crabb snarled.

"You're under arrest, Crabbie."

"For what?"

"Breaking the Official Secrets Act."

Crabb laughed out loud. "Horseshit. *Horseshit!*" he roared. "You're not arresting anyone. And my friends here, those who've shared drinks with me this evening, may feel you're being a bit rude." Crabb indicated the two sturdy men standing with him. "They may not let you put your filthy hands on me."

Again Christopher spoke gently. "Lionel," he said. "They're all my officers." He nodded to them. "Wren Third Officers Lawson and Bertram and Lieutenants Marsh and Wilmot. They're a cover team, old chap, detailed to protect you from yourself."

Crabb looked at his four drinking companions first in shock, then in sadness. Suddenly it all fit together. The shame and humility were instantly visible on Crabb's face.

"Then who's Foster?" Crabb asked.

"I wish I knew," Christopher answered. "But maybe it's not even important." Crabb looked crestfallen. Christopher put a hand on the smaller man's shoulder. "Come on, Crabbie," he offered. "You can sleep it off on *Victory*."

"Aye, aye, sir," said Crabb.

"Thank you, Commander." Christopher turned to Wilmot and nodded. The two officers extended hands to Crabb and escorted him from the bar. The Wrens followed.

Christopher turned disconsolately away from them and took Crabb's place at the bar. Jemima moved in next to him and for a long minute neither of them spoke. When the barman appeared in front of them, Christopher ordered a black and tan for each of them.

When it came, they drank deeply and observed another long silence.

"Well, at least he's safe now," Jemima said suddenly. "Can't come to any harm."

"My thoughts precisely," he responded.

And they drank again. For several minutes neither spoke. Then, "I'm terrified," Christopher said. "I know something's going to happen."

"Christopher . . ."

"There's a huge piece missing to this thing," he said, suddenly animated. "Look. Nothing fits together. Why would they kill a man like Roger Garin? And why would they attack *us?* Specifically, you and me? Us. What's the point of the raid on

403

Birdham? And above everything else, where does Crabb fit in?"

She shook her head. "Bloody von Ostenberg. *He* knows. And he'll damned well die before he talks, Rawlins' injections notwithstanding."

He finished his pint. She watched him. Then her own thoughts began to run away with her. "Time to go," she said suddenly. "I've got some last-minute rounds to make on my duty girls." She finished her own drink and stood.

"I'll walk out with you," he said.

They returned to their car and drove back to the dockyard. They walked the three hundred yards to *Victory*. The Soviet warships were some seventy-five yards to their left and seemed peacefully content. There was little activity upon them. A few lights here and there. It looked almost like a summer cruise.

As Jemima went her own way, Christopher boarded *Victory*. He reported his presence to the officer of the day, then went to his cabin, the one once used by Captain Sir Thomas Masterman Hardy, who had commanded *Victory* at Trafalgar.

Christopher was so tired he ached, so emotionally spent that his head throbbed. Where *would* the attack come?. And *when?*

He collapsed onto his bunk. Into his mind flashed the memory of an old captain under whom he'd served for a very brief period on Atlantic convoy during the war. This captain had the acknowledged navy speed record for getting to the bridge at night on the sounding of action stations. One night Christopher had learned how the man did it: he never took any of his clothes off, not even his sea boots when he slept.

On this night, as the eighteenth of April neared its conclusion, maybe Christopher had a premonition. Or maybe he was too tired to undress. But when he lay down, he was fully clad in navy blue battle dress and shoes. He slept instantly, his beret on a hook just above his head, waiting for the call that would surely come.

THIRTY

Baron Wilhelm von Ostenberg, his face ashen, lay motionless on his bed at Birdham. Two Queen Alexandra's Nursing Sisters stood by. A marine captain was at the door.

Jemima spoke very quietly. *"Willy, mein Lieb. Deis ist Tania. Deine dich liebende Frau."*

The room was lit only by a small red lamp, part of the night alarm system. Jemima sat on the edge of von Ostenberg's bed. As she spoke, the German's eyes flickered and opened. They went wide, as if he were hallucinating.

She sat on the edge of his bed. She wore a black dress, heels and two rows of pearls. Von Ostenberg's gaze was dull. She took his hand. His wrist was limp and deathly. With her other hand, she brushed his head. "Willy, my Willy," she continued softly in German. "It is Tania. Your Tania. Your wife has come back to you."

Jemima leaned forward and kissed him. She straightened his sheets. For several minutes, while he made no verbal response, she spoke of their life together before Hitler — before the war, before her death.

"In Berlin in 1945, Willy," Jemima continued, "if I hadn't let those Soviet beasts have their way and rape me — seven of them. Willy, *seven* — they would have ripped me to pieces." Jemima's German was soft with the inflections and tones of Bavaria. "But I cooperated. Then I escaped. Now I've found you again."

The nursing sisters and the marine captain stared at the performance. It was worthy of the West End.

She kissed him once more, but with greater passion. Her hand drifted onto his left thigh. There was a response, almost undetectable at first, then stronger.

"Tania!" von Ostenberg blurted suddenly. It was half a gasp, half a plaintive cry. "My dearest wife, Tania." He spoke again in German. She let him place a hand on her knee, beneath her dress.

"Yes, Willy. I am safe and well. I escaped the Red Army. The British have protected me."

Clearly, the man was dying. Slowly, Jemima knew, the Section was killing him to get their information. She was revolted, but also thought of the innocent lives at stake.

He managed to pull himself up onto one elbow, then placed both arms around her. He pulled Jemima to him and kissed her squarely on the lips, exerting himself considerably. One of the sisters looked on very anxiously. Jemima gently pulled free of his grasp and let him lay back.

"My dearest, darling Tania," he said.

"I will come back to you later this evening, Willy," she said. "We will sleep together."

"Why not now?" he asked.

"I have a dinner party, Willy," she said. She reached for her purse, which was on a bedside chair. "It is Wednesday, April 18. The Russians are here in Portsmouth harbor. They have invited me aboard the *Ordzhonikidze*."

"You are going on their ship?" He tried to pull himself up again, greatly agitated.

"Yes."

"But you will not be safe."

"Of course I will." She laughed. "I am protected by the English. And I will be with Marshall Bulganin and Secretary Khrushchev."

"No!" he said. Von Ostenberg had understood, but was befuddled. He studied Jemima again. His hand left her knee and he fingered her pearls. "No," he repeated. "If you are alive—"

She pulled away. "Silly man," she said. "I will return later. We will make love and—"

"I forbid you to go! It is too dangerous!"

"Aboard the *Ordzhonikidze?*"

"Yes."

"Silly," she insisted again. She pulled away from him and gathered herself, standing up. "We are guarded by the Royal Navy. Nothing can get through, Willy."

Von Ostenberg lay back. His breathing became labored. A sister took his pulse, then shook her head.

"There isn't long to go," the nurse said softly.

For some reason, von Ostenberg heard through the narcosis. "No, there is not much time," he said in English. "And all the might of the British Navy cannot stop it. It is preordained."

"What, Willy, *what?*" she asked, returning to German.

Von Ostenberg eased back onto the bed. Jemima could feel the consciousness fading from the man, perhaps for the final time. She placed a hand on his leg, but he was quiet. She was failing and she knew it. His secrets would remain within him.

"What, Willy, please?" she said, her voice urgent and strained with emotion. "If I am in danger from the Bolsheviks again, you must tell me. If you love me, Willy, you must tell me!"

She reached to his brow and gently mopped it. The German was rolling in sweat.

"Panavich," he said so softly that she could barely hear. "Panavich in Kronstadt."

Jemima was frozen. Marie, her head cocked, barely heard either. The two women searched each other's faces.

"Willy?" Jemima said again. "Willy?" She shook him. There was no response. She shook him harder and again he didn't move. For a moment, she thought he was dead. But his breathing was very deep and even. Jemima looked to a nurse, who stepped forward as summoned.

The nurse reached down to von Ostenberg and felt his pulse. She held an eye open for a moment, then let it close.

"You'll have to come back, ma'am," the nurse said. "He really has to rest."

Still fully clothed, Christopher sat up on his bunk. His head pounded. On less than two hours of sleep he took the signal from Angela.

"From Miss James, sir," Angela said. "First Priority Immediate on direct security line from Birdham."

Christopher thought he'd misheard. What could Jemima have been doing at Birdham? He struggled to shake himself awake, then read the signal. It was a transcription of Jemima's conversation with von Ostenberg. He read it carefully, then read it again. For a few moments, he said nothing. Then he came to life.

"Angela, tell Sir Desmond and Colonel Sainthill to report to the section office in the Great Cabin. Now. And you as well."

Eight minutes later, Christopher had Morton and Sainthill assembled. Angela read Jemima's signal aloud. Creighton turned to Morton.

"Who's Panavich?" Christopher asked.

411

Morton stopped lighting his pipe, and spoke, what was for him, unusually quickly. "Comrade Igor Panavich has been a resident in the Kronstadt area for many years. He survived the Stalin and early Khrushchev purges. We've done business with him since 1946. He hates the Bolsheviks. Stalin executed a Polish ballerina with whom he was in love during the war. It seems that Beria raped her before carrying out the sentence."

"Is Panavich a party official?"

Morton nodded and put his pipe in his pocket. "He's commissar for naval appropriations in Lenningrad. He would have little trouble getting mines or divers into the Kronstadt naval base. I believe I need say nothing else—" Morton's voice tailed away.

"Mines of American manufacture attached to the Soviet ships in Kronstadt before leaving the Soviet Union. Then the mines are there now," said Sainthill incredulously.

Morton nodded.

"God almighty," whispered Christopher. He looked out of a cabin window. He saw the *Ordzhonikidze* and her two escorts a long broadside away.

"But what about the attacks on us? And von Ostenberg? And the White Russians?" asked Sainthill.

"A classic 'false flag' job, Tim," Morton answered. "Scapegoats. Someone to do some dirty work, then take the blame. The plot originated within the Soviet Union." Morton glanced back to

Christopher. "Better inform Brother Serov. Can't keep this from him."

"No. Of course not." Christopher looked to the chronometer on the bulkhead. Oh-one-thirty. He felt a surge in his stomach. "We're going to have to evacuate the ships," he said.

Morton snorted a cynical little laugh. "Doubt it," he said.

"Why?"

"First, Eden would never stand for it."

"Sod Eden! He's done nothing but make things more difficult."

"The Russians won't stand for it, either," Morton said. "Look, what if we go to Admiral Kotov and tell him what we think is down there? He'll never believe the mines were attached in Kronstadt. Plus, what if the mines *are* American, as I suspect they are. See the implication in that? See what the Russians will claim? And suppose the Americans get wind of the situation? Suppose some hawk in the Pentagon gets trigger happy? The Americans are still the only people who've ever *used* the Big Bomb."

Christopher considered it for several seconds. "You're right," he finally said. "The Russians will stay with their ships no matter what."

"I'll tell you one other thing, Christopher," Morton concluded softly. "Something that didn't make sense until the last few hours."

"What's that?"

"I had an intelligence report back in February

concerning an execution in Lubyanka prison. Two Americans. Smugglers. Rumor had it that Serov pulled the trigger himself."

"So?"

"So someone, maybe Panavich, had two Americans smuggle the American mines into the Soviet Union. Then he gave the smugglers away, the KGB arrested them and Serov dispensed justice. Very neat."

There was a knock on the door. Christopher answered. Lieutenant Nigel Wilmot came in.

"Sir, Khrushchev and Bulganin have just gone back aboard the *Ordzhonikidze,*" Wilmot said. "There was a hitch at Claridge's. Some Lithuanian demonstrators got into the hotel. General Serov wasn't willing to risk their sleeping in London, so they've returned here in absolute secrecy. No one knows. Certainly not the press."

Christopher was still for a long moment. Then he dismissed Wilmot. "God Almighty," he whispered, almost to himself.

Creighton stood with his hands on his hips. He stared at the bulkhead, then turned back to Morton. "If those mines are down there, they have to be removed. They could detonate at any moment."

"And those of us who survive could be looking at World War III."

Christopher and Desmond Morton held each other's gaze for what seemed like an eternity. They read each other's thoughts. Then Christopher came alive and turned to Angela.

414

"Angela, rouse up the electrical officer and tell him to supply two RG lights and receivers, under-water pattern. Then contact Commander Webb. He has a limpet mine, U.S. make, which we gave him for analysis. Tell him to bring it here quicker than that."

"Yes, sir." Angela wrote furiously on a notepad.

"When all that's in motion, make to Charle-magne, repeat Serov, the Author and the Prime Minister: 'Believe limpet mines attached to Soviet ships in Kronstadt. Detonation time and date un-known. Bears One and Two sleeping aboard *Ordzhonikidze* tonight. Two Section divers will at-tempt to detach and disarm." He glanced at his watch. "Estimated time commencement of opera-tion, ETCO 0215 GMT. Have you got all that?"

"Almost, sir." She continued writing, finished the signal. Christopher turned to Sainthill.

"Tim, if you please, silent and dark run, bring the ship to action stations."

"Very good, sir." Sainthill came to attention, then doubled out the door.

Angela finished writing. She looked up. "Is that all, sir?"

"No," Christopher said. "It's not. Before anything else . . ." She poised her pencil. *"Get Crabb.* Send him in here at the rush. Find out where Wilmot stashed Crabb's diving gear and have that sent here as well. Then do the same for my gear."

Her eyes were wide. She coaxed her fingers into writing.

"Now, move!" Christopher said. Angela flew out the door.

When the room was quiet again, Creighton turned back to Morton.

"There are dozens of ace divers at Vernon," said Christopher. "But I have to use Crabb. He's the best there is. Once he's sober."

Morton nodded.

"Well," Christopher said. "You heard everything. Anything I forgot?"

Morton answered after a second's thought. "Only a prayer," he replied.

They said one.

THIRTY-ONE

Three minutes later, Crabb entered, accompanied by Surgeon Lieutenant Commander Billings. Crabb was bleary-eyed and subdued. He sat heavily on a vacant chair and looked around, unimpressed. "Now what?" he asked.

The doctor spoke first. "I've given him a shot of amphetamines," Billings said. "It should hit him in another five minutes." Creighton nodded. "I'll give him another one later on if it's necessary."

The doctor departed. Crabb's gaze wandered around the great cabin of *Victory*, then settled uneasily upon Christopher. "What's this all about?" he asked, glaring at the younger man.

"Crabb, you've just been recalled to the RNVR Active List," said Christopher. "So you'll call me 'sir,' for a start. Do you understand?"

Crabb's attention drifted away for a few seconds, then returned to Creighton. He looked contemptuously at the thirty-one-year-old captain. "Bugger off, man," Crabb said.

Christopher sprang forward, grabbed Crabb by the shirtfront and yanked him to his feet. "Now, listen to me!" he snapped. "If you want to waste your fucking life wallowing in alcohol and self-pity, that's your business. But you're not going to waste mine. Further, you're being given a chance to redeem yourself. You're going to do something for your country and your Service. You've done it before and you've won decorations for it. So you're bloody well going to do it again. Right now!"

Christopher released Crabb and shoved him back into the chair. Crabb was dazed, but sobering. Next Creighton tried kindness and compromise.

"You'll also be paid, Lionel. A thousand pounds. Just what you were counting on."

Crabb was rubbing his chin, perking up slightly. Christopher fleetingly wondered how Paymaster Branch would feel about him promising money without any proper authority. No matter. He'd pay it from his own pocket if necessary. Or Sir Desmond would. Or Mountbatten. It hardly mattered.

"What about the money I already took?" Crabb asked warily. "From Foster."

"For all I care, keep it," Christopher answered.

"Then who's this job for?" Crabb finally asked.

Christopher recalled Crabb's flagrantly Royalist sentiments. The truth positively glowed within him. "For the Queen," he answered.

"She knows I'm going to dive?"

418

"Yes."

"How could she know?"

"I just sent her a signal saying so," said Creighton. Crabb stared Christopher in the eye. Christopher nodded slowly. "I did, Crabbie. Sir Desmond will verify that. God is my witness."

Morton looked up abruptly. His gaze was reproachful. "Seems to me," he said, "that God may be getting ready to clobber all of us if we don't get on with things."

But Crabb never took his eyes off Christopher. Creighton had hit Crabb directly, right in the heart, with the appeal of service to the Sovereign. For the first time, Christopher knew he was going through.

"What's the job?" Crabb asked.

"Just about the same as you thought you were going to do anyway," replied Christopher. "Only this time it *will* be for the Admiralty."

"A survey?"

"To start with, yes. We believe that there are mines on the hulls of the Soviet ships. We're going to look for them. If we find them, and I think we will, we disarm and remove. Or the other way around, as the case may be."

"What sort of mines?" Crabb asked, slowly coming around. "Limpet?"

Christopher nodded.

"English? Russian?" Crabb asked.

"American."

Crabb raised his eyebrows. "How long have they been there?"

419

"Too long. Probably several days."

"It barely matters," Crabb said sardonically. "They've either blown or they haven't."

"A reasonable option," said Christopher, his voice heavy with irony. In the corner, to Christopher's right, he saw Sir Desmond stifle a grin. The performance was vintage Lionel Crabb. Nothing excited him, and he was slowly easing into an operational mood. If Christopher could only get him into his old form, he would be the best diver in the world again — at least for one more morning.

The door opened. Lieutenant Commander Webb and his assistant Lieutenant Peter Page, the reigning experts of the Vernon mine section, entered. Webb carried a package. Christopher turned toward them.

"Hello, gentlemen," Creighton said. "Thanks for getting here so promptly."

"Good morning, sir," they said in unison. Christopher stole a look at the clock. Oh-two-twenty-seven GMT. The minutes were ticking wastefully away. For the first time he felt a brief tumbling sensation in his stomach. He recognized it. Fear. Fear that this job wouldn't get done. The time span was impossible. The minutes would tick off that clock and the whole harbor would blow. He wondered whether Angela had transmitted the messages yet to Serov, Mountbatten, Eden and the Queen. Miss efficiency herself! Of course she had.

"I brought the mine *and* the report, sir," Webb said succinctly. "I can guide you through both." He hesitated for a half-second, surveying the surroundings. He did not recognize Desmond Morton or the small rumpled man on the straight-backed chair. "We can set up here," Webb suggested, "or wherever you'd like."

"We'll work here," answered Christopher. "No time to move unnecessarily."

Lieutenant Page began to unwrap the package. Creighton took the occasion to continue.

"I must officially warn both of you," Christopher said, "that this is on the highest level of secrecy. In the future, you will be able to discuss it with no one at all other than myself or Lord Mountbatten. Not even each other, not even other people you might now see in this room."

"Aye, aye, sir," they both replied. Lieutenant Page pulled the limpet mine and the report from the package. Instinctively, Crabb's eyes widened as he saw the contents. Creighton studiously avoided introducing either officer to Crabb, though it was probable they knew already who he was.

The package was completely unwrapped. "Right," said Christopher. "Let's hear all about it, then."

Webb took over behind the desk. He held aloft the limpet mine seized by Colonel Sainthill's team in France. "This is a US coded 2CG," he said. "It's about a year old. The most recent mine the Americans manufacture. *One* of these could close Portsmouth harbor for two months."

Commander Webb was one of the presiding experts on mine warfare, not just in the Section but within the entire Royal Navy. When he'd been younger, he'd been an expert diver himself. Now he taught, but he taught well. He explained every aspect of the US 2CG's manufacture, its explosive power, its magnetic components and its methods of attachment and removal from a steel hull. As he spoke, Webb took the mine completely to pieces. Its explosives had long since been replaced by a dummy charge.

Webb exhibited every part of the mine relevant to the coming operation. He handed pieces to Crabb and to Christopher, insisting that they get the feel of the pieces in their hands. Everything would feel different underwater and handled through rubber gloves, but all three men were cognizant of Webb's technique of instruction: the more familiar a man was with a mine, the less chance there was of a mistake.

Finally, Webb explained the timing mechanism. With the thin end of a demagnetized screwdriver, the instructor showed Cobb and Creighton how the timer might be deadened. Then he reassembled the mine and turned it over to the two divers.

"Have a go at it," he said.

Creighton went first. "Ever seen one of these before?" he asked Crabb.

Crabb shook his head. "Never," he answered. But his attention was focused now. He was still unshaven and his hair dirty and matted. But he was stone sober and concentrating.

Christopher took the mine apart and put it back together. Then he repeated the procedure. Crabb watched. So did Webb. So did Lieutenant Page, Owl and Colonel Sainthill.

Crabb took the mine. He broke it down thirty seconds faster than Christoper and reassembled it with equal speed. When Crabb repeated the procedure, Christopher was relieved to see that Crabb hadn't lost his natural aptitude with a mine, though it would be much more difficult underwater and much slower. But Christopher was glad he'd chosen him for the job. Crabb may have been broke, boastful and dissolute, but these qualities applied only to dry land.

"Here's a big problem," Crabb said.

Christopher waited. So did Webb.

"When this mine is magnetized to a surface, it will have to be disarmed before any attempt is made to remove it. Otherwise it will explode."

Crabb indicated how the timing mechanism, once set, was virtually inaccessible. Then he said, "Wait a minute." He looked sidelong at the mine. "Hey, Webb," Crabb said, "give me that long thin thing you were using."

Webb handed him the demagnetized screwdriver. Christopher stood an inch away from Crabb and leaned over him as Crabb worked. Two minutes passed. Then five. Then more. Crabb was fiddling with the timer.

Crabb set the timer and inserted the head of the screwdriver from various angles. Each time, the timer clicked loudly, indicating detonation. On Crabb's third attempt, the timer stopped ticking.

But there was no click. No detonation.

"The mine's vulnerable to a long, thin blade," Crabb said. "And it has to enter sideways, practically from eighty degrees to port. Look at this, sir. You can do it this way."

Crabb moved the mine to Christopher.

"It's a tricky fucker, this one," Crabb said. "But it can be neutralized. It's essential you keep the head of the blade right home until you've removed the mine from the hull. Then you can neutralize it from the back. Otherwise, if you take it out or it slips before removal, detonation is almost certain."

Christopher tried it twice himself. As he worked, a lieutenant arrived at the door with the diving equipment. Christopher saw the hands of the watch on his wrist. Oh-three-oh-two. He broke into a cold sweat. There just wasn't any *time*.

"Okay. I've got the hang of it," Creighton said. "What else?"

"Where's my fucking suit?" Crabb asked.

Christopher nodded to the pile of equipment that had been left by the door. Crabb walked to it. He pulled his own gear away from Christopher's. He picked up his newly devised oxygen recycling set and looked at it very critically. Then he turned his scrutiny upon Christopher's equipment.

"You're not going to wear that useless submariner clobber, are you?" Crabb asked. He gestured contemptuously at the Sladen shallow-water suit and a DSEA breathing set.

"I'm used to it," replied Creighton.

"The oxygen recycler is much better," Crabb insisted. "No telltale bubbles on the surface."

Creighton was about to answer that the bubbles hardly mattered since Serov had been notified anyway. But Crabb had no need to know about collaboration with the Russians. It would only have infuriated him. So Christopher stuck with a technical response.

"Bubbles won't show up on radar," he said. "And on your recycler, the maximum depth is thirty-two feet. Any more and you're courting trouble." He turned to Webb. "How many feet does the *Ordzhonikidze* draw?" he asked.

"Twenty-five feet. Same as the *Sverdlov*." It was Crabb who answered, not Webb. "I ought to know. I've been under it." Crabb grinned impishly. "I'm using my own equipment," Crabb said. "That's final."

Creighton looked back to the clock. Oh-three-oh-eight GMT. *Why can't time stop?* he wondered. *Just this once.*

"All right, Crabbie," Christopher said. "As you wish."

Crabb smiled slightly. "We've got RG, I assume."

"You assume right. Brand new. The light straps to the chest, the receiver to our backs. Viewer to one eye. It will light up the underwater like a strong green moonlight."

"Then let's get rigged out and get to work," Crabb said. He was wide awake now.

As Crabb pulled on his oiled long johns and then

his black rubber suit, Christopher observed him closely. The man who'd partaken in the degrading scene at the Queen's Hotel the previous evening had mysteriously vanished. Returned was the pride, strength and courage that had won Crabb a fistful of medals against the Germans and Italians a decade earlier. But now that Crabb was back where he loved to be—facing a dangerous operation for the Royal Navy—he was renewed. And a renewed Lionel Crabb was as good a diver as ever lived.

The two men were ready. They left the great cabin. Lieutenant Page gave them duffle coats to wear when they emerged on the dock. Their oxygen cylinders, masks and fins had already gone down to King's Stairs Jetty, where they would be able to enter the water unobserved. They came to the gangway and slipped into the coats.

Christopher heard a woman's voice. He turned. It was Angela, crossing the quarterdeck. "Captain, sir!" she called. "Immediate for Christopher Robin!" Angela ran to him and handed him two signals. He tore open the envelopes.

The first was from Mountbatten:

YOU HAVE MY FULL SUPPORT.
GOOD LUCK.

CHARLEMAGNE

The second was from Prime Minister Eden:

I REPEAT: YOU ARE NOT TO APPROACH

ANY RUSSIAN HULLS. INFORMATION ON MINES IS FALSE AND CIRCULATED TO CAUSE PANIC AND DISCORD BETWEEN RUSSIAN AND ENGLISH LEADERS. AGAIN I REPEAT: YOU ARE NOT TO APPROACH ANY RUSSIAN HULLS. COURT-MARTIAL WILL FOLLOW FOR ANY NAVAL PERSONNEL WHO DISOBEY. ACKNOWLEDGE.

EDEN

Christopher read the message swiftly, then reread it. He crumpled it and handed it back to Angela.

"Angela," he said evenly, "make to Prime Minister, repeat Charlemagne and the Author: 'Regret Christopher Robin operational protecting hulls. Cannot be contacted.' Sign it yourself."

"Aye, aye, sir." She disappeared again.

Christopher and Lionel Crabb walked slowly down the gangway together. Sainthill and Desmond Morton watched from the quarterdeck.

As Christopher walked, his gaze lifted. *Victory* was at a long broadside distance from the *Ordzhonikidze*. Between the dockyard buildings, he was surprised to notice that the Russian ship was calm and normally lit. He could see sailors on the deck and assumed Khrushchev and Bulganin were asleep in their quarters.

Suddenly, he was amazed. What stupid games were the politicians now playing? Serov had received word, *hadn't he?* A signal Wren officer had delivered it aboard the Soviet cruiser. Were Khrushchev and Bulganin so stubborn that they would stay aboard no matter what the risk? It didn't make sense. There was no activity aboard the *Ordzhonikidze* to suggest that anything was amiss.

For a moment, Christopher stopped, letting Crabb trudge on ahead of him — an improbable short, squat figure masking a diving suit with a duffle coat. Christopher scanned the harbor. He looked at sleeping Gosport, Portsmouth, then raised his eyes toward Fareham Lake. It was all so peaceful. So still. And yet, he knew:

If the mines were in place, they had probably been set well in place, beneath the magazines of the warships. If one mine detonated, every bit of ammunition on that ship would go, also. *Ordzhonikidze* would be blown to pieces, Bulganin and Khrushchev dying in the conflagration. The two other Russian ships would blow in a chain reaction. And so would every other Royal Navy ship within five hundred yards, including *Victory*. Christopher quickly counted four of them.

And then? The political ramifications for a world newly entered into the Atomic Age? Christopher could only guess in horror.

If there was any consolation to Christopher, it was his own fate. His death, and Crabb's, would be instantaneous. At the first mistaken nudge of any live mine, they would be obliterated. It would be so fast that they wouldn't feel a thing. Just, he imagined, a big red nothingness.

Lord God, he thought as he continued to walk. *It's all come down to this.* He contemplated it as a man with a chronic illness might, viewing the end of his life.

He walked several paces behind Crabb. He thought of his mother and sister living in Kent and wished he'd spent a few days with them recently. He thought of his boyhood, Churchill and the war.

"Christopher . . . ?" Jemima's voice.

He turned. She ran toward him. Gone were the pearls and the black dress. She was back in uniform, her face both frightened and beautiful in the reflected lights from the harbor. There was so much to say, yet so little that could be said.

"You're marvelous," said Christopher. "Your information may save us yet."

She nodded. "Angela told me everything. I called on my transceiver on the way here."

Christopher started to walk and she walked with him. His duffle coat fell back. She saw the diving suit and shuddered. They caught up with Crabb and arrived on King's Stairs at the same time.

"What if the mines are not the American type?" she asked. "What if they're a sort neither of you know?"

Crabb gave her a nonchalant half smile. He clapped his hands sharply. "Bang! I should think!" he laughed. A man with little to lose.

Christopher looked at Jemima. He couldn't say any of the things he wanted to. Instead he gave her a wink and a slight wave of the hand.

429

She spoke for both of them. Or rather, she didn't speak. She moved her lips, and he read the message.

"I love you," her lips said.

Christopher fought with emotions that he didn't know he had. He wrestled mightily, and he won. He became again the captain speaking to his deputy commander. "Take command in my absence, Number Once," he said gruffly.

"Aye, aye, sir," acknowledged Jemima and stood smartly to attention. Crabb's words echoed in her ears. *Bang, I should think!*

And Christopher was gone, walking down the King's Stairs with Crabb toward the water.

She walked away quickly toward *Victory*, her pace increasing with each step. She almost hurdled up the gangway and out onto the quarterdeck where the Officer of the Day and his ratings were keeping watch. She looked across to King's Jetty but it was impossible to see anything. She then looked to the Russian ships, half-hidden by the dockyard buildings. But all was quiet. *For how long?* she wondered. Suddenly, desperate to do something, an inspiration moved her. She looked aft at the bare flagpole.

"Mr. Johnson!"

"Yes, ma'am," the Officer of the Day answered.

"Would you say that the operation on which the Captain and Commander Crabb are engaged is 'an action'?"

"Most decidedly so."

"And an action by the crew of *Victory?*"

"Yes, ma'am."

Tim Sainthill and Desmond Morton appeared close by.

"Mr. Johnson! Hoist the battle ensign!" she ordered.

"Aye, aye, ma'am," he said. "Yeoman!"

The yeoman and his mates, standing close by on their action stations, had already heard. They pulled the ensign from its locker and doubled aft onto the poop deck. In ten seconds the white ensign of Her Majesty's Fleet guided smoothly upward.

"Battle ensign hoisted close up, ma'am," the yeoman reported.

"Very good," she acknowledged.

As she had at incalculable other times in naval history, HMS *Victory* showed her colors to the enemy. Only this time, the enemy lurked beneath Portsmouth harbor, deadly, faceless and — as it had been since this operation began — virtually invisible.

THIRTY-TWO

Christopher Creighton and Lionel Crabb walked slowly down the four flights of steps that led to the harbor. Crabb went first. They were one hundred seventy yards north of the *Ordzhonikidze,* the nearest Russian vessel. They were out of view of everyone except each other.

Christopher spoke softly, reviewing. "We swim to the cruiser first," he said. "I'll examine the port side for mines; you check starboard. If either of us find one, I'll surface and signal *Victory* by RG. You start disarming while I check the destroyers. If the check on the destroyers is positive, I'll start disarmament there. If negative, I'll come back to the cruiser and start at the other end." They started together down the final flight of steps to the water. "If we're lucky, we'll meet in the middle with the job done."

And if we're not lucky? Both thought of that

question. Neither asked.

"Luck," said Crabb, obliquely addressing the point, "is something I've had in short supply recently, Captain."

"Find some tonight, Crabbie," Christopher said.

Crabb reached the water first. There were no emotional glances or comments. Crabb fixed his mask in place, checked his equipment a final time and slid into the water. In five seconds, he'd drifted out into the shadows.

Christopher drew a deep breath. Many times in his life he'd faced death or contemplated it. His Catholicism had always been a comfort, but had never dispelled the fears any man has of dying. Never, however, had he before entered the final stage of an operation with such an extreme sense of dread as tonight. Perhaps it was because he was a man now in his thirties, a man who'd come to understand mortality and the fallibility of human flesh, a man who'd attended too many funerals of too many friends.

Something told him he would die this night. He raised his eyes and drew a second deep breath. He looked around Pompey harbor, or what he could see of it. He could not prevent a quick glance at Haslar Hospital across the water, nor could he help cringing at the extreme pain of the burst appendix he'd left there during the war.

Then he thought of the DSEA tank at Gosport, and how he'd nearly drowned in it.

Then a more recent image appeared before him,

that of the Russian sailors breaking out carbines on the decks of their ships. That bastard Serov, he suddenly thought. What game was *he* playing? Christopher guessed that the Soviet crews had not been notified of an operation beneath their ships. Meaning, they would jolly well shoot if they saw divers.

Mountbatten's words flashed back to steady him. *Your job, young Christopher, is not to wonder about diplomatic policy, but rather to help further it.*

Yes, sir, he thought. He entered the water several seconds behind Crabb. Little Lionel was fifteen yards ahead of him, steadily moving through the dark like an alligator.

The water was cold as ice. As usual, it trickled down the neck of his Sladen shallow-water suit. It wasn't dangerous, just a major discomfort. For years, ever since he'd first started diving, Christopher had tried to plug the leak at the base of his neck. He had failed yet again. He moved twenty yards from shore and felt the slight ripple of a wake left by Crabb. He wondered who was following whom. Then it occurred to him that Crabb's suit would be well caulked and watertight. There were little touches the student never completely learned from the master. In the darkness of the water, as he turned around the bend in the harbor and saw the massive silhouette of the *Ordzhonikidze,* Christopher was suddenly filled with admiration for the squat little diver in front of him. Whatever else

Crabb was, he was his own man. Christopher respected him for it.

There was a gentle flood tide flowing against them. But it offered no hazard as they flippered toward the Soviet ships. In the distance, Christopher could see slight movement on the deck of the *Ordzhonikidze*. A Russian sailor with a rifle on watch. As Christopher had told friends many times, he'd done just about everything in the waters around Portsmouth: but dying from a Russian bullet was something he'd never envisioned.

They were halfway to the cruiser. The water trickling into his suit had reached his waist. In another few minutes it would be freezing his balls off. Then everything would turn numb. He suppressed a shiver. He saw the Russian with the rifle more clearly now and knew that he and Crabb would both have to submerge within another minute. He cursed the apparatus he carried. He would be leaving bubbles. Crabb, suspicious forever of the Soviets, had brought the oxygen recycler, which couldn't be detected from the surface. There was little doubt in Christopher's mind who the better prepared diver was.

The great hull of the Soviet cruiser loomed darkly in front of them, a seagoing megalith with deck lights. Crabb treaded water and turned toward Christopher. Crabb made a gesture which indicated he was about to go under.

Creighton nodded, but motioned also to the RG eyepiece. With his hand, Crabb gave a gesture of understanding; then both men fixed their eyepieces to the left sides of their masks. Without any gesture at all, they switched on the RG lamps and receivers. The infrared beam, viewed through the eyepieces, lit up the *Ordzhonikidze* with an eerie green glow. The hull itself was a mixture of hundreds of strange shades, colors and shadows.

Crabb turned and nodded a final time. Then he dived. Christopher followed, enjoying an irrational sense of safety once he was underwater.

Christopher's own thoughts were magnified by the dull pressure of the water upon his head and body. He moved forward but in a serpentine pattern, scared now that a direct line of bubbles would give him away. For a moment he lost Crabb, and for a moment after that he was disoriented. But when he studied the underwater through the RG he could see the hull of the Soviet ship twenty yards before him. And also, he could see Crabb.

Christopher looked at his watch. Oh-three-fifty-six GMT. There wasn't time. There simply would not be time. He surged ahead through the frigid water. His entire genital area was numb now.

They moved together closer to the hull. Then they touched it. Christopher watched Crabb. Crabbie's instincts were uncanny, combined with his experience. He gestured to Christopher to follow him. There were strategic points on any ship, Christopher knew, where a mine would cause maximum damage. There were spots where—

Crabb whirled and pointed. They both saw the

437

first mine together. Christopher's stomach surged. There it was. The theory of mines and mine disarmament had just been replaced with the reality of both.

Crabb went to the first mine and touched it gently. It had been well camouflaged, but was clearly visible through the RG receivers. Both divers moved in very close and scanned. In a very minor way, Christopher was relieved.

Crabb nodded and made a thumbs-up gesture. It was the American limpet they'd practiced upon. US 2CG. The two men shared a small glimmer of hope.

Methodically and expertly, Crabb went to work with his de-magnetized screwdriver. Christopher glanced at the contours of the *Ordzhonikidze*'s hull, then drifted gently to the surface. He broke through as slowly as possible to make no noise, though from his position beneath the tip in the ship's bow, he could not be seen from above.

In silhouette before the lights of a sleeping Portsmouth, *Victory*'s yardarm showed clearly. Christopher aimed his RG light at it and flashed the call sign: K for Kanga.

He flashed continuously. Two seconds. Five seconds. *Come on, Angela. Come on, Joan.* Eight seconds. Creighton barely breathed.

Then through his RC receiver, he could see a small green light flashing on his bearing. It signalled V twice. *Victory* was ready to receive.

***

From *Victory*'s yardarm, Angela and Joan were receiving Christopher's signal on their own RG's. Jemima anxiously walked the poop deck below.

"Acknowledge," said Angela to Joan.

Joan nodded and flashed back a double R, while Angela climbed down to Jemima. "Mine positive, ma'am. American type. Disarmament proceeding."

"Thank you, Angela," acknowledged the deputy commander, standing rigidly still. *All right!* she told herself. *So it*'s the American type. But they still have to be disarmed!

Jemima wished she could relax. She was shaking all over. Help came in the form of Tim Sainthill. "Here, madam acting captain," he said. He gave her a cup of coffee.

"Thanks, Tim," she said, taking it. "You always arrive in the nick of time."

He gave her a big smile and half a bear hug. "That's what Royal Marine Commando colonels are for," he said. He turned to Angela. "Yours is on the sextant box."

"Thank you, sir," she said.

"Oh, and Angela," said Jemima. "When you've had a good swig, make to Charlemagne from Kanga, repeated Lord High Admiral, Prime Minister and Serov, and relay the captain's signal."

"Aye, aye, ma'am," confirmed Angela. She went off to the signals office, taking her coffee with her.

Jemima walked across the deck to the main-to'-gallant mast and climbed to the yardarm. She looked across at the Soviet warships, so near and in such danger. It made no sense that they had not been evacuated long ago. Sir Desmond had tried to explain the reasons. She hadn't accepted any of them. What stupid bloody game were they all playing, those politicians and diplomats? They would be responsible for killing everybody. Christopher, Crabb and all of them; and she had no illusions as to her own immediate danger. *Victory* lay one-and-a-half cables from the *Ordzhonikidze*. What Villeneuve failed to achieve at Trafalgar might well be achieved here by a slip of Christopher's fingers.

She looked around the harbor. To Gosport and Hardway, up toward Fareham Lake and Porchester, Portsea and — . It all seemed so quiet and peaceful — difficult to comprehend that it all might suddenly ignite.

Christopher reached *Smotryashchi* within a minute, forgetting that she was moored tightly alongside the cruiser. In comparison to the *Ordzhonikidze*, she was quite small. The water was dark, still and deafeningly quiet. *Why,* he wondered, *was the greatest danger always accompanied by solitude and vast sheets of silence?*

He switched on his RG, and by its green beam made a thorough survey of the hull. He was relieved to find nothing. Not one mine. He completed the search in twenty minutes. Then he swam on to *Sovershenny*. It took him another thirty minutes to examine the entire hull. Again, no mines. Both men

440

had been in the water for more than an hour. Christopher looked at his watch. It was 0448 GMT.

His senses began to race. He swam back to Crabb, who had a mine in his hand. He gave Christopher a thumbs up and let go of the limpet. It disappeared into the murky slime of Portsmouth harbor. Christopher held Crabb's shoulder and indicated that they should surface for a moment. They surfaced together, close up under the cruiser's bow. Only their heads were above the waterline.

Christopher spoke in a whisper. "Destroyers negative," he said. "What about the cruiser?"

"Eighteen mines," reported Crabb nonchalantly. "Nine on each side."

"Eighteen! How many have you disarmed?"

"One."

Christopher was transfixed. "That'll take us well into daylight!"

"So we should get back down there, right?" Crabb calmly asked. "No use talking about it. I looked at the fuse on the one I disarmed. They're going to go at around 0700."

Suddenly the water around Christopher was ice cold again. He saw little hope of defusing seventeen more mines in two hours. His hand broke the surface and he looked at the glowing dial on his watch. Oh-four-fifty-nine.

"It goes faster as you work, sir," Crabb said. "Come on. Let's get back down there. Watch me. I'll show you how. QED."

Crabb disappeared beneath the water and Christopher followed.

He stayed with the smaller man as Crabb started on the second mine on the port side of the *Ordzhonikidze*. Christopher thought of Khrushchev and Bulganin sleeping somewhere above them. He wondered why he and Crabb were in freezing water on an April morning risking their lives for the Russians. And Mountbatten's words came back . . . no individual lives more important than completing our operation, including yours or mine. If Christopher hadn't been honor bound to that arrangement, he realized, he wouldn't have been down there. He crowded close as Crabb went to work on the second mine. He had to be absolutely sure that he followed the technique.

Crabb's hands worked with astonishing dexterity. The second mine took sixteen minutes. Christopher waited and studied Crabb's method on the third mine. As Crabb proceeded, Christopher mentally did the next step ahead of Crabb. When each mine was disarmed, Crabb dropped it. It sank harmlessly. Other divers would recover it later.

Christopher tapped Crabb on the shoulder and indicated he was going to work. He followed the hull down to the cruiser's stern. He took out the demagnetized screwdriver and attached the securing line to his wrist. He set the RG light and the receiver so that the green beam focused on the mine a foot in front of his face. Then he began.

Christopher's heart pounded in his chest. He squeamishly moved the outer casing off the mine about one sixteenth of an inch, then worked the blade of the screwdriver carefully in from the eighty-degree angle Crabb had used. He slipped the blade forward in a tortuously slow insertion, praying that the blade would not trip the wrong mechanism.

How would it end, he wondered. Would he even feel the killer shock waves that would precipitate his death? A vision returned to him of the World War, of men blown to tiny pieces by a direct hit from an aerial bomb.

The blade slipped farther in. Beneath his suit, his sweat merged with the icy water that continued to leak at his neck. He gave the screwdriver a final gentle prod and he thought he felt the timing mechanism.

He *did* have the timing mechanism. His other hand was flush against the mine. The ticking had stopped. Now he held the screwdriver in place as his other hand detached the mine from the *Ordzhonikidze*. It took several minutes more. With the limpet mine separated from the steel hull, Christopher reached to the back of the mine and removed the detonator. Then he released it. He wasted several seconds by watching the mine drift harmlessly down into the black silt in the bed of the harbor.

One down. His confidence perked up. He glanced down at Crabb, who was proceeding much more quickly. Christopher turned to his second mine and repeated the same laborious, meticulous procedure. For a second time, he was successful. He removed a third and it seemed almost routine. He occasionally glanced at Crabb again. They finished on the port side of the hull and moved to starboard.

Now it almost seemed easy. The two divers worked efficiently and confidently, barely glancing at each other. As Christopher removed his sixth mine, he spent a few extra seconds studying the timing mechanism. And he froze. There was almost not time left on the mine he'd held in his hands. He removed the detonator and dropped it as if it had been contaminated. He moved back from the hull and scanned with his RG beam. Six mines remained. Three for each of them. Then he looked at his watch. It was 0631 and Christopher had to summon every bit of his strength and courage.

Six mines. Approximately thirty minutes. He motioned to his watch. Crabb jerked his head up and down. Yes, he was aware of the time also. In the green glow, Christopher could see Crabb's face through his diving mask. The man's eyes were drawn and haggard. He looked suddenly like a cadaver. And when Christopher gave him a pat of encouragement, he realized how quickly Crabb was breathing.

Then he noticed the worst sign of all. He was working faster than Crabb now. Crabb was fading. Or tiring. Or growing ill. Or in trouble.

Please God. Just four more, he found himself praying. A glance to his left and, *Hurry, Crabbie, God damn it, hurry!*

Christopher removed two. It was 0649. Crabb

444

had only removed one in that time. Above them, it was dawn. There could be no surfacing now. None at all. The Russians would shoot at anything that moved near the ships. No question about it. Christopher stared at Crabb. The man's hands were motionless. Crabb had stopped. What was wrong?

Then Crabb reached for the second of his two remaining mines. His work was labored now, fading, slow and clumsy. Christopher did the only thing he could. He worked frantically on his own final mine, and it slipped away from the Russian hull at 0654. When he removed the detonator, he saw that the timer had almost completely elapsed. One mine remained and it was in front of Crabb. Christopher knew that it was set to go at any moment, too.

Christopher looked at Crabb. For a moment he froze. Crabb was clutching his throat and his stomach. He was ignoring the sole remaining limpet. Crabb was in trouble.

Christopher swam to him immediately. Crabb, however, had panicked. He made a violent gesture toward his oxygen recycler, then bolted toward the surface. Christopher grabbed him. Surfacing in the daylight would be in plain view of the Russians. There would be bullets. Soviet frogmen. And it would look for all the world that British divers had planted a mine on the *Ordzhonikidze*.

Creighton pulled Crabb back, but Crabb was above him in the water. Crabb's foot kicked into Christopher's face. It jarred the RG eyepiece and

Crabb broke free. But Christopher was by far the taller and faster. He grabbed Crabb and pulled him back down.

Crabb was frantic and Christopher knew it. He also knew that Crabb had no chance. If he broke to the surface, the final mine would never be removed properly. It would blow. If the magazine ignited, the Russian ships, the British ships and a third of Portsmouth would go with it. Christopher knew what he had to do. But he fought his duty for as long as he could. Then Crabb made it easy. The squat little man clutched for his diver's knife as he continued to struggle violently.

Mountbatten's words flashed: . . . *no individual lives more important than completing this operation* . . .

Christopher reached for Crabb's oxygen cylinder. He held Crabb as tightly as he could, as tightly as he'd ever held any man or woman in his life, and he shut the valves that supplied and recycled Crabb's oxygen. Christopher bit down so hard he was afraid his teeth would shatter. He also felt something tight inside his chest and that, too, felt like it would burst.

Crabb struggled less now. The fight was going out of him, and with it passed Crabb's consciousness. The frenzied struggling — the desperate desire to survive — was weaker in Crabb. His knife dropped and his hands clawed for his air supply. But Christopher would not — *could not* — give it to him. Even returning to King's Stairs was impossible. There wasn't time. The final mine would blow.

Christopher Creighton could feel Crabb's body shudder violently. Then he felt consciousness leave the little man, with a final pathetic spasm. Then it was over and all Christopher had in his hands was a body. He saw his watch. 0659. The life of a man he dearly cared for could terminate within a matter of minutes. But the struggle was over. Years of Christopher's training took over. He acted now on instinct, clinically detached from what he was doing.

He was a naval officer completing an operation, he told himself over and over. A shipmate had fallen. But he must not abandon his trust.

Crabbie himself would have agreed.

Christopher put his safety line around Crabb and tied a bowline. The two bodies were attached to each other. Crabb couldn't float to the surface because Christopher's weight held him.

Creighton did not find it difficult to swim back to the remaining limpet, despite towing Crabb. He found its disarmament the easiest of them all. Maybe he was numb to them; maybe he'd mastered the technique. He clipped off the final mine and held it up. There was no time left on the fused timer. He let it go and drifted down with the rest of them.

Christopher swung around and turned to the north. The tide was now ebbing gently, but he hardly noticed it as he swam toward King's Stairs. He went twenty yards with no incident, then thirty. Suddenly he felt a pull.

Crabb's body was suddenly and inexplicably buoyant. It was pulling toward the surface and Christopher couldn't stop it. He turned and pulled on the lifeline to try to keep Crabb's body down, but he had no leverage. They both were floating dangerously to the surface. Christopher could see the brightness of dawn above him. Then Crabb's body broke the surface.

Christopher stayed beneath the water line and grabbed Crabb by his oxygen cylinders. All Christopher could think of was that a misrouting of oxygen had caused the problem. Creighton turned a valve and rerouted the air supply. Slowly Crabb began to sink again. Christopher pulled him back under—*far* under—and now swam as fast as he could for King's Stairs. He waited for Russian carbine bullets to break the surface over his head. But if there were any, they were not close to him.

Seven minutes later he arrived back at King's Stairs. He staggered up the first two steps. He pulled Crabb's body from the water. It was 0723.

One of his young Royal Marine commandos saw him. "Get a van or a car and the surgeon," Christopher said. "At the rush."

The marine doubled off. Christopher looked at Crabb. He undid his diving suit and ripped Crabb's head and upper chest out of it. He felt for a neck pulse. It was negative. Christopher started to break.

"No, Crabbie. For Christ's sake, no!" he said, more as a prayer than anything. He lifted his old friend in his arms and carried him to the first stone

448

landing. He laid him out lengthwise. Crabb's face was white, his eyes open and numb. Christopher pressed his lips to Crabb's and began mouth-to-mouth resuscitation.

Christopher worked furiously, pressing on Crabb's chest with an open hand. He breathed, he prayed, he implored. Anything to get Crabb to start breathing. Not that much time had elapsed. His church taught him about miracles. He prayed for one here. He implored.

Come on, Crabbie! Breathe, Crabbie! Move, Crabbie! Don't die, Crabbie!

Sainthill and Trott arrived. So did Angela and Jemima. Sir Desmond was there a few seconds later. By some sixth sense or from the corner of his eye, Christopher was aware of them. All of them. They stood and watched, as dazed as he was.

Christopher pumped Crabb's chest and forced the air back into his lungs. For several minutes he did everything he knew how to do. Only when he saw Surgeon Commander Billings racing down the stone steps did he stop.

Billings knelt by Crabb. Christopher sat on the stone steps. The doctor made a quick clinical examination. He looked at Christopher.

"I'm sorry, sir," Billings said. "He's dead."

Christopher looked at the man in the black diving suit for several seconds. His eyes misted. No one moved.

Christopher looked back over the water and turned his face away from the small group above him. The tears streamed now. He clutched at his face to hide the tears, but they flooded past his fingers. He shook all over. Two young marines appeared on Sainthill's orders and lifted Crabb's body from the stone landing.

No one came to Christopher. No one dared.

It took him several minutes to gather himself and to realize again that he was the captain commanding this operation. He told himself that his duty still mattered. He climbed the steps and found Colonel Sainthill.

"You must be responsible for him," Christopher said. "Freeze him in absolute secrecy until we hear from Charlemagne."

"The Russians saw something in the water, sir," Sainthill said. "They sent divers over the side of their ships."

"Deny everything," said Christopher.

"Very good, sir."

"They never saw us. We weren't there. Nothing happened," Christopher explained.

"Yes, sir," Colonel Sainthill said again.

Christopher turned. "Angela?" he asked.

The signal Wren appeared. "Sir?"

"Make to Charlemagne, repeat the Author, Prime Minister and General Serov. 'Eighteen mines disarmed and removed. Soviet ships *Ordzhonikidze*, *Sovershenny* and *Smotryashchi* are clear — I say again — are clear.' "

"Aye, aye, sir." She started to move, but Christopher held her arm.

"And Angela, make an additional signal to Charlemagne, no repeats, eyes addressee only. 'During operation Commander Lionel Crabb became ill and obstructed disarmaments of mines. It became imperative to kill him."

Angela's eyes widened and rose to meet Christopher's. Her pencil stopped. His other officers stood still.

"That's all," he said to Angela. He felt like collapsing.

"Yes, sir," she acknowledged.

Christopher did not look at them. Not even Jemima. He picked up his gear and stumbled up King's Stairs, then crossed the dockyard toward *Victory.*

"Mr. Page," said Sainthill to the marine lieutenant standing by, "transport this body in the highest secrecy to the special morgue in Cosham. To be held under our directions."

"Sir," said the lieutenant affirmatively.

Sainthill took a last look at Crabb and shook his head. With Jemima, Angela and Morton, he walked after Christopher. Reaching him, Sainthill took his diving gear and Jemima put his duffle coat across his shoulders. Then she and Angela put an arm through his on either side. He did not resist.

Behind them, Lieutenant Page presided over Crabb's body, lying underneath a blanket, finally at peace.

Reaching *Victory,* Christopher crossed the quarterback and went immediately up to the poop deck.

He looked back to King's Jetty. Lieutenant Page's driver had reserved his fifteen-hundredweight truck to where Crabb lay. Three marines lifted the blanketed body into the back of the truck. They bolted up the backboards and pulled down the rear canvas section.

Then, with no plan or preconceived notion, Christopher acted upon the sheer training and instinct of a naval officer.

"Chief yeoman," he said clearly, "stand by aft."

"Aye, aye, sir," said the chief yeoman of signals. He doubled across the quarterdeck, up the ladder and across the poop deck to the afterrail. Christopher pulled his beret out of his duffle coat pocket and put it on.

At King's Jetty, Lieutenant Page and a sergeant had climbed in the front seat of the truck. They drove toward the dockyard gate.

Christopher walked forward as the truck made to cross *Victory*'s starboard bow.

"Chief yeoman," said Christopher.

"Sir!"

"Dip the ensign."

"Aye, aye, sir," said the chief yeoman.

Christopher saluted and the ensign was lowered to the regulation distance of one third. The rest of them stood silently to attention. Creighton wanted to say a prayer, but couldn't think of any words.

The truck carrying Crabb slowly passed *Victory* and disappeared under her bows.

Christopher's hand came down and the ensign

was rehoisted close up.

He looked up at the three Russian ships. There was activity on all of them, bordering on excitement. But it was eight bells in the morning watch and activity was to be expected. Otherwise the waters of Portsmouth harbor were clear and still, rippling very gently on the ebb tide.

Out of force of habit, Christopher glanced at his watch. It was 0802 GMT, sunny and clear on an April morning. He glanced back toward the Russian ships, his face drawn and haggard. He squinted in the dazzle of sunlight upon the harbor.

THIRTY-THREE

Though the entire M Section in Portsmouth was dead tired from the night watch, the next day's duties did not change. The watch was maintained rigorously upon the three Soviet ships, and the ring of steel remained operational.

Christopher was too tired and too grief-stricken to sleep during the day. He kept a quiet vigil in his cabin aboard *Victory*. His shift was punctuated only by signals.

The one from Charlemagne arrived first. YOU HAVE ACTED IN THE BEST TRADITIONS OF THE SERVICE, Mountbatten said. It did nothing to assuage Christopher's sense of loss. What, he kept asking himself, could he have done differently that might have spared poor Crabbie's life? He couldn't find anything.

The message from Prime Minister Eden arrived five in the afternoon. It was ominous: MEET WITH

ME TOMORROW 20TH AT DOWNING STREET, 1100, Eden wired. Christopher grimaced and pondered his dismissal from the Royal Navy. In his depressed, fatigued state, he saw the bitter irony of it all: he would take Crabb's place, the unfairly dismissed career diver crawling penniless from one London pub to another.

Later in the evening, General Serov arrived unannounced aboard *Victory*. The KGB leader was his jovial, grinning self. He pumped Christopher's hand. After dinner, Serov cornered Creighton.

"I want you to know," Serov said, "that Comrade Khrushchev himself is aware of what happens this early morning. He wishes convey personal appreciation. He wanting thank you personally before leaving England."

"Very kind of him, Ivan," Christopher said. "But he needn't. I'm certain he's very busy."

"But he's insisting," said Serov.

Christopher shrugged. "So be it," he said. Serov held in his hand a snifter containing a fifty-year-old Armagnac. In the middle of the brandy were a pair of ice cubes. Creighton held Serov in a tight, critical gaze. "Comrade," he said, "something bothers me."

"Please tell me."

"Why were your ships not evacuated? Your leaders took such an unnecessary risk being aboard, as did your sailors, as you did yourself."

Jemima appeared at Christopher's side. Serov sipped his drink.

"Never informed," Serov said.

"What?"

"I personal had no knowing diving operation until this morning," said Serov. "Otherwise, most certainly would have led Comrade Khrushchev and Comrade Bulganin to safer quarters."

"But you were signaled that the operation was in progress," Creighton said.

"Yes," Jemima added. "Angela sent the signal by Second Officer Joan Prewitt. Joan delivered it personally aboard *Ordzhonikidze*."

But Serov shook his head ruefully. "Yes. But after the earlier threat to my leaders at Claridge's, I had to return to London. I not come back here until eleven this morning. No one empowered to receive signal in my absence."

"Well," said Christopher, shaking his head. "If that's your communication system, you'd better improve it. Your leaders might have died because of it."

Serov nodded, raising his before-dinner brandy as a toast. "But they did not. Thanks to heroism of Captain Christopher and Commander Crabb."

A few moments later, all five sat down to dinner in the great cabin. Christopher and Jemima, Morton, Sainthill and Serov. The meal was fine, but the atmosphere was greatly subdued. Afterward, Christopher saw Serov off and returned to the great cabin. He sat with Desmond Morton. At least this evening Khrushchev and Bulganin were in London, far outside of Christopher's responsibility in Portsmouth.

Creighton sat with Sir Desmond and chatted. A few minutes later, Angela rapped at the door and entered.

"Excuse me," she said. "There's a message from Birdham. It came in on the direct security line."

He looked at her. But she handed it to him so that he might read it himself.

VON OSTENBERG DEAD, it said. He read it out.

Christopher blew out a long, exhausted breath. He crumpled the message and handed it back to her.

"That's that, I suppose," he said. She agreed. Sir Desmond looked his way, nodded and said nothing. Angela departed.

"So who planted those limpets, Uncle Desmond?" Christopher said through his exhaustion. "Who got Crabbie killed? I want to know. And my one source has just expired."

Morton stared out the panoramic window behind Nelson's desk, the window that overlooked the harbor. He broke a silence after several minutes.

"It's easy to blame it on Panavich, isn't it?" he asked. "But would a little Naval Commissar in Kronstadt engineer something as grand as that? I don't think so. As an explanation, that just doesn't satisfy."

"No," Christopher said. "It doesn't. But who then?"

Morton was very quiet, staring at the water and saying nothing. Then he turned. "Well, it's very simple, isn't it?" he asked. "Someone else, other than White Russians, who wanted Khrushchev dead. Right?"

The great cabin was quiet. They looked at each other. Then Jemima said, "I think I'll play a courtesy visit to *Ordzhonikidze* sometime tomorrow. There are some questions I want answered."

The fact was, Khrushchev had been enjoying himself.

At Victoria Station, at one-thirty in the afternoon, Prime Minister Eden was on hand to welcome his Soviet guests. The reception was formal and polite, if not enthusiastic. Too much had happened since Geneva.

A motorcade moved quickly through the streets of London and attracted nowhere near the attention that police and security officers had feared. There were the pro-Communist groups and anti-Communist groups along the route, but there were no crowds packed behind police barricades. A noisy throng congregated near Claridge's toward the Russians' hour of arrival, but police dispersed them toward Grosvenor Square. Khrushchev was never aware of them. At the hotel, the First Secretary of the Communist Party of the Soviet Union found the royal suite on the tenth floor very much to his liking. From room service, he ordered champagne and smoked salmon, discovering that the Scottish fish compared very nicely to the Norwegian type he normally favored. Khrushchev made a note to devour a good deal of it on the day he'd visit Edinburgh and Glasgow.

Through Soviet Ambassador Jacob Malik, British Foreign Secretary Selwyn Lloyd arranged a last-minute dinner party — strictly informal — at Claridge's that same evening. Bulganin and Khrushchev eagerly accepted. The table of honor also included Andrei Gromyko, a first deputy foreign minister; Paval Kumykin, deputy minister of foreign trade; and Nikolai Mikhailov, the minister of culture. Joining Eden and Lloyd in representing Her Majesty's government were Sir William Hayter, the ambassador to Moscow, and the Marquess of Reading, the minister of state in the Foreign Office.

There was a second and a third table for the wives and families of Khrushchev, Bulganin and the English diplomats. Included in the latter were Commander Trott and Third Officer Holmes. Another table was reserved for Kurchatov, the physicist, at which he met members of the British scientific community.

The diners were served langoustines, beef Wellington, jugged hare, clarets, cheeses, salads, sorbets, port and coffee. After dinner, Eden toasted his guests and stressed the grave danger to world peace posed by the disagreements in the Middle East. Aloud, Khrushchev replied through his interpreter.

"If you do not like wars," Chairman Khrushchev replied, "you must be very careful not to start one." In the silence that followed, Khrushchev grinned broadly.

After dinner, as the guests mingled with one another, Lady Hayter asked Khrushchev what his most favorable impression was of England so far. He answered again through his interpreter.

"The long stretches I saw of little red brick houses," he said, thinking back to his train ride to London. "They reminded me of my boyhood in the Donbas. My father was a miner. He worked in a mine in the Donbas region. The housing there was built by a Marxist Welshman, John Hughes."

The wife of the ambassador nodded cordially and walked away. Khrushchev was still smiling as she left.

Late on the morning of the nineteenth, Khrushchev, Bulganin and part of their delegation returned to London and toured a wire factory at Reading. After lunch, political discussions continued at Westminster. The recurring subjects were Egypt, Germany, disarmament and peaceful coexistence. Each side politely accused the other of impeding progress.

The day was otherwise quiet, at least in London. Much newspaper space went to members of an organization called the League of Empire Loyalists. Five of their members went to 10 Downing Street to present the Prime Minister with a ten-foot-high wooden spoon, a wry protest against Eden's dinner with the Soviets the previous evening.

The inscription upon the spoon was noteworthy: HE MUST HAVE A LONG SPOON THAT MUST EAT WITH THE DEVIL. Eden recognized the quotation from *Comedy of Errors*. He was in good enough spirits to accept the spoon.

Khrushchev heard about the gift and saw pictures of it in the newspapers. The quotation he didn't understand, nor did his interpreter. But the ten-foot spoon amused him greatly, so he took it as some sort of approval of Eden's action and subsequently, Khrushchev reasoned, approval of himself.

The fact was, he thought the spoon was terrific. So did John Trott, who included it in the report he later made to *Victory*.

Christopher, reviewing the events in Portsmouth of the last forty-eight hours, expected the Prime Minister to be at his worst in London on the morning of April 20. Creighton was braced for a raving, screaming interview. Eden entered the room, chipper and smiling. "Good morning, Creighton." Christopher rose. "Please sit. You must be ungodly tired, my dear fellow."

Christopher sat. His reaction was guarded. "Thank you, sir," he said.

Eden sat also. The Prime Minister pursed his lips and eyed Christopher in complete silence for what seemed like two full minutes. Christopher swore to himself that he would let Eden speak first.

"The visit is going very well, you know," Eden said. "The Russians, I mean. We already have promises on trade agreements, technological and cultural exchanges. Mr. Khrushchev even agrees that some formula must be found to ease the problems in Egypt and the Middle East." Eden's fingers tapped on his desk. "Do you know, I was applauded by a crowd on Brook Street when I left Claridge's last night. That was the first applause I've received in public for seven months, Captain." His white eyebrows arched slightly. "I do believe the pendulum is swinging back my way. A man can only be pilloried for so long."

"I'm very glad, sir."

Eden leaned back in his chair and reassessed Christopher, his eyes squinting slightly. He retreated in tone. "Yes, I'm sure you are." Several seconds passed. "So *you* didn't tell the Russians? About the mines?"

Christopher lied carefully. "They appear to have found out independently."

Eden nodded. "Good. I'm glad. I would have been most upset if you had flagrantly contravened the most vital of my orders." Christopher remained studiously silent. "And I'm certain that Admiral Mountbatten would have been upset greatly, also."

"Yes, sir."

"But there were other orders, however. Regarding the hull. And you did approach the hull."

"Yes, sir."

"Against my specific orders!" Eden's voice rose,

just as Christopher had heard it rise many times in heated Parliamentary debate.

Creighton waited for the onslaught. "That's absolutely the case, sir."

Eden surveyed him for a long, long moment, his face frozen. "Well, I'm damned glad you did," he said softly. "If you hadn't, it seems likely the bloody mines would have gone off, doesn't it? And then where would we be?" He paused. "We're damned lucky to have sailors who can think for themselves at a critical moment. Orders, I suppose, are like rules. Made to be broken."

Christopher, observing his own brand of quiet diplomacy, did not answer.

"This whole affair is to receive a complete security blackout," said Eden suddenly. "As if it never happened." Christopher nodded and sighed with relief. "Unfortunately, Crabb shot his mouth off rather widely before making his final dive, as you reported to me. There are already rumors going around concerning his disappearance. We will be taking some precautions. You know, to cover Crabb's whereabouts."

Christopher nodded.

"It will be made to appear upon the Queen's ledgers that aside from your M Section officially not existing, it was utterly passive during the first four months of this year. Thus you will destroy all written records of your operation."

Creighton nodded again.

"Everything here will be doctored to suit. Specifically including Cabinet papers. Nothing will be left to the inevitable priers and troublemakers."

Christopher couldn't resist. "By that, sir, I assume you're referring to the Opposition. Mr. Hugh Gaitskell."

Eden's eyes focused tightly on the naval officer. "Why, yes! I had no idea you followed politics, Captain, but that's exactly what I had in mind. Questions will be asked in Parliament, and we bloody well won't answer them. The Opposition voices will be loud and shrill, but what's the old expression? 'The hollow vessel makes the most noise'?"

Christopher smiled. Eden laughed, greatly amused by his own sense of humor. Then, with swiftness that astonished Christopher, Eden turned very serious indeed, almost in a preachy patronizing manner.

"It's very simple, Captain. This story mustn't come out for a very long time, if ever. If it did, hardly anyone would believe that you and Crabb weren't down there attaching the mines yourselves. Ridiculous, of course. Our friends—the Americans, the Canadians, the Australians—would believe us, but it would barely matter. Khrushchev and Bulganin told me privately last evening that if the story of the limpet mines reached the public, they would be forced to take extreme action to maintain their position in the Communist world. That's understandable, isn't it? That's politics." Eden paused. "So they want us to cover and so do we. Our records will show that Crabb was conducting tests in the Portsmouth area of a new piece of diving equipment. An oxygen recycler. If we have to, we'll admit he was there. But *without,* I hasten to add, the knowledge or approval of Her Majesty's government. The record will show that he apparently drowned and his body has not been recovered. This," Eden concluded proudly as he inclined forward, "will tie in with Crabb's boastings of the previous evenings. Thus we can publicly declare he was in the harbor, yet admit that he should *not* have been. Are you still with me, Captain?"

"I'm right beside you, sir."

"Good!" Eden sprang to his feet. "Because here are my final orders."

Christopher rose, too, and waited.

"In pursuance of final cover," said Anthony Eden, "you will return Commander Crabb's body to the sea. You will do this immediately and in such a manner as to ensure that he finishes up at the same place he would have if you'd left him in Portsmouth harbor."

Christopher walked down the steps at the end of Downing Street fifteen minutes later. He turned left for the Hole. He decided to look in on the subsection there, but his real purpose was to be again with men and women he trusted. And he wished to make a signal to Charlemagne, seeking approval of the Prime Minister's orders.

As he walked up the familiar route, past the Foreign Office and Clive Steps, he pondered what Eden had proposed to him. *Operation Rub Out,* it was to be called. Christopher was sickened.

He could not comprehend why returning Crabbie to the waters would have any beneficial effect on cover. He would await wisdom from above on this one. Yet he knew that he might have to wait for a good long time.

THIRTY-FOUR

During that afternoon, Charlemagne signaled his reluctant approval of Eden's orders. Jemima gave Angela, Joan and their staff the task of dealing with secret reports, logs, notes and signals concerning Rub Out. All were to be removed, expunged, shredded and burned, except for one copy of each. That one was to be held in top security until Christopher wrote his report to Mountbatten. Then the one official record would go into the Section's Secret archives, kept by Desmond Morton. No one knew the location other than Morton and Mountbatten.

The papers that had been removed were to be replaced by cover documents fabricated by Section members. These would attest to the nonexistence of those who concocted the documents.

It had never happened. It was pure make-believe. Jemima detailed Trott to bring home these points to

469

all who had participated. Similarly, every man and woman involved again signed his agreement to the Official Secrets Act. After dinner that same day, in the great cabin of *Victory,* Christopher gave a comprehensive review of Eden's orders to his senior officers. Christopher set the next morning at 1000 as the time they would meet with two experts and settle Crabb's fate.

When the meeting concluded, Creighton slouched back in his chair behind Nelson's desk. He looked at the exhausted faces around the room. He felt his own spirit sag.

"We're off duty," he said. "Let's get out of here. Who's joining me for a run ashore? Café Royal for dinner, then some music at the Jokers' Club."

They were a party of six. Christopher and Jemima, Sainthill, Morton, Angela and Joan. All wore civilian dress. Trott was left aboard in temporary command, and Morton expressed the hope that he didn't get suddenly carried away in a fit of anti-Bolshevism and open fire on the Soviet warships with a *Victory* fifty-two-gun broadside, half her full complement. Sainthill considered that this would be well nigh impossible, as *Victory* lay almost bows on to the warships, with several buildings in the way. Joan felt that Commander Trott might not necessarily appreciate that.

At the Café Royal, each chose independently from the menu, but all had champagne on Christopher's insistence. The grape got to them and soon they were relaxing and joking. Dinner over, they walked along Osborne Road to the Jokers' Club. It was a popular navy haunt, and Christopher knew it well. During the war he'd gone there often and played the piano, mostly for his own enjoyment, but sometimes to add to his meager pay as a midshipman and sublieutenant in the early forties.

That evening, the Jokers' went wild. Christopher played again, and almost the entire clientele sang the songs of World War II. Later he transposed to the jazz of the twenties and thirties and the place turned into a stomp joint. Jemima sang "Yankee Doodle Dandy" and forgot the words halfway through. Angela and Joan did a "Dolly Sisters" act, pulling their skirts right up and doing the most extraordinary gyrations. Even Sainthill joined in gamely, but only managed to get in the way. Desmond Morton astounded everyone by singing Jessie Matthews songs from the thirties. He then insisted on performing Bach's "Ave Maria" in a high falsetto at a dead slow tempo despite Christopher's attempts to get a beat into it. After many requests, mostly from Jemima, Christopher really gave renditions of Fats Waller, Teddy Wilson, Charlie Kuntz and Carroll Gibbons. And the requests came rolling in, as they always did.

Jemima watched him. This was the first time he had played the piano since she came for him at Father John's in New York's Greenwich Village in January. A lifetime had gone by since then. Now he was warm and relaxed. A glow had come into his eyes and color into his face. Both of them knew that to him this was an art and a profession which almost equaled that of being a sailor, of being in the Royal Navy. But it would never exceed it. That's how it had always been. And always would be.

The finale was to astound them all. Three Russian sailors on a run ashore from the *Ordzhonikidze* wanted everyone to sing Russian folk songs. They were amazed when their halting requests were translated into action by Jemima, with Christopher's replies relayed back to them in perfect Russian. After the "Volga Boatman" and two revolutionary songs, one sailor suggested that the three girls should join the Soviet Navy. They had lady sailors, the three Russians proudly told them. Joan said she believed they had them here as well.

The evening ended with everyone singing "The Internationale." And the irony was not lost on any of the M Section members. "God Save the Queen" didn't even rate a mention.

At 1000 hours the next morning, back under strict discipline, the same party plus Trott sat round the table in the great cabin of *Victory*. One other officer joined them: Lieutenant Commander David Cummins. He was an ace navigator and oceanologist possessing the coveted letters FIN after his name, Fellow of the Institute of Navigation.

Only one item was on the agenda. On Angela's paper, it read: *The returning to the sea of Commander LPK Crabb (DD), RNVR.*

Cummins was visible through the thin haze forming in the cabin from Owl's pipe smoke. Absently, Christopher was reminded of a similar haze on the waters around Portsmouth on summer mornings.

"Well," Cummins answered, "if the object doesn't get enmeshed in the many underwater obstructions in that area, it would be carried out of Langstone harbor, eastward along the southern stretch of Hayling Island and into Chichester harbor. There it would most likely run aground on the one of the many shoals of sandspits."

Christopher backtracked. "What underwater obstructions?" he asked. "What's down there?"

"For a start, sir, three sunken wrecks. The tug *Irishman,* the dredger *Excelsior* and the bucket dredge *Withern.*" Cummins pointed to his chart. "There are many jagged edges here to snag a drifting body."

After a moment, Morton posed the question that was on all of their minds. "On balance," he asked, "would you say that it was *more* likely or *less* likely that such a body would be caught on one of those obstructions?"

"Much *more* likely, sir."

"Why so certain, Mr. Cummins?" asked Jemima.

"Because I've been down there, Miss James," he answered. "I've seen what's been snagged already."

Several questions followed, most from Christopher and Desmond Morton. When there was nothing further to extract from Cummins, Christopher dismissed him.

For a few moments the M Section officers looked at each other. Christopher could not bring himself to make the summation. Eventually Morton took it up. "So we are going to ensure that he *does* get caught on an obstruction, are we?" he posed quietly.

Christopher looked around the table. There was no word of dissension.

"At Langstone?" queried Morton.

Christopher nodded gently.

"Then if we attach Crabb to one of these wrecks," Morton continued, "is there some sort of strap, some sort of attachment, which we could rely on to wear through and release him? Say in fifteen to eighteen months?"

"One could be easily made," replied Sainthill. "I've used this type of thing during the war on some of the 'Double Cross' operations. My straps were for objects, not bodies. But it shouldn't make any difference." He thought for a moment. "One of my officers in the dirty tricks department will come up with what we want."

Again, silence gripped Nelson's great cabin. Christopher looked to Trott and finally spoke. "This is your specialty, Commander. What do you need?"

Trott answered quickly. "Three divers and two days, sir," he said. "I'll need to reconnoiter the harbor. I'll do it under the cover of checking the wrecks in Langstone. We'll pinpoint the best position for attachment. If Colonel Sainthill is ready with his straps, I can attach within forty-eight hours."

"Do you have three first-rate divers?"

"I have a *flotilla* of them," said Trott, a trifle piqued. "I need only the straps and your orders, sir."

For a moment, Christopher's gaze dropped down to his fingers. "All right," he said at length. "Let's do it."

Nikita Khrushchev had always disliked socialists. This evening, which was centered upon a crashingly dull dinner with the leaders of the Labour Party at the House of Commons, had done nothing to dispel his feelings. First there had been a toast to the Queen with this lamentable English whiskey which the English themselves liked to blame on the Scots. Then there had been roast lamb, exactly the way Khrushchev didn't like it: red and undercooked. Didn't they know that Eastern Europeans liked their meat brown or gray? Khrushchev considered the raw lamb the worst meal he'd endured since the previous November, when he'd visited Latvia and the local party secretaries served him ground reindeer meat.

Then, to make the meal worse, there was the endless string of suggestions by the Labourites that they were the chosen representatives of the working classes. How dare they! There was not a working-man among them! The Labour wives bothered Khrushchev, too. They were much too dowdy to suit his image of western womanhood. He liked the Conservative women much better. They were more sure of themselves, more aware of who they were. If Khrushchev wanted dowdy women, he mused, he would have visited Bulgaria. During the high points of the meal, Khrushchev was bored; during the low points he seethed. But what could be expected of a local Socialist party who stood before a meal and reverently saluted a sovereign with a cloying yellow liquor?

Khrushchev's mind wandered. During the dinner at Chequers two days earlier, Mrs. Eden had asked him what kind of missiles he had. "Will they fly a long way?" she had inquired.

Khrushchev had answered truthfully. "Yes, they have a very long range," he had said. "They could reach your little island or go quite a bit farther." The remark had found its way into the newspapers within forty-eight hours. The press was making a big things of it, even as far away as Washington and New York. So much for an honest answer in a nation where the government was so impotent that it couldn't even muzzle its own newspapers.

Khrushchev looked around the dining hall, where some of the Labour MP's were getting to their feet after the meal. He had nothing but contempt for these people. He thought back to something he'd said in Germany a year earlier, when the membership of Walter Ulbricht's Socialist Unity Party was demonstrating a little truculence. "The way to make them obedient, Walter," Khrushchev had told him, "is to shoot some intellectuals." That remark had traveled around, also resulting in a renewed dedication to Marxist principles.

Khrushchev got to his feet and the rest of the delegation followed. Even Bulganin, who'd stopped doing anything without consulting the Party Secretary. Khrushchev looked around the room. He smiled. Yes, there was something about this meeting which again made him think of shooting intellectuals.

He started working his way toward the door, bread crumbs on the front of his suit — he wore one of the gray suits on this occasion — and a bit of grease from the lamb at the corners of his mouth. Suddenly Hugh Gaitskell was next to him. Gaitskell was the leader of the Labour Party and, as such, had been one of Khrushchev's chief irritants that evening. Gaitskell sidled directly in front of him and rudely handed him an envelope. Khrushchev looked angrily at the Englishman. In the Soviet Union, handing a man a sealed envelope after dinner was never a sign of deep friendship.

The English and Soviet interpreters crowded around, as did members of the Labour and Communist parties.

"What is this?" Khrushchev asked.

"A list of Eastern European socialist politicians who have disappeared over the last two years, Mr. Khrushchev," Gaitskell said in a belated attempt at tactfulness. "I wonder if you would be able to advise us of their whereabouts."

Khrushchev's stubby finger jammed its way into the envelope. He tore it open. His face reddened. He scanned a list of three dozen names. These English socialists were uncanny in their lack of common courtesy. Every man on the list had been shot. Not all at the same time, but shot nonetheless. Why did these spiteful Labourites insist on holding *him* responsible for these fools who'd behaved in a manner that left him no choice but to execute them?

"Wherever these men are," Khrushchev answered graciously, "I'm sure they are as happy as pigs rolling in shit."

There was a lull as the interpreter conveyed the remark to Gaitskell. Gaitskell's face reddened. For a moment, Trott thought he might have to act as a referee.

Later, in his suite at Claridge's, the First Secretary's telephone rang. It was Eden. The Prime Minister was tickled to death that the Russians' first contact with the Opposition had ended in disaster.

"Comrade First Secretary," Eden inquired gently through an English interpreter, "how did your evening go?"

"It was not everything it might have been," Khrushchev answered, diplomatic for once.

Eden sighed. "Those Labourites," the Prime Minister commiserated. "I apologize for them. They have no manners whatever!"

A well-purchased hauling sling lowered the crate

into the motorboat alongside King's Jetty in the dockyard. Inboard, two petty officers secured it for the sea. It was raining and the battered crate was marked "RN/Equipment." Seventy-seven miles to the northeast, Khrushchev was suffering through the lamb.

Trott was at the helm of the launch. He turned the boat in the water and the Section members on the dock disappeared. It was a remarkably dark night, Christopher noted, matching his mood completely. he was thankful he knew these waters so well. It was a small consolation.

Well clear of Portsmouth harbor, they turned eastward. Trott was less than a talkative soul, and Christopher offered no conversation himself. The only lights were the small red and green navigation lights plus one round white light on the launch. It was a lonely, suicidal spot on a black, wet, cold evening. Christopher felt alone with his own thoughts and the muffled chugging sound of the launch's engine.

He wished fervently that this was the end of this filthy business. Crabb had risen gloriously to the challenges of his final operation, carrying out his part with perfection and courage. Not another diver in the Navy could have so quickly taught Christopher how to disarm those American mines. Without Crabbie, the harbor would have blown.

And what, Christopher asked himself for the millionth time, had Christopher done for Crabb in return? When Lionel had fallen into trouble with oxygen poisoning combined with exhaustion, Christopher had killed him.

Mercifully, he wondered? Or had it been an act of witless cowardice, a failure to think of anything better to do?

"God Almighty!" he murmured sotto voce to himself, his head shaking for greater emphasis. His hand was on the edge of the equipment crate, numb as the cold rain swept across it. "God, God, *God!*" Well, he'd decided, it would all be in the report he gave to Charlemagne. No hiding behind accidental drowning or the old, "Sir, Crabb became ill . . . There was nothing I could do . . ." routine. He would expose everything in his report, detail how he'd closed Crabb's air valves with his own hands and abide by Mountbatten's judgment.

But beneath his remorse, beyond his bereavement over Crabb's death, there remained Christopher's anger.

"We're here," said Trott softly.

They turned to port, past Eastney Ferry, and into Langstone harbor. Up ahead, in the water like a crimson specter, was a red marker buoy. On the other side of it, coming into a grayish, ghostly focus through the rain, was a small skiff. In the water, like strange apparitions, were the faces of three Royal Navy divers.

Creighton looked at the men. They moved through the water like serpents, the sound of their strokes hidden by the rain. Two of them boarded the launch and picked up crowbars. They looked at

Christopher.

"Let's get on with it," Creighton said.

They opened the box as Trott held a battery lantern. Crabb's body was nestled tightly therein, his head to one side, like a large bird with a broken neck. He wore the diving suit he had died in and his legs were folded slightly up. The length of the box had been the same as Crabb's height.

Christopher looked at his friend a final time. He said nothing. Crabb's eyes were closed tightly and the flesh of his hands and head was sallow, made even whiter by the harshness of the lantern. The straps, the ones Colonel Sainthill had designed, had already been fitted to the dead frogman.

Trott and Christopher assisted the two divers in taking Crabb from the box. Using weights, they placed him in the water. Christopher watched Crabb disappear beneath the surface. He saw his face for several seconds after he went under.

Christopher closed his eyes and made the sign of the cross

Trott saw him and grinned faintly. "I never took you for a religious man, Captain," Trott said, an edge of accusation to the remark.

Christopher looked back to him with no apologies. "Shut your mouth, Trott!" he said.

"Yes, sir," said Trott, looking back toward the water.

After six minutes the job was done. Crabb had been lashed to the wrecked *Withern,* which lay below the red buoy. Crabb had his resting place but only a temporary one. When Sainthill's straps released, he would drift. Hopefully he would travel into Chichester harbor, past the COPP depot at Sandy Point, the secret commando unit to which Christopher had belonged during the war and at which Crabb had instructed him how to dive.

It's all in the mind, Crabb had once said. *It's all confidence. Always tell yourself it's just an exercise. Then you can relax and get on with it.*

Christopher hoped Crabb's soul was enjoying a more peaceful journey.

The divers boarded their own boat. Trott swung the launch around and headed back toward Portsmouth. They moved resolutely through the darkness. The wind kicked up and the rain was sweeping and freezing.

It was when the lights of Portsmouth harbor faded into view that the events of the past days suddenly flew apart for Christopher for a final time, then reassembled. It struck him both coldly and dumbly. There was no specific impetus that suddenly put things together before him, no grand epiphany, no jolting comment that Trott or anyone else had made. Just a sudden comprehension of what he'd done.

When the launch touched the dockside, two seamen took it over. Christopher was off it in a flash, looking toward *Victory,* then glancing at his watch.

It was 2200 on April 24, meaning it was already 0330 in New Delhi. Perfect. Mountbatten would receive the signal as he awoke.

It read, *A Crabb rests.*

Much later, Christopher sat on a stone step just above the waterline at the foot of King's Stairs. He was not far from the spot where Crabb had died. The rain was falling heavily now, but Christopher was oblivious to it. He wore no protective clothing. The rain dripped through his hair, soaked his uniform and mingled with the seawater at his feet. He sat quietly and made no movement, like a man at a wake. His body and soul had been turned to stone. Jemima appeared unnoticed and sat down beside him.

"Christopher?" she said. He didn't reply. "Christopher . . . ?"

She sighed. Then she took off her raincoat and wrapped it around his shoulders. She sat down next to him. In less than a minute, she too was soaked. But she didn't care. She sat there with him, keeping a silent watch.

The night hours passed, until the sun rose up behind the Southsea bight and the rain faded with the dawn.

Then Christopher got up and went back to *Victory.* Jemima followed. His silent vigil was over. Maybe now, she prayed, his grief for Crabbie might lessen and soon fade.

THIRTY-FIVE

On April 25, at five-thirty in the afternoon, Christopher and Jemima arrived at Claridge's in London. Serov greeted them affectionately, in the front downstairs foyer a few steps inside from Brook Street.

"My friends," he said. "Please be coming in this direction."

He escorted them quickly across the foyer to the lifts. A terrible flap had occurred in the British press over Serov's presence in the country. He was supposed to have left already. Yet he was in overwhelmingly good spirits. He wore an ill-fitting dark suit that looked almost formal, but wasn't. For a fleeting moment, he looked like a nineteenth-century dandy.

"Hurry, hurry," Serov scolded, leading them into the elevator.

Christopher extended his arm to Jemima. "Can't

turn down a friendly invitation, can we?" he asked.

She took his arm.

Serov had three of his agency's best gorillas not far behind him. High cheekbones, long arms, short legs. Christopher could spot top Russian hoods in the dark. He and Jemima accompanied Serov to the elevator, where two more KGB officers stood.

Serov spoke to his employees in Russian. "Just the three of us, please," he said. Christopher and Jemima joined him in the elevator. It ascended.

As it rose, Serov made a point of small talk. "The First Secretary has an exasperation today," he said. "With Mr. Eden in the government complex, he viewed a portrait like Czar Nicholas II. I believe it was in a reception area, close by Prime Minister."

Christopher thought for a moment. "That was a portrait of George V," he said. He thought of Mountbatten. "The Czar's cousin."

"The First Secretary changed subject immediately," Serov explained in ingratiating tones. "Very unpleasant. Reminded Mr. Eden that King's cousin was killed during our Revolution."

"I'm sure Mr. Eden is aware of it," Christopher said.

Serov's smile wavered slightly. Serov had marvelous antennae, Christopher noted. He already expected trouble. Then the elevator door opened.

Serov took Christopher and Jemima down a corridor past several more Soviet and British security personnel. At the end of the corridor, at the corner suite, he stopped and rapped sharply at a door.

A voice responded from inside. Serov identified himself and latches fell from within. Jemima and Christopher waited as Serov stepped in first. Then, extending an arm, Serov bade them enter also.

There were three other people in the room. One was an interpreter, a large hulking man with closely cropped blond hair. Christopher recognized him from the intelligence reports that had preceded the Khrushchev visit. The man was also Khrushchev's personal bodyguard. The second man in the room was Bulganin. The third was Khrushchev, who grinned when he saw Christopher.

The two Russian diplomats stood. Serov introducted Christopher as Jemima remained behind him. Khrushchev went into a short speech, which Jemima translated in a condensed version.

"He's thanking you," Jemima said, "for your 'vigilance and courage' in protecting the three Soviet ships." She paused. "Protecting them from czarist hoodlums," she translated.

Christopher felt his face go into a mask. Serov, he noticed, was staring directly at him.

Khrushchev turned and snapped his fingers to the interpreter. The bodyguard pulled two small boxes from his suit pocket. He handed one to Bulganin, who handed it to Khrushchev. The First Secretary opened it and beamed.

Then Khrushchev turned it toward Christopher and showed it to him. Christopher was amazed. The box contained a medal, a round silver disk suspended on a crimson ribbon. Upon the silver was a peasant woman holding a carbine.

Now Bulganin spoke. He spoke English in very measured, deliberate tones. "This is Soviet Order of Red Star," he said. Khrushchev nodded. "For conspicuous services in the defense of the USSR in war or peace," Bulganin said. Then he reverted to Russian as he addressed Jemima.

"There is a second medal," Jemima interpreted. "One for the brave man who died. Commander Crabb. The President wishes to know who will accept it for him."

Christopher thought for only a moment. "You take it for him, Miss James," he answered, "And hold it in trust for Crabbie."

Jemima translated for the Russian leaders. They both nodded. Khrushchev pinned the Red Star on Christopher while Bulganin pinned the other on Jemima. The Russian medals hung strangely next to their British decorations. Then both Khrushchev and Bulganin shook hands with Christopher and Jemima, embraced and kissed them.

Then they were back in the lift, riding down again with Serov, who remained silent. When the elevator stopped on the main floor and the door opened, Christopher looked at Serov and spoke.

"That was your idea, wasn't it?" he asked.

Serov smiled. "You deserving honor by more ways than two," he replied. "You having dinner and drinks with me?"

"I think not, Comrade Ivan," Christopher said. "But what I would like is a private word."

There was a moment that Serov did not understand. Then he realized that his own security people had been cut off from him. Christopher reached to the control lever on the elevator and let the door slide shut.

"Please come quietly, Ivan," Christopher said. "That's the only way you'll be able to save your life."

Instinctively, Serov groped for the elevator's control. But when his hand landed upon Christopher's, he understood that the younger man was much stronger, and in no mood for a discussion.

The elevator rose to four. Christopher opened the door. There were M Section security people in the corridor. Christopher quickly whisked Serov to room 405. Jemima followed them in and closed the door.

Serov found himself in a vestibule, then in a single room with yellow wallpaper. The room smelled of pipe smoke. In a chair sat Sir Desmond Morton.

"I believe you know Sir Desmond," Christopher said. Serov was wary, but cordial. Somehow, he knew what was happening.

Jemima took a seat at a desk that faced Serov. The KGB chief was left to stand, awkwardly. Christopher moved behind Jemima, glancing out the windows down onto Brook Street before he began.

"Comrade Ivan," Christopher said, turning, "on the night of the eighteenth-nineteenth, Commander Lionel Crabb and I removed eighteen American-made limpet mines from the hull of *Ordzhoni-*

kidze."

"This I knowing, Christopher."

"It was you who had them planted there," Christopher said. "Commander Crabb died during the disarming operation. Your objective was to assassinate Comrade Khrushchev, whatever the cost. Dozens of Soviet and British sailors and many innocent civilians, as well as Comrade Khrushchev, would have died had the mines detonated. Similarly, you might have started another major war."

Christopher walked to within striking distance of Serov. "I ought to tear you apart myself, just as I tore apart your KGB commander during your raid on Birdham—your clumsy attempt to murder and silence von Ostenberg."

Serov said nothing. His expression darkened and he stared angrily. "You are speaking lies, Captain Christopher." Serov walked across the room and sat heavily in a large armchair. Two section officers guarding the door watched him closely.

"Under British law, you are a prime accessory to several serious crimes," Christopher continued. "Diplomat or not, you can be held here. Or, I can go back downstairs and turn over every bit of evidence to Comrade Khrushchev. I suspect your liquidation will then follow in record speed."

There was a long silence in the room.

"Or," Christopher said, "you can cooperate with us. That will be the easiest for you. We even understand why you've acted as you have. We're prepared to deal accordingly." Christopher looked to the sofa

490

and nodded. "Sir Desmond?"

Morton's face tightened and his eyes burned. He drew a tight gaze upon Serov. Nothing sparked Morton like a shot at sticking it to the duplicit Russians. Nothing. He'd even brought out a bottle of vodka for the occasion.

"Comrade General Ivan Alexandrovich Serov," Desmond Morton began in an angry rasp. "I will start three years ago. It's early 1953. Stalin's health is failing. He suffers a stroke. For one reason or another, Stalin never recovers. They bury him quickly. Most of the Soviet Union breathes a huge sigh of relief. After some ten to twenty million deaths since the 1930s, the greatest butcher of the twentieth century is safely buried."

Serov gave a terse nod.

"Immediately the jackals start to congregate. Malenkov had been designated as Stalin's personal heir. But he's not liked within the Party. Further, he starts to move too quickly, too crassly. The other men with access to power Molotov, Beria, Bulganin and Mikoyan—block Malenkov's rise. They divide the power among themselves, then name another man, Khrushchev, to the position of First Secretary of the Party machinery. They do this for a simple reason: they have underestimated him. They feel they can always control the coarse little Ukrainian."

Morton frowned thoughtfully.

"But quickly a split develops in the government. Malenkov holds tightly to the Party machinery and the old Stalinists support him. Beria still controls internal security. And Khrushchev represents the Party. Clearly, Malenkov and Khrushchev are scared witless of Beria. So are thousands of others. So they turn on him, denounce him, discredit him and shoot him. Now what is left is Malenkov and Khrushchev. They parry with each other for eighteen months. Then Khrushchev, carefully playing upon the strength of the Party, forces Malenkov's resignation. But to please the Stalinists, he appoints Bulganin to Malenkov's old position as Chairman of the Council of Ministers. This is one year ago. Bulganin supports Khrushchev but is acceptable to the Stalinists as well."

Serov looked almost bored. "And that is situation with which your Russian guests arrived," he said. "Your knowledge the same as mine."

"Backtrack again," Morton urged. "Witness Khrushchev when he first came to the leadership of the party. He set free thousands of political prisoners. He allowed the small farmers to make profits with their surplus. He liberalized the stage and the theater. He became powerful enough to have Beria shot, influential enough to personally denounce Stalin. The head of the government. Bulganin is his lackey. The head of the secret police, you, Comrade Ivan, are his trusted fellow Ukrainian. But there is a problem. Khrushchev is becoming the new Stalin. The new Czar, as it were. The Supreme ruler whom no can challenge. So a decision is made. Khrushchev is to be murdered. What better place than in

492

the West? What better scapegoats than a few surviving White Russians, a handful of German mercenaries and the Royal Navy? What better way than to have hired American agents to bring the mines from California to Russia. There, these agents are arrested and murdered in Lubyanka prison by you and your KGB. The mines are then sent under KGB escort to Kronstadt, where they are attached to the Soviet ships by Panavich's divers. Once in Portsmouth, the Royal Navy protects the hulls so that the mines will never be discovered."

Serov sat stonily quiet.

"Simultaneously," Desmond Morton added from where he sat, "your coconspirators, Molotov, Malenkov, Kaganovich and Voroshilov, are all in Finland, conveniently and innocently inspecting a third-rate factory."

Serov glanced around the room, weighing the faces of the four Englishmen and one English woman who stared at him. Literally, he was cornered.

"You had one of your KGB killers murder poor old Roger Garin," Jemima said contemptuously. "He knew there was a power struggle shaping up in the Soviet Union: The KGB and your coconspirators against Khrushchev. Roger knew and you had him murdered so that he couldn't tell anybody."

"Similarly," said Christopher with surprising politeness, "you had a bomb planted aboard *Seabird*. You didn't do it yourself, obviously, but one of your agents did. It was meant to kill Miss James and myself, throwing security operations into a shambles on the eve of the Soviet visit."

"You were off the *Ordzhonikidze* when the mines were timed to detonate," Morton said. "But you cleverly arranged for Khrushchev and Bulganin to be back aboard. You *knew* of the danger. You knew an operation was in progress to remove the mines. Yet you ensured that your leaders would not leave the cruiser."

"It is untrue," said Serov, rising unsteadily to his feet. "Never received signal! I knew nothing of mines! Informed you already that —"

Christopher turned to Jemima. "Number one!" he said to her.

On the table before Serov, Jemima presented the evidence. She laid before him a small slip of paper, a Soviet navy signal officer's receipt.

"I was given this when I went on a courtesy visit to *Ordzhonikidze* on the morning of the twentieth of April," she said. "The Soviet and British navies are exercising close cooperation at this time. Therefore, I had no difficulty in getting a copy of this receipt, Comrade Serov. It is the official record from your own communications office. You signed for that signal. You read it. It's on your ship's records."

Serov was very silent. The *coup de grace* was almost played.

"Why didn't you do anything about this receipt?" Christopher asked. "Why didn't you destroy the evidence?"

494

The Serov silenced continued.

"Maybe your forgot?" suggested Jemima helpfully. "In your hurry to get off *Ordzhonikidze,* maybe you left it in your cabin. And when you remembered, you believed it didn't matter. It would be destroyed with the ships." Jemima paused, before playing her trump. "You were wrong, Comrade General Ivan Alexandrovich Serov. It was found in your cabin and given to Captain Zoltov."

"Russian ships, British ships, Russian and British sailors, and many, many of my Section, men and women, to be killed! Blown to pieces! For your Machiavellian ambitions!"

Christopher's fury was mounting, and Jemima watched him anxiously. Quickly Morton defused it.

"I wonder," mused Desmond Morton aloud, "what First Secretary Khrushchev will say when we present him with all this!"

A line of sweat broke across the Russian's forehead. "Admitting nothing," he answered boldly. "But ask you. What do you want?"

"In exchange for Crabb's life, Comrade General!" Christopher's tone was icily menacing. "I want your soul."

Jemima pushed an engrossed legal document toward Serov. It was a confession, drafted in English by Desmond Morton and the section's senior solicitor. It was in English and Russian, the latter translated by Jemima. Attached was an agreement drawn in like manner. Serov would pass along all classified KGB documents requested by M Section for the rest of his life. If he failed, the case against him would be turned over directly to Khrushchev. If Serov refused to sign, he would be placed under arrest at that minute and the same evidence would be turned over to the Soviet government.

Serov turned white when he read the document. He looked up at Christopher. "You would have KGB Director as your double agent?"

Creighton nodded, his arms folded across his chest. "You have fifteen seconds to make your decision, Comrade General," he said. "Please make the wise one."

Less than a minute later, an ashen-faced Serov emerged from Claridge's room 405. He walked by himself to the elevator, leaving behind the signed confession in the custody of Sir Desmond Morton.

At 0900 two mornings later, the Russian leaders—their three ships and themselves intact—left Portsmouth harbor on the morning tide. They had been in British waters for slightly more than nine days.

First Officer Jemima James stood with Captain Christopher Creighton high up in a tower of Fort Blockhouse, a fine vantage point to view the departure of the tiny Soviet armada. Christopher had a pair of powerful binoculars. He could watch the Russian ships all the way past Spithead to where they would turn east up the Channel toward the Straits of Dover. From there, the path was clear to the Baltic.

As the *Ordzhonikidze* passed between Vernon and Dolphin, Soviet sailors closed up on deck, waved to their British counterparts and were both unaware how perilously close they might have been to a war. Christopher saluted as the ships passed. Jemima followed suit. They stood and they watched until the Russians passed Selsey Bill and disappeared. As Christopher saw them pass Langstone harbor, a pang of sadness hit him. Jemima could tell and squeezed his hand. Yet no one aboard any of the vessels was any the wiser.

When the three Soviet ships passed south of Brighton, an aircraft with British markings appeared on the horizon. At first the aircraft startled the Russian sailors, particularly when it began a low dive toward the small Soviet flotilla. But then it waved its wings in salute. The aircraft circled, then swept low over the Soviets a second time.

In the airplane a handsome man, his black hair turning to silver, peered intently out of the window. He studied the Russian ships with great professional interest each time the aircraft made a pass.

Then the man looked back to his pilot. "All right, Burrows," he said. "It's been six bloody weeks. Let's get home."

"Aye, aye, sir," the pilot acknowledged.

"And Peter," he said to a young man in a Royal Navy uniform sitting next to him, "make to Christopher Robin from Charlemagne: 'Meet tomorrow, Saturday, 28 April, 1100 hours Birdham.' "

"Aye, aye, sir," said the young man.

"Seems as if we've missed all the fun."

"Fun, sir?"

"Yes. Great fun."

When Mountbatten came aboard the Section HQ at Birdham the next day, the officers of the M Section were there to greet him. Charlemagne was tanned and rested. He had a kiss for Jemima and Angela.

A short time later, he settled down with Christopher in the Section library. Christopher said nothing and waited.

"I've read your report, Christopher, and I don't need to tell you that your entire section has done very well. You, Jemima, Angela, Trott, Sainthill, Webb . . . everyone. Commander Crabb, also. We owe a debt to him, the Squad, and to Sir Desmond. All of you. I've noted your recommendations for awards. I'll do my best to get all of them through."

"Thank you, sir."

"I'm not at all happy about one section of the report, however. You claim to have killed Commander Crabb."

"Yes, sir."

Mountbatten leaned back in his chair. He held a single pencil lengthwise in the fingers of his two hands. He studied it as he spoke.

"It would seen to me that you were under much too much pressure at the time to accurately assess your action. You had one limpet mine left to disarm. And you had a struggling, dying man on your hands. Am I correct?"

"You are, sir, but—"

"Do not interrupt me. In addition you had been underwater for almost two-and-a-half hours, well past the danger limit for a concentrated dive. Is that also correct?"

"It is, sir."

"Then faced with the real possibility of the last limpet mine detonating, together with the obvious results, I cannot possibly accept that you were able to make a completely reliable report on the incident. It seems to me that you tried to cope with Crabb and disarm the live mine. In doing so, Crabb was inadvertently killed. Your prime responsibility was to prevent an explosion in the harbor. And that is what you did, properly and correctly."

Christopher remained silent.

"Your report will be suitably amended," he ordered. "And Christopher. I don't want to hear anymore about it. Ever. That's a direct order."

"Aye, aye, sir," Creighton replied quietly.

"Do you fully understand me?"

"As much as I ever will, sir."

Mountbatten's eyes twinkled for a moment. "Yes. Right. And now, Serov."

Christopher waited.

"Your achievements in regard to him have been

nothing short of astounding," Mountbatten continued. "But now you must do the hardest thing of all: you must forget about him. All of you. It's Desmond's concern now. He'll route the KGB intelligence in the way he thinks best. He is our top expert in these matters. The rest of us are amateurs. We should be glad to be rid of the responsibility."

"I thoroughly agree," said Christopher.

"Right," Mountbatten said again. He heaved a sigh of relief and leaned back from the desk. "Now. Important matters: where's the damned coffee?" He looked at the door and called out. "Angela! Coffee!"

There was no immediate response.

"I don't think Angela is the coffee girl today, sir," Christopher said.

"No?" Mountbatten's busy eyebrows ascended.

"Not since your return, sir. We have a new cook in the section, sir. Temporarily. A classically trained *chef* more than a cook, in fact."

"What the hell has the cook to do with me?" Mountbatten asked.

The door opened behind Mountbatten and Marie entered with a tray. "Here I am, my Lord," she said. She put it on the table as Mountbatten, speechless, whirled in his chair. "Freshly brewed coffee with walnut *kaschka*. A treat which little boys on school holidays used to like at Ekaterinburg."

"Marie . . ." he said. He was on his feet with arms open. She came to him and he kissed her. They embraced. Christopher quietly left the room.

Had the tide of history not interfered, the man and woman before Christopher might have been husband and wife for the better part of the twentieth century.

In the early morning two days later, a Royal Navy frigate edged away from Watering Island in HM Dockyard and headed steadily toward the entrance to Portsmouth harbor. Travelling as the Countess Czapaska, and escorted by Colonel Sainthill and Commander Trott, was the woman M Section knew as the Grand Duchess Marie of Russia. The two naval officers would see her on this warship to Cherbourg, and then by special car to Cannes. There she would be reunited with her grandson Alexis, the proclaimed Guardian of the Imperial Throne. When Trott and Sainthill were satisfied that all local security arrangements were in order, they were to return.

Standing side by side on the southwest jetty were an admiral, a captain and a Wren First officer. They saluted as the frigate increased revolutions. From the bridge, Marie waved in return, and they all waved too.

Christopher watched silently. He drew back for a moment, and out of the corner of his eye, he saw Mountbatten's face. It was both sad and joyous. Marie continued to wave, a graceful graying grandmother.

They watched for several minutes. Then the figure

of Marie became very small and suddenly the ship was gone toward Spithead, just as the Soviet ships had vanished several days earlier.

Jemima saw Mountbatten shiver. She was almost certain that there was a glistening in his eye. He turned and caught her looking. He smiled.

"Come on," he said. "In a sudden and inexplicable mood of generosity, your commander-in-chief has decided to buy you breakfast at the Queen's Hotel."

"Scrumptious," said Jemima. Mountbatten put his arm through hers. Christopher did the same from the other side and all three walked toward Mountbatten's car.

"I'll have you both know," Jemima said, sounding off, "that it is strictly against Queen's Regulations for Naval Officers to link arms with Wrens in uniform. And further—"

"If you don't stop rattling on, Jemima," Mountbatten interrupted, "I shall whack your behind. And that is *also* against Queen's Regulations."

Christopher laughed out loud and Jemima glared at him. But she shut up.

As they drove out of the dockyard gates, Christopher looked back. Everything seemed still and quiet. The place was at peace. And in the background, Nelson's flagship, *Victory,* seemed to sparkle in the flood of morning sunlight. It was almost as if the ship herself were aware that once again, she had presided over a magnificent naval triumph.

EPILOGUE

In the days that followed, the sighting of a lone frogman in Portsmouth harbor on April 19, 1956, was reported in the English press. Questions were asked in both Parliament and the daily papers. On the fifth of the following month, Her Majesty's government made a stunning admission.

Commander Lionel Crabb, no longer an officer in the Royal Navy, had been employed the morning in question as a civilian to make a "test dive" in Stokes Bay, about three miles from where the *Ordzhonkidze* was berthed. His mission was to test some new diving equipment, specifically an oxygen recycler. Crabb had not returned and was "presumed dead." It was not known who had hired Crabb, but Prime Minister Eden, responding to the growing number of inquires now made in Parliament, stressed that Crabb's dive "was done without the authority of Her Majesty's ministers." Subsequently, an apology was issued on May 10 to the Soviet Union.

The explanation satisfied no one.

In Parliament and in the press, certain questions recurred with disturbing regularity:

Who *had* hired Crabb? What had been his actual mission? What was the involvement of Her Majesty's government? What knowledge of Crabb's dive was shared by the Admiralty, specifically by the First Sea Lord? (As the *Daily Mail* twice reminded its readers in editorials, Mountbatten always knew *everything* concerning the Royal Navy, its operations and its divers . . . even, the newspaper stressed, its retired divers.) Further, why was a clumsy attempt subsequently made by Portsmouth police to remove Crabb's hotel registration? Who ordered the attempt?

And above all, where was Crabb? Was he really dead, or, as some cynics suggested, had he defected to the Soviet Union following some mysterious operation?

Thirteen months later, three fishermen in Chichester harbor spotted something black with a wet, rubbery sheen bobbing in the water. They thought it might be an old tire. But when their seven-ton lugger sailed closer, they discovered that the object in the water was a headless, handless corpse decaying in a Pirelli diving suit.

Out of decency, they hauled the unfortunate human remains aboard their ship. When they reached shore, they notified Chichester police. The fishermen were astounded when a statement was forthcoming from the local constabulary within thirty minutes.

"This is not just an ordinary body. There are security, political and other reasons for caution." A coroner's inquest was held Tuesday, 11 June. Though the head and the hands of the body were missing, the coroner "positively" identified the corpse as that of Commander Lionel Crabb, "who was last seen, by a witness called today, on April 17, 1956, in London."

No evidence was heard about the last two days of the missing frogman's life, April 18 and 19, in Portsmouth.

When the inquest adjourned, Alastair W. Geddes, the solicitor retained by Crabb's mother, had a brief statement for the press.

"There have been irresponsible conjectures regarding the last operation which Commander Crabb was engaged in prior to his disappearance. It is desirable therefore to emphasize that every piece of evidence in our possession points to the fact that this gentlemen died, as he lived, in the service of his country."

Could he elaborate?

"No. I cannot say more. My hands are tied."

It had all gone according to the official plan which Christopher Creighton had himself helped draft.

Ten years later, there was one more footnote. In March of 1967, ten miles from Portsmouth harbor as the tides run, Mrs. Margaret Bull was shrimping on the beach. She found something half buried in the sand. She though it was a large sea shell and pushed the sand away from it. Moments later, she screamed, having unearthed a human skull.

Pathologists determined that it had belonged to a "man of about fifty" and it had probably been in the ocean for five to a dozen years. Because the lower jaw was missing and there were but four unfilled teeth in the upper, a positive dental identification was impossible. But so, skeptics reasoned, were a lot of things.

In June of 1957, fourteen months after the attempt on Khrushchev's life in Portsmouth, Malenkov, Molotov and Kaganovich made a second and more blatant attempt to rid themselves of Khrushchev. Again taking advantage of Khruschev's absence—this time *he* was in Finland—they convened a secret meeting of the Presidium of the Central Committee and moved for his resignation.

Khrushchev rushed back to Moscow. With the help of Marshall Zhukov, the Soviet Minister of Defense, he succeeded in transferring the question of resignation to the Central Committee, where he had innumerable allies.

After a week of bitter struggle, from June 22 to

29, Khruschev won. The entire "anti-Party" group was stripped completely of their political and governmental powers. Later in that same year, Khrushchev boldly turned on Marshall Zhukov and removed him from office. As an anticlimax, the faithful Bulganin was relieved of his duties in March of 1958.

With that move, the prophecy feared by the men who had conspired to murder Khrushchev in Portsmouth had come to fruition. Holding the posts of First Secretary of the Central Committee, CPSU, Chairman of the Presidium of the Central Committee, and Chairman of the Council of Ministers, Nikita Khrushchev was the supreme dictator of the Soviet Union, unquestioned in his authority in the same manner as Stalin. In the close tenure of power that followed, Khrushchev used his folksy and irascible style to threaten the West with nuclear annihilation whenever he saw fit.

Khrushchev himself remained in power until October 15, 1964, when he too fell victim to a purge. He lived out his life in the Ukraine and died of natural causes in 1971. In his memoirs, he recalled his trip to London and the Crabb Affair.

Comrade General Ivan Alexandrovich Serov, first director of the KGB, kept the bargain made in London in April 1956. Over the years that followed, top-rated secret information flowed from Moscow to Desmond Morton, then to proper authorities. At no time was it more valuable than in 1962, when Kremlin estimates of their own naval strength were leaked through the British Admiralty to the United States Navy, which then confidently blockaded Cuba during the missile crisis of that October. Shortly thereafter, the leak in Soviet intelligence was traced to Serov. He was liquidated in February of 1963.

The Grand Duchess Marie, Empress of Russia in Exile, died in Rome, December 14, 1970. But before she died, she extracted a solemn promise from her grandson Alexis that he would not publicize her true identity until ten years after her death. Alexis kept his promise until February 1981, when he declared himself.

His Imperial Highness Prince Alexei Romanova Dolgorouky, Duke d'Anjou Durassow and Pretender to the Throne of All the Russias, now lives in Madrid, a few blocks east of Calle Seranno.

Jemima James retired from the Women's Royal Navy in 1966. She lived in Oxfordshire for many years, where she received Christopher from time to time. She emigrated to Canada in 1970, upon the death of her mother and the sale of her family property. She never married. She lives now in Vancouver.

Christopher Creighton lives in the south of England under a different name. He is currently at work on a third novel and, when asked when—if at all—he retired from active duty to his Queen, his country and Royal Navy Intelligence, he simply smiles and declines to answer. He has no set schedule other than one.

Each year in the early morning of April 19, he travels to Portsmouth harbor. At King's Stairs Jetty in the Royal Navy dockyard, he stands for a moment and says a silent prayer. Then he casts a single red rose into the water at the position where Crabb died. It might be of remembrance for all the brave comrades who've fallen for England. But those who note the date know better, aware that the single rose floating with the tide in Portsmouth harbor is for a particularly brave man—truly one of the New Elizabethans, who was spared so often by the sea, only to be claimed by it at last.

ACTION ADVENTURE

SILENT WARRIORS   (1675, $3.95)
by Richard P. Henrick
The Red Star, Russia's newest, most technologically advanced submarine, outclasses anything in the U.S. fleet. But when the captain opens his sealed orders 24 hours early, he's staggered to read that he's to spearhead a massive nuclear first strike against the Americans!

THE PHOENIX ODYSSEY   (1789, $3.95)
by Richard P. Henrick
All communications to the USS *Phoenix* suddenly and mysteriously vanish. Even the urgent message from the president cancelling the War Alert is not received. In six short hours the *Phoenix* will unleash its nuclear arsenal against the Russian mainland.

COUNTERFORCE   (2013, $3.95)
Richard P. Henrick
In the silent deep, the chase is on to save a world from destruction. A single Russian Sub moves on a silent and sinister course for American shores. The men aboard the U.S.S. *Triton* must search for and destroy the Soviet killer Sub as an unsuspecting world races for the apocalypse.

EAGLE DOWN   (1644, $3.75)
by William Mason
To western eyes, the Russian Bear appears to be in hibernation — but half a world away, a plot is unfolding that will unleash its awesome, deadly power. When the Russian Bear rises up, God help the Eagle.

DAGGER   (1399, $3.50)
by William Mason
The President needs his help, but the CIA wants him dead. And for Dagger — war hero, survival expert, ladies man and mercenary extraordinaire — it will be a game played for keeps.

Available wherever paperbacks are sold, or order direct from the Publisher. Send cover price plus 50¢ per copy for mailing and handling to Zebra Books, Dept. 2297, 475 Park Avenue South, New York, N.Y. 10016. Residents of New York, New Jersey and Pennsylvania must include sales tax. DO NOT SEND CASH.

THE FINEST IN FICTION
FROM ZEBRA BOOKS!

HEART OF THE COUNTRY   (2299, $4.50)
by Greg Matthews
Winner of the 26th annual WESTERN HERITAGE AWARD for
Outstanding Novel of 1986! Critically acclaimed from coast to
coast! A grand and glorious epic saga of the American West that
NEWSWEEK Magazine called, "a stunning mesmerizing perfor-
mance," by the bestselling author of THE FURTHER ADVEN-
TURES OF HUCKLEBERRY FINN!
   "A TRIUMPHANT AND CAPTIVATING NOVEL!"
                         —*KANSAS CITY STAR*

CARIBBEE   (2400, $4.50)
by Thomas Hoover
From the author of THE MOGHUL! The flames of revolution
erupt in 17th Century Barbados. A magnificent epic novel of
bold adventure, political intrigue, and passionate romance, in the
blockbuster tradition of James Clavell!
   "ACTION-PACKED . . . A ROUSING READ"
                         —*PUBLISHERS WEEKLY*

MACAU   (1940, $4.50)
by Daniel Carney
A breathtaking thriller of epic scope and power set against a
background of Oriental squalor and splendor! A sweeping saga
of passion, power, and betrayal in a dark and deadly Far Eastern
breeding ground of racketeers, pimps, thieves and murderers!
                 "A RIP-ROARER"
                 —*LOS ANGELES TIMES*

*Available wherever paperbacks are sold, or order direct from the
Publisher. Send cover price plus 50¢ per copy for mailing and
handling to Zebra Books, Dept. 2297, 475 Park Avenue South,
New York, N.Y. 10016. Residents of New York, New Jersey and
Pennsylvania must include sales tax. DO NOT SEND CASH.*